PRAISE FOR
MATEGUAS ISLAND

D1500721

"Native Ameri   e of suspense and horror in the multifaceted Mateguas Island, the story of the Anderson family who is forced to relocate to rural Maine where they face a rising evil that could destroy not only their family, but the world....Surprising twists and turns and a powerful old box filled with magic: these are the elements of a fine horror story that slowly builds its plot with believable protagonists and engrossing color. Any who like horror stories and gothic fiction will find Mateguas Island an exceptional read"

D. Donovan, Senior eBook Reviewer, *MIDWEST BOOK REVIEW*

"...a frightening read that only gains in intensity the further you dare to go."

H. William Ruback, author of *the SHORT of it...*

"MATEGUAS ISLAND will draw you into its world, page after page. Read it tonight after the sun sets and darkness grips your home."

Robert James Jackson, author of *Moon Strike* and *StoneRealm*

"MATEGUAS ISLAND by Linda Watkins is a suspenseful novel that quickly pulled me in with well-developed characters, a tight plot and a fascinating story line...One of the best I've read in this genre. It kept me up reading late into the night."

Darlene Blasing, author of *Bargain Paradise*

"MATEGUAS ISLAND is a crisp story for a stormy night when the house is creaking, rain is rattling on the window panes and you just know Something is Out There."

J. Scott Payne, author of *A Corporal No More*

"From the first goose bumps when you learn of the old Indian woman's death to the final conclusion of this book, Linda Watkins keeps you mindful of that macabre presence waiting for you just beyond the shadows where things can and do turn deadly."

Steve LeBel, author of *Bernie and the Putty*

"I was immediately transported to this rocky sea-side setting and the sense of isolation was conveyed easily. There is just enough suspense to keep the reader hooked...I would recommend this book to anyone looking for a good page-turner to curl up with!

Melissa Miles, *Melissa's Reviews*

"...This story had me from the second page of the book. The characters are well written; Miss Watkins weaves a terrifying tale of Native American lore. Keeping me in suspense the whole time, this book had me staying up late into the night. If this is a first book for Linda, I can see great things in her future.... Check out this book, I don't think you will be disappointed. I know I wasn't."

Patricia, *L.S.K. Sweetheart Reviews and BOOKS TO CURL UP WITH BLOG.*

Mateguas Island

A NOVEL

LINDA WATKINS

East Baton Rouge Parish Library
Baton Rouge, Louisiana

Editing by Kristina Circelli (www.circelli.info)
Cover design: H. William Ruback (www.incolordigitaldesign.com)
Background photo: Linda Watkins (www.mateguasisland.com)
Interior formatting: Mallory Rock (www.malloryrock.com)

Published in the United States of America by Argon Press
Library of Congress Control Number 2014933260
ISBN 978-0-9910554-4-9 (PB)
ISBN 978-0-9910554-5-6 (EB)

ARGON PRESS

www.ArgonPress.com

ACKNOWLEDGEMENTS

I would like to thank all my "readers" who provided me with such valuable insight and encouraged me to keep going! Most especially, among these are my best friend, Marge LeBel, and my sister, Susan. I don't know what I would have done without either of you. I also want to thank my editor, Kristina Circelli, who helped me form the final version of Mateguas.

To my writing group - thank you all for your support and guidance through this amazing journey of discovery. And, finally, special thanks to Steve LeBel for providing me with his computer expertise and advice. Without him, the publication of this novel would not have been possible.

For Splatter

All proceeds from this book will be donated to the
Raison d'être Fund for Dogs.

*"If once you have slept on an island
You'll never be quite the same"*

- Rachel Field

OCTOBER

She rolled over to check the clock. *It's time,* she thought, nodding to herself. Careful not to disturb the man who lay beside her, she silently slipped out of the bed and tiptoed over to the closet. Reaching up to the top shelf, she pulled a small black box from under a pile of linens. She stared at it for a moment before removing the lid, revealing its contents. Inside, on a satin pillow, lay a small bone knife with a carved handle. Slowly, she lifted it from its resting place and tested the blade against the tip of her finger. A drop of blood at once appeared. Smiling grimly, she grasped the hilt firmly in her hand and walked to the bedroom door. As she left the room, she looked back over her shoulder at the man who was still asleep. She loved him and did not want to lose him. She prayed he'd keep his promise.

Quietly, she padded barefoot down the stairs and out the back door. When she reached the middle of the lawn, she turned, facing east. As if summoned, the moon appeared from behind a cloud, its sickle shape glowing with preternatural brightness. Standing motionless, she turned her gaze toward the sky as the autumn wind whipped her nightgown around her slender form.

She took a deep breath and stood up straight. She was ready. Slowly, she raised her arms to the sky in supplication and began to speak....

THE FERRY

SIX MONTHS EARLIER

"Is that the island, Daddy?"

Bill Andersen glanced down at his eight-year-old daughter, Terri, and smiled. "Yes, honey," he replied, putting his hand on her shoulder. "We should be docking in about fifteen minutes."

They stood by the rail in the bow of the commuter ferry to Mateguas Island on the way to their new home. There was no bridge to this island - access was only by boat.

Bill gazed out over the water, watching as they neared the island's craggy shoreline. It was a beautiful sight - waves crashing against the rocks, spray shooting into the air, and everything sparkling in the late afternoon sun. But it was cold. A shiver ran down his spine.

"Daddy, what does *Mah-tuh-gwoss* mean?" asked Terri as she leaned over the railing, her long blonde braids whipping around her head in the brisk sea breeze.

"I don't know, sweetie, just some Indian name, I suppose."

Terri looked at her father with disappointment, a frown on her face. He was supposed to know everything. She was the more analytical

3

of his twin girls, always questioning and expecting answers to be readily forthcoming. Sophie, who was sitting inside the cabin with her mother, tended to be the quieter, but more creative, of the two. When they were together, Terri usually took the lead with Sophie trailing happily along behind her.

Bill adored his daughters and prayed this new home would be good for them. The elementary school they would attend was one of the last of Maine's fabled "island schools." After that, they would have to get up at dawn to catch the ferry to the mainland and take the bus to the middle school in town. It would be quite a change for them, but he hoped it would be for the better.

His thoughts were interrupted by a deep voice coming from behind them. "Mateguas means 'rabbit' young lady."

Bill and Terri turned toward the speaker.

A tall man, Bill guessed his age at around fifty though his face was so weathered by sun and sea, he could have been younger.

"Rabbit?" replied Terri. "That's a funny name for an island. Why is it called that? Are there lots of rabbits there?"

"No, honey," the man said. "You'll see the occasional jack rabbit, but that's about it. The Indians who settled here, the Abenaki, named the island. You see, they worshipped the Rabbit. He was the ruler of The Land of the Dead. But don't let that scare ya - he was pretty much a good old boy, that Rabbit. Not like some other Abenaki spirits."

"What other spirits?" asked Terri eagerly.

The man laughed. "Oh, honey, those stories are for late at night when you're safe at home with a warm fire crackling in the woodstove and you're surrounded by your loved ones. Then's the time for tales of the Mskagwdemos!"

"What's a *muh-skog-day-moose?*" asked the little girl with some anticipation.

A plain-looking woman on the other side of the bow turned to the man. "Now don't you go telling your tall tales and scare that poor child, old man!"

She shook her finger at him and then looked at Terri. "Don't you mind him, honey. He thinks he knows just about everything there is to know about the Indians and their legends. But most of it's just a bunch of hooey!"

"Are there Indians on the island?" asked Terri.

"No, honey, they all left. Moved to Quebec many years ago. You might still find an arrowhead on the beach, though, if you look real closely." The woman smiled at Terri, then turned to Bill. "Are you folks Janie Morgan's kin?"

"Yes, she was my aunt," said Bill, offering his hand. "I'm Bill Andersen and this is my daughter, Terri. My wife, Karen, and my other daughter, Sophie, are inside."

"Name's Pete McKinney," the man said, shaking Bill's hand. "The one over there with the mouth is the wife, Louise."

Louise frowned at her husband, then looked at Bill and smiled. "Happy to meet you. And please accept our condolences for your aunt. She was a grand lady. It was a sad thing when she passed. We are all going to miss her. Are you and your family just here for the summer or are you planning on staying year-round?"

"Oh, we're here to stay - uh, I mean, year-round," replied Bill.

"Good, we need more year-rounders. Girls be going to the island school?"

Bill nodded. He was about to reply when he heard the cabin door open and a tall, slim blonde with cool blue eyes emerged from inside.

"Bill, it looks like we'll be docking soon. Are you sure there's no taxi service to take us up to the house?"

"Pete, Louise, this is my wife, Karen," said Bill. "Karen, this is Pete and Louise McKinney."

Karen nodded and smiled, then turned back to Bill, looking at him questioningly. "A taxi, Bill?"

"No, Karen. We talked about this before," he replied with a hint of irritation. "The taxi only runs during the 'season' and that doesn't start till the Fourth of July. I'll jog up to the house and get the car. It's only a half-mile."

Karen frowned and pursed her lips, obviously annoyed at the inconvenience.

Pete watched the couple carefully - the tension between them being almost palpable.

"Hope you don't mind me putting in my two cents," he interjected, "but you're going to have a pretty hard time getting Janie's car down to the wharf. When she took ill, she put the car away in the garage. Battery's most likely dead and I expect it probably needs oil and air in the tires, too. Why don't you let Louise and me give you a lift?

Our truck will hold all of you and your stuff and it's on our way anyway."

"That's very kind of you. We'll take you up on it," said Bill.

Karen nodded to Bill and to the McKinneys, thanking them, and went back into the cabin. She did not smile.

Bill sighed, worried about how his wife would adapt to life on the small island. She was a California girl used to all the conveniences.

How's she going to make it here with no movie theaters, no malls, and just one small grocery store? And there's only a single burger joint and a seafood takeout place. She's a woman used to dining in the finest of restaurants. Staying home all the time is not going to sit real well with her, that's for sure.

He frowned as he gazed at the rocky shoreline. It was spring now but it wouldn't be long before winter came and, with it, the cold. And there would be snow.

Oh, yes, the snow. That'll be tough on her, too.

Inside the cabin, Karen sat stiffly on the wooden bench next to her daughter, a frown on her face. She glanced around the room, which was about half full. Most of the people in the cabin were elderly or looked working-class. In their hands or sitting at their sides were ugly canvas bags jam-packed with groceries and God knew what else.

Soon, I'll be one of them, she thought, shuddering.

She looked toward the bow of the boat and could see her husband through the window in animated conversation with some of the islanders. Her frown deepened.

This isn't going to be easy. Moving to this god-awful place so far away from everything. And Bill - I can't help it. Every time I look at him, I just get so mad.

Thinking about this, she mentally chided herself. *But why am I so angry? He lost his job because of the recession. Well, at least that's what he tells everyone. But, I know him and I'm sure somehow he was responsible - he did something - something he's been keeping hidden from me.*

"Mommy, are we there yet?"

Brought back to reality by the sound of her daughter's voice, Karen smiled. "Yes, honey, I think we're coming in now."

Outside, Bill and Terri observed the boat's captain as he expertly maneuvered the ferry up to the small dock. As the deckhand tied up the boat, Karen and Sophie emerged from the cabin. Bill turned when he heard the door open and reached out to his wife. She looked down at his hand for a moment then moved away, over to the rail, and stared at the mainland behind them. A stiff breeze whipped her hair around her head and she clutched her sweater tightly to her neck to ward off the chill. Bill sighed, a look of frustration on his face.

Making note of the silent exchange between the new couple, Pete turned to his wife and raised his eyebrows. In response, she gave him a stern look and an abbreviated shake of her head.

When the ferry was securely tied up to the dock, the Andersens carried their belongings to Pete's truck. Karen watched the activity on the wharf as Bill and Pete carefully loaded everything into the back. The other passengers from the ferry had debarked and were carrying their canvas bags and pulling their wheeled carts to their cars, chatting amiably with each other on the way.

At the end of the wharf, Karen noticed a group of men standing beside a boat loaded with what she guessed were lobster traps. One of the men nodded in her direction and another, whose back was to her, slowly turned around.

He wore a baseball cap that partially obscured his features, but she guessed he was about Bill's age. He had on jeans and rubber boots and, despite the cold, wore only a light windbreaker over his tight T-shirt. His body appeared lean and well-muscled. Their eyes met and they stared at each other for a moment. Then a slow, suggestive grin started to grow on his face as his eyes began to travel up and down her body. She felt the beginnings of a blush and tore herself away and turned back to her husband, who had finished the loading and was helping their daughters into the back of the truck.

"Karen, you hop in next to me," called Louise, squeezing over toward her husband, who was behind the wheel. With relief, Karen climbed into the front seat of the truck. Her daughters were giggling and she turned her head and smiled as she watched them through the window. They were obviously excited to be riding in the back with their father.

As they drove away from the wharf, they passed the group of men standing by the lobster boat. Karen could hear them laughing as they went by and she deliberately kept her eyes straight ahead, refusing to look in their direction. However, she could feel him still watching her, arms folded across his broad chest and that slow, sexy smile lingering on his face.

In the back, Bill put his arms around his daughters' shoulders, hoping they didn't catch a chill. The sun was warm, but there was a blustery ocean breeze, a remnant of the winter just past. It was early May and, though it was beginning to warm up, there was still a long way to go until the heat of summer arrived. Bill planned the move for this time of year, hoping to stave off the high cost of heating oil they would experience in the winter. Once a successful software engineer, he also prayed he could find work on the mainland, hoping the marketplace here was not as glutted with tech types as California's was.

A fresh start, he thought as the truck pulled away from the wharf to take them to their new home.

AUNT JANIE'S HOUSE

From a distance, the property was impressive. The house sat on the highest point of the island, overlooking the sea. It was an old farmhouse and, on closer examination, they could see it was sadly in need of painting and repair. Because of its proximity to the ocean, the wind off the water would be their constant companion. This weather phenomenon was pleasant during the hot summers, but could be bitter cold in wintertime.

Karen examined the large, overgrown perennial beds that lined the walkway. *What a mess! These are going to need a lot of work.*

Shaking her head, she turned and walked to the side of the house, gazing at the yard in back. It was good sized and park like, the edges ringed with blackberry and raspberry bushes. Behind these lay dense woods.

She wrinkled her nose. *Smells musty - cold and damp.*

Turning back to the entryway, she noted one of the front steps was broken and the screen door hung dangerously askew. *Christ, the place is practically falling apart. How am I supposed to live here?*

9

As she continued to stare at the broken step, Bill and Pete walked over to the garage. Inside, they found the auto covered with dust and cobwebs that had accumulated over months of disuse.

Pete frowned. "Louise and I need to get a move on now, but we'd be happy to come by in the morning and help you get Janie's vehicle started."

"That'd be great," replied Bill, shaking the older man's hand.

He watched as the McKinneys drove away then turned back to his wife, who still stood at the bottom of the front stairs, Sophie by her side. Terri was on the porch, peering in the windows.

"So this is the paradise you've brought us to," Karen said irritably. "We would have been better off on welfare in California."

"Don't be so quick to judge," Bill replied. "At least this place is paid for and we can fix it up - maybe it's all just cosmetic. I bet the inside is better than the out. The Aunt Janie I remember was a meticulous housekeeper. Let's get our stuff inside. From the look of the sky, I'd say it might rain."

Karen looked up and was surprised to see dark thunderheads rapidly approaching from the mainland. "Where'd that come from? It was sunny when we got off the boat."

Bill smiled. "Weather can change rapidly out here, hon."

Karen sighed and nodded. "Okay, girls," she said to her daughters. "You heard your father. Let's get our things inside."

The family began to move their belongings into the house and Bill was pleasantly surprised by what they found. The front door opened into a large entryway with wood floors painted a soft buttercup yellow. Wallpaper in a floral pattern adorned the stairway leading to the second floor. From the living room at the front of the house, a large picture window looked out at the sea, creating a focal point for the room. The furniture was old but in good condition, mostly antiques. A woodstove insert sat in the fireplace, promising cozy winter evenings. In the dining room, a built-in china cupboard adorned one wall and a large oak table sat in the middle of the room. The kitchen was good-sized but not especially efficient.

Karen shook her head in dismay as she noted the minimal counter space. *Sweet Jesus, how am I going to cook in here? That stove is ancient and the sink is barely usable. They'll have to be replaced. But how? Where will we get the money with Bill out of work?*

She sighed then examined the refrigerator, which, like the stove, was old, but appeared to be in decent working condition. Off the kitchen, at the rear of the house, was a family room. This comfortable-looking space had an additional woodstove and a modern flat-screen TV. A mudroom off the family room led to the back door and stairs down to the yard.

On the second floor, the front bedroom, like the living room, looked out onto the ocean through a large bay window. It was a spacious room, furnished with a queen bed and large dresser. A small closet sat at the far end.

Karen noted a large crack along the rear wall and frowned in distaste. Then she turned to the window and stood silently watching the sea.

"Honey, are you all right?" Bill asked, approaching her from behind, putting his arms around her. "I know this move has been hard on you."

Karen stiffened in his embrace. "Don't patronize me, Bill."

She pulled away from him and turned, looking toward the doorway. "Now where have those girls gotten to?"

Terri and Sophie were busy exploring the other rooms on the second floor. The back two bedrooms were located on either side of the master bath. One room, closest to the front porch, was square shaped. After a brief examination, the girls dismissed this room as too small and boring. The other bedroom, which looked out over the backyard, was much more spacious and shaped like an "L." Inside were twin beds, one at each end, two nightstands and an antique dresser. There was a small walk-in closet on the wall next to the bath.

"This is ours!" exclaimed Terri as she lay down, testing one of the beds. Sophie followed suit and the little girls nodded at each other.

"You can have one end and I can have the other, Ter. It'll be like we have our own rooms but we'll still be together."

Finding the beds comfortable, they checked out the closet and determined it was large enough to hold their things. Their explorations ended when they heard their mother call and they dashed off to find her.

"Well, what do you think, Ter, Soph? Do you want to each have your own room or share?"

Terri and Sophie looked at each other and burst out laughing.

"Mommy!" exclaimed Terri. "Of course, we want to be together! What a silly thing to ask! We love the L-shaped room. Can we have it, Mommy, please?"

Karen laughed with them. "Of course you can. How silly of me to think you might want rooms of your own. That'll come in time, I'm sure, but not now."

Just then a clap of thunder shook the house.

"Okay, troops, bedrooms decided, we better get the rest of our stuff inside before the rain comes," said Bill. "I think we may be in for a heck of a storm."

Bill was right. The rain began quick and hard and the wind was soon keeping pace.

THE CELLAR

Karen made herself busy in the kitchen unloading the groceries they'd bought on the mainland while Bill and the girls brought the last of their meager belongings into the house. Intermittent thunder disrupted the steady beat of rain and wind against the windows and roof as they worked.

"Bill, it's getting cold in here. How come the heat isn't on?" asked Karen as she organized things in the pantry.

"Don't know," he replied. "I made sure the oil tank was full before we left California and I asked the attorneys handling the estate to have the furnace checked. They said they did it, but who knows? The furnace is in the cellar. I'll go down and see what's what."

The cellar was located off the kitchen. It was not a finished basement, nor could it really be called a basement at all. Basement was too good a word for it. It was a cellar, perhaps the epitome of all cellars. The floor was rock and dirt, uneven and damp. Bill observed an ancient sump pump in one corner that appeared well used.

Looks like we can expect some flooding down here, he thought ruefully, noting the furnace and oil tank were raised up on concrete blocks. *Most likely it happens in the spring when the snow melts off.* Watermarks on the walls confirmed this hypothesis.

Shaking his head, he walked over to the boiler, which sat in the center of the room next to the chimney. It was pretty much a mystery to him, having never seen an oil burner before.

Oh shit, I don't have the foggiest idea how this thing works, he thought in disgust as he examined it. Noting a big red button on the front of the machine labeled "Reset," he pressed it. The furnace roared to life.

I'll have to ask Pete for the name of someone who can service this monstrosity, he thought, feeling pleased with himself.

Turning from the furnace, he noted trickles of water beginning to seep through cracks in the old stone foundation. *Guess I'm going to find out if that sump works tonight, too.*

Gazing at the furnace, the pump, and the condition of the cellar in general, he shook his head again and took a deep breath. *Maybe Karen's right; maybe we've bitten off more than we can chew. But what's done is done. Time to stop complaining and make the best of it.*

With renewed resolve, he turned to go back up the stairs but stopped, noticing something curious. On the wall next to the bulkhead door were marks etched into the stone. From a distance, they looked like Aboriginal cave paintings or crude symbols of some sort. But, in the poor light of the cellar, it was hard to tell. Squinting to see better, he noted that the stone they were etched on was part of the foundation, yet somehow it looked different than the rest. He began to walk over to get a better look when Karen called to him.

"What's taking you so long? We need you up here to help with the unpacking while I make dinner. Also, a nice fire in the woodstove to kill the chill would be appreciated!"

"I'm coming," he replied, deciding to leave his investigations for another day, perhaps when he could open the bulkhead door to let more light in.

Yeah, that's what I'll do, he thought as went upstairs to help his wife.

Karen prepared sandwiches, a salad, and chips for dinner,

wanting to leave serious cooking for another day when she had time to get acquainted with the ancient stove. Before they sat down to eat, Bill brought in some dry wood from the mudroom and started a fire in the living room woodstove. Chores done for the time being, the family gathered around the old oak table for their first meal in their new home.

"Wait," said Bill, getting up from the table. "Something's missing."

He went into the kitchen and came back with a bottle of champagne he had kept hidden to surprise Karen. He grabbed four old jelly jar glasses from the china cupboard, opened the bottle with a loud "pop," and poured half glasses for him and his wife and little sips for the girls.

"A toast," he said, raising his glass. "To our new home and our new life as islanders!"

The girls giggled and lifted their glasses. With some reluctance, Karen raised hers.

As they all drank, lightning flashed outside, followed by loud thunder. The wind howled. The storm was in full swing.

THE GIRLS

After supper, Terri and Sophie left their parents by the fire and went upstairs to their new room to unpack. They found the small walk-in closet empty except for several wire hangers. The back wall was lined with shelves and Terri decided this would be a good place for their shoes. As she placed a pair on one shelf, she noticed a loose board on the back wall. Naturally curious, she pushed on the board and was amazed when it slid sideways to reveal a secret hiding place.

"Sophie, come here," she whispered. "Look what I've found."

The two girls knelt down and peered into the opening. Inside was a wooden box. Terri carefully slid it out onto her lap, examining it.

The box was rectangular in shape, the size of a sheet of notebook paper, and three inches deep. On top were carved several symbols: a crescent moon, what looked like a bolt of lightning, and a rain- or teardrop. And the box was locked.

Terri shook it gently to see if there was anything inside, laughing when she heard and felt things move.

"There's stuff inside it, Soph. And look - it's got two locks. Someone must have wanted to make sure no one opened it!"

Terri pointed to the key-type lock that was integral to the box and an additional small padlock that was secured to a metal strap that was wound around it.

The girls tried to slide the strap off, but it was wrapped too tightly.

"I wonder what's in it," said Terri. "You think it might be a treasure?"

"We have to find the keys," said her twin enthusiastically. "Should we tell Mommy?"

"No, let's not. Let's keep this our secret. We found it in our room, so it's ours."

"Yes, but it might contain grown-up things and Mommy should know."

"No, Soph, it's ours," said Terri, adamantly. "Pinkie swear you don't tell Mommy or Daddy!"

"Okay, Ter," her twin agreed reluctantly, sighing. "I pinkie swear."

The girls entwined their little fingers, then turned their attention back to the box. Sophie ran her hands over the carved symbols. "What do think these mean?"

"Don't know, Soph. Maybe what's inside will explain. We've got to find those keys!"

Both the girls puzzled over where the keys might be.

"Since the box was hidden, I guess the keys are probably hidden, too. What do you think, Ter?"

Terri nodded in agreement.

Curious and excited by their discovery, they decided to put their unpacking aside and search the room to see what they could find.

First, they looked in the obvious places - the bureau and nightstands, but those were all empty.

"If I were an old auntie lady, where would I hide a key?" asked Sophie. "I wouldn't put it under the bed, 'cause then I'd have to bend down and everyone knows old people can't bend."

"Maybe it's taped to the bottom of one of the dresser drawers," replied Terri.

Acting on this suggestion, they pulled the drawers out to check, but again came up empty-handed.

17

Next, they examined all the other walls and shelves in the closet, hoping to find a second hiding place. But they found none.

"They could be anywhere in the house," said a frustrated Sophie. "And maybe the old witch had the keys in her pocket when they buried her!"

"She wasn't a witch. She was an auntie and she was Daddy's auntie so she couldn't have been a witch," replied Terri, indignantly. "Maybe she hid them in the bathroom - in the medicine cabinet."

For lack of a better idea, the girls ran to the bathroom, but the cabinet, too, was empty. Returning to their room, they sat on their respective beds and tried to solve the puzzle of the missing keys. Despite Sophie's belief that old people couldn't bend, they looked under the beds and under the mattresses too. Again, they came up empty.

Running out of ideas of places to search in their room, Sophie tiptoed into their parents' room and looked in the nightstand, dresser, and closet while Terri stood guard listening for footfalls on the stairs. Then, they searched the third small bedroom, again to no avail. It was getting late and they were frustrated and tired.

"This is crazy," complained Sophie. "They've got to be here somewhere."

"Let's think," added Terri. "What would Nancy Drew do?"

The girls had a whole set of Nancy Drew mysteries, a gift from their maternal grandmother, and even though the stories were dated, they enjoyed them tremendously and admired the young sleuth.

Perplexed, Sophie put her head in her hands and thought for a minute. Then a big smile broke out on her face. "She'd look in the floorboards! For a hidden compartment in the floorboards!"

The girls looked at one another and dove to the floor. Raising dust balls and cobwebs as they went along, they searched and searched, and just when they were about to give up, Terri's fingers found a knothole in one of the boards under the dresser. She put her thumb in the hole and pulled. The board loosened and finally came out. Sitting in the recess was a key ring.

"I got it!" she exclaimed in delight.

She was about to reach into the hole to extract the key when Sophie heard someone coming up the stairs.

"It's Mom and Dad!"

Quickly, Terri pulled her hand back, leaving the key ring in its hiding place, and replaced the board. Hearing the footsteps coming closer, the girls hopped onto their beds just as their mother entered the room.

"Looks like you girls didn't get too much done," Karen said, pointing to the unpacked boxes that littered the room. "Well, it's time for bed now, girls. You'll have to finish up in the morning."

Karen noticed the dirt and dust on the twins' clothing and hands. "My, oh my, how did you two get so dirty? Well, it's too late for baths. Both of you get into your PJs and march into the bathroom to brush your teeth and wash up. I'll make up the beds - then it's lights out! We'll think about baths in the morning."

The girls followed their mother's instructions and marched into the bathroom. Karen put fresh linens and blankets on the beds and soon the twins were settled and ready to sleep. Bill joined Karen and together they said goodnight to their daughters.

"Sweet dreams, munchkins," Bill said as he kissed them goodnight. "Tomorrow's a big day - lots of unpacking to do and we have to get you two registered for school."

"No whispering, reading, or anything tonight," instructed their mother. "Just get a good night's sleep. Your father and I will be up shortly. Love you."

She kissed her daughters on the cheeks as Bill turned out the lights and shut the door. When she heard her parents go downstairs, Terri whispered to her sister, "We'll see if the keys fit tomorrow."

"Just like Nancy Drew," responded Sophie as she yawned, rolled over, and fell into a dreamless sleep.

It took longer for Terri to fall asleep, her mind focused on the carved box and what it might contain. She lay awake listening to the wind and rain as the storm raged outside. Sometimes it felt as if the wind was calling to her and she had an urge to get up and go outside to answer it. But fatigue from the long day finally won out and she pushed those thoughts from her mind and drifted off to sleep.

Her sleep, however, was not dreamless. Sounds of moaning and pitiful cries for help invaded her mind causing her to toss and turn. She woke up at one point, gasping for breath, and called out weakly for her mother, but no one answered. Afraid to go back to sleep, she thought about waking her twin, but did nothing. Finally, exhausted, she fell to sleep again and this time, luckily, no visions or sounds disturbed her.

BILL & KAREN

As Terri struggled with sleep, her parents tried to relax downstairs, a fire crackling soothingly in the living room woodstove. The heat it generated held back the ever-pervasive dampness that was the price for living next to the ocean. Karen sat in an overstuffed chair facing the picture window, watching the storm outside. Behind the sound of the wind and rain, she could hear the pounding of the waves against the shoreline.

Nice sound, she thought as a single tear ran down her cheek, *but wrong ocean.*

She took a sip of her wine. Deep in thought, she was startled to feel a hand on her shoulder.

"Karen?" Bill asked, bringing her back to reality.

She shuddered and turned to look at him, her eyes liquid and full of tears. "What?" she asked, pulling away from his touch.

Bill sat down on the sofa opposite her. "Listen, I know you're tired and not altogether happy with this move, this house, but we're here now and we need to make the best of it. We need to talk about what's ahead. Maybe make a list of things we have to do, set priorities, that kind of stuff. I can't do this alone. I need your help, your input."

Karen laughed. "Not altogether happy? No, I guess I'm not altogether happy." She turned away from him and gazed out the window again. "And what am I not altogether happy about? Just about everything, as far as I can see - this house, this island, the weather. Did I leave anything out? And, Bill, don't be such a geek with your lists, prioritizing everything. Why can't we just live for a change? Let what happens, happen? I'm tired of all this planning and worrying about consequences. I just want to relax and let life take its course. Can't we give it a rest for one night? God, this place is claustrophobic!"

She turned back to face him and her anger melted away. "Oh sweet Jesus, Bill. You look like a puppy I've just kicked. I'm sorry if I hurt you. I'm trying. Please, I'm trying. I just need time and some space. This is all new to me. I miss my home, my things, my life."

Bill moved toward her, but she stiffened again, rejecting him. "And please, don't smother me. You absolutely smother me with your understanding and tolerance. I don't deserve it. Just believe I love you and our girls but give me time to find my own way. Please."

Bill stood and stared at her as she turned again to gaze out the window, shutting him out. He started to speak, but thought better of it and, with a quiet sigh, left the room.

Hearing him leave, Karen's head fell to her hands as tears streamed through her fingers. She held her breath and then, slowly, exhaled. Her life was changing and she didn't like it.

Do I still love him? I just said I did, but was that a lie? She shook her head in frustration, returning her gaze to the sea. She knew she had just hurt her husband unnecessarily. *But isn't he to blame for putting us in this position? Isn't he somehow culpable?*

She sighed. The answers were nowhere in sight. All she was sure of was that, for this night, she needed a temporary halt to the forces that were pulling at her soul.

So, she closed her eyes and leaned back in the chair listening as the storm raged, around and inside of her, and salty tears dried on her cheeks.

Leaving Karen alone, Bill sat down in the family room to try to get some work done. After fifteen minutes of doodling, he put down his laptop and got up to start a fire in the woodstove. He was angry - angry at the way Karen was treating him. It had been a rough day for all of them and her attitude didn't help at all. He tried to put aside his irritation, but her words kept coming back to him. Finally, admitting he was too wound up to accomplish much, he got up and walked to the dining room.

I need a drink, he thought as he searched through the china cupboard, assuming that was where his aunt would have stored her liquor. Behind a half-full bottle of port, he found an unopened bottle of Jack Daniels, covered in dust. He grabbed one of the jelly jar glasses and, wiping the bottleneck with his shirt, poured himself a healthy drink. As he turned to go back to the family room, he stopped in the doorway and gazed at his wife. She still sat in the chair by the window. Her eyes were closed and her arms were wound tightly around her body as if she were trying to keep herself from breaking apart. He thought about waking her, but decided not to.

Back in the family room, he stood at the window watching the storm as he sipped his drink. The wind was fierce, driving the rain against the house and roof. An old ship's bell his aunt had mounted by the door clanged annoyingly. He felt a chill and realized that cold air and dampness from the cellar were seeping up through the floorboards into the room. He stoked the fire in the woodstove and added more logs. When it was ablaze again, he took his drink and sat back down on the sofa.

Leaning back, he closed his eyes. *How did we ever end up here?* He sipped his drink as his mind retreated to a time two years prior when he'd thought he had the world in the palm of his hand.

With a Masters in Computer Sciences, Bill had been a rising star in Silicon Valley, and had been given the opportunity to be the lead developer on a new software package. It was an important assignment for one so junior in the company and, if he succeeded, there was a promise of a promotion, possibly to senior management. Everything moved along smoothly and at the time of the launch, his boss, Sloane, invited the whole research and development division for a party at his club to celebrate. Bill and his team were treated to a round of golf before the festivities began. Karen and the other wives and girlfriends were going to join the group later, when the party started.

The day couldn't have gone better and Bill was relaxing with Sloane over drinks when his cell buzzed. He pulled it out to see who it was. "It's Karen," he explained. "I'd better take this." He got up from the table and walked over to the window.

"Hey, babe. What's up?" he asked.

"Sophie's spiked a fever and Terri is starting to sniffle and complain," she replied, sounding frustrated. "I talked to the doctor and this could go on for on for quite a while. I'm sorry, hon, but I think I'd better sit this party out. The girls need me here."

"You sure? Can't the babysitter take care of them?" he complained. "It would just be for a couple of hours; you can leave early. I need you with me tonight. It's important, Karen."

There was dead silence on the line for a minute. Then he heard her sigh. "This isn't open for negotiation, Bill. I'm NOT going to the party. These are our children and they're sick. You'll be all right without me."

He was about to say more - try to persuade her to come when she told him to hold on for a minute. He could hear muffled voices in the background and then she came back on the line.

"That was Terri. She's sick to her stomach, her face is all flushed, and she feels feverish. I have to go. Make my excuses. Have a good time, but don't drink too much and drive carefully. I'll see you when you get home."

Not waiting for a reply, she'd hung up. He remembered standing quietly for a moment gazing out the window. He'd wanted her to be with him. It all meant nothing if she wasn't there to share in his success. Feeling a bit angry, he'd returned to Sloane and, ignoring his wife's advice, ordered another drink.

Soon the party began in earnest and he had more than his usual share of the freely flowing alcohol. Everyone was congratulating him, clapping him on the back, and he felt like he was on top of the world. Then, there was Julie. She was Sloane's new trophy wife, about ten years younger and very attractive in a Vegas sort of way. She'd flirted with him when they'd socialized before, but Karen was always there to see nothing ever got out of hand. But tonight was different. Karen wasn't there and he'd had too much to drink. In the end, it was all really nothing, but that prick, Marty, saw them.

He was always jealous of me, thought Bill. *Probably couldn't wait to tattle to Sloane.*

In the weeks following the party, everything stayed pretty much the same at work, but there was no mention anymore of a possible promotion. Bill finally relaxed, thinking he was in the clear and was surprised when, after the recession hit, the company decided to downsize. He was one of the first to get his pink slip and the reference letter he got from Sloane painted the picture of a mediocre employee and even hinted there might be a drinking problem. Bill tried to talk to him about it, but Sloane refused to meet. About six months later, the whole company went belly-up, but Bill was sure if he'd still been there he could have networked himself into another job. As it was, he'd remained in the unemployment line for two years with no real prospects in sight. He'd never told Karen what really happened at that party, but somehow, he was sure, she knew he was partly to blame for the subsequent unraveling of their lives.

Watching the fire in the woodstove, he sipped his drink, deep in thought. *Sloane's reference really killed any chance I had. If only Karen hadn't bailed on me that night, we wouldn't be here now. We could have kept this place as a summer home.*

He thought some more about his wife as he drank. She'd treated him like a pariah in the months after he was laid off. He remembered how she reacted when he'd suggested maybe she could get a job temporarily until he could find something. In response, she'd stared at him long and hard.

"So, you want to stay home now and be Mr. Mom? Well, I don't think that's going to happen. As I recall, you're supposed to be the breadwinner. Maybe you're just not trying hard enough." Then she'd exited the room, conversation over.

So, he'd tried harder, sending out his resumé to anyone and everyone and watched as the rejections piled up. Soon, their beautiful, but heavily mortgaged, home was threatened with foreclosure. When the first notice came, Karen had been shocked.

"What's this, Bill?" she'd asked her voice laced with panic. "It can't be right, can it? You have to fix it!"

He remembered looking at the notice, his mind racing for some way to make it disappear. "Kar, maybe your father can help. Maybe he could float us a loan. I'll pay it back, with interest, as soon as I get a job. I just need a little more time. Will you talk to him?"

The look in her eyes gave him her answer before she spoke. "I'll be damned if I go begging to that man and his skanky wife for anything. What about your parents? Maybe they can help?"

"Kar, you know they can hardly make ends meet themselves. If I asked them they'd try, but they can't afford it and I won't do that to them."

"Well, you figure something out," she'd said, tossing the notice at him. "And do it now!"

The next few weeks had been difficult, Karen barely speaking to him. Then came word of his aunt's death and his inheritance.

Aunt Janie really saved our lives, he thought, thankful.

He finished his drink and yawned. It was time to stop reliving the past and get on with the future. Resolved to try to make the best of things for his family, he lay down on the couch. The rhythmic sound of the rain and the warmth of the fire combined with the alcohol were making him drowsy. He tried to put Karen out of his mind for once and stretched out, closing his eyes. Soon, all too soon, he was asleep.

MORE DREAMS

As he slept, Bill slipped into a dream state and his dream began, as most do, benignly. He was out for a run. It was a beautiful, bright, sunny day and, while the landscape was familiar, he really couldn't quite place it. He was alone, running at an easy pace, enjoying the scenery. The road was dirt and winding. As he rounded a bend in the road, he glimpsed a figure running ahead of him and could tell by the shape and gait the runner was a woman. His heart soared. Had Karen come out for a run with him? It had been so long since they'd gone for a jog together. He called to her, but she did not turn or slow her pace. He tried to catch up to her, but as soon as he got close, she ran out of reach again.

As he jogged along, following the figure ahead of him, he began to notice the landscape start to change dramatically. The trees that lined the road now appeared to be closing in, their branches threatening to block his path. All around him, the bright sunlight was fading and dark shadows loomed. He tried to run faster, but he gained no ground. Bewildered, he looked down at his feet, surprised at what he saw. The dry dirt road had turned into a muddy morass and his pace slowed to a crawl as he attempted to pull his feet free. Struggling and beginning to feel a bit panicky, he looked up. The woman ahead of him had stopped. She turned toward him, and when he saw her face, his mouth opened in surprise. This was not Karen. No, this was something else - something unclean, something foul.

He tried to turn to run away, but his feet would not move. He looked up again. The woman was walking toward him. An odor of decay filled his nostrils and fear washed over him. She was coming closer and closer, her hands reaching out, reaching for him. He opened his mouth to scream....

He woke up with a start, choking back the scream that was about to erupt from his chest. He sat up, drenched in sweat.

What the hell was that all about? he asked himself as he got up and went into the kitchen for a glass of cold water.

As he drank, he tried to remember the dream, but it had already begun to fade. All he could recall was he had been running and there was a woman involved. He walked back to the family room and stood at the window, looking out. It was still night but the storm outside was winding down. He could no longer hear the wind, and the rain was just a soft pitter-patter on the roof.

Cooled off, but exhausted, he lay down on the couch again and fell back asleep. This time, however, he slept peacefully and there were no bad dreams to disturb his slumber.

MORNING

Grrump, pssssst, grruump, psssssst. Bill woke up to the sound of the sump pump clearing out the water that had seeped into the cellar overnight.

Well, at least one thing's working, he thought.

He was still stretched out on the couch where he had fallen asleep and was covered by a soft rose-colored afghan.

Where did that come from? Did Karen put it over me?

Thinking of his wife, his mind returned to their exchange the night before.

She called me a 'geek.' So big deal. I am a 'geek,' always have been, always will be. And she married me. With her looks, brains, and personality she could have had anyone, but she picked the 'geek.' Maybe it's time she got used to it!

He got up and popped a pod into the coffee maker. While it brewed, he looked out at the morning sky. The house faced east so they would always get the sunrise, not the set. This morning, after last night's rain, the sunrise could prove to be spectacular. He went upstairs and rummaged through boxes until he found his sweats. Changing from his rumpled clothing, he noted the bed had not been slept in. Back downstairs, he saw his wife still curled tightly in the chair facing the sea, fast asleep.

He took his coffee and went outside, down the driveway and across the street to the beach, where the air was salty and fresh. It was low tide, so he sat on one of the exposed rocks to witness the sun as it crept up over the horizon. As he watched, he tried to remember the strange dream that had disturbed his sleep the night before. Deep in thought, he was startled by the sound of a car door slamming. He turned to see a young woman with a mass of curly red hair emerge from a beat-up old Volkswagen bus. With the girl was a beautiful Irish Setter that virtually exploded from the car and took off down the beach.

"Freckles, you get your butt back here," the girl yelled. The dog paid her no mind and ran into the surf, playing with the waves that lapped the shore.

A look of surprise flashed across her face when she saw Bill sitting on the rock. "Hi there," she said. "I hope we aren't disturbing you. Haven't seen you before. Are you Jane Morgan's nephew?"

"Boy, news sure does travel fast here," he replied, standing up to introduce himself. "We just got here yesterday! Yes, I'm Bill Andersen, Janie's nephew, and you aren't disturbing me in the least. That's some beautiful dog you've got there."

"Thanks," she said giving him a bright smile. "I'm sure Freckles appreciates the compliment. There's a bunch of us who come to this beach regularly to exercise our pups. We're here early in the morning, pick up poop, and promise not to make a nuisance of ourselves. Hope you won't mind if we continue to come here?"

She was standing close to him, feet apart, hands on her softly rounded hips. She was young - no more than twenty-five or six, wearing tight jeans and a sweatshirt. Although her top was over-sized and baggy, Bill could see the gentle rise and fall of her generous breasts as she spoke. Her face, framed by that mass of red curls, was pale, a rash of freckles splashed across her cheeks. Her eyes, a startling shade of green, seemed to dance seductively as she smiled at him. But it was her lips, so full and pouty, that he found infinitely beguiling. He couldn't take his eyes off her. He began to feel himself stir, his mind so overwhelmed by her presence that he could barely comprehend what she was saying.

"So what do ya say? Can we still bring our pups here? Bill?"

At the sound of his name, Bill pulled himself together and tried to focus on her words. "Oh, yeah, sure. No problem. It's a public beach anyway, isn't it?"

She curved her lips in a tantalizing smile, eyes sparkling with amusement, as if she were fully aware of the effect she was having on him. "Yeah, it's public. However, there's a leash law on this island and we don't want anyone complaining to the selectmen and getting them to enforce it. Thanks for understanding."

She broke eye contact with him and gazed longingly across the road to the house on the hill. "Glad someone has moved into that old house," she said wistfully. "I've always loved it. Hate to see island homes go to rack and ruin from disuse." She returned her gaze to him. "Oh, I forget my manners; I'm Maggie Maguire of the Irish Hill Maguires."

Bill nodded and looked at her quizzically. "What's Irish Hill?"

"Oh, I forgot you're a newbie," she laughed. "Irish Hill is a group of homes on the north end of the island. I live there, as do most of my relatives. We're all pretty inbred here – you know, it's sorta like living in Appalachia. You met my uncle yesterday, my mom's sister's husband, Pete. He and Aunt Louise and my folks will probably be showing up at your house around mid-morning to help you get that car started."

As they talked, two more cars pulled up. A short heavyset woman with two yellow labs got out of one and a tall gray-haired woman with a golden retriever emerged from the other. Maggie's Setter ran up the beach, greeted the new arrivals, and went off with them to play in the water.

Maggie pointed to the heavyset woman, "Bill, this is Kari McKinney, Pete's sister, and this is Alice Dougall, my cousin by marriage. Like I said, we're all kinda inbred here. Ladies, meet Bill Andersen, Jane's nephew."

Kari extended her hand, "Welcome to our world, Bill. Hope you enjoy island life."

"Likewise," said Alice, shaking his hand.

Introductions completed, the two women turned and joined their dogs, who were frolicking in the surf.

Giving him one more lingering smile, Maggie turned, tossed her head, and started to jog down the beach to join her friends.

Watching that girl walk away just might be the high point of my day, he thought. Then his mind returned to Karen and guilt started to seep back in. Sighing, he reluctantly got up to return to the house.

As he stood, Maggie turned her head and yelled back at him. "Hey, Bill – remember – there's no secrets on this island."

"I'll remember," he yelled back, laughing as he watched her run down the beach with her dog. Wishing he could be that carefree, that young again, he finished the last of his coffee. He knew he was just procrastinating. He couldn't avoid facing Karen any longer. Reluctantly, he turned away from Maggie and began what seemed like a very long walk home.

TERRI

The little girl lay in her bed, eyes tightly closed, feigning sleep. Her night had been anything but pleasant. Dreams the likes of which she had never known plagued her mind and now, as she lay huddled under her blankets, she wished she were back home in California. The fear she felt was new - she was the brave twin. This shouldn't be happening to her.

I'm not a scaredy cat. I'm not a scaredy cat, she repeated over and over in her mind. *Sophie's the scaredy cat, not me. NO, NOT ME!*

Yet she was scared - frightened by something elusive - something that, in the light of day, she couldn't fully comprehend.

The bedroom door opened. "Get up, sleepyheads," said Karen. "Time to rise and shine!"

Sophie groaned and rolled back over in her bed, pulling the covers over her head. Terri sat up and stared at her mom.

"What's up, Terri-bug?" asked Karen using her pet name for her daughter. "Is something wrong? Are you feeling sick?"

"I called for you last night, Mommy, but you didn't come. You didn't come! Where were you? You didn't come! I needed you. Where were you?"

Karen looked closely at her distraught daughter. "Oh, honey, Mommy fell asleep downstairs. That's why I didn't hear. I'm so sorry. Why did you need me? Were you sick? Did the thunder scare you?"

Terri didn't want to tell her mother about the dreams. She really couldn't remember them, anyway. "I woke up and I wasn't sure where I was and I got scared. But I'm okay now."

Karen gave her daughter a long hug. "You're sure you're okay? Nothing else's going on that I should know about?" She looked at Terri with a mother's eyes.

Terri glanced down at the bed, then straight up into those eyes and lied. "No, nothing else. I just forgot where I was."

"Okay, then. Let's think about taking those baths we missed last night," said Karen, laughing. "Who wants to try out that old claw-foot tub? After baths, I'll make waffles - maybe even with chocolate chips! What do you think of that?"

"Yummy, yummy, Mommy!" exclaimed Sophie. "I'll always go first for chocolate chips!"

Karen tussled her daughter's hair. "Okay, Soph, I'll go draw your bath."

As soon as Karen left the room, Terri grabbed Sophie's arm. "Remember your pinkie swear. Don't say anything about the box to Mom. It's important you don't. Okay?"

"I won't. I promise. Now lettgo my arm! You're hurting me!"

Terri looked down at her hands. Indeed, they were clutching Sophie's arm tightly. When she let go, vivid red marks branded the place where her fingers had been.

"Bath's ready," called Karen from the bathroom. "And, Terri, you're next, so don't disappear on me."

When Sophie was finished, Karen cleaned out the tub and refilled it for other daughter. Once in the tub, the little girl pulled the shower curtain closed and sunk down, letting the hot water relax her.

Reluctantly, she tried to remember the dreams, but all that came to her conscious mind was the sound - a horrible moaning sound like nothing she'd ever heard before. It was as if someone or something was in terrible pain. And there was the smell - an odor of something horribly rotten and decayed. It made her physically ill to think of it and she jumped from the tub and retched into the sink, but nothing came up but bile.

I've got to stop thinking about it, she admonished herself. *It was only a dream.* She once again sank down into the hot water and willed herself to relax.

"Come on, Terri-bug, time to get out of the tub before you shrivel up like an old lady," Karen exclaimed as she opened the door to the bathroom. "Breakfast's almost ready, so let's get you dried, dressed, and braided!"

Terri let her mother enfold her in a big white towel and, forcing a smile, dried herself off and went to the bedroom to get dressed. Karen towel-dried and then braided her daughter's long blonde hair. Terri's hair was always braided. Sophie, on the other hand, liked to let hers run wild and free. Their preference for different hairstyles was one sure way to tell the girls apart.

Dressed and braided, Terri tried again to put her dreams behind her and went downstairs with her mother and sister to help with breakfast.

BILL & KAREN

Unable to put it off any longer, Bill slowly walked back to the house. *Maybe she's packed her bags. Maybe she's going to leave and take my girls.*

Bill had been with Karen for twelve years and he could not imagine life without her. However, he knew her leaving was now a definite possibility. *I have to make things right for her. Turn back the clock somehow. Get us back to where we were.*

Unfortunately, the "how" of doing this eluded him. However, even if she decided to leave, one thing was certain in his mind - he wouldn't let her take his kids from him.

No, I'll fight her tooth and nail if it comes to that, he decided.

Entering the house, he could hear Karen and the girls talking and laughing as they prepared breakfast. Those sounds, ones he had heard a thousand times before, were now like music to his ears. He walked to the kitchen and stood in the doorway watching as Karen and Terri cooked while Sophie set the table.

Hearing him enter, Sophie turned and leapt into his arms. "Daddy, where have you been? We're having waffles with chocolate chips!"

Karen turned. She looked contritely at him and started to speak, but Bill silenced her with a wave of his hand. "Let's leave it for now, Karen. We've been under a lot of stress lately. We need time to unwind. I know all this has been tough on you and the girls, but it's going to get better, you'll see."

Karen looked at him, her eyes turning cold. "Sure," she said flatly. "Now go wash up. Breakfast's just about ready and we've all got a long day ahead of us."

After breakfast, Bill sat down with his laptop to work on his job search. Finding work was his number one priority. He couldn't make things right for his family until he had his self-respect back. He got the Internet up and running and settled in to check out the employment market on the mainland. Disappointedly, there wasn't much in his field. He found a couple of possibilities and faxed his resumé off to them.

While her husband worked on the computer, Karen and the girls finished unpacking and began inventorying what was in the kitchen cupboards. Working hard, they lost track of time and were surprised when they heard a truck pulling up the driveway. Bill looked out the window. It was Pete McKinney, his wife, Louise, and another couple.

"Karen, it's Pete and Louise," he said as he went to open the door for their new friends.

Pete made the necessary introductions. "Bill, Karen, this is Rusty Maguire and his wife, Emma. I brought Rusty along 'cause he's just about the best mechanic on the island."

Rusty was a man of medium height with shocking red hair, peppered with gray. Bill took his age to be around fifty-five. His wife, Emma, obviously had once been a real beauty who had given way to stoutness as she aged. When she smiled, he could see laughter in her eyes and dimples in her cheeks.

Bill shook hands all around while Karen stood mute. "Rusty, you and Emma wouldn't be Maggie's parents, would you?"

Karen looked at him quizzically. "Maggie? Who's Maggie?"

"Oh, I forgot to tell you. I met her this morning down by the shore. She and some of her friends were exercising their dogs."

"Yup," said Rusty. "That's our girl all right. Always running off at the crack of dawn with that dog of hers. Hope she didn't make a nuisance of herself. She can be a bit forward, if you know what I mean. You'll probably be seeing a lot of her since you have those cute little girls. Maggie's the headmistress of our elementary school here on the island."

"Okay, guys, enough jabbering," interjected Pete. "We need to get our rears in gear and get that car started for Bill. Ladies, if you will excuse us."

Bill helped Rusty and Pete unload their tools from the truck and then headed to the garage while Karen and her guests went into the house.

"Oh, by the way, Bill," said Pete. "Rumor has it you're looking for work on the mainland. Is that right?"

Bill nodded, surprised his situation was already common knowledge around the island. Then, he remembered what that girl had said earlier about secrets and a smile broke out on his face.

"My cousin, Phil," Pete continued, "works in sales for the Omicron Software Corporation over in town and he says they're hiring. The salary's not much; you make the real money on commission. But the icing on the cake is they have a good benefits package and the hours are pretty much your own, which is helpful when you're commuting from this island. If you're interested, Phil would be happy to recommend you to the sales director."

"I would be most grateful for the introduction," Bill replied. "Sales isn't really my field, but software is, so I think I could hack it."

"Okay, great, I'll have Phil set it up. Just give me your cell or landline and I'll have him call you."

Bill wrote down his number and gave it to his new friend as the three men proceeded to work on Aunt Janie's car. Like most year-round residents' cars, the island vehicle was old and full of rust. Islanders kept their good cars on the mainland and Aunt Janie was no exception. In town, she had a two-year-old Toyota hybrid.

Sales, Bill thought disparagingly. *Well, beggars can't be choosers. I'll take what I can get now and keep looking for something better.*

The men worked on the car for about an hour until it was purring like a kitten. Rusty also looked at the lawn tractor to ensure it was running properly. Bill got the name of a man to service the boiler and planned to call him later that afternoon. The mechanical work done, the boys headed back to the house where Karen was getting an earful about life on the island and dozens of survival tips for the winter season.

"Okay, Louise, time to hit the road," said Pete. "We got work to do on the boat."

Louise and Emma got up to leave and the couples exchanged the usual pleasantries as they walked to Pete's truck.

"Listen," said Bill. "I really appreciate your help today. Why don't you all come to dinner some night later this week or next? I promise you Karen's a great cook."

Pete looked at Louise. "Mother, the social calendar's your prerogative. Any time that's fine with you is fine with me."

"Rusty and I will have to beg off," said Emma. "I'm having a medical procedure done tomorrow, nothing earthshaking mind you, but I'm supposed to stay off my feet for a couple of weeks. We'll be happy to take a rain check though."

"Friday would work for us, if that's okay with you, Karen," said Louise. "And you have to let me bring a salad. Hate to come to someone's house for dinner empty-handed."

"Friday's fine, and we'll take that salad. Say six o'clock?" Karen responded, laughing.

"Sounds great. Looking forward to it," said Pete as he backed the truck down the driveway and waved goodbye.

The morning had quickly disappeared and, after lunch, Karen decided to take the girls to the town hall to register them for school.

"Maybe, if we're lucky," she said, "we can get them in class by this afternoon. I don't want them to miss any more school than they have to."

Bill agreed, but opted to stay home and continue to work on the computer.

Karen got the girls dressed for school and loaded them into Aunt Jane's old car and took off for the town hall. The registration process went smoothly, as the clerk already had the girls' transcripts.

"Any chance they can join class this afternoon?" Karen asked.

"I think that would be fine," replied the clerk. "Why don't you take these transcripts with you. Give them to Maggie Maguire. She's the head teacher. She'll make sure your daughters get settled in okay."

Karen followed the directions given her by the town clerk and was soon parked in front of what was once a church that now served as the schoolhouse.

"Okay girls, here we go. You be on your best behavior for your new teacher," instructed Karen.

Terri and Sophie hopped out of the car, eager to see their new school. Karen looked them over, tried to calm down Sophie's unruly hair, straightened Terri's braids, and marched them into the schoolhouse.

It was a one-room structure. On the back wall was a large blackboard divided into sections. There were twelve students in the room with three adults. The students were separated into three groupings, not necessarily by age. A young woman with red hair pulled back rather haphazardly into a scrunchie looked up from the group nearest the blackboard. Seeing Karen and the twins, she stood up and beckoned to them.

"Hi," she called out. "You must be the Andersens. Nancy at the town hall phoned and told me you were on your way. I'm Maggie Maguire, the head teacher here."

Karen looked the young woman over. She was about twenty-five or twenty-six and was wearing a light, cotton dress that buttoned up the front. Her shapely legs were bare and she wore flip-flops on her feet. For makeup, she wore only a little lip gloss, but she really didn't need anything else. She was attractive in an earthy sort of way, and not at all what Karen expected.

"Yes, I'm Karen Andersen and these are my daughters, Terri and Sophie. Girls, say hello to Ms. Maguire."

Terri and Sophie, in unison, greeted their new teacher.

"Actually, all the kids call me Maggie, so you can put the 'Miss Maguire' in your pocket for now! We're pretty informal around here. Are those the girls' transcripts?" Maggie pointed to the brown envelope Karen was holding. Karen nodded and handed it over.

"I'll take these home tonight and study them and put together a lesson plan for each of the girls. You see, since we're so small, we have a great teacher-to-student ratio and we can formulate individual learning programs for each student. This allows them to progress at their own speed and not be stifled by the age-induced classroom structure. We do, however, make sure they can pass the State exams that are formulated by age. So, don't you worry about that, Mrs. Andersen."

Karen nodded again. "You'll see that Terri has advanced placement in math and Sophie's verbal and language skills are off the chart for her age. In addition, both girls score very highly on spatial and cognitive skill tests. I don't want them to fall behind."

"They won't," replied Maggie. "I'll make sure they stay on track both intellectually and socially. Our kids always do very well on their tests and continue to do well once they reach the mainland."

Maggie gave Karen a quick tour of the classroom and introduced her to the two teachers' aides who were working with the children.

"What time do the children get out of school?" Karen asked. "So I know when to pick them up."

"Oh, the bus will take them home," Maggie explained. "We know where you live. They should be home around three forty-five. And the bus will pick them up at eight-fifteen tomorrow morning, if that's all right with you?"

"That would be fine," replied Karen as she turned to her daughters. "Okay, Terri, Sophie, you have fun and mind Miss Maguire, I mean Maggie."

She embraced each girl in turn and watched as Maggie took them by the hand and led them to the table set up by the blackboard, where four other children around their age sat. She watched as they settled in and, satisfied she had done all she could, turned and left the building.

KAREN MAKES A DECISION

Karen stood in the school parking lot staring at her "new" car. It was an old Honda Civic, so ancient it didn't even have a CD player. She'd had a Toyota Highlander hybrid back in California, with all the bells and whistles - at least she'd had it until Bill lost his job and the repo men came.

I hate this place, she thought. *I hate everything about it. Everything.*

She sighed, got into the car, and just sat, her mind in turmoil. She didn't want to go home. And "home," what was "home" now?

That damp and smelly old house, filled with those ugly antiques. How am I supposed to stand that? And what will life be like having to take that uncomfortable old ferry over and back every time I want to go to the store? And what will I do if Bill actually manages to get a job? There'll be no car for me to use on the mainland on weekdays. How will I ever get away from this place? What is there for me to do here anyway? Will I be expected to be like those women who came over this morning? Emma, she seemed all right - fairly well educated. But Louise, well, she's lucky if she graduated from high school. And what do they want me to do? Will they expect me to join some ladies' group and knit sweaters, help with potluck dinners, get involved with the church? What kind of life will that be? It certainly won't be the life I'm used to, the life I want back.

Karen, the daughter of a prominent San Francisco physician, was an only child and had been pampered from the day she was born. Her parents delayed having a family until her father had established himself in his medical career and, when Karen came along, they were delighted and made sure she had the best of everything. She went to private schools, wore the prettiest clothes, was a member of the local soccer club, took gymnastics - basically enjoyed all the advantages her parents could afford.

Her life seemed perfect until, at age twelve, her parents divorced. Her surgeon father succumbed to the usual cliché - an affair with his scrub nurse, a woman twenty years his junior. When the woman found out she was pregnant, he packed his bags and moved in with her, leaving Karen and her mother high and dry. When all the wrangling and name calling was done, Karen's mother got the house, a healthy amount of alimony and child support, and custody of Karen, who only saw her dad every other weekend and for a month each summer.

Karen hated her dad's new wife and was equally unhappy with her new half-brother and sister when they came along. She barely endured the time she was forced to spend at her father's, calling her new siblings "the evil spawn." She was glad when she graduated from high school and could go off to college and get away from all of them for good. She vowed she would never get divorced. When, and if, she ever trusted any man enough to marry him, it would be for good. She took the vow "till death do us part" literally and was determined no child of hers would go through what she did.

Scoring in the 95th percentile on her SATs, she was accepted at Stanford and majored in Languages, envisioning a glamorous career as a translator off in some foreign land. She spent her sophomore year at Stanford's campus in France, learning to speak the language fluently.

As an undergraduate, she was popular, dating mostly star athletes or young men prominent in other aspects of campus life. Her experience with her parents' divorce left her suspicious of men and she found it difficult to maintain a relationship. She had one serious boyfriend during her senior year, but that ended when the boy moved back east after graduation. Karen was a west coast girl and she planned to keep it that way.

She stayed on at Stanford in their Masters' Program and, during her first year of graduate work, met Bill at a party at San Jose State. A classmate had cajoled her into attending and she was thinking of leaving early when she noticed a young man enter the room. He was nice looking, tall and slender with tousled sandy hair. She could tell by the way his clothes fit he was athletic, most likely a runner. He wore black glasses that gave him a serious look, but he had a ready smile and was quick to laugh. Overall, he was a very appealing package.

As she examined him, he turned in her direction. They watched each other for a few seconds then he walked away. Disappointed, Karen decided it was time to escape the party and go home to Palo Alto. She began looking for the friend she came with when she felt a tap on her shoulder. She turned to find the young man with the black glasses standing before her, offering her a beer.

"Hi," he said. "I saw you were empty-handed so I thought I'd get you a drink. I'm Bill Andersen. I'm in the graduate program here in Computer Sciences."

She smiled shyly at him and took the drink, thanking him. As they chatted, she discovered he was in his second year of grad school. He was a couple of years older, having had to work part time to finance his undergraduate education, but now was on full scholarship. He spoke enthusiastically about his field and she could sense he couldn't wait to graduate and make his mark on Silicon Valley. As they talked, she became attracted to his lively sense of humor and gentleness. In addition, he had an aura of confidence, but in a way that was not obnoxious.

When it came time for Karen and her friend to leave, he asked for her number. She gave it to him readily and, by the time she arrived home at her apartment, there was already a message from him asking her out for the following weekend. They dated for the next two years while Karen worked on her degree and, for the first time, she let herself fully trust a man, feeling safe and secure in the love he felt for her.

Bill got his Masters and soon landed a lucrative position with a start-up in Silicon Valley. The day he got the job, he asked Karen to marry him. She accepted his proposal and they were wed two weeks following her completion of graduate school. The wedding was an elaborate affair, paid for by her dad and his wife. They honeymooned at her father's beach house in Monterey and it was there Karen finally lost her virginity. Bill was the only man she had ever known intimately and she was sure he'd be the only one she would ever know.

No glamorous translator jobs available, Karen settled for a position as a secretary with a Palo Alto law firm and, for two years, she and Bill worked and saved until they had the down payment for the home of their dreams in pricey Los Gatos. The home was located halfway between their respective places of employment so it made commuting easy. On their first night in their new home, Karen got pregnant and nine months later, the twins arrived.

Karen hated her job at the law firm and was happy to quit and become a full-time mother. When the twins were old enough for pre-school, she entered the social life of Los Gatos with rounds of shopping, tennis, and lunches with friends. She and Bill entertained often and she was an excellent hostess. She took pride in her lovely home, stocked with all the latest conveniences, her children who were precocious, and her husband, a rising star in the software business. Everything was perfect until the unthinkable happened - Bill lost his job and everything went south from there. Now, they were here on this god-forsaken island, trying to pick up the pieces of their life and start over again.

I could leave. I could just take the girls and leave, she thought as she started the car. She drove until she found a public "right of way" to the shore and turned down the dirt road, parking at the end. She walked to the beach and sat on a rock overlooking the sea, alone with her thoughts.

I could take the girls back to California. Mom would help us at first. I'd probably have to take classes to get my skills back, but I could do that. Then I could get a job, maybe as a translator this time.

But she knew Bill would never let her take the girls that far away. He was a good father and he loved his children.

He will not let them go, not easily. There'll be a fight and the losers will be Terri and Sophie. No, I can't do that to them. I won't let them grow up the way I did, visiting Dad on weekends, resenting both parents for ruining their childhood. There has to be another way.

Karen stared out at the sea before her, mesmerized by the sound of the waves.

I could give it six months. I could try, really try, for six months. Maybe I can make this work.

It was early May now and six months would take her to the beginning of October, just before the snow started. Snow, just the thought of it sent shivers up her spine. Snow to her was Lake Tahoe and skiing, not shoveling the driveway.

If I can't make it work by the middle of October then we'll leave. Before the snow. Yes, six months, and I will really try.

Thinking about it, she realized to "really try" would mean inviting Bill back into her bed. Their sex life had been nonexistent for the past few months. The same scenario replayed itself - he made overtures and she rebuffed them. She was angry, so angry with him for ruining their fairy tale existence, just the thought of intimacy was repugnant.

But, be fair now, girl, she admonished herself. *The layoff wasn't entirely Bill's fault. Yeah, he had a part in it - something he won't talk about, but it was the recession, too. I should be mad at the government, the bankers, the Wall Street fat cats, not Bill. Yes, to make this work, I have to invite him back in, even if it means feigning orgasm. Yes, if necessary, I can do it. I've done it before and, maybe, just maybe, I won't have to.*

Bill had always been a considerate lover, always concerned for her pleasure, and they enjoyed a very healthy sex life before he lost his job. *Maybe we can get that back, but if not, I can always pretend.*

She stood, feeling like a weight had been removed from her chest, and took a deep breath. "I've made a decision," she said aloud. Then she laughed. "Well, actually, I've made a decision not to decide. Not much of a decision, but it's better than the nothing I had before." Smiling to herself, she vowed she would really try - for the sake of her children and her marriage; she would try to make this work.

Feeling better than she had since their arrival on the island and full of resolve, Karen returned to her car and the road that led back to her new home and her family.

MAGGIE

It was the end of the school day and Maggie watched her charges get on the bus for home. She was vigilant, making sure none of the little ones went missing. Five years on the mainland had taught her that. Even though it was only early May, the island day-trippers were beginning to appear, and not just on weekends. Therefore, she had to be careful with the safety of the children, and she was.

The last to get on the bus were the Andersen twins. *Such cute little girls and smart, too,* she thought. *Terri, the one in braids, seems to be more serious and studious while the other one, Sophie, is a bundle of laughter.*

And the mother. What was her name again? Oh, yes - Karen - a tall, slender, attractive blonde with very cool blue eyes. Yeah, Bill scored there. But the iciness is not just in her eyes. It's in her manner, too.

Maggie shook her head and went about closing up the classroom, thinking about the aura of aloofness she sensed in Karen. *She's like some of the summer people. Thinks she's too good for mere mortals like me.*

Maggie had been born and bred on the island. Her mother was one of the summer people who married an islander. That's the way it usually went - summer girls married island boys, while summer boys married anybody but island girls. Rusty Maguire fished for a living and was good at it, so they lived pretty well. Maggie was an only child and her parents doted on her. She had her mother's good looks and her father's shocking red hair and, as she grew up, she developed into a strikingly beautiful young woman. Her parents were strict with her and discouraged any involvement with summer boys, insisting she date only islanders. However, cursed with a rebellious streak, she often snuck out and hung with the summer crowd anyway and after one of those parties, lost her virginity at age fifteen. But the romances never lasted. September came and those privileged young men returned to their homes in California, Boston, New York, or wherever there were private schools and gated communities. They went back to their debutantes and left island girls like Maggie alone and broken-hearted.

She did well in school and her parents saved in order to send her to college on the mainland. With the help of a scholarship, she was able to live on campus, but it was not enough for her to be a full-time student. To supplement, she waited tables at a local restaurant and, in five years, earned her degree and teaching certificate. During her last two years at school, she became involved in a torrid affair with one of her professors, a married man. Eventually, his wife found out about it and confronted Maggie at her place of work.

In the end, as could be expected, the professor refused to leave his wife and left Maggie alone and humiliated. Word of her affair got back to the island. Her parents, embarrassed by their daughter's conduct, pressured the island's school board to offer her a job so they could keep an eye on her. Because teaching jobs were scarce then, she had no choice but to accept and had held the position for close to two years now.

Since social life on the island was limited, she often escaped to the mainland, usually hanging out in one of the working-class bars that peppered the waterfront. Occasionally, she picked up some guy and let him take her home, but these were all just one-night stands. Since the professor, she'd shied away from any serious entanglements, but now she was beginning to feel the need for something more.

As she exited the schoolhouse, her thoughts turned to Bill Andersen. *He's a hottie, for sure. Really good-looking. A little nerdy with those*

47

glasses, but nice eyes and bod. Has that California look about him - fit, tan, and well put together. Yeah, looks like he knows who he is and where he's going, like he fits inside his own skin. Gosh, when I first saw him sitting on that rock, it was like a thunderbolt hit me. And he felt it, too. I could see it in his eyes. Now the only hurdle I have to get over is the wife - that tall, cool blonde.

She shook her head. *Another married man? Lord, what is wrong with me?*

Nevertheless, she sensed all was not well with the Andersen marriage. The story of Karen's coolness to Bill on the boat had already gotten the gossips' tongues wagging and she sensed he was troubled when she'd interrupted him that morning. Rumors of his family's financial woes had also made the rounds and she knew money problems could be hard on a marriage, even a good one. Moreover, there was that feeling she got when she was talking to him.

Yes, I could see the desire in his eyes. He wants me, just like I want him.

She got in her car, thoughts in turmoil. *Well, I won't go there unless he makes the first move. And, if that happens, well, we'll just let the chips fall. Yes, I'll just wait and see what happens. It's a small island. I'll run into him again.*

Smiling to herself, she backed out of the parking lot and headed home, her mind full of hope and possibilities.

KAREN & BILL

Bill was repairing the front step when he heard the car come up the driveway. He had been worried about Karen. It was three o'clock and she should have been back long before this. He breathed a sigh of relief when he saw her emerge from the car.

"Where did you find this?" she asked, pointing to an old gas barbecue that now stood on the front patio.

Swallowing the questions that wanted to tumble from his lips concerning her whereabouts, Bill replied, "I found it in the garage. I got it cleaned up and I think it will work okay - just needs propane."

"It's probably so old it doesn't have a CD player either!" Karen replied, chuckling to herself about the reference to her "new" car.

"Huh? A barbecue with a CD player? What are you talking about?"

"Private joke," she answered as she walked over to where he was working. She leaned down and kissed him lightly on the lips. Then, humming to herself, went into the house.

Bill sat down on the steps, a look of surprise on his face. *She kissed me for no reason at all. When was the last time that happened? And her attitude - making jokes? Well, at least I think it was a joke. Something about a CD player? Whatever she did after dropping the girls at school seems to have mellowed her a bit and I'm thankful for that! It hasn't been fun walking around on eggshells all the time, never knowing what might set her off. Maybe the sea air and natural beauty of this place are beginning to have an effect.*

Shaking his head, he went back to work on the step, his mind turning to other things. His afternoon had been a productive one. Almost as soon as Karen and the girls left for the town hall, he received a call from Pete's cousin, Phil. They'd chatted about the opening at Omicron and the company in general. Phil said his manager, a Mr. LeFleur, was expecting to receive Bill's credentials by the end of the day. Bill got the company's fax number and, after thanking Phil, sent off his resumé to LeFleur. About an hour later, while he was working on the porch, he received a call and set up an interview for Monday morning.

In preparation for the interview, Bill did some research on the firm. Omicron was a young and vibrant company focused on developing products to modernize the New England fishing industry. It also produced software for companies involved in alternative energy - wind and solar, a rapidly growing field that Omicron intended to grow with. The sales job would mean a lot of time away from home and some overnights on the mainland, but LeFleur had hinted it could lead to a position in Research and Development when an opening came up. If that happened, he would have an inside track and a way to return to his chosen career path.

Pleased with himself and the progress he'd made toward obtaining employment, Bill continued to work on the step. As he hammered, Karen came to the door.

"The girls should be home by bus around three forty-five. When they get here, if they're not too bushed from their first day at school, maybe we can go find that store and see if they sell propane. I have chicken thawed for dinner and it might be fun to barbecue."

"Sounds like a plan. I'm almost done here. What did you think of the school?"

Karen pursed her lips and frowned. "I'd say it was primitive by our standards, but the teacher-to-student ratio is good and the Maguire girl says she's going to fashion individual lesson plans for each of the girls so they can learn at their own pace. We'll have to keep close tabs on the work they're doing, make sure they don't fall behind or are short-changed. Their education comes first. If they don't get what they need here, we'll have to think about home schooling or a school on the mainland."

The subject of home schooling was not a new one for them. Both Karen and Bill had first-class intellects. Back in California, had private school not been an option, they might have chosen this path. It was concern for the girls' social development that made them choose a private school.

"And, your friend, the Maguire girl," Karen added. "Well, she's a real piece of work. I don't think she wears a bra. And the flip-flops, just a tad too bohemian for my taste."

Bill laughed. "I just met her once, Kar, that hardly qualifies her as my friend! But seriously, these island schools have a very good reputation. Don't you remember the research we did before we got here? Ninety-five percent of the students from these schools go on to get college degrees and that's significantly higher than the normal public school population. However, if this school or the teachers can't cut the mustard, then I'm with you on the home schooling thing. Our girls are just too bright to fall by the wayside, intellectually."

Bill turned his attention back to his carpentry work. "There," he said as he pounded the last nail in place. "I think that'll do it. I'll tackle the screen door tomorrow and see if I can get that old scooter I found in the garage running. It would be nice to have an alternative form of transportation available and it might be fun in the summer."

"That'd be cool. It's been a long time since I've been on a bike."

"You've ridden a motorbike?" asked Bill, slightly surprised.

"Before your time. Now, we have the McKinneys coming for dinner tomorrow night. I think I'll go to the mainland and pick up some steaks. That should be an adventure. We can do them on the grill. And maybe something for dessert. It's still too chilly for ice cream - how about a pie or cake? And a nice wine. What do you think?"

Bill thought briefly about their meager bank account and then about the sudden change in Karen's attitude and decided not to upset the applecart by seeming stingy right now. In any case, if he got the sales job, there would be a paycheck soon. Besides, they deserved a treat, didn't they?

"Make that two bottles of wine, maybe a nice cab or pinot and a chard."

They chatted a bit more about the McKinneys before Bill told her about his upcoming job interview. Karen seemed delighted and gave him a hug and another brief kiss. He was about to put his arms around her when they heard the sound of the school bus at the foot of their driveway.

The twins exploded from the vehicle, laughing and giggling as they ran to greet their parents. They were bubbling over with enthusiasm about their new school, new friends, and, to Karen's dismay, their new teacher. Just why she didn't like that girl, she couldn't explain, but the animosity was there and she sensed it was mutual.

"There's only fifteen kids in the whole school and three teachers!" exclaimed Terri.

"And Maggie - she wants us to call her Maggie, Daddy," explained Sophie. "Well, she's our teacher and she's going to make up lessons just for us. Mine won't be the same as Terri's or any other kid's. It will be just for me!"

"And there's a garden we will get to plant next month and we'll bring stuff we grow home to you, Mommy!" offered Terri.

Karen was glad to see the animation in Terri's eyes. She had been worried about her daughter, thinking she was coming down with something or was possibly psychically tuned in to the discord growing in her parents' relationship. However, now she seemed like her old self, full of confidence and joy.

"Okay, kids, we want to hear all about it," said Bill, patiently. "But first we need you to hop in the car and go with us to the general store to see if we can rustle up some propane for the grill. Mom wants to barbecue chicken tonight!"

"Oh, boy! Barbecue! I love barbecue!" exclaimed Sophie.

The girls hurried to stow their backpacks and then jumped into the car. The Andersens, on an even keel for once, headed off in search of propane.

THE GIRLS

After dinner, Sophie and Terri told their parents they had homework and retired to their room. Once there, they put their classroom assignments aside and turned their attention to more important things - the strange box and the keys they'd found. When they were sure they were alone, Terri reached under the dresser and opened the compartment in the floorboards. She removed the key ring and showed it to her sister.

"Look, Soph, two keys," she whispered.

The girls examined the keys carefully. One was quite small, the size one would expect for a jewelry box. The other was larger and looked like a standard house key.

Sophie retrieved the box from its hiding place in the closet.

Looking at the locks on the box, Terri frowned. "I don't think this is going to work. I think the little key will fit, but the other is way too big for the padlock."

She tried the smaller key and it did fit the box's lock but, as she expected, the other key was too large.

Sophie sat thinking, her face a study in concentration. "Makes sense. If you go to all the trouble to lock the box twice and hide the keys, why would you hide both keys in the same place? Nancy Drew wouldn't do that. She'd hide the keys in different places."

Terri nodded, pleased with her sister's reasoning. "If one key on that ring is a house key, maybe the missing key is on another ring with the car keys."

"Or, on a ring with another house key!" offered Sophie.

"Mommy and Daddy have those key rings. We'll have to find a way to check them out without them knowing. We'll have to be sneaky!"

"We could get in trouble. We have to be very, very careful!"

Terri nodded. "We have to think about this to make sure we don't get caught. Let's do our homework now and we can brainstorm later."

Sophie nodded and the girls hid the box and keys back under a pile of T-shirts in the closet and pulled out their homework.

Their first assignment was simple and designed to help Maggie get to know them better. They were each to write a short autobiography, including their impressions about moving to the island. The idea behind this assignment, from their teacher's point of view, was to assess their language skills as well as to find out something about them so she could more accurately meet their needs, both intellectually and socially.

Terri sat with pencil in hand, looking out the window as she composed her thoughts. The storm and the dreams that accompanied it were gone. The low-pressure system that dominated the atmosphere when they arrived had slid off to the north, leaving a high-pressure system in its place. With the high came clear skies, warm days, and cool nights. Although Terri did not make this connection, she knew she again felt like her old self, her malignant dreams virtually forgotten.

Time flew as the girls worked on their essays. When they finished, they exchanged papers and, not surprisingly, their writings were nearly as identical as their faces. They giggled and put their work away in their respective backpacks to be turned in the next day.

"Homework all done? Want to share it with me?" asked Karen as she walked into the room.

"It's all done," chirped Sophie. "And it was just writing. Nothing hard like math or geography. When that comes along, you know I'll need your help."

"You okay, too, Terri-bug?"

"Yup, Mom. Everything's a-okay here!"

"All right, then, let's get you all ready for bed. Your dad will be up in a minute to tuck you in."

Karen made sure the girls were washed and settled in bed when their father came up.

"Get a good night's sleep," said Karen. "You've got a big day ahead of you - a full day of school. The bus will be here at eight-fifteen so it's off to dreamland for both of you."

Kisses goodnight were given, lights went out, and Terri and Sophie drifted off to a peaceful, quiet sleep, their dreams benign and full of hope.

BILL & KAREN

The girls in bed, Karen cleaned up the kitchen and sat down to make a grocery list for her trip to town. Bill was in the living room by the woodstove, laptop in hand. They were both tired, physically and emotionally, the events of the past few days having taken their toll.

Bill looked at his watch. "It's going on ten, honey. I think I'll hit the sack. What ferry are you taking tomorrow? Don't forget to get the mainland car keys from me or you'll be stuck over there without transportation. I'll have to call the dealership and see about getting another set for you."

Bill thought for a moment about offering to go with her, but decided against it. She'd asked him not to smother her and he was determined to try to abide by her wishes.

"I think I'll take the nine-thirty," she said, checking the ferry schedule tacked on the refrigerator door. "I can come home on the one o'clock. That way I'll have time to clean up the house before the twins get home. Can you try to get that screen door fixed tomorrow? And make sure the grill is ready for the steaks I'm going to buy. Think I should call it a day, too. I'm feeling a bit tired."

Together, they went upstairs to their room overlooking the ocean.

The sea is calm tonight, thought Karen as she changed into her nightgown. Brushing out her hair, she watched her husband as he emptied his trouser pockets onto the dresser. *Okay, it's now or never, girl. Time to "try."*

She put down her brush and walked up behind him. Putting her arms around his waist, she leaned her body into his back. She felt him stiffen in surprise and then slowly relax into her embrace. He turned around in her arms and gazed into her eyes questioningly. In response, she reached up, put her hand behind his head, and pulled him to her in a passionate kiss. They stood entwined for a few moments then he pulled away from her and put his hand on her cheek in a gentle caress.

"Are you sure?" he asked. "I don't want...."

"Sssh, Bill," she interrupted him. "Just shut up and make love to me now."

He tightened his arms around her, holding her close. "I love you," he said as he nuzzled her neck and ran his hands down her back.

She leaned her head back as he kissed her neck, then turned in his arms so her back was to him and gave in to sensation as his hands and lips caressed her body. As they made love, the wind, as if in harmony with their rising passion, began to pick up and the sea, once calm, came to life again.

SCHOOL DAYS

Karen woke to the sound of her daughters giggling in the room next door and in that half second between sleep and consciousness, felt content. Then, reality washed over her and the smile that had been playing at the corners of her mouth turned upside down. She'd let Bill make love to her and, she had to admit, she'd enjoyed it. Nevertheless, that did not change how she felt about the situation she found herself in.

Try, she told herself. *Really try.*

None of this was lost on Bill, who had been awake for some time. He knew the closeness they'd felt after making love might not carry forward into the light of day and that she was still on the verge of leaving him. However, it had been a start - she had let him back in, at least for a while.

Sitting up in bed, she turned to him. "You awake, Bill?"

He nodded as he rolled over to face her. "What time is it?"

Karen glanced at the clock. "It's time to get up. I'm going to get a shower and start breakfast. You wake the girls."

She put on her robe and left the room. Bill shook his head as he got up and threw on his sweats. It was like last night never happened. Sighing to himself, he did as she instructed and left the room to get his daughters ready for school.

The bus arrived promptly and picked up the girls. Karen kissed her daughters goodbye, giving them the lunches she had made for them. When the bus arrived at the schoolhouse, Maggie stood by the front door waiting to greet her charges.

"Now it's Terri in the braids and Sophie without? Am I right?"

Terri and Sophie giggled and nodded.

Maggie smiled. "Got that homework assignment done for me, kids?"

The girls dutifully handed over their papers. Maggie thanked them and took their homework to her desk to study. The girls' transcripts had been impressive and she knew keeping these intelligent young ladies from getting bored would be a challenge for her, one she looked forward to.

She read Terri's paper first, finding it very well written, focused, and direct. Sophie's was also well written, but more imaginative. Noting the sameness in the girls' essays, she also saw hints of some dysfunction in the family following the decision to move to the island.

So, the rumors about trouble in the Andersen marriage may be true. She made a mental note of this and planned to watch the girls carefully to try to head off any emotional difficulties that might develop because of their parents' disharmony. She also thought again about Bill Andersen — and those thoughts had nothing to do with school.

The morning went by swiftly for the Andersen twins, who excelled in scholarly pursuits and had missed the challenges of school and the companionship of other children their own age. Having been out of school for close to two weeks, they'd missed their soccer practices, music lessons, and all the other activities that filled their days back in California. Being in class again, with its routines, brought back a sense of normalcy.

Halfway through the morning, Maggie took the children outside to exercise and play. There were not enough students for team sports, but there were tennis and basketball courts on the school grounds. A volunteer islander came twice a week during the spring to instruct the children in tennis and Maggie would usually get three or four kids involved in an abbreviated game of basketball. While it was different from what they were used to, the twins found it more fun and less intimidating than sports at their old school.

Maggie explained that during the summer months, the school held programs that included children who were just there for the season. There would be golf clinics, sailing lessons, gardening classes, and other activities the girls thought sounded fascinating and looked forward to participating in.

After exercise, it was lunchtime and the twins sat down to eat the sandwiches their mother packed for them. As they ate, they considered ways to "borrow" their parents' keys.

"When he's home, Daddy usually leaves his keys on the dresser with his spare change," offered Terri.

"But today, Mommy has those keys. We have to do this when they're both home and that could be scary."

"Maybe tomorrow, you could distract Mommy and Daddy while I grab the keys and try them out. I could do it real fast, if we planned it okay."

"Won't you be scared? We could get in big trouble."

"We'll make it work, Soph. You can pretend you fell down or something and hurt yourself. I can already be upstairs watching from the window. When you have their attention, I'll get the keys, try them in the box, and be done in less than five minutes. No one will ever know."

Sophie took time to think about this plan. "It might work. But you would have to be quick. You know Mommy always knows when I'm fibbing."

"Yeah," nodded Terri. "I know, but I'll be quick. You know how quick I can be."

"What's going on here, ladies?" asked Maggie as she stopped by the girls' table. "You two look thick as thieves."

Both girls blushed and stammered that they were just talking about their schoolwork.

Maggie nodded. "Well, it's time to get back to that schoolwork. Lunchtime's over. Terri, you're with me for some advanced math work, and Sophie, you go over there with Beth's group. They're working on Haiku poems this afternoon and I think you're going to like that."

The twins nodded and did as Maggie instructed and spent the rest of the day working hard at their lessons, the problem of the keys set aside for the time being.

Before they knew it, it was time to go home. Packing up their belongings in their backpacks, they boarded the bus, sitting close to the rear. Behind them were two boys around their age. One of them promptly pulled on Terri's braids.

"Hey, new girl," he said. "Don't you live in that old haunted house where those old ladies used to live?"

Terri turned in her seat, slapping at his hand. "Leave my hair alone!"

The boy blushed. "Sorry about the hair. I'm James and this is Scott. I know you live in the house on the hill where old lady Morgan lived. My dad tells all kinds of Indian ghost stories about that house. People have gotten lost in those woods and never been seen again!"

Terri and Sophie exchanged surprised looks as the bus pulled up at the curb.

"This is our stop," said Scott. "We'll see you Monday."

"Yeah, if the Indian ghosts don't get you over the weekend!" laughed James as he reached again for Terri's braid.

"Leave my hair alone!" she yelled and then turned to her sister. "Indian ghosts! Sophie, we need to find out about this!"

"Yeah. I'm scared of ghosts."

"Maybe that friend of Daddy's who's coming to dinner knows something," suggested Terri. "He talked a lot about Indians on the boat over."

Just then the bus pulled up at their house. "Andersens!" called the bus driver and the girls collected their things and ran up the driveway to their home.

BILL

After dropping Karen at the wharf, Bill began work on the screen door. Though he was a computer nerd, he was also handy with tools. His father had made sure all his sons knew how to wield a wrench and had schooled them in carpentry and basic home repair as well.

Bill was the son of working-class parents. His mother and father were both employed at the telephone company - Dad out in the field and Mom as a secretary. They worked hard and made good wages, which afforded them a ranch-style house in a small town about an hour's drive from San Francisco, where they lived and raised their three boys. Bill was the youngest and grew up in a house full of laughter and noise. He was the more cerebral of the boys, his older brothers being the "jocks" in the family. That's not to say Bill wasn't athletic; no, to the contrary, he excelled in track and field. He enjoyed long-distance running, relishing the solitude as well as the physicality the sport afforded. It was not uncommon for him to get up before dawn and go for a ten-mile run. This activity helped him clear his mind and organize his thoughts for the day ahead.

Even as a small boy, he was fascinated with computers and when he was ten, he managed, with the savings he had accumulated, to buy his first Apple. From that moment on, he was hooked. Computer science was his field and he planned to excel in it.

His parents saved what they could but were unable to afford for him to go away to college. Obtaining an academic scholarship to San Jose State, he commuted from home. In addition, to help defray the cost of his school expenses, he secured a part-time job at a local bookstore. This prevented him from carrying a full class-load and he graduated in five years, not the usual four. But he did so with honors and, as a result, earned a full scholarship to graduate school at San Jose in Computer Sciences.

Bill's social life was full and he dated a lot of girls, both in high school and college, but never had a serious relationship. His focus was on his future career path and he was determined not to let romance derail his plans in any way. But that all changed when he went to a certain house party at San Jose in his second year of grad school.

The party was, for the most part, the usual crowd Bill hung out with. He got there late, almost not going at all. He was talking to friends when he noticed a tall, slender blonde he had never seen before staring at him. She was wearing a Stanford sweatshirt and blue jeans that she filled out nicely. She was small-breasted and looked lean and fit, like a runner. As he stared at her, the thought ran through his mind that if he could just have one ten-mile run with that girl by his side, well, he might just have found nirvana.

He broke contact with her cool blue eyes and went to the bar, got two beers, and ambled over toward her. She introduced herself as Karen Collins and they chatted while sipping their drinks. A band made up of local students began to play and Bill asked her to dance. By the time she had to leave, Bill knew he had to see her again. She was "the one" and, with her by his side, who knew what he could accomplish. He got her number and called her as soon as he got home.

They were married after she got her Masters. Their life together was a dream come true and, when the twins were born, that was just the frosting on the cake. Everything was perfect until the economy went sour and the recession reared its ugly head. Then the layoff came and Bill found himself with a crumbling marriage and no real prospects for the future.

His Aunt Janie's demise couldn't have happened at a better time. He was surprised when the attorney in Maine contacted him, as he hadn't seen his aunt since his wedding. She had traveled even though her partner of many years, Lisbeth Boucher, was undergoing chemo for breast cancer. Lisbeth survived and lived for several more years but, unfortunately, the malignancy returned and she passed away, leaving Janie alone. The loss of her partner sent Bill's aunt into a decline and she succumbed to pneumonia eleven months later.

Bill remembered fondly the time Janie and Lisbeth had visited his parents when he was in high school. His mom and dad did not approve of the relationship between the women, but Bill enjoyed spending time with them. Janie was an artist of small renown and Lisbeth was a published poet. A French Canadian by birth, Lisbeth laid claim to Indian blood dating back to the 1700s. The warmth and generosity of spirit the two women exuded as a couple made a strong impression on Bill, whose upbringing had been quite conservative.

After learning he was her heir, Bill regretted he had not kept in touch with his aunt. Cards at Christmas and birthdays, the birth announcement of the twins, was the sum total of their relationship for the past ten years. Even so, she had left him all that was hers - the house, the land, and everything that went with it. That "everything" included a small bank account that enabled his family to make the move and survive until he found employment. He was grateful to his aunt and prayed she and Lisbeth were now reunited in some better world.

When all the legal papers were signed, the lawyers had given him a thick folder full of documents related to the house, cars, and other property. In that folder were two envelopes addressed to him. The handwriting on one he recognized as that of his aunt. The other was a mystery. Bill knew he had to read them, but for some reason he kept putting it off, his guilt at not keeping in touch eating away at him.

He thought about these things as he finished the screen door repair. *Yes*, he told himself. *I have an obligation to read what Janie wrote, guilt or no. I'll do it soon, tomorrow or maybe the next day.*

A TRIP TO TOWN

Karen found a seat alone on the ferry away from all the islanders who were conversing around her. She planned to do her shopping at a natural foods market just outside of town and maybe stop at a wine shop that was nearby. Back in California, she'd done her shopping at the boutique grocery stores that lined the streets of small towns like Los Gatos and Saratoga.

Well, at least I can still get organic produce here, she thought.

The ferry soon arrived in town and Karen made her way to the parking lot and her car. The Honda's backseat was full of canvas bags like the ones she noticed on her first ferry ride.

I guess those bags are what I use to carry my groceries back to the boat and then to the car on the island. How inconvenient. How can people live like this? She frowned, shaking her head. *Well, I guess I'm living like this now and, so far, I don't like it in the least.*

She sighed as she got into the car. *Let it go, girl. You're back to civilization, however primitive. Just enjoy yourself. Make the most of the day.*

Resolved, she drove first to the market and was pleasantly surprised with what they had to offer. When done there, she stopped at the wine shop next door and picked up the libations for the dinner she was planning. Shopping done, she found she had plenty of time to do some exploring. She left her car and groceries in the parking lot by the ferry terminal and began to investigate the shops along the waterfront.

Intrigued and pleased by the number of restaurants she found and the variety of cuisines represented, an idea began to form in her mind.

We could easily come to town for dinner once a week. Maybe every Saturday night, like a date night. We could leave the girls with a babysitter and Bill and I could have an evening out alone - maybe even go dancing. I'll ask him when I get home. Next Saturday, yes, we could start next Saturday.

Smiling and feeling happy for a change, she checked her watch then hurried to catch the afternoon ferry.

Bill got into the car to pick Karen up at the ferry.

I hope everything went okay with her, he thought as he backed down the driveway. *Maybe this trip to town will improve her mood.*

Driving to the wharf, he thought about his daughters and wondered how they were doing in school. He tried to picture the schoolhouse from Karen's description and envision his children in it. Then, he thought of Maggie with her bright green eyes and generous smile.

No, better not to think of her, he scolded himself, but her image seemed to have been burned into his consciousness.

On the drive back to their home, Karen chatted gaily about her day in town, telling Bill about all the restaurants she'd seen and the shops she'd explored.

"We could go to town once a week for dinner, hon," she gushed. "Try out a new restaurant each week. I'm sure we can find a babysitter for the girls. It would be like we were going on a date. Now, I know we have company tonight and I've probably broken our budget on the steaks and wine, so I know this week is out of the question, but a week from Saturday - could be go? Could we, Bill, please?"

As she listened to herself speak, Karen began to feel disturbed. *Christ, I'm almost begging him. Is it that important to me?*

Bill smiled at her. "Of course we'll go. We can ask Pete and Louise about the babysitter situation tonight and I'm hopeful I'll have a job by then, so we may be able to afford a little R&R. You pick the restaurant."

Karen threw her arms around him and hugged him tight. "Thank you. This will be good for us. You'll see."

The rest of the afternoon passed quickly as the Andersens prepared for their company. Bill made sure the grill was spotless while Karen cleaned the house. Soon the girls were home and running up the driveway into his arms, bubbling over with talk of their first full day of school. Karen questioned them closely about their lessons, the classroom routine, the other children in the school, and, of course, their teacher, Maggie. The interrogation over for the time being, Karen went back to the kitchen to finish preparations for dinner.

"Terri-bug and Sophie-slug," she called, "come in here and help Mommy make a berry pie."

The girls gladly came to her aid because they loved berries and knew their mom would let them sample them.

"Ter, you roll out the dough and Soph, you wash up the berries - but don't eat them all!"

Bill watched through the doorway as the women of the house worked. He had always marveled at what a great homemaker and hostess Karen was. She seemed to have a genuine instinct as to how to make a person feel comfortable. Tonight was a perfect example - she had not set the table with their best, fancy linens. No, she used more casual ones that she anticipated were in sync with the McKinneys' lifestyle. In addition, the flowers she put on the table - not an ornate bouquet - but, rather, simple daisies and wildflowers in a jelly jar. The wines she had chosen were moderately priced vintages, but she had also bought a six-pack of Coors in case her guests preferred beer. A bottle of Coke, something they would never buy for themselves, now sat in the refrigerator in case someone requested a soft drink. In addition, the place settings - Karen had chosen not to use their best crystal, but instead chose a potpourri of different wine glasses, an eclectic style that represented the casual atmosphere she was trying to project.

The steaks she selected were thick, beautiful ribeyes that Bill was sure set him back a pretty penny. With the steaks, Karen was serving baked potatoes with all the trimmings and steamed vegetables. In addition, she was counting on Louise for a wonderful salad and, for dessert, would be the homemade berry pie.

Bill smiled. Yes, his wife knew how to entertain and he enjoyed watching her as she set the scene for the dinner that evening.

As they worked, Karen resumed her questioning of the girls about their school. "What about homework? What have you brought home for the weekend?"

"We have some math problems, some geography reading, and some English," answered Sophie.

"Good," Karen replied. "I'm available to help you with the math or anything else."

"Oh, no, Mommy!" Sophie exclaimed. "Maggie says we are not to get any help from our parents. She wants us to try to figure out the problems all by ourselves and, on Monday, we'll show her what we did. If it's wrong, she'll show us the right way to do it. She says we'll learn better that way."

Karen raised her eyebrows, not sure if she liked this new teacher's techniques. "Well, my offer still stands - if you need or want my help, I'm here."

Overhearing this exchange, Bill decided to add his thoughts on the matter.

"Hey, Kar, I heard you talking with Soph about her homework and Maggie's approach to it. Maybe we should just butt out for now and see how it goes. We can always discuss it with her later if we don't feel her methods are working for our kids. But, maybe her approach will help the girls learn more independently and prepare them better for real life. She seems to be a very intelligent, progressive teacher."

Karen turned and stared at him. "So, now you're the education expert? Sticking up for your girlfriend, the multi-talented Ms. Maguire? I'm sure she fills out a pair of jeans quite nicely, but you just admire her brain. Right?"

Bill kept his head averted from Karen's view so she wouldn't see the blush that was spreading across his cheeks. She always knew. How she knew, he couldn't guess, but she seemed to have a sort of radar when it came to women he found attractive. He remembered one of the girls' soccer games that they had attended. The high school cheerleading squad was practicing on the field next door and one of the young women struck Bill's fancy. As Karen watched the soccer game intently, he snuck peeks at the girl, admiring her youthful, athletic body. Thinking he was unobserved, he was surprised when Karen, never taking her eyes from the game, whispered under her breath, "Don't even think about it, Bill, not in your wildest dreams." Then she'd added, chuckling, "And she's jailbait, too, and you know I would make sure you didn't get a 'get out of jail free' card!"

Yeah, he sighed to himself, *she always knows. Didn't she watch me like a hawk when we used to socialize with Sloane and his wife? She senses my attraction to Maggie so it's probably better I drop the subject of the girls' homework for the time being. Let her have her way.*

"I think I'll go up and shower," he said changing the subject.

"That's a good idea," said Karen, smiling. She knew she'd scored a hit on him about that Maggie creature. "It'll be six o'clock in no time. I'll be up to change soon and you can make sure the girls are presentable."

The McKinneys arrived promptly at six. As promised, Louise brought a beautiful salad with vinaigrette dressing on the side. Bill offered drinks and found Karen was right, Pete was a Coors drinker. Louise accepted a glass of chardonnay. While Karen gave Louise a tour of the house, Bill and Pete sat outside discussing the merits of propane over charcoal and the best way to barbecue steaks. The weather was mild and the girls were playing croquette and trying not to get too dirty.

Soon, dinner was ready and everyone sat down at the big oak table to enjoy each other's company and the meal.

STORY TIME

After dinner, Karen and Louise cleared the table while Pete, Bill, and the girls moved over to the living room. Bill started a fire in the woodstove and they sat watching the ocean and talking. Soon, Karen and Louise joined them, bringing coffee.

Terri, who had been curiously quiet throughout the evening, looked at Pete and suddenly asked, "On the boat, Mr. McKinney, you said the island was named after a rabbit that ruled the dead. Can you tell us more?"

Pete smiled at the little girl. "Yes, that's right, honey. Abenaki legends tell us that The Great Spirit, or creator, gave life to humans and, from the dust of his body, created Glooskap and his brother, Mateguas. He gave these boys the power to create a good and prosperous world. However, Mateguas went a bit to the dark side and, as a result, was killed. But, because of the power that had been given to him by the Great Spirit, when he arrived at The Land of the Dead, he became its ruler and, in that role, he gave his brother spiritual guidance from beyond the grave. That's how I heard it told. Lots of these legends have roots in real events, but the events happened so long ago that the stories have changed and changed again over the years."

"Are there other Indian stories about this island? Are there any about our house?" asked Terri.

Bill looked at her quizzically. "What do you mean, Terri? Has someone been teasing you? Trying to scare you?"

Terri sat up straight. "Not scaring me, Daddy. I'm not a scaredy cat! But one of the boys on the bus said our house was haunted and that people went into the woods and were never seen again."

Pete eyed Terri with interest. "Well, you know, there is a legend that involves this property, but it's a spooky one. Are you sure you're up for it?"

"Oh, yes," squealed Sophie. "Tell us, tell us. We won't be scared, will we, Mommy?"

"Well, as long as it's not too frightening," said Karen.

Louise gave Pete a "look."

Pete smiled back at her. "Don't worry, Mother, I'll keep it 'G' rated."

She nodded to him and then it seemed that as one, the Andersens leaned forward, giving him their full attention.

"Well, okay," he began. "It happens that this land that you're living on was once Abenaki land. As I told you before, they were the tribe that first settled this island way, way back when. The hill your house is built on, and the land surrounding it, were the property of an Abenaki woman. She didn't live here though; she lived deep in the woods behind your house. This knoll, where the house stands now, was barren. Abenaki legends said that, as the highest point on the island, it was closest to the Great Spirit and, therefore, sacred. Of course, all this meant nothing to the white man."

Pete paused to take a sip of his coffee. "Okay," he continued. "This Indian lady lived here peacefully until around 1850 when Maine and lots of other places saw an influx of immigrants coming over from Ireland because of the great potato famine and subsequent economic depression. They came here hoping to find the good life. One of these, a man named Fergus Maguire, came to Mateguas to try his luck as a fisherman and he set his sights on this knoll to build his home."

"Pete, was this Maguire related to Rusty?" interrupted Bill.

"Yes, he was Rusty's great-great-great or something grandfather. Well, to go on, this Fergus Maguire wanted the land and convinced the Indian agent on the mainland that the Abenaki woman was wasting a valuable resource and, together, the two of them swindled her out of her property. Fergus took the hill and dry land surrounding it, leaving her with just the swamp beyond the woods. As you can imagine, this did not set well with her.

"But Fergus didn't care. He proceeded to clear the land and build his house. Not the one you live in now, but a small saltbox right here on the hill. Your foundation may be partially the same, but the rest is different."

Pete's mention of the foundation reminded Bill of the marks or writings on the rock wall in the cellar. He made a mental note to go down and take a better look at them soon.

"Well," Pete continued. "As Fergus and his friends worked on the house, numerous instances of bad luck seemed to befall them. Tools went missing, fires broke out, and other mishaps kept occurring. After one bad fire that set the building back quite a bit, Fergus decided he had had enough. You see, he blamed the Indian woman for all these misfortunes - thought she was a medicine woman, one who conjured up evil spirits.

"So, one night, he and some of his buddies took torches and hammers and went into the woods in search of her. Oh, I forget to say - the woman didn't live alone. No, she had a child, a little boy. Okay, no one really knows what went on that night, but it's believed that when Fergus found the woman and her son, he and his friends murdered the both of them. Drowned them in the swamp. After, they burned all of her belongings in an effort to cover up their crime."

"Did the police come to get him?" asked Terri.

"No, honey. Most of the Abenaki had already left the island at that time and none of the white people really cared about the woman and her child, so nothing was ever done by the law about it."

"That's not right," said Sophie indignantly.

Pete smiled. "I know, honey, but that's the way things were back then. Okay, where was I? Yes, after the murder, Fergus got his house built and, seeing he had some success fishing, sent back to Ireland for his family - a wife and two kids. It's said they lived very happily for a year or two, but the kids were always complaining of hearing someone moaning and crying for help. They heard these sounds usually during a nor'easter so their ma said they were just hearing the sound of the wind."

At the mention of the moaning, Terri stiffened, remembering her dream. She leaned closer to hear more.

"So it happened, one night when a storm was brewing, the wife and kids went down to the hall or someplace like that, maybe church, to help with a potluck dinner or something. While they were away, Fergus and a couple of his friends began partaking of spirits at the house. As the storm intensified, they started to hear someone wailing and crying for help outside. Well, by this time, Fergus and his buddies were pretty well liquored up and they felt duty bound to save whoever was doing all that caterwauling. So, they grabbed their lanterns and headed out into the storm. The cries were coming from deep in the woods but that didn't deter them and eventually they found themselves at the edge of the swamp. No one knows what happened then, but one of them boys showed up later that night, his hair gone completely white and spouting gibberish from his mouth. Another was found two days later, deaf and dumb. He stayed that way till he died."

"What happened to Fergus?" asked Terri.

"He was never seen again. The townspeople searched the woods and the swamp for days, but found no trace of him. Fergus' wife never set foot on the property again. She moved with her children to the mainland, remarried, and never came back to the island. Said it was cursed. Her kids, though, came back, tore down the old saltbox and built the house you live in now. They never lived here though. They sold the property to some summer people and, with the proceeds, built new homes on what came to be called 'Irish Hill' on the north end. That's where the Maguires and their people still live today."

"And was that the end of it?" asked Karen. "Just one guy, who was a murderer, getting lost in the woods doesn't seem to justify calling our house 'haunted.'"

"Hang on there, Karen," said Pete with a laugh. "I'm not done yet. Haven't gotten to the good parts. Okay, well, those summer people that bought the house, they had a child, a little girl. For a few years, they only came to the island for the 'season' so there weren't no trouble. However, one year, they decided to stay the fall to see the leaves turn. Well, the weather in September and October can be iffy seeing it's still hurricane season and that year one of those storms traveled up the coast to Maine and the summer family was here when it arrived. Night of the storm, the folks tucked their daughter into bed and retired to the living room to ride it out. Around midnight, people say, they heard the back door slam. Thinking it was the wind, they secured the door and went back to doin' what they were doin' before. Come morning, they looked for their little girl, but she was nowhere to be found. Her bed was empty and, search as they might, she was not in the house. Again, the townspeople searched the woods and the swamp, but that child was never seen again.

"As you might expect, the summer people abandoned the house and put it up for sale. A childless couple purchased it in the early 1900s - I think they were from Pennsylvania. They weren't rich folks, so to make ends meet, they rented out a room to a young man who worked as a sternman on a lobster boat. He stayed for the season, from June till November. Nothing happened for a couple years, but then one night he went missing during a big storm. And, like Fergus and the little girl before, no trace of him was ever found.

"By now, this house had garnered quite a reputation, but the couple stayed on alone here for several years. Then, one night, during a nor'easter, the husband started complaining that someone outside was in trouble, that he could hear her crying for help. His wife heard nothing. Well, the old man was about to put on his coat and go out into the storm to help whoever it was, but his wife stopped him. To keep him inside, she got his rifle and told him she would shoot him dead if he moved a muscle to go outside. She was so adamant, he believed her, and he sat there with the rifle pointed at him till dawn. Once the sun came up, the man couldn't remember why he had wanted to go out in the storm so badly at all."

"Okay, now, the house went up for sale again and sat vacant till a consortium bought it in the 1920s and used it as a boarding house for summer visitors. It remained in that fashion until 1939 when the war broke out. You see, during the war, the island was pretty much taken over by the army and this house was used as an office of sorts. After the war, it sat vacant again until around 1950 when it sold to summer people. Then, in 1970, as you know, your aunt bought it. Her partner, Lisbeth, was very interested in all the old legends, her being part Indian herself."

"But what happened to those people that were lost?" asked Terri. "Did anyone ever find them or their bones?"

"No, no one ever did," replied Pete. "But there is an Abenaki legend that tells of a swamp woman, called a Mskagwdemos, who is a sorta ghost that abides in swamps and lures victims to her with cries for help. She's an evil being and no man or child foolish enough to attempt to come to her will ever return. The local Indians and folks who set store in Abenaki folklore believed the woman who was killed by Fergus, upon arrival at the Land of the Dead, petitioned Mateguas to become a Mskagwdemos so she could avenge the death of her child. And, once that hag got rid of old Fergus, well, she just kept on killing, cause that's what swamp women do."

"Why always during a storm?" asked Bill. "Is that just a coincidence or does it mean something?"

"There's some differing opinions about that," Pete replied. "One legend says she needs a storm to gather the energy to cry and moan and compel a man or child into the swamp. On the other hand, some believe it is the storm itself that is to blame. The storm awakens her from a deep sleep and, because of her hunger, she sets off a-crying and a-moaning, luring victims to her.

"In any case, there's been no problem here that I know of in decades. Some people think that the Mskagwdemos, well, she still lives back behind your woods and is waiting for someone to hear her cries so she can lure them into the swamp and kill them."

"Okay," said Karen. "Say she's still back in the swamp, waiting. If that's so, then there must be some sort of Indian magic to keep her at bay. Most tales of good and evil illustrate a balance between the two. So there must be some good magic that can protect the innocent."

Pete nodded. "Now that you mention it, there is a tale that says there are prayers that can be said to the Great Spirit to keep her from plying her trade. These prayers need to be recited from the high point on the island - your property - at the apex of the storm. I'm sure there's some other mumbo jumbo that goes along with them, but that's a moot point now since any knowledge of the prayers has been lost over time. I heard tell that they were once written down and locked away in a sacred box, but no one has ever seen such a thing."

At the mention of the box, Terri and Sophie looked at each other. Sophie started to speak but Terri silenced her with a look and a subtle wiggle of her little finger, reminding her sister of her pinkie swear.

"And that's all I know, kids," said Pete. "Maybe some of the older folks around here know more, or maybe, if you're real interested, Betty Jones, our librarian, might be able to help. As for me, I don't put much stock in this old legend. I think it's just a bogeyman story to keep kids and drunks out of the swamps at night. Hope that I didn't scare you kids so's you have nightmares tonight?"

"Well, that was some story - wasn't it girls?" said Bill. "Our house has a claim to fame."

"Or infamy, more like it," said Louise as she glanced at her watch. "Oh, my gosh, look at the time. It's nine-thirty, way past your bedtime, old man. We'd best be getting along if we're going to work on your boat tomorrow."

"Guess I just talked myself out of a good night's sleep," laughed Pete. "Hope you all have sweet dreams tonight, despite my story telling. And, Karen, thank you so much for the delicious dinner. It was a real treat to have a night away from this old woman's cooking!"

"Oh, come on now, you know you love my cooking," chuckled Louise. "But I give you my thanks also, Karen. The dinner was wonderful and I'll admit it was nice to get away from the stove for the night."

As Bill and Karen walked the McKinneys to the door, Bill turned to Pete. "You said that story was the 'G-rated' version. What other version is there?"

Pete laughed. "It's an 'X,' and I won't be telling it except in the light of day!"

Bill laughed with him, clapping him on the back. "Someday, you'll have to tell it to me."

When they reached the door, Louise turned to Karen. "Thanks again, Karen."

She started out the door then stopped abruptly. "Oh dear, I almost forgot - a week from tomorrow, on Saturday, there's going to be a potluck dinner/dance down at the Hall. It's a benefit for the library and we're asking a five-dollar donation from the adults and either a salad, main course, or dessert. Kids are free, of course. We hope you and Bill and the girls can make it."

Karen was about to decline when Bill cut her off. "Of course, we'd be delighted to come. Sounds like fun and a good way to meet people. Why don't you put us down for a dessert, if that's okay with you, Karen?"

Karen stared at her husband, her mouth curved down in a frown. "Did you forget, dear, we already have plans for that night."

"Oh, we can go to town for dinner anytime," Bill said, not catching her expression. "This will be great for us and good for the girls, too."

As he spoke, Karen's face closed down, all expression leaving it. This was not lost on Louise, who was watching her reaction carefully. Bill, however, was oblivious to the sudden change in his wife's mood.

"That'd be wonderful, Bill," said Louise. "A dessert. I got it. Dinner's at six, dancing follows later. Thanks again for the wonderful meal. Next time, our place." She gave Karen a quick hug and got into the truck and, with her husband, slowly backed down the driveway and headed home.

TROUBLED TIMES

After putting the girls to bed, Karen went silently into the kitchen to finish cleaning up from dinner. When she was done, she poured herself a glass of wine and sat down at the kitchen table.

How could he do that to me? He treats me like I don't exist, like I don't count, like I don't have feelings. He can't do that. It's not right. I won't let him treat me that way. I won't.

She finished her wine and poured herself another glass. As she sipped, she played the scene on the porch repeatedly in her mind and, with each iteration, her anger and outrage grew. Finally, finishing the second glass of wine, she got up and walked into the living room where Bill sat hunched over his laptop.

"I'm going to bed," she said flatly.

Busy, Bill didn't look up at her. "I'm just finishing up, hon. I'll be with you in a minute."

Not acknowledging him, she went upstairs, checked on the girls, got washed, and put on her nightgown. When Bill came up, she was standing facing the bedroom dresser mirror, brushing her hair.

"I think that went very well tonight, don't you?" he asked. "And all those old stories, weren't they a hoot! Hope they didn't scare the girls. And next weekend will be fun, you'll see. We can do dinner out any time."

Karen's hand stopped midair as her whole body went rigid. She stood motionless for a second, then slammed the brush to the dresser, upsetting a glass of water. The glass fell to the wooden floor, shattering with a loud crash.

Next door, Sophie and Terri were startled awake by the sound of the breaking glass. Then they heard their mother's voice.

"How dare you, how dare you!" she yelled. "If you think I want to go to some old hillbilly dance with a bunch of yahoos from God knows where, well, you've got another thing coming!" As she spoke, she took two steps toward him, brush now upraised in her hand.

Bill stared at her, shocked by her sudden anger. "You're overreacting, Karen. There's no reason to be so upset. Like I said, we'll do dinner the week after. It's no big deal. In addition, I think it's important to go to this island function. We need to try to become a part of this community."

Karen took another step toward her husband. "I will NOT!" she yelled.

Bill stood his ground, his anger building. "Yes, you will," he said, raising his voice. "You WILL go to the dinner/dance, you WILL make a cake, a pie, or some other sort of fucking dessert, and you WILL pretend you're having the time of your life! By God, Karen, you WILL!"

She glared at him. "You can't talk to me like that. You can't make me go. You don't own me, or MY girls! We'll - I'll take them and...."

"You'll what, Karen? What'll you do? Say it, just say it!"

Karen raised the brush and leaned toward her husband. "Don't push me, Bill. Don't you push me!" she threatened.

Seeing the brush raised as if to hit him, Bill closed the distance between them and grabbed her roughly by the wrists, forcing the brush from her hand. He tightened his grip as he glared back at her.

"Don't threaten me, Karen," he said in measured tones. "If you want out so bad then, well, so be it - go! I love you, but if this is what life is going to be like, then go ahead, get out, but don't think you're going to take my girls. That WILL NOT happen. I'll fight you every inch of the way. Trust me, you'll regret it. You WILL regret it. I WILL NOT let that happen!"

They stood still, frozen in their anger, for what seemed an eternity, eyes locked on one another. Then, Karen looked down at his hands, still holding tightly onto her wrists.

"You're hurting me, Bill," she said in a soft voice, anger replaced by pain.

Bill looked down at his hands, not realizing how tightly he had been holding her. He let go. Her wrists were a bright red and threatened to bruise. Karen didn't look up at him. She rubbed her wrists, turned, and lay down on the bed, hugging a pillow to her chest. She did not move or speak. Bill started to say something, but stopped himself. There was no giving in this time. No, this time it was too important. So, instead, he turned and walked out of the room.

Terri and Sophie huddled together in Terri's bed listening to the argument next door. Their parents rarely fought and, when they did, Daddy usually caved and let Mommy have her way. However, this time, they sensed it was different. Mommy was so mad and Daddy did not seem to be trying to placate her, to compromise, as he usually did.

When they heard their father leave, Sophie began to cry. Terri tried to calm her sister, holding her tightly. Both girls were scared - not in the way Pete's stories had frightened them - that was fun scared. No, this was different. They were both mortally frightened they were going to lose one or both of their parents - that Mommy would go as Daddy told her she could; or, that Mommy would take them away and they'd never see Daddy again. So, they clung to each other till sleep finally came over them and it wasn't till much later that Sophie returned to her own bed.

THE MORNING AFTER

It was near dawn when Bill woke up. After the fight, he had gone downstairs, poured himself a drink, and sat in the living room, nursing it, as he watched the waves in the moonlight. When his glass was empty, he returned to bed, exhausted, and fell instantly to sleep. When he awoke, Karen still lay curled up around a pillow at the far side of the bed. The anger that had lain dormant in both of them for so long had finally reached the surface and erupted in an explosion that might be irreparable. Bill threw on his sweats silently, deciding he needed a run. Before he went downstairs, he cracked the twins' door to see how they were. He breathed a sigh of relief when he saw them sleeping peacefully, each in their own bed. He loved them so much and he was worried they might have overheard the argument the night before.

I won't let them go, he vowed to himself as he quietly closed the door. *Karen won't take them away, not without a fight.*

The twins were not asleep when their father looked in, though they pretended to be. When they heard his footsteps going down the stairs, Sophie sat up in bed.

"Terri, are you awake?"

Terri sat up, too. "Yeah, I'm awake. Are you okay, Soph?"

"Oh, Terri, is Daddy leaving?" Sophie whispered. "Is he leaving us?" Tears sprang into her eyes when she heard the front door close.

"I don't think so. You wait here. I'll check."

Terri jumped out of bed, tiptoed over to the spare bedroom, and peered out the window that faced the front of the house. To her relief, she saw her father standing in the driveway, running gear on, doing his warm-up exercises. She hurried back to Sophie.

"He's going running, that's all," she said to her distraught sister. "Soph, he's just going for a run. He'll be back. Daddy won't leave us, he won't. Now, we need to go back to bed. Mommy will be up soon and she'll come to wake us."

"Okay, but I won't sleep. I know I won't," whispered Sophie.

Next door, Karen still lay on the far side of the bed, curled up around a pillow that was wet with tears. She had not moved since she had lain down the night before, nor had she slept. The anger she'd felt had given way to a profound despair and her eyes, red and swollen from silent crying, were testimony to that. Now, she lay staring at the wall next to her. Occasionally, she glanced down at her hands. Her wrists were encircled with vivid bruising from the pressure Bill had applied to them.

How could he have hurt me so? He's never laid a hand on me in anger before. But what about me? Was I really going to hit him with that brush?

The answer, she knew, was "yes." She'd wanted to bash his face in, to hit him and hit him, and keep on hitting him until she stopped the words that were coming from his mouth. She'd wanted to silence him, possibly forever.

Where did all that anger come from? It's not like me to blow up like that. Sarcasm is my usual weapon, not violence. And, why was I so upset about that dinner in town anyway? It wasn't really that important, was it? No, that's wrong, it was important. It is important.

She remembered how she felt when she'd stepped off the ferry in the harbor. *It was as if I were walking out of a fog into bright sunlight. And when I had to get back on, to return to this island, well, the fog returned, and I felt like I was suffocating. There's something wrong with this place. I felt it the first night. It's like someone or something is watching me and my girls and waiting, yes, watching and waiting. Getting off this island is important, but how can I explain that to Bill? All I have is a feeling, a sense of foreboding. There's nothing solid, nothing concrete that I can point to and say, "This is wrong." Even if I could, would he believe me?*

No, she acknowledged to herself, after last night, he wouldn't; there was no way. She knew she was alone in this.

No, not alone. My girls. I have to think of them. They have to come first. What will happen to them, if I let them down? I know I should get up and go to them, but I can't move, I just can't. Bill threatened me and he hurt me. That's so unlike him, just like my anger was unlike me. How far will he go? How far will I go?

Her weary mind could find no answers so she hugged the pillow tighter and stayed where she was. With tears continuing to course down her cheeks, the bed and the pillow had become her only sanctuary, and feeling increasingly helpless, she sank deeper and deeper into despair.

THE GIRLS

Next door, Sophie and Terri sat on their respective beds waiting for the sound of their mother coming to wake them or for their father to return. He'd left a little after dawn and it was now going on seven-thirty and there'd been no sound from their mother's room.

"I'm scared, Terri. You heard them last night. Maybe Daddy hurt Mommy. Maybe she needs help."

Terri mulled this over for a minute. "Okay, Soph, you get dressed and I'll go check on Mommy. If she's hurt, we'll call 911. Okay?"

Sophie nodded.

Terri walked down the hall to her parents' room. The door was ajar. Quietly, she opened it and peered inside. At first, it seemed to be empty, but then she noticed the lump on the far side of the bed and recognized the form of her mother. Karen was totally covered by blankets, curled tightly in a ball around one of the pillows. Worried, Terri ran to her mother's side and knelt down next to the bed. Her mouth opened wide in shock when she saw her mother's face, almost unrecognizable from the redness and swelling caused by her tears.

"Mommy?" she said softly.

Karen's eyes fluttered open and it seemed to take her time to focus and recognize her daughter. She put her hand out to Terri, revealing the vivid bruising around her wrist.

"Oh, Mommy, Daddy hurt you!"

Upset, Terri moved to embrace her mother. She sat on the bed and cradled her mother's head in her lap, both of them crying now.

"No, Terri-bug, you're wrong. Daddy didn't hurt me," Karen whispered. "It was an accident. Daddy didn't hurt me on purpose. It was my fault."

Terri looked down at her mother's wrists; the bruising was turning an angry purple color. And her mother's face - so swollen and red from crying. The little girl felt a profound sadness and, again, fear entered her heart.

"I love you, Mommy," she cried. "Please don't go away. Don't leave us, Mommy!"

The sound of anguish in her daughter's voice woke up something in Karen and she tried to pull herself together. Sitting up, she took Terri in her arms.

"I'm not going anywhere, Terri-bug. I'll never leave you and Sophie, I promise. I will always be here for you."

As they hugged each other, a small, frightened voice came from the doorway. "Is Mommy all right?"

Karen turned and saw her other daughter peering around the half-opened door, her face contorted in fear and anxiety. "I'm here, Sophie," she said gently. "Come to me."

The little girl ran to her mother and threw herself into her arms. Karen folded her arms around both her girls, hugging them tightly and whispering words of reassurance.

Eventually, she separated herself from the twins' embrace and looked them in the eyes. "Terri, can you do something for Mommy?" When both her girls nodded in unison, she went on. "I need to take a bath and have a cup of coffee. Terri, you know how to use the coffee maker. Can you make a cup and bring it to me in the bath? Be careful, the coffee will be very hot. And Sophie, can you get breakfast for yourself and Terri, just cereal and juice? After my bath, I'll be downstairs to clean up, so don't worry about that. Can you girls do that for Mommy?"

Both girls nodded again and ran off to do their mother's bidding. When they were gone, Karen slowly got out of bed, her body stiff and sore from lying in one position for so long. She walked into the bathroom and was shocked to see how she looked. As she drew a hot bath, she thought about her daughters.

Somehow, I have to make things right for them, give them back the security that we took away so brutally last night. But what about Bill? Where is he? Has he left me? No, he told me to get out. He wouldn't leave.

She got into the tub and, as she sank down into the hot water, she made a vow to herself. *I have to protect my girls. Yes, that's my job, to protect them and I will.*

She sighed and let her battered mind relax in the heat of the bath and put aside, if just for a short time, her fear and anxiety about the future - the future of her marriage, but more importantly, the future of her children.

LONG-DISTANCE RUNNER

There was a light fog hanging over the island at daybreak that gave everything an otherworldly look. The sun crept over the horizon, creating a hazy, muted light that contributed to the surreal atmosphere. The wind was calm. And Bill ran.

He didn't know where he was going. He was just running - running away from what he'd done the night before.

I hurt her; I physically hurt her. How could I do that? What in the name of God is wrong with me?

He had never abused a woman before, yet he'd hurt Karen, the red marks on her wrists left by his fingers haunting him.

She's going to be bruised, bruised badly. All because of me. Yes, she provoked me, but that's no excuse, no excuse at all.

His father's voice echoed in his mind. "You never raise a hand to a woman, son, never hit her, never use your physicality to subdue her. That's just not manly. It's a cowardly thing to do."

Yet, that's just what I did. No, didn't hit her, but I hurt her just the same. There's no difference. I should have walked away. Why did I get so mad? She threatened me with that brush. She was going to hit me with it, for sure. Where did all her anger come from? I know she's been unhappy and not excited about this move, but that can't justify the fury she expressed last night. It was almost as if she was another person. But even her irrational anger is no excuse for the way I responded.

The steady rhythm of his feet hitting the pavement helped to clear his mind. He thought of how, after he'd let go of her, she'd just lain in bed, huddling under the blankets, curled tightly in a ball, as far away from him as she could get.

If only she'd reached out for me, I would have begged for her forgiveness. She looked so fragile, like if I touched her she would shatter into a million pieces. How did we come to this? Even at our worst in California, after the layoff, we never hurt each other this way. It seems as if from the moment we set foot on this island, we've been at odds with each other. I've got to find a way to fix things. But how?

No answers came to him so he just kept running, running as if his life depended upon it.

At home, Terri brought her mother a steaming hot cup of coffee while Sophie set the table for breakfast. When Terri returned to the kitchen, she saw the questions in her twin's searching eyes. "She looks better, Soph. She stopped crying and she smiled a little when I gave her the coffee."

"Her wrists, oh, Terri, her wrists. Did Daddy do that? How could he hurt Mommy like that?"

"Mommy says it was an accident. She says that Daddy didn't do it on purpose. She said it was her fault."

As she spoke, the door to the family room opened and their father walked in. His hair was wet and there were stains under the arms of his sweatshirt. His face shone with perspiration.

"Dadd..." Sophie started to call, then abruptly stopped, closed her mouth, and stared down at her cereal bowl.

Terri looked up as her father entered the room. She locked eyes with him for a second before greeting him. "Hi, Daddy," she said in a soft voice.

Sophie continued to stare at her cereal, her eyes welling up with tears. Terri gave her a stern look, then turned back to her father.

"So what's up with the cereal, munchkins?" he asked, well aware of his daughters' distress. "No cheesy eggs, no pancakes?"

"Mommy doesn't feel well," responded Terri a bit defiantly. "She's taking a bath. She told us to have cereal and that's just fine with us. Isn't it, Sophie?"

Sophie nodded briefly as she continued to stare at her food.

"It's okay, Terri," said Bill in a soft, calm voice. "Cereal's fine, but if you want some cheesy eggs, I can make them for you. What do you say? How about you, Soph?"

Sophie finally looked up at her father, the wetness in her eyes threatening to erupt. "Oh, Daddy," she cried, then broke off and looked down at her food again, tears on her cheeks.

Bill knelt down beside her and put his arms around her, hugging her tight. "It's all right, Soph," he crooned. "Everything's going to be fine. Hush now, honey, there's no need for tears."

As he held Sophie, Bill looked up at Terri and reached out for her, but she moved slightly away, letting him know she was not about to forgive him so easily.

They were all startled when they heard footsteps coming down the stairs. As Karen entered the room, Terri got up and walked over to her, putting her arm around her mother's waist.

Karen was wearing gray sweats and her hair, usually so carefully coifed, was still wet from the bath and pulled back into a ponytail. Her face bore no makeup and was ravaged and swollen from the emotions of the night before. She looked at Bill for a brief moment then dropped her gaze to the floor. The baggy sweatshirt she wore concealed her wrists and it seemed to Bill that she was standing so as to keep it that way. Terri led her to the table and helped her to sit down.

"Mommy, do you want some cereal or juice? I can get it for you."

Karen gave her a small, shaky smile. "No, Terri-bug. Mommy's not hungry, but could you make me another cup of coffee?"

"I've got that, Terri," said Bill, getting up and putting a pod in the coffee maker.

As it brewed, he turned to look at his wife. She sat at the table, her head bowed. As much as he tried to will her to, she would not look at him. He felt helpless, at a loss for what to do.

She looks so frail, so beaten down, he thought guiltily. *If I do or say anything, I might make things worse.*

The air in the room hung heavily with tension, so he decided to see if he could somehow defuse it.

"Guess what I found in the garage while I was working yesterday?" he asked. When no one responded, he went on. "Well, I found a couple of old forks and baskets for digging clams and I thought it might be fun for us to try our hand at it this afternoon. The tide will be right and I got some tips on where the best clam flats are while I was out running."

"Don't you need a license to dig clams?" asked Karen, still staring down at her coffee.

"Yeah, you're right, hon, but I think we'll be okay. I stopped at the store during my run because I forgot to take water. I guess the store is quite a meeting place in the mornings. Anyway, I talked to some of the guys there and one of them was the clam warden. He said he'd cut me some slack today if I promised to pick up the license next week. He also gave me those tips about the clam flats. So, guys, what do you think? Do we put on our clam diggers and go get ourselves some dinner?"

"Sounds like fun," Karen responded, trying to force some enthusiasm. She still did not look at him.

"Okay, it's a plan!" said Bill, again trying to lighten the atmosphere in the room.

"Girls," said Karen looking at her daughters. "When you finish your cereal, go up and get washed and put on jeans and sweatshirts. I think it's a little cool outside today. Get out your slickers and rubber boots, too, just in case that fog doesn't burn off. Can you do that? And Sophie, don't forget to brush your teeth - two minutes - no more no less. I'll be up to help you when I've had my coffee."

Terri and Sophie nodded and went back to finishing their breakfast. Bill walked over to the refrigerator, got out eggs, milk, and cheese and started to make his own. "Last chance for cheesy eggs!" he called to Karen and the twins.

"No thanks, Daddy," responded Sophie. "We've got our cereal."

Karen said nothing.

The twins quickly finished their meal and left the kitchen, glad to be out of the tension-filled room.

When Bill finished cooking, he took his plate and walked over to the table where his wife sat silently staring at her coffee cup. As he approached, she reached for the cup and the sleeve of her sweatshirt rucked up, revealing the dark bruises that encircled her wrist.

Bill's mouth fell open in shock. *Oh my god, that's what I've done to her.*

He dropped his plate on the table and knelt down beside her. Gently, he took her hand in his and bent down to lay a soft kiss on her bruised wrist.

"I'm sorry. I'm so sorry, hon, I didn't mean...."

A tear fell on her wrist.

She slowly raised her head and looked at him. As their eyes met, she entwined her fingers in his and gently squeezed.

"It's okay," she said. "It's going to be okay."

They stared at each other, silently, for what seemed a lifetime. Then Karen unclasped her hand from his.

"You eat your breakfast. I'll go up and make sure the girls are okay. You look like you could use a shower and fresh clothes. I need to change, too."

"Karen, I..."

"Not now, Bill. Later. We'll sort this all out later. Right now we have to take care of our girls."

Bill nodded. "You're right. Later, we'll talk later. I'll finish here and be up to shower and change."

Karen nodded as she stood, giving him a soft smile.

Once upstairs, she found her daughters had not followed her instructions. On the contrary, they sat huddled together waiting, frightened about what might be happening downstairs. Karen sat down opposite them, taking their small hands in hers.

"Terri-bug and Sophie-slug, everything's okay. There is nothing to be frightened of. I will always be here for you. Your father will always be here for you. You are our world and we will not let anything hurt you, ever. I'm so sorry you heard all that last night and I promise it will never happen again. I will see to that and I will keep you safe."

She opened her arms and her girls fell into them, hugging her.

"Squeeze me any tighter, and I'll break in two," she laughed as she tightened the embrace. Then she sat up. "Okay, now let's get washed and dressed. Jeans and sweatshirts 'cause we're going to get dirty! Dig out your boots and slickers, too. But first - teeth, faces, and hands. And make it snappy. Dad will be up to shower soon."

The girls broke into their first genuine smiles since the night before and, laughing, ran to the bathroom to get ready.

Karen sat on the bed watching them. *I will protect you*, she thought. *With my dying breath, I will protect you.*

CLAM DIGGING

While Bill showered, Karen changed into jeans and a clean sweatshirt. She dried her hair and, again, pulled it back into a ponytail. She searched through her dresser until she found an oversized pair of sunglasses.

Anyone looking at me will know for sure I've been crying. Yes, in five minutes, the fact that Bill and I have had a fight will be all over this damn island. Feeling frustrated, she stared at her reflection in the dresser mirror. *Oh god, I'm so tired, I don't really want to go anywhere. But I have to do it - do it for the girls. Going out as a family will illustrate to them that Bill and I don't have any immediate plans to split up and that their world is still secure and safe. But is that the truth? Is there any future left for our marriage?*

Closing her eyes briefly, she took a deep breath, then put the sunglasses on the top of her head and turned to go downstairs.

When Bill was dressed, he gathered up all the things they

would need for their outing and loaded them in the car. Karen made sandwiches and packed them along with snacks and cold drinks in their cooler.

"We're going to North End Cove," Bill announced as he backed the car down the driveway. "That's where the warden, I think his name was Andrew something, said the best clamming was."

The fog still hung stubbornly over the island, refusing to give way to the sun that was trying to break through. The air was damp and heavy, but the wind remained calm. The Andersens arrived at their destination around eleven a.m. There were already several cars parked at the beach, giving the impression this was a popular spot. The family unloaded their things while Bill surveyed the beach. It wasn't a sandy beach; the area they were going to was muddy and Bill could see several groups of people already busy clamming.

"Boots on, guys!" he exclaimed. "It looks pretty yucky out there."

The girls and Karen complied and pulled on their boots while Bill put on his. They grabbed the forks and baskets and trudged their way through the muddy sand.

"Look for holes in the sand, girls," Bill explained. "That's how the buried clams breathe, through those openings. So, the more holes, the more clams."

Sophie and Terri squished through the muddy sand, giggling as they walked, looking for holes. They soon found a promising area and Bill proceeded to dig with the clam fork. Karen followed suit using the other one, but the digging was hard for her given the state of her wrists. Smiling, she put on her game face and tried her best.

"Okay, girls," said Bill. "Now it's your turn. Get in there and see if you can find any clams. But put your gloves on first."

The girls put on the canvas gloves Bill had brought along and began to ferret out the clams. They were all concentrating on the work at hand when a voice came from behind Bill.

"Those clams under two inches, you need to put back. They're babies and it's illegal to pick 'em."

Karen looked up, frowning. Standing close behind her husband was that Maggie creature, her face framed by a mass of disorderly reddish curls, a mischievous smile playing on her pouty lips. Bill turned to see who was behind him and when his eyes met Maggie's, Karen could swear those green eyes flashed hungrily.

"Oh, Maggie, do we have to?" cried Sophie.

"Yes, honey. It's the law and if everyone took the little ones, there wouldn't be any to dig next year."

"Shouldn't you be home grading papers or making lesson plans?" Karen asked bluntly, standing up and moving between Maggie and her husband.

Maggie, surprised to find Karen very much in her face, felt it prudent to take a couple of steps backwards, widening the distance between them. As she moved, she made a mental note of those big, dark glasses Karen wore despite the fact there was no sun.

"Oh, I'm just here with my dad, digging clams like everyone else. Weather permitting, this is a regular excursion for us. Sort of a father-daughter bonding thing." She laughed then turned away from Karen and smiled down at Bill. "Well, I'll leave you folks to your fun. Hope you get enough to make a good chowder. Careful with the broken clamshells, kids, they can be sharp and can give you a nasty cut. And don't forget to soak those suckers really well, else wise you'll end up with a mouth full of grit and sand. Uck, nothin' worse than gritty clams."

Before she turned to walk away, Maggie looked down once again at Bill.

"Thanks for the tips," he said, staring into her green eyes. "Nice to see you again."

"Oh, it's my pleasure, Bill," she said, tossing her curls and looking back over her shoulder. "My pleasure, indeed!"

She gave Bill one last smile and then sauntered over to where her father was filling his clam basket. Karen watched her walk away and was surprised at the depth of animosity she felt toward that girl.

Following Maggie's directive, the girls sorted through the clams and put back those that were too small. Karen knelt back down and resumed her digging.

Bill watched his wife out of the corner of his eye, surprised by her apparent jealousy. *Maybe there's hope for us yet*, he thought, a smile playing on his lips.

A MEANINGFUL DISCUSSION

The family filled their baskets, rinsed the clams, and went to the real beach for their picnic.

It's turned out to be a good day, thought Bill. *Karen's exhausted, yet she's putting on a good front for the kids - willing herself not to let them down. I wish I could cradle her in my arms and comfort her, but I'm afraid that would just bring on a fresh bout of tears. She needs to sleep. It's time to bring this to an end so she can get her rest.*

"Okay, guys," he said. "Let's pack it up and head for home. I think your mother could use a little nap."

Karen smiled gratefully at him. "I could use a little rest. That be okay with you, Terri, Sophie?"

"Sure, Mommy," replied Terri. "Soph and I can work on our homework. If we get it done today, we won't have to do it tomorrow!"

They packed up the car and took the short drive home.

"You go on up to bed, hon," said Bill as he helped her out of the car. "The girls and I can take care of the clams and the cleanup."

"Okay, I think I'll do that," Karen replied, leaning toward him and placing a soft kiss on his cheek.

Once upstairs, she lay down on the bed, exhausted, and fell asleep almost as soon as her head hit the pillow. When she woke up, it was dark out. She checked the clock - she had slept for six hours, right through dinner. Shaking her head, she got up and walked to the girls' room. They were already in their PJs, sitting on the floor playing an old-fashioned board game.

"Hi, Mommy," chirped Sophie. "Did you have a good nap?"

"Yes, honey. Did your dad get you dinner?"

"Yes, Mommy," replied Terri. "Daddy made us tacos and chips. They were really, really good but he didn't make them so hot that we'd get sick."

"Good," said Karen. "Now, just another half hour, then it's lights out. Okay?"

Her daughters nodded and Karen left them to their game and went downstairs to face her husband.

Bill was sitting in the living room staring out the window, deep in thought. He turned when he heard Karen on the stairs. Her face looked better, the swelling and redness fading. Her wrists, however, were now turning a yellowish purple color and looked worse than ever. A fresh wave of guilt washed over him.

"Feeling better, honey?" he asked. "Did you get a good rest?"

"Yes, I think I am. Thanks for letting me sleep. And, I have it on good authority that the girls enjoyed their dinner. Maybe I'll let you do the cooking more often."

Bill laughed. "Hopefully not! Can I get you anything - a glass of wine?"

Karen sat down in the overstuffed chair. "That would be nice."

Bill left the room, coming back a couple of minutes later with a bottle of red wine and two glasses. He poured the wine and sat down opposite her on the couch. For a few minutes, they sat quietly, staring at each other.

Finally, Bill broke the silence. "We need to talk. We need to figure out what's happening to us."

Karen took a sip of her wine and nodded. "Bill, you might think I'm crazy or just making excuses, but ever since we got to this place, I've felt different somehow - angry, out of control. I can't explain it, but I know when I went to the mainland yesterday, well, it was the first time I felt okay - the first time I felt like 'me.' And when I had to come back, it all just started up again. It feels so claustrophobic here - like the walls are closing in on me and I'm close to panic half the time. That's why the trip to town for dinner was so important. It gave me something to look forward to - something to keep me going during the week.

"Bill, I don't like who I'm becoming. I want myself back. I want our marriage back. I know it sounds insane, but it was like it wasn't me in the bedroom last night. I wanted to hurt you, hurt you badly. But that's not me. I would never...." Her words trailed off as she took another sip of her wine, her face an obvious mask of pain and confusion.

Bill leaned forward, listening intently to what she was saying. Hadn't he felt the same way - sort of disoriented, out of control?

"I know," he said. "I know. I've kinda felt it, too. But last night, oh God, I hurt you. I can't believe it. I don't react like that. It's just not the way I'm made. It makes me sick to think about it, how I hurt you. It just must be the stress of the move and everything. What else could it be? We just have to get a grip and remember what's important: our marriage, our girls, and our life together. Things will get better once I'm working. You'll see. If you really can't stand it here, we'll move. We'll sell this old place and find something on the mainland. Once I get a job, everything will change. Things will get better, Kar, they will."

"If I really can't stand it here, we'll move?" she asked hopefully.

"Yes," he said nodding. "Once I'm making good money again, then we can consider moving. It may take a while for me to get established, understand that, but yes, we'll move. If you can't stand it, we'll get off this rock and find a new place where you can be happy."

Karen really smiled at him for the first time since the fight the night before. "Thank you," she said gratefully.

"Until then, if you have to go to the city every day to feel good, then do it. Don't stay cooped up here feeling isolated. If there's nothing to do here, go see a movie, go to a museum, anything. I want you to be happy. Your happiness and the girls', that's all I want."

Karen nodded as she sipped her wine and watched as Bill got up to turn out the lights.

But what about that girl? You want her, too, almost as much.

She tried to push the image of that mass of red curls and flashing green eyes out of her mind and reached for his hand as she got up out of the chair. They embraced carefully, each fully aware of the delicate nature of their relationship. Bill took her face in his hands and gently caressed her checks with his thumbs. Karen leaned forward and accepted his kiss and, then, hand in hand, they went up the stairs to bed.

THE JOB INTERVIEW

The rest of the weekend went by quickly, Karen and Bill working at their relationship, trying to rekindle the love they'd once felt for each other. The twins relaxed, happy to see the new closeness between their parents. Soon, their minds turned again to the mystery of the locked box, but they were unable to find an opportunity to get their hands on their parents' keys.

On Monday morning, Bill rose early. His interview with the software company was at nine o'clock and he planned to take the seven-thirty boat in order to have time to get his act together before it started. He knew his future was riding on this one interview - his marriage, his children - it all came down to this. He dressed carefully, suit and tie, the whole nine yards. Karen was up as well, knowing how important this was for her family. Moreover, it was her ticket off the island, too, so she was there to provide whatever support she could.

"How do I look?" he asked when he came downstairs.

Karen gave him an appraising look. *He's a handsome man, even more so when dressed in a suit. As he ages, he just gets better. Funny how that is - men, if they keep in shape, just get better looking over time, while women get crows' feet and sagging breasts and butts. At thirty-six, Bill is much better looking than when I met him twelve years ago. Yes, there will always be some young girl, one like that schoolteacher, waiting in the wings, waiting for an opportunity to pounce and steal what's not hers.*

Karen vowed to herself she would not let that happen.

"You look great. If your interviewer were female, you wouldn't have to say a word. How about a light breakfast to take the jitters away? Just a little coffee and toast." She knew he was nervous and would not want to eat a full meal.

"I think I'll pass on the toast," he replied. "Just coffee, hon. I don't have much time anyway. I'll stop someplace in town and review all the research I've done on the company so it's fresh in my mind and grab a bite then."

Cup in hand, Bill kissed Karen goodbye and headed for the ferry to town.

Once Bill arrived downtown, he walked until he found a deli and enjoyed another cup of coffee and a Danish while he reviewed his notes on the history and makeup of Omicron Software. Convinced he knew as much as anyone about the company, he paid his check and headed for the company's main office, five blocks away. He arrived at eight forty-five am, as planned, fifteen minutes early for his appointment. After announcing himself to the receptionist, he took a seat to wait. He was not seated long when a rotund gentleman around forty-five years old entered the room.

"Bill?" the man asked.

When Bill nodded and stood up, the man came forward, shook his hand, and introduced himself. "I'm Henry LeFleur," he said as he pumped Bill's hand vigorously. "Let's head down to my office where we can be comfortable. After we talk, I'll give you a tour of the plant."

LeFleur's office was spacious with a wonderful view of the city. He indicated for Bill to have a seat at a small table in the center of the room. He picked up a folder from his desk and sat down across from Bill.

"Coffee?" he asked.

Bill declined, but thanked him for the offer.

"Nice suit," LeFleur said. "We're not quite that formal here, but I do appreciate your trying to make a good impression. So many people don't bother nowadays. However, if you take the position, it's nice, pressed jeans, a good-looking shirt, and sport coat. Nikes are okay, too. Oh, except in winter when it's down vests and boots," he chuckled, then he opened the folder and the interview began in earnest.

After about an hour of questions, answers, and general discussion about the software industry and Omicron's place in it, LeFleur closed the folder and looked Bill squarely in the eye. "You know, you're vastly overqualified for this position."

Bill's heart sank. It was going to be another rejection. How could he face Karen and the kids?

"But," LeFleur continued, "I'm going to hire you anyway; that is, if you want the job? Before you answer, let me remind you that this position means you might have to spend some nights away from home during the week. That doesn't sit so well with some guys' wives. Friday is our paperwork day. That means you'll spend every Friday here in the office - that is, unless you have some fantastic deal to close. I like my people to be able to get home to their families on weekends and that's why I chose Friday for the paperwork day. So what'd you think? Going to climb aboard the Omicron express?"

Relief washed over Bill. "Yes, sir, if you're offering, then I'm accepting."

LeFleur smiled. "Unlike a lot of our brethren in Silicon Valley, our company has been doing quite well over the past couple of years. I expect we will be hiring soon in R&D and it would be a feather in my cap to already have a superstar on the payroll. So, you just hang in there, make sales, learn as much as you can about our business, and you'll have an inside track when something opens up. Now, how about that tour?"

After the tour, Bill was taken down to Personnel, where he filled out all the required employment and benefit forms. By mutual consent, it was decided he would start work the following Monday, his first day to be spent in orientation.

Paperwork complete, Bill had time to spare before the next ferry home. He thought about calling Karen to let her know the good news, but decided to surprise her instead.

In a jubilant mood, he picked up a chilled bottle of champagne and bought a bouquet of flowers from a vender on the wharf. Celebratory materials in hand, he rushed to make the afternoon ferry.

MAGGIE

Maggie sat at her desk reviewing lesson plans for the week ahead. Each child worked at his/her own pace, so each had a unique plan. Each plan assured that the child could pass the State exams but also allowed those who could, to move ahead of their peers. The Andersen twins were examples of this.

Those girls are smart as whips, she thought.

She'd cajoled the town clerk into letting her see all the registration information on the twins, so she knew quite a bit about Karen and Bill's background. She knew Karen had attended Stanford and held a Master's degree. She also knew Bill had an advanced degree.

That's where those kids get their smarts. Terri must get her math aptitude from Bill and Sophie probably gets her verbal skills from her mom. And Karen has a Master's from Stanford - gosh, that has to be worth its weight in gold. Maggie shook her head. *Why didn't she take care of the family after Bill lost his job? She could have kept them going, but, instead, she let them flounder onto rocky shores. That just doesn't seem right. Not what I would've done.*

Her mind turned to the clamming encounter on Saturday. Karen had been wearing those big, dark glasses, even though there was no sun to speak of.

Only reason for shades on a cloudy day is if you just got your eyes dilated or had cataract surgery, she mused. *And I'm pretty sure Karen had neither. More likely, Bill popped her a good one or she'd spent the night crying. In either case, it's just another nail in the coffin of that marriage.*

She remembered, however, how Karen reacted to her flirting with Bill. *That woman got right up in my face - no hesitation at all. Like a lioness protecting what's hers. Yeah, I've got to be careful around her.*

Maggie sighed. *What am I doing anyway? Bill's married, end of story. I've been there, done that, and got the proverbial T-shirt and a shitload of pain to boot. Do I really want to go down that path again?* She shook her head. *Yeah, I think I do. There's just something about him, something special.*

But that wasn't all of it. Somewhere deep down she could feel there were forces moving around her that she didn't understand, but felt compelled to obey.

We belong together. He knows it and, I think, Karen knows it, too, and that's why she's so dangerous.

She sighed again and tried to put her thoughts aside and concentrate on her schoolwork. However, her mind kept drifting - drifting back to Bill Andersen.

A WALK IN THE WOODS

After Bill left for his interview, Karen felt at loose ends. She had no friends on the island, no one to do anything with, the house was clean, there were no meals to prepare, and the children were in school.

What am I going to do with my days here? Maybe I should take up fishing, she laughed to herself.

It was a fine day out, sunny with a bit of a cool breeze, so she decided to work in the gardens. An avid gardener, Karen's home in Los Gatos had been surrounded by beautiful flowerbeds she tended regularly.

Maybe I can make something of these despite the short growing season, she thought as she surveyed the perennial beds at the front of the house.

She found some old gardening tools in the garage and proceeded to get to work, weeding and transplanting as she thought necessary. When that was done, she walked to the backyard where there were two raised beds she planned to use for vegetables. Surveying the size of the beds, she made a mental note to find a nursery next time she went to town to pick up seedlings.

Leaving the raised beds, she walked the perimeter of the yard. Just before the woods began, there was a row of blackberry and raspberry bushes. Interspersed, at odd intervals, were wild blueberries. All of these plants were overgrown and in serious need of tender loving care.

If I can get these things in shape, we'll be knee-deep in berries by mid-summer.

She went back to the garage and rummaged through the tools until she found a pair of loppers and some pruning shears, then proceeded to go to work on the bushes.

As she pruned one particularly strange, unruly bush, she noticed, through its thorny branches, a trail leading into the woods. The footpath appeared to be in much better condition than the bush that concealed it and Karen wondered if there was some sort of volunteer trail-making brigade on the island. The pathway looked wide and inviting and the sun seemed to sparkle on the ground as it streamed down through the canopy of branches created by the treetops above. As she gazed down the trail, Karen was surprised to see a rabbit hop out of the woods in front of her. It turned and stared at her for a moment and then scampered down the trail.

It was so comical, Karen laughed. *Well, should I be Alice? Bill won't be back for a while, I have on my sturdy shoes, and my hands are beginning to ache from all the pruning I've done. Yes, I will. I'll be Alice and follow that damned rabbit into Wonderland!*

She used the loppers to cut back the branches that were hiding the trail, then put her gardening tools and gloves in the basket she'd found in the garage and stepped onto the path.

The air felt crisp and clean in the forest as she walked. Along the sides of the trail, growing around the trees, were scatterings of beautiful wildflowers - Lady Slippers, Blue Bells, and others. *Why are they all in bloom so early in the season?* she asked herself as she knelt down to look at the flowers more closely. Lost in thought, she was startled when two white-tailed deer leapt across the path in front of her. Almost immediately following the deer, another rabbit hopped onto the trail. Like the one before, it stopped and stared at her for a moment, then hopped away.

Mmmmm, I think I may have wandered into a freaking Disney movie, she thought, smiling to herself.

As if to confirm her thought, two bluebirds swooped down out of the branches above to hover, just for a split second, before her eyes. She shook her head in wonder. *Wait till I tell the girls about this.*

Standing up again, she continued strolling down the path, enjoying all the sights, sounds, and smells of the forest. Finally, the trail came to an end, opening up onto a lovely meadow. In the middle of the meadow was the most beautiful pond she had ever seen. It was ringed by wildflowers and looked magical with the sunlight flashing off the water. Dragonflies flittered by and she laughed as a silver fish leapt into the air, its scales lighting up like a rainbow in the afternoon sun.

She stood entranced by the pond, losing track of time. Finally, she looked up at the sky but could not see the position of the sun through the canopy above. She checked her watch - it read a quarter after eleven.

But that was when I left the yard, wasn't it? Damn thing must have stopped. I'd better get going. I have to be home when Bill gets there. We can always come back another day.

She was about to turn to leave when she felt something warm seeping into her sneakers. Curious, she looked down at her feet.

Her mouth fell open in shock. She was standing almost ankle deep in noxious mud.

Where did that come from? she asked herself as an odor of rot and decay began to fill her nostrils making her feel slightly nauseous. She slowly pulled her feet from the muck that encased them; careful she didn't lose her shoes in the process. When she was free, she looked up again and her sense of alarm intensified. The lovely meadow and the pond were gone - vanished!

Oh, my god! What's happening? It was there. I know it was.

She stared, horrified, at what was now a marsh-like swamp - dark and dismal and reeking of corruption. Vicious black flies and mosquitoes swarmed above the tepid water and she could see vile-looking snakes moving sinuously in and out of the rotting vegetation.

No bluebirds here, she thought as her confused mind tried to comprehend what had happened. She suddenly felt an urgent need to get home - home to safety. Adrenaline coursed through her body as she stepped back onto the trail and turned to go.

A murder of crows began to shriek in the treetops, the sound sending chills down her spine. She quickened her pace, wanting desperately to put the swamp and the horrible cacophony of the crows far behind her. Suddenly, without warning, a large owl swooped down and grasped her gardening hat in its talons.

She screamed, her fear intensifying as the chorus above her shrieked even louder.

That could have been my head, she thought, her mind swirling in disbelief. *What in God's name is happening? The forest - how could something so beautiful change like that - change into something so dark and menacing? Am I losing my mind? I've got to get out of here!*

She began to run for home, but the wide, well-manicured trail was now narrow and winding, tree branches seemingly reaching out to block her way. All around her it was getting darker and harder to see the path, the canopy above somehow closing in and blotting out the sun. She stumbled over a root that rose up out of nowhere and fell heavily onto the path. As she hit the ground, her hand caught on a jagged piece of rock, slicing open her palm. Catching her breath and wincing from the pain, she knelt in the dirt, cradling her injured hand to her breast. She reached into the pocket of her jacket for a tissue to stem the blood flowing from the wound, but could find none. She pushed herself to her feet, drops of blood falling freely to the forest floor. As they soaked into the earth, the crows suddenly became silent and the trees around her seemed to shudder and sigh. A strange sense of peace began to wash over her mind, but then a vicious hoot from an owl pierced the stillness around her.

Terror again seized her and she forced herself to move, running again - this time harder and faster. After what seemed an eternity, in the distance she saw the strange bush that marked the beginning of the trail. As she approached it, she was dismayed to see its thorny branches again blocking the entrance to her yard and to safety.

I cut those damned things back, her mind screamed. *I know I did. How did they grow again so fast? Those thorns will tear me to pieces.*

She stood frozen in indecision not wanting to be wounded by the thorns when, from behind her, she heard the sound of the owl again - this time closer and more menacing. Her fear spurred her into action. She pushed herself into the bush mindless of its barbs, trying to force her way back to the yard. As she struggled to get through, her blouse caught on one of its branches and, for a moment, she was trapped. Panic threatening to overwhelm her, she labored to get free, ripping her blouse and scratching her arms viciously. Finally, the branch gave way and she stumbled to the safety of the yard. Breathing heavily, she fell to the ground, her mind in shock.

What just happened? Am I going mad? Was it a hallucination? A brain tumor?

Catching her breath, she slowly got up and, leaving her gardening basket where it sat, stumbled into the house. Once inside, she breathed a sigh of relief. She was safe.

I need a drink, she thought as she went to the liquor cabinet and poured herself two fingers of Jack Daniels, neat. She threw her head back, tossed the liquor down, and sank into the overstuffed chair, letting the warmth of the alcohol relax her weary body. She sat still for several minutes trying to wrap her mind around what happened in the woods. Unable to comprehend the experience, she walked back to the liquor cabinet and made herself another drink, this time with ice and a splash of water.

Drinking at two o'clock in the afternoon. Next thing I'll be getting tattoos and piercing my navel.

She sat down again and tried to assess the damage she had done to herself. Her shoes were ruined, as were her socks. Her jeans were muddy and there was a tear at the left knee. Her shirt, torn by the thorns, was a disaster.

Shaking her head, she looked down at the cut on her palm. *Oh, that looks nasty. I'd better get this cleaned up before it gets infected.*

She got up and went upstairs, drink in hand. In the bathroom, she stripped off her soiled clothing and got into the shower. The hot water soothed her as she scrubbed herself well, trying to erase the odor of decay that still seemed to cling to her. Finally feeling cleansed, she tended to her hand and the numerous scratches and abrasions caused by that bush's thorns.

"What a mess I am," she said as she studied her body in the bathroom mirror. "What will I tell Bill? I can't tell him the truth, if, indeed it is the truth. He'll have me locked away in the loony bin for sure. And what did really happen? I know what I saw - it was beautiful, but it changed and turned rotten, like an overripe piece of fruit, nasty and disgusting. And that owl, it almost got my head! I could have died out there."

She gathered up her clothing and put them in the hamper then changed into her sweats and went back downstairs.

Hallucination or brain tumor? Which would I prefer? she thought, laughing to herself. *A brain tumor would get me sympathy, but would probably kill me. A hallucination would make everyone doubt my sanity and probably land me on some shrink's couch or, worse, institutionalized. No, it's better I keep this all to myself right now. Bill and I have enough on our plate already without muddying the waters with doubts about my sanity or health. I'll just have to make up something to explain all the scratches and the cut.*

She finished her drink and went about cleaning up the muddy footprints she had left on the rug. She was just finishing when she heard the car in the driveway. Bill was home.

A CAUSE OF CELEBRATION
& A LITTLE WHITE LIE

Karen watched through the window as her husband parked the car, thoughts of her afternoon misadventure swept from her mind.

I'll think about it tomorrow, she decided and then laughed. *Another literary connection - first I'm Alice, then I'm Scarlett. Maybe I do belong in the booby hatch!*

As Bill got out of the car, she noticed how he moved - there was a little spring to his step that had been missing for the past two years.

He got it! she thought as a big smile broke out on her face. *Best I let him tell me himself.* She sat back down in the overstuffed chair and waited.

Bill walked into the house, champagne in one hand, flowers in the other.

"Karen," he called.

"I'm in here, Bill," she answered from the living room.

As he walked through the doorway, the smile on his face disappeared when he took in her appearance - scratches on her face and neck, her hand bandaged. "What the hell happened to you?"

Karen smiled. "I got into a fight with a rose bush and, as you can see, the bush won."

"That explains your face, but your hand, how did you hurt your hand?"

"Oh, that. I tripped over my gardening basket and cut my hand on the pruning shears. It'll be okay, nothing serious. Just another day in the life of Karen the Klutz! Now, what's up with you? Bubbly, flowers? You got a hot date or something? Got something to tell me?"

Bill smiled. "You are now looking at a member of the employed! I got it! I start next week."

Karen stood up and walked over to him. She put her arms around him and kissed him softly on the lips, taking the flowers from his hand. "Well, what are you waiting for?" she asked as she turned away. "Let's celebrate. Open up that bubbly while I put these in water."

Bill popped open the bottle and poured a glass for each of them. Karen placed the flowers, now in a crystal vase, in the center of the table.

"To us," he said, handing her a glass of champagne.

"To the working man!" she exclaimed as she raised her glass and drank. She smiled at him. "Seriously, Bill, I'm so very proud of you. I know this job is not what you want and that you're doing this for the girls and me. Please know how much we appreciate it."

As she spoke, she moved closer to him. He put his arms around her waist.

"What time is it?" she asked.

Bill looked at his watch. "Three-fifteen. Why?"

"We've got a half hour," she replied with a twinkle in her eye.

"A quickie?" he asked as he moved his hands to her buttocks and pulled her close.

She answered him by reaching up and pulling his head down to meet her welcoming lips.

"Grab the champagne," she laughed. "Hurry!"

She took his hand and together, giggling like teenagers, they ran up the stairs.

THE LOCKED BOX

Sophie and Terri walked up the driveway, surprised neither of their parents was there to meet them. As they neared the house, Terri turned to her twin and whispered, "Remember, when Mommy's cooking, you distract Daddy, keep him talking to you. I'll be upstairs and I'll check out the keys on his key ring. I'll only need five minutes. Can you do that?"

"I'll be scared, but I can do it. You just be fast in case Mommy wants us to help cook or set the table or something."

Terri nodded and wiggled her little finger at Sophie. "Remember, pinky swear."

Sophie sighed and nodded, not completely happy with the situation.

The girls were interrupted when their parents, both looking rather flushed, burst through the door. Karen was laughing and their dad looked more relaxed and happy than he had in a long time.

"Sophie-slug!" he exclaimed, grabbing his daughter's hands and twirling her around. "And Terri-bug! Now it's your turn."

"Daddy, you got the job!" cried Terri with delight.

Bill nodded and gave both his girls a hug.

Karen stood on the porch, smiling as she watched her family. *Finally, things are looking up for us.*

A moment later, a large crow landed on the lowest branch of the maple tree that stood at the foot of the driveway. It stared at her intently for a moment, then began to caw loudly. The sound sent a shiver up her spine as she remembered her experience in the woods just hours before.

Better not to think about that now, she told herself. *Be Scarlett, girl, just be Scarlett.*

Putting her anxiety aside, she checked her watch and, noting the time, went inside to start dinner.

When Terri saw her mother go into the house, she gave Sophie a knowing look, then turned to her father. "Daddy, I think I'm going to go start on my homework."

"Okay, sweetie," he replied, giving her a quick hug.

She skipped up the stairs into the house after her mother. Bill was about follow, but Sophie grabbed his hand.

"Daddy, can you help me understand something?"

Bill knelt down beside her. "Sure, honey, what's up?"

Upstairs, Terri listened to be sure Sophie was playing her part. When she heard her dad's voice, she knew the coast was clear and tiptoed into her parents' room and was surprised to see their bed was mussed up. This puzzled her because her mom was a stickler for neatness and would never let a bed go unmade.

Another mystery, she thought but quickly made herself focus back on getting the keys.

On the dresser, as she had expected, were a small pile of change and two key rings. On one, Terri identified a house key and a car key that bore the Toyota logo. Knowing these were not the keys she was looking for, she turned her attention to the second key ring. This one was one of those stretchy beaded bands that looked very old and well used. On it was three keys. Terri identified one as another house key and the second as the key to the island car. The third was a mystery. It was smaller than the others and lighter.

This must be it! she thought.

She took the keys and tiptoed back to her room. Once there, she pulled the box out of the closet and tried the little key in the padlock. "It works!" she exclaimed. She was tempted to sit down and open the box right away, but she didn't.

It wouldn't be right to do it without Sophie, she scolded herself. Resolved to wait, she hid the box in the closet again and snuck back to the front bedroom, returning the key ring to the dresser.

Satisfied everything looked the same as it had when she first came in, she left the room and went downstairs. She smiled when she looked out the window and saw Sophie and her father sitting on the porch having an animated discussion. Sophie looked up and Terri nodded to her. Then, she walked over to the kitchen to see if her mother needed any help with dinner.

Later, after supper, Karen sent her daughters upstairs to complete their homework. Once safely in their room and secure in the knowledge that they wouldn't be observed by their parents, Sophie turned to her twin, eyes wide in anticipation. "Did it open? Did one of the keys fit?"

"Yes," Terri answered. "It was just like we thought and I took the padlock off so we don't lock it up again by mistake. And I didn't peek. I waited for you. You did real good with Dad, Soph, real good."

Sophie beamed at the praise from her sister. "Can we look now?"

Terri thought for a moment. "I think we'd better wait till later, when they think we're asleep. You know how Mom likes to come up and help us with our homework even though she's not supposed to."

Sophie looked disappointed but nodded, knowing Terri was right. Their mother did have a habit of surprising them while they were doing their lessons and she might be mad if she found out they were hiding stuff from her. Sighing, Sophie pulled out her homework and, with Terri, began to complete their assignments. True to form, about a half hour later, Karen appeared in their doorway with an offer of help.

Before they knew it, it was bedtime and they were soon washed, tucked in, and kissed goodnight. After their parents went back downstairs, Terri sat up in bed.

"I think it's safe now," she whispered. "We have to be really quiet, Soph, and not turn on any lights. I have my flashlight here in my bed. You stay there and I'll come to you."

Terri got out of bed, turned her flashlight on, and made her way to the closet to retrieve the box. Once she had it securely in hand, she sat down beside Sophie on the bed. They looked at each other and then, together, opened the box. Terri turned her flashlight on the contents.

On top, wrapped in tissue paper, were three cornhusk dolls. The dolls looked very old and very fragile.

"It's a family," whispered Sophie. "A daddy, a mommy, and a little girl or boy."

Very gently, Terri lifted the dolls out of the box and examined them closely then handed them to her twin. "Do you think they're toys, Soph?"

"Don't know," she replied setting the dolls aside. "What else is in the box?"

The next item was a document that was rolled up and tied with a blood-red ribbon. It looked to be very delicate and was yellow with age. Sophie carefully untied the ribbon and unrolled the parchment. On it were crudely drawn symbols - three figures that looked something like the cornhusk dolls, a crescent moon, a teardrop, a lightning bolt, a large rabbit, and other pictures or symbols the meaning of which eluded the twins.

"I bet it tells a story in pictures," whispered Sophie. "Like those Egyptian writings we saw on the Discovery Channel."

Terri nodded as Sophie rolled the document back up and retied the ribbon and set it aside with the dolls. Turning her attention back to the box, she pulled out an envelope. On the front were written the words *"Mateguas Prière."* Inside, they found three sheets of notebook paper. On the first was written,

Mateguas Prière

> *Oh, Mateguas Grand Père de la Mort, entend ma prière.*
> *Entendre la prière de cette mère pour sa famille.*
> *Ce soir, la Mskagwdemos manèges la tempête.*
> *Elle lance l'éclair, elle hurle el tonnerre, elle lave la terre de ses larmes, et elle a faim pour la famille de cette mère.*
> *L'homme qu'elle appelle pour qu'elle puisse coucher avec lui et de lui voler sa semence.*
> *L'enfant, elle demande à téter à son sein.*

Cette mère pourrait garder sa famille en sécurité.

Cette mère permettrait de protéger l'homme et l'enfant, comme ils sont incapables de se protéger de la fureur des Mskagwdemos.

Cette mère supplie la grande Mateguas de miséricorde.

Avec ce couteau fait à partir des os de l'orignal sacré, cette mère va faire le sacrifice pour le Grand Père de la Mort, afin qu'il puisse prendre pitié d'elle, et restaurer sa famille à elle.

Son sang rend fertile la terre de sorte que les gens, qui a tant aimé par Le Grand Mateguas, va prospérer.

Oh, Grand Père de la Mort, entend ma prière.

"I think that's written in French," said Terri. "I recognize some of the words from that class Mommy made us take last summer."

"Yeah, I remember," replied her twin. "Boring!"

Terri laughed as she unfolded the second paper. On it, they found more writing, again in French.

Mateguas Prière

1) *Tracer un cercle autour de vous sur la pelouse à l'aide de la poudre de sang.*

2) *A l'intérieur du cercle, dessiner les symboles croissant de lune, coup de foudre et de larme.*

3) *Placez la famille (poupées) à l'intérieur du cercle, face à l'est.*

4) *Réciter la prière Mateguas, toujours face à l'est.*

5) *Quand vous venez au sacrifice, prendre le couteau d'os et couper ouvrir votre paume - ne bonne et profonde, car il fait saigner dans le terre. Appuyez sur paume de la terre tout en continuant a reciter la prière.*

6) *La terre doit prendre votre sang et être nourri par elle.*

7) *Continuer la récitation de la prière et le sacrifice de répéter jusqu'à ce que le soleil se lève.*

8) Si vous faites toutes ces choses correctement, votre famille sera retournée, sains et saufs a vous.

Mais toujours face à l'est, quoi qu'il arrive, ne pas tourne autour!

On the third sheet was a drawing of a circle inside of which were, again, the dolls and the crescent moon, teardrop, and lightning bolt symbols. Outside the circle, written in French, were what the girls believed were the directional indicators - North, South, East, and West. The family in the drawing faced east.

The girls marveled at these documents and were intrigued by the mystery that they implied. Terri carefully refolded the papers and returned them to their envelope. She put them aside along with the other objects and turned back to the box. At the bottom were two more items.

The first was a small glass bottle filled with a reddish colored powder. A tiny spoon was attached at the neck. The bottle was old and looked hand-blown and the twins handled it with great care. The top was sealed with wax and secured again by a gold wire from which the silver spoon dangled.

However, it was the final object in the box that made them both gasp.

"Oh, look, Sophie," cried Terri as she held up a small bone knife. "See how it's carved!" The handle was of intricate design and bore the now familiar symbols - the moon, lightning bolt, and teardrop. Like the other items in the box, it was very old - the bone yellow with age.

"Listen," said Sophie, her head turned toward the door to their room. "I think I hear Mommy and Daddy. They'll be up here soon and you know they'll check on us."

Terri looked at the clock. It was late. "You're right. Let's put this stuff away and get to bed. We can study it again tomorrow."

Sophie nodded in agreement and the girls returned the treasures to the box and secreted it again in the closet. Terri tiptoed back to her bed, hid the flashlight, and pulled up the covers, feigning sleep. Only minutes later, their door opened a crack and they knew their father was checking on them. After a moment, he closed the door again and, relieved they hadn't been caught, the girls drifted off to sleep, their dreams filled with the mystery that was unfolding around them.

GARDEN THOUGHTS

The next morning the twins overslept and had to be rousted out of bed.

"Hey, you guys, better shake a leg right now or you'll miss the school bus," yelled Karen when she realized they were still asleep. "How come you're both such sleepyheads this morning? Now, up and at em!"

Still tired, the girls reluctantly did as their mother commanded.

Downstairs, Bill was having breakfast. Karen came down shaking her head. "I don't know what's gotten into those girls, sleeping this late. I bet they got up after we put them to bed and played a game or something. We'll have to keep better tabs on them from now on."

Bill nodded. "Hon, I'm going to go to town today to meet with Phil, Pete's cousin. I want to try to get a head start on things so I'm completely prepared on Monday."

Bill had explained to Karen the night before about the car situation on the mainland. He would need the car Monday through

Thursday so, until they could afford a second vehicle, she would only have access to it on Fridays and weekends. This did not sit too well with her, but she grudgingly acknowledged it was necessary. If she went to town during the week, she would have to hoof it or take public transportation. Bill also explained there would be times he would have to stay over on the mainland because he might not make the last ferry home. Again, Karen grudgingly gave her acceptance.

With the anticipation of a regular paycheck coming in, Bill and Karen's relationship settled into an uneasy truce. The joy and delight they'd experienced when he'd announced his success at the interview was short-lived and soon they resettled into their old pattern: Karen, edgy and quick to anger; and Bill, walking on eggshells around her. Adding to the tenuousness of their relationship, Bill really didn't buy her explanation for her appearance on Monday - the scratches on her face and neck, the cut on her hand.

She's hiding something from me, he thought. *Something or someone really shook her up.*

The girls safely on the school bus, Karen drove Bill to the ferry. When she returned home, she busied herself outside making notes on the flowers that were in the perennial gardens and deciding what would stay and what would go. She also made a list of plants and other gardening items she needed, including the vegetable seedlings and compost for the raised beds out back.

As she worked, her mind journeyed back to what she had begun to think of as her "experience" in the woods. It now seemed surreal and illusory, the fear she had felt dissipating.

I don't think I'm losing my mind. No, that can't explain it. The whole thing, well, it seemed like I was being tested, like my strength was being assessed. I was frightened, no doubt about it, but I overcame it, didn't I? And I really didn't get hurt - just that cut on my hand and a few scratches. Nothing life threatening. If somebody was trying to hurt me, well, they could have done a much better job. No, maybe I just imagined it all, like in a dream.

She shook her head and returned to her lists. Finally, finished, she went back inside. The girls wouldn't be home until school was over and Bill wouldn't be back until five o'clock. She sighed and sat down in the overstuffed chair, watching the waves hit the shore, trying to let her mind go blank. However, echoing strangely in her memory was the soft hoot of an owl and try as she might, she couldn't let it go.

A PLAN

At school, Sophie and Terri sat down by themselves for lunch. They hadn't had a chance to talk since they'd narrowly escaped detection the night before.

"We need to find out what's in those papers," said Terri as she opened her lunch. "If only Daddy would let us use the Internet without being supervised."

Terri was referring to her father's rule that the twins be under strict supervision whenever they searched or played on the Web. There was no access to the Internet allowed without a parent, teacher, or other responsible adult in attendance.

"I know," sighed Sophie. "But maybe we can get online at the library? Mommy might allow it and I don't think the librarian will bother us if we're real quiet."

"Good idea, Soph," said Terri, clapping her twin on the back. "Maybe we can get Mommy to take us on Saturday. We can copy down the words we don't know and try to find a translation program online.

Then, maybe we can figure out what it all means. We can tell Mommy it's for a project at school."

Sophie nodded vigorously and, glad they had a plan, dug into her lunch. Soon, it was time to return to their lessons, but today, even Maggie noticed, they were not focusing on the work to be done. No, they both seemed lost in their own thoughts, giving off an aura of secrets shared – no outsiders allowed!

The rest of the week went by quickly for the Andersens. Bill focused on his new job and finding out all he could about the customers he was inheriting and potential new accounts in his territory. Karen concentrated on her gardens, picking up numerous plants and materials at a local nursery. She had the front beds all organized and was working on getting the vegetable beds ready for planting. The girls had their school and homework and they looked forward to Saturday because their mother had agreed to let them spend the day at the library.

When they were alone, Terri and Sophie spent what time they could copying down the French words and phrases they wanted to translate. Studying the documents, they believed the first one was some sort of prayer, perhaps the one that their dad's friend, Mr. McKinney, had spoken about that would keep the swamp woman away.

Saturday soon came and Karen loaded the girls and their notebooks and schoolbooks into the car and drove them to the island library. Karen went in with them and introduced herself to the head librarian, Betty Jones. Betty gave them a brief tour and Karen was impressed at how modern and well stocked the facility was.

"So, it's okay with you if I leave them here to work on their project for a couple of hours?" Karen asked.

"That's just fine," the librarian replied. "I'm here all day so I'll keep an eye on them. And don't worry, we have strict controls on Internet access for youngsters so they won't get into any trouble in that area."

Satisfied, Karen gave her girls a kiss. "Now you both mind Ms. Jones and don't make nuisances of yourselves. You have the cell, Terri.

If you want me to pick you up earlier, call me. And don't leave the library, okay?"

"We'll be fine, Mommy," said Sophie, giving her mother a quick hug.

Karen looked both of them over again. "Okay, I'll see you later," she said as she turned and walked out the door.

Terri and Sophie didn't waste any time. As soon as their mother was gone, they approached the librarian.

"Ms. Jones?" said Terri.

"Yes, honey," she replied. "What can I help you with?"

Taking a deep breath before continuing, Terri explained to the librarian that they were working on a project that involved translating a document. Betty smiled and directed them to a free program on the Internet. It was hard work for the little girls, but they actually finished much faster than they'd anticipated and, with time to spare before their mother came to get them, turned their attention to their real homework.

KAREN

After dropping the girls off, Karen went home to make what she called "The Yahoo Cake" for the potluck dinner/dance being held that evening. She was still not happy about having to attend this social engagement, but couldn't think of any reasonable way to get out of it.

I could cut off my hand, she thought ruefully. *However, they'd probably get me out of the hospital in time to make the festivities. I just can't win with this one.*

As she put together the ingredients for the cake, she thought about her situation. With the kids in school and Bill working, she'd be on her own a good chunk of time and there was only so much gardening and housework she could tolerate.

Maybe I can find some sort of volunteer work on the mainland, she mused. *I need something other than shopping to get me away from this place during the week. I could take some courses at the local college and then get a job myself.*

She knew she had refused to return to work back in California, mainly out of stubbornness and anger, but now, getting away from this island was more important to her than her precious pride.

When the cake went into the oven, she sat down at the computer to see what she could come up with to fill her days. Unfortunately, her search did not bear fruit.

Yes, there's a local college with an array of courses, but the ones I'm interested in aren't scheduled at times that coincide with the ferry or the girls' school. I could take some of them from home on the Internet, but that won't get me off this damned island, which is the only real motivation for taking them in the first place.

That left volunteer work. Checking out the various opportunities, she was again disappointed.

Oh shit, all of the animal shelters are in the suburbs. Without access to a car, I can't get there to do any dog walking or kitty cuddling. The only other thing available is at a homeless shelter and I don't think I'd really do very well ladling out soup.

Disgusted, she turned off the computer and walked back to the kitchen just as the timer went off. She took the cake out of the oven and set it out to cool before frosting it. Checking her watch, she went upstairs to refresh her makeup before driving to the library to pick up the girls. As she brushed her hair, she again thought about her "experience" in the woods. It had faded somewhat, like an old photograph, and the terror she'd felt had mutated into a strange sense of wonder.

It all started with that rabbit, she thought, remembering how it had turned and stared at her. *It was like it was daring me to step on that trail.*

Then she remembered the sense of acceptance she'd felt from the earth and forest when the blood from her hand seeped into the ground. The memory left her slightly dizzy and she sat heavily on the bed and bent over, putting her head between her knees. Breathing deeply, she quickly recovered, trying to shake off renewed doubts about her sanity.

Get a grip, girl. It was all just an illusion - like a dream. It won't happen again. You're okay.

Taking another deep breath and feeling like her old self again, she stood up and went downstairs to go pick up her children.

THE DANCE

Late Saturday morning, while Karen was baking the cake, Bill went for a jog. He ran for a while, enjoying the freshness of the sea air. When he reached the intersection where the town grocery store was located, he decided to go inside and grab a cold drink.

The store was a busy place. There were several trucks parked outside and a group of men was sitting at a picnic table, enjoying coffee and conversing. Bill recognized Rusty as one of them and walked over to say hello. Rusty greeted him warmly and introduced Bill to his friends.

"And, Bill, this bad boy here is Dexter Pierce," he said, pointing to a rugged-looking man with startling blue eyes.

"Dex to my friends," he drawled, offering his hand. "Nice to meet you, Bill. However, I'd much rather be sitting down with that pretty woman of yours. I would surely like to get acquainted with her!"

There was a mischievous twinkle in his eyes and Bill sensed that, while this man was not classically handsome, he was probably quite attractive to women. He had an aura about him - rakish good looks and a very sexy smile.

Rusty shook his head. "Now, Dex, don't you be giving Bill the wrong impression. He's just joshing you, Bill. Our Dex likes to think he's quite the ladies' man."

Dex laughed. "You and that pretty woman coming to the dance tonight?"

"Yeah, we'll be there," Bill replied. "Karen is baking a cake for the potluck. We'll have the kids with us so I don't know if we'll stay for the dancing or not."

"Oh, you got to!" insisted Dex. "We have a good old time. After nine o'clock, the bar opens and we really rock out! And I'm hoping to get a dance with your pretty wife."

Bill laughed, wondering what Karen would think of this character. "Well, maybe, we'll stay for a while. Karen has been wanting a night out on the town and this might be just what she needs."

As he spoke, he knew it was a lie. Karen was still not enthusiastic about the evening ahead of them and her idea of a night out was just a wee bit different than a local dinner/dance. Glancing at his watch, he made his excuses to Rusty and the other men and began his jog home.

Even though she was not looking forward to it, Karen dressed carefully for the evening. She knew it was important to make a good impression with the locals if just for Bill and the girls' sakes. Since it was casual, she put on jeans and a sweater. She pinned her blonde-streaked hair up in a French braid and put on a large turquoise pendant, with earrings to match, that she'd purchased when the family vacationed in the southwest. She dressed her daughters similarly, jeans and sweaters and, for a treat, French-braided their hair, too.

Bill was waiting in the living room when they all came downstairs. "Wow!" he exclaimed. "You all look great. Every man and boy there is going to be jealous of me tonight with such a bevy of beauties on my arm!"

Karen smiled at the compliment as the girls giggled and blushed. "Thanks, hon, we do try."

She walked to the kitchen and got the cake while Bill teased Terri and Sophie a little more. "Ready, Bill?" she called. "We don't want to be late."

"Okay, kids," he replied as he took his daughters' hands. "Mom says it's time to get this show on the road!"

The hall the event was held in was a large building for such a small island. Tonight, the main room was full of rectangular tables laid out with place settings. Off this room was another, half as large, housing a small bar, dance floor, and elevated stage area. Out back, a long farmhouse porch lined with rockers looked out on a yard with a small playground for the children. Beyond this yard, was a path to the beach.

When the Andersens arrived, the dining room was already full of people, some sitting, others standing, but all in animated conversation with one another. Several women were in the kitchen putting together the meal. Louise saw Karen arrive and beckoned her over.

"Sadie," she said to one of the women in the kitchen, "get an apron for Karen. Honey, we're going to put you to work!"

Karen put on the apron and, with a wry smile, joined the ladies in the kitchen. Bill took the girls outside where some of the children from their class were playing.

Watching his girls, Bill was surprised to feel a tap on his shoulder. He turned around to see Dex leaning against the porch rail, a wicked smile on his rugged face.

"Now where's that little woman, Bill?" he asked. "You know she's the only reason I came to this thing."

Bill laughed. "I'm afraid she got shanghaied by the kitchen squad. She'll be out later and I'll be sure to introduce you."

"I'm going to hold you to that one, Bill. And after dinner, you come out on the porch alone. Me and the boys got something for you and it's kinda mandatory if you want to be a real islander."

Bill looked at him quizzically. "Is this something that's going to get me in trouble?"

"Mayhap it will and mayhap it won't," Dex replied with a wink. "But keep it a secret, okay?"

Bill nodded.

"Okay," said Dex. "We'll see you all later."

Dex turned and went back inside just as Pete came through the door and walked over to Bill.

"I saw you in conversation with Mr. Pierce, Bill," he said. "You watch out for that one. He's a damn good fisherman - none better on this island - but he has a bit of a wild streak in him. Ladies love him, though, so keep a close eye on your wife."

Bill laughed. "I don't think I have to worry about Karen. She can take care of herself."

"Well, don't say I didn't warn you. Listen, I've got places saved for you all with Louise and me, if I can get her out of the kitchen. I see she's corralled Karen in there, too."

The two men talked for a short while longer until it was announced that dinner was served. Bill rounded up the girls and, together, they joined Karen and Louise in the dining room.

As she sat down, Karen glanced around the room. The conversation was lively and she could see Bill and the girls were having a good time. As the meal progressed, she smiled and spoke when spoken to, but she just couldn't seem to get into it.

There's nothing wrong with these people. So, why can't I just relax and try to be one of them? She didn't know the answer, but one thing she was certain of, she was glad that schoolteacher wasn't there. *Yeah, if that Maggie creature were here, I'd have to endure Bill ogling her all night and that would be anything but fun.*

Soon the meal was over and some of the older folks and ones with small children said their good-byes and went home. Those who stayed moved over to the barroom, where an old-fashioned jukebox sat in the corner. The real music wasn't scheduled until nine o'clock and the local group that was playing was just setting up.

Bill, Karen, and the girls followed the crowd into the room. Several of the men went out onto the porch to smoke and Bill remembered Dex's invitation. Pete picked out several songs on the jukebox and, when the music started, whirled Louise out onto the dance floor. Soon, several other couples joined them.

Bill turned to Karen and took her hand.

"Shall we?" he asked, leading her out onto the dance floor.

As they danced, he was distracted by a commotion at the entrance to the room. Several young people had arrived, apparently coming just for the after dinner party. At the center of the group, he could see a mass of red curls and he couldn't help but stare as Maggie entered the room. Simply dressed in jeans and a plaid shirt, she was breathtaking. She turned and locked eyes with him, opening her mouth slightly and pushing her lower lip out in a pout. Then, laughing, she broke into a beautiful smile. Bill quickly tore his eyes away and turned his attention back to his wife and his dancing.

As the song ended and he was leading Karen off the dance floor, he felt a slight tap on his shoulder.

"Mind if I cut in?" Dex asked, reaching for Karen's hand. "Bill, aren't you going to introduce me to your lovely wife?"

Karen looked up to see who had taken her hand, her eyes widening in surprise. *It's that man from the wharf - the one who eyeballed me so shamelessly when we first arrived.*

She felt herself begin to blush and a mischievous twinkle began to dance in his eyes as if relishing her discomfort. She glanced down at the floor, trying to pull herself together, then looked back up at him, giving him one of her most fetching smiles. He laughed knowingly, squeezing her hand lightly.

Unaware of the silent exchange going on between his wife and his new friend, Bill responded. "Karen, this is Dex Pierce and I've been warned not to leave you alone with him!"

Karen smiled at her husband. "I think I can take care of myself, Bill. Nice to meet you, Dex."

"The pleasure is all mine, princess," he replied as he led her back out onto the dance floor. The jukebox began playing an old fifties tune and Dex spun and whirled Karen about with ease. She was surprised to find herself laughing and enjoying this man immensely. Too soon, the number ended and Dex obediently returned her to her husband. But before leaving, he took her hand, bowed low, and placed a light kiss on the back of it.

"That was truly special, princess," he said, giving her a wink. Then he turned to Bill, made a motion with his thumb toward the porch, and sauntered away.

"What was that all about?" asked Karen, indicating the gesture Dex had made to Bill.

"Oh, just some sort of island initiation for me," Bill replied, laughing. "Hope it doesn't involve a snipe hunt."

"Well, I think it's about time I got the girls home and into bed. You stay and do your boys' thing. Do you think you can get a ride home?"

"Sure, and if not, I can always walk. It's not too far."

They gathered up their sleepy daughters and put them in the car. Bill leaned in the window and gave Karen a kiss. "Thanks for being such a good sport tonight, honey. Next Saturday, it's you and me alone in town for sure. I'll just do this thing with Dex and be home before you know it."

Karen smiled, returned his kiss, and then backed out of the driveway for home.

Bill watched as Karen drove away, then walked around the building, out to the porch, looking for Dex. He soon found him sitting in the far corner in the shadows with a couple other men around the same age.

"Thought we'd lost you," said Dex when he saw Bill come into view. "Come on over here and have a seat."

Dex made the necessary introductions and offered Bill what appeared to be a clear liquid in a mason jar the men had been passing around.

Bill looked suspiciously at the jar, raising his eyebrows. "White lightning?" he asked.

Dex and the other men laughed. "White lightning is a ladies' drink compared to this stuff! We just call it Mateguas hooch and you're not a real islander until you partake of it! So drink up, my friend, drink up!"

Bill looked at the jar again, hesitated a moment, then took it from Dex with a smile. He nodded once and tossed it back. He felt the fire from the alcohol immediately and couldn't help but choke and cough. This brought peals of laughter from Dex and the others. Not wanting to be outdone by these guys, Bill girded himself, raised the jar again and drained it, then passed the empty back to Dex with a steady hand.

"Holy shit, Bill," exclaimed Dex. "One was enough. You trying to kill yourself? Hey, maybe that's not a bad idea, then that pretty woman of yours would be available."

"Not going to happen," laughed Bill, beginning to feel the effects of the alcohol.

Dex replenished the jar from a jug he had under his chair and the men commenced passing it around again. Bill took a couple more swigs and was surprised when the door to the hall suddenly burst open and Maggie walked out onto the porch. She looked around, and, seeing Dex and the men in the corner, walked over to them.

"Thought I'd find you here," she said to Dex. "The constable just arrived and if he finds you out here with that hooch, you're going to wind up in the county jail for sure."

"Thanks, kitten," Dex replied. "Bill, it's been fun. I'll have to take you out on the boat sometime. You're a good sport."

"I'll look forward to it," said Bill as Dex and his friends grabbed the jug and took off across the lawn to their trucks.

Bill watched them go and then stood up. Maggie was standing next to him, so close he could smell her perfume; it was more intoxicating than the hooch he'd just consumed. A lock of his hair fell across his eyes and she reached up and brushed it away. Her touch was electric. He started to take a step toward her, but staggered, the alcohol taking its toll on him. She stepped in and slid her arm around his waist, steadying him.

"Whoa there, California," she said. "Looks like you may have had a tad too much of that hooch. Think you could use some sea air to clear up that fog that's gotten into your brain."

Bill nodded and let her lead him down the short path to the beach.

Once there, they stood watching as the moon sparkled off the water and the waves lapped the shoreline. Maggie's arm still lay lightly around his waist and he could feel her heat through his clothing. Head clearing, he turned to her, meaning to thank her, but she turned at the same time and they found themselves facing each other, their bodies almost touching. She held her moist lips just slightly apart, a softness coming into her eyes. Without thinking, he placed his hand under her chin, tilting her head slightly back, and leaned down and kissed her gently. She wrapped her arms around his neck and returned his kiss with passion as he pulled her body close to his. The kiss seemed to go on forever, but the spell was soon broken by the sound of someone calling out his name.

He pulled away from her. "It's Pete."

"Go," she said softly. "It's okay. No, wait. Give me your cell."

Bill handed her his phone, trying to pull himself together. She quickly opened his address book and typed her number in.

"Now you have no excuse," she said, handing the cell back to him. She leaned in and kissed him again, quickly. "Now go. Go before he gets here."

Bill nodded and turned to walk back down the path. Maggie stayed on the beach, staring out at the sea. Halfway back to the Hall, Bill ran into Pete.

"Hey, buddy," said Pete. "I was looking to see if you needed a ride and got a bit worried what with Dex and that hooch and all. You okay?"

"Yeah," Bill replied, slurring his words a bit. "Guess I tried too hard to be one of the boys. Had to get some sea air to clear my head. I'll take you up on that ride. Don't think I want to be walking home feeling like I do now. That hooch is powerful stuff."

Pete laughed. "Like I warned you, you gotta watch out for that Dex. And keep your eye on Karen, too. That boy jokes around about wanting your woman, but if he got the chance, look out! He's been the cause of more than one marriage goin' south around here, believe me. Well, let's get this show on the road. Louise is waiting!"

"I'm ready, and thanks, Pete. I really appreciate the lift and your watching out for me."

KAREN

At home, Karen tucked her tired girls into bed. Sophie had practically fallen asleep while Karen was unpinning her hair. Once she had them settled, she went back downstairs to wait for Bill. She poured herself a glass of wine, grabbed a book, and sat down in the overstuffed chair facing the window. It was dark out, the moon hidden behind a cloud. Listening to the waves hitting the shore, she wondered what mischief Dex had in mind for her husband.

That guy is really a piece of work, she mused. *He's very good looking and sexy. And he knows how to handle a woman.*

Her mind drifted back to the dance they'd shared, reliving it with a smile on her face. She could almost still feel his hand on her waist as he'd twirled her out and pulled her back.

Nice eyes and smile. If I wasn't married, I just might give him a run for his money.

The thought made her laugh, then her mind turned to the other islander who had made an impression on her that night.

That girl, always that girl.

It had not been lost on her when Maggie entered the room. She'd felt Bill stiffen just the slightest bit while they were dancing and, as they turned, she'd caught sight of Maggie's red curls. She frowned as she thought about the girl.

Bill always has had a bit of a roving eye, but I don't think he's ever acted on it. There was Sloane's slutty wife - but I think that was all her, not him. However, this girl - well, there's just something about her. She might be a problem. Yes, she's different and I'm right to worry about her.

Karen sipped her wine and checked the clock. It was getting late. She was about to pull out her cell and give Bill a call when she heard a car door slam. A moment or two later, Bill entered the room, a little unsteady on his feet.

"Uh-oh," she said, smiling. "I think someone's had a little bit too much to drink."

"Moonshine," he said. "White lightning or something damn near like it. Said I had to drink it to be one of the boys. But, I showed them! I drank it right down and asked for more!"

He took a step toward her, laughing when he lost his balance.

"Whoa, I think I need to lie down."

Shaking her head, Karen helped him upstairs, got him undressed and into bed.

"Thanks, honey," he mumbled as he rolled over and closed his eyes.

Karen sighed, put on her nightgown, and got ready for bed.

As his wife lay down beside him, Bill, not quite as drunk as he appeared, thought about the night just past and about Maggie.

God, it was nice to put my arms around someone who was eager, yes, so eager, for my touch. And her lips, held just slightly apart, so wet, so soft, and so inviting. Oh, yes, those lips promise something. But will I take her up on it?

With that unanswered question rolling around in his mind and with the memory of a warm soft body held close to his, he reached out to put his arms around his wife and let himself drift off into a dreamless sleep.

MAGGIE

Maggie left the beach and walked back to the hall, reliving in her mind the kiss with Bill. She started up the steps to the porch when a voice came at her out of the darkness.

"Now, you wouldn't be going down to the beach all by yourself on a fine night like this, would you, girlfriend?"

Maggie turned toward the voice. "You mind your own business, Dex Pierce. Where I go and with whom I choose to go with is no concern of yours!"

Dex laughed. He was sitting on the porch swing and, with a wave of his hand, indicated for her to join him. She sat down next to him and rested her head on his shoulder as he put his arm around her.

Maggie had known Dex her whole life. He always treated her like a little sister, teasing her with one hand while protecting her with the other. After the fiasco with the professor, Dex had been the one she went to for solace and he had gladly leant her his broad shoulder to cry on.

"Seriously," she said, "you won't say anything, will you? I surely don't want to be the talk of the town again. My parents will disown me."

Dex gave her a squeeze. "No, I won't. Scout's honor. But you sure you know what you're doing, kitten? He looks pretty much married, if you know what I mean. And his wife, now I wouldn't mind getting into some of that, but she looks like she's not the sharing kind."

"I know," sighed Maggie, "but I just can't seem to help myself. There's just something about him. It's like it's fate - like we're supposed to be together. Oh, gosh, Dex, I don't know."

"Now, sugar, you know you're just horny," he said, laughing. "He's the only new cock on this rock and, girl, you just gotta go for it!"

Maggie burst into laughter, hugging him. He hugged her back and then turned her face to his, suddenly serious. "Just you be careful, girl. I pride myself on knowing women and his wife, well, I see a strength in her that I don't think even she realizes is there. You just watch your step around her."

Maggie nodded, taking his impressions of Karen to heart. When it came to women, Dex was usually right.

"I will, Dex, I will," she said as she laid her head back on his shoulder, her mind again reliving Bill's kiss and knowing that, despite Dex's warning, she would seek him out again.

SUNDAY MORNING

"Oh, sweet Christ," moaned Bill, waking up with a fierce hangover. His mouth felt full of cotton and his head was pounding. *Why did I drink that shit? Need aspirin right now and coffee.* He rolled over. Karen's side of the bed was empty. He glanced at his watch.

Holy crap, it's ten o'clock! I've slept half the day away.

Out of bed, he headed for the bathroom, downed some aspirin, and drank a couple glasses of cold water to rehydrate. Then, he jumped in the shower to try to wash away the hangover. Finally, cleaned up and dressed in his running gear, he ventured downstairs to see what his family was up to. He found Karen in the kitchen finishing the breakfast dishes.

"Well, you finally decided to get up," she said when he entered the room. "Want a raw egg and a beer to kill that hangover?"

"Thanks, but no thanks, just coffee, please," he replied, sitting down at the kitchen table. "Boy, I really made an ass of myself last night. I get drunk at the first island function I go to. That sure makes an impression. The whole island is probably laughing at me by now. I'm sure glad Pete stayed to get me home. I'd probably be sleeping it off on the beach somewhere, waiting for the tide to get me."

Karen laughed and placed a steaming mug of coffee in front of him. "Well, you had some help. That Dex, I think he's a wild card. You were just trying to be one of the boys and I don't think anyone's really going to hold that against you. But if you do it again..." Her voice trailed off as she smiled.

Bill laughed then winced. "Ooh that hurt! Think I'll go for a run to sweat the bad stuff out of my system."

He quickly finished his coffee, gave his wife a kiss, and went out the door.

She watched as he jogged down the driveway, shaking her head. *That Dex*, she thought, remembering his blue eyes and that slow, sexy smile. *Yes, he's a wild card, for sure.*

With their dad out for a run and their mother busy in the kitchen, the girls slipped upstairs, behind closed doors, to try to solve the puzzle of the ancient box. They again studied the papers, trying to determine their meaning. They'd translated many of the words, but putting it all together was difficult. They also wondered about the bottle and its contents.

"The French word *sang* means blood and the word *poudre* means powder," said Sophie holding the little bottle in her hand. "So, this stuff must be something called 'blood powder.' Yuck!"

"Sounds nasty," agreed Terri. "Maybe you use this stuff to draw a circle like in the picture and that's what the spoon is for. Or maybe you use the spoon to eat the stuff. What do you think?"

Sophie made a face. "I don't think you eat it. At least, I won't! I think you draw with it and you probably have to draw these other things, too," she said pointing to the crescent moon, lightning bolt, and teardrop. "We should give this box to Daddy so he'll be able to protect us if anything happens."

"No, if we give it to anyone, we give it to Mommy. The prayer talks about the *mere* not the papa. The only dad in it is Mateguas and he's the dad of the dead!"

140

"But it's the daddy who always protects the mommy and kids, everyone knows that," objected Sophie.

They argued about this for a while then, getting bored, Sophie began to play with the cornhusk dolls, giving them names and creating a story around them. Terri, however, was more interested in another item from the box - the small bone knife. She looked at it intently, weighing it in her hand. Then she lifted it into the air, her arms spread wide. "Oh Mateguas," she intoned, "great dad of the dead...."

Sophie looked up at her, alarmed. "You better be careful! You might cut yourself."

Terri laughed. "With this? This old knife couldn't cut butter! Watch!"

As she spoke, she took the knife and pointed the blade at her fingertip. Jabbing it forward, a look of surprise flashed across her face when the blade easily sunk into her flesh. Instantaneously, blood oozed from the wound, dripping down the shaft of the knife. Terri watched, mesmerized, as the knife began to glow and grow warm in her hand. Her blood, flowing freely and covering the knife blade and shaft, began to pulsate with light. Slowly, she started to move the blade toward her finger again.

Sophie, her eyes wide as saucers, sat frozen as she watched her twin. Horrified by what was happening, she quickly lashed out her hand and knocked the knife from Terri's grasp. As soon as it left her hand, the strange glow disappeared and it was just an old knife again, lying on the floor, bloodied.

The moment the blade left her hand, Terri seemed to come out of the strange trance she had slipped into and stuck her finger in her mouth to try to stop the bleeding.

"I think we'd better put all this stuff away, Terri," said Sophie. "And I think we should tell Mommy."

Terri gave her sister a hard stare. "You pinkie swore!" she said vehemently. "This stuff is ours! But, I agree, let's put it away. That knife is weird. If something bad happens, then we can tell Mommy or Daddy. Okay?"

Reluctantly, Sophie agreed and the girls carefully returned the dolls, knife, and powder to the box. Then they hid it away again, under a pile of T-shirts, in the back of the closet.

HELLS' ANGELS?

Bill and Karen both got up early Monday morning. Karen prepared a hearty breakfast, wanting to give her husband a solid foundation for his first day at work. Bill dressed carefully in pressed jeans, madras shirt, lightweight beige sport coat, and topsiders.

When he entered the kitchen, Karen looked up and remarked, "You look good enough to eat! Now sit down and have breakfast."

"Can't," he replied as he grabbed a cup of coffee and a piece of toast. "Gotta make the next boat. I don't want to be late on my first day."

Karen looked at the meal she had prepared and sighed. "Okay, but at least have some juice. I'll put some coffee in your commuter mug so you can drink it on the boat."

Bill handed her his cup and grabbed a quick glass of juice as he got ready to leave.

After she drove Bill to the wharf and the girls were off to

school, Karen wondered what she might do to fill the hours until they came home. The night before she'd written out a short list of things she needed at the store and, since she had nothing else pressing to do, decided to try out the island market. She dressed in jeans and a sweatshirt, pulled her hair back into a ponytail, grabbed her wallet and a windbreaker, and drove off to the store.

She was studying the products on the shelves when she felt a sharp yank on her ponytail. Startled, she turned to find Dex standing behind her, a mischievous grin on his face.

"Well now, pretty lady, we meet again and so soon. Perhaps 'tis fate?" He had a flirtatious sparkle in his eyes and Karen couldn't help but laugh.

"Oh, I don't know about that," she replied with a smile. "Unless you think picking up laundry detergent constitutes fate."

"Well, stranger things have happened on this rock. Speaking of which, has anyone given you the nickel tour yet?"

Karen shook her head. "Bill and I have driven around a bit, but we really haven't taken the time to do any real exploring."

"Say no more, pretty lady, my chariot is at your command! No better guide could you have than one born and bred here." As he spoke, he took her hand and bowed low like a courtier, a wicked smile on his face.

"I don't know. It's a tempting offer, but..." Her voice trailed off.

"No buts allowed, pretty lady," he said as he grabbed her hand and pulled her toward the door.

Once outside, he pointed to an old, but well-kept, Harley Davidson motorcycle. "My chariot," he announced proudly.

Several men were standing on the store's porch drinking coffee and watching the drama play out between the two of them. It looked to Karen as if they were taking bets as to whether she would get on the bike or blow Dex off. She looked his ride over carefully. It had been years since she'd been on a motorcycle. Back at Stanford, before Bill, she had had a boyfriend who rode a hog. On weekends, they'd motored up and down the California coast, north to Mendocino and south to Santa Cruz or Big Sur. She loved the sense of freedom she'd felt on the bike and, now, was sorely tempted by Dex's offer. She turned and looked at him.

"Helmet?" she asked.

"Why, you can have mine," he replied, a bit surprised, and handed her his helmet.

Karen began to put it on, but her ponytail got in the way. With a flick of her wrist, she pulled off the scrunchie that held it in place and, leaning forward, shook out her hair and placed the helmet on her head. This action brought hoots, hollers, and wolf whistles from the audience on the porch and some of the men were digging in their pockets for money to pay off the winner of the bet.

Dex laughed and mounted the bike. "Hop right on, princess, and don't be shy. Just put your arms around my waist and, if you get scared, just hug me tighter. I won't mind. Oh no, I won't mind!"

Karen laughed and got on behind him resting her hands lightly on his hips. "Okay, show me this rock!" she demanded and with a roar they were off to the laughter and applause of their audience.

For the next two hours, they rode around the island, stopping at numerous points of interest. Dex was a great guide, informing Karen of local history and customs. He showed her the best beaches and the best hiking and biking trails on the island. He seemed to know the history of every house they passed and some of his revelations about the locals left her in stitches. She couldn't remember the last time she had laughed so much or felt so relaxed. Surely, she hadn't felt this good since coming here and, she suspected, it was much longer than that.

This guy really has a way about him, she thought, smiling to herself.

At close to noon, Dex pulled into the boatyard where there was a little store with picnic tables outside.

"Now, princess, might I interest you in a little lunch? This store sells sandwiches and cold beer and I, for one, could go for a brewski right now."

"That sounds great," said Karen as they parked the bike and walked into the store.

The clerk at the counter was a pretty young thing who couldn't have been more than eighteen. They picked out sandwiches and Dex grabbed a couple of cold beers from the cooler and walked over to the cash register. Karen watched as he spoke with the girl while she rang up the sale.

Such a flirt, she thought as she watched him tease the clerk until she was all flushed and giggling.

They took their lunch outside and sat down at one of the tables, talking as they ate. Like most men, Dex liked to talk about himself and Karen was surprised to learn he had a college education.

"I had it all planned out," he explained. "Med school then a residency in Neurology. Hoped to be a big time doctor down in Boston or New York. But fate intervened. My parents were coming to see me at school and a big rig jackknifed in front of them. They were killed instantly."

He went on to describe how he inherited not only his father's boat, but also all his debts. Those debts, coupled with his student loans, defeated whatever dreams he had about becoming a physician.

"But, I'd always had a knack for fishing and, in those days, there was plenty of money to be made. So, I took Dad's boat and became a full-time fisherman. I did all right and in a few years paid off all the debts and loans."

He spoke with pride about his house; how he tore down the one he was raised in and built a new one of his own design. He'd lived there and fished ever since. He was thirty-six now, same age as Bill, but said he'd never been involved in a serious relationship with a woman. Oh, he was good with the ladies, no doubt, and could always be counted on to leave a party with the prettiest girl there, but marriage and settling down were not part of his game plan for now.

As they talked, Karen was surprised to find him to be an intelligent, articulate, and sensitive man. He was an outrageous flirt, to be sure, but underneath she sensed there was much more depth to him.

He questioned her about her motorcycle riding experience, having noted she knew how to handle herself on the bike, and she entertained him with numerous stories of rides she had taken with the "before Bill" boy.

"So we were stopped in this cafe on the way to Mendocino, getting a beer, when a group of Hell's Angels walked in. They came right up to Mike and starting asking him about his ride. They grabbed some beers and, before we knew it, we were tagging along with them all the way up the Mendocino coast until they turned into the interior. So I guess you can say I've ridden with the Hell's Angels!"

They both laughed. Reluctantly, Karen glanced at her watch. It was time to go.

"Dex, I've got to get going. The girls will be home from school soon. I can't tell you how much I've enjoyed this afternoon. Thank you so much for suggesting it."

145

Dex looked at her and smiled. "It's my pleasure, princess, and this was way special for me, too. It's not too often I get to spend the day with a beautiful and intelligent woman. Lot of people think men just want to spend their time with blithering idiots with big breasts and butts, but not me - it's the brain that makes a woman beautiful in my book. So, please, it's me who should be thanking you.

"And," he went on, "if you can put up with my teasing and flirting, I would love to take you out on my boat some day and show you what a real fisherman does for a living. Rest assured, I'll respect you as a married lady, so there would be nothing for you to worry about in that regard. However, be warned, every now and again, I just might try!"

Karen blushed, flattered by his words and manner. "I think I'd like that," she replied in a soft voice.

"I knew you were an intelligent woman!" laughed Dex. "Boat's in the yard right now getting repaired. Should be back in the water in about a week. I'll be in touch."

They cleaned up the debris from their lunch and deposited it in the trashcan by the entrance to the store. Then they hopped back on the bike and headed back to where Karen had left her car. As she opened the car door, he laid her hand across his palm, made a courtly bow, and placed a gentle kiss on the back of it.

"M'lady," he said softly.

She gazed into his eyes and laughed. "You are a piece of work, Dexter Pierce, you know. Thanks again for the day."

With a wave of her hand, she backed out of the parking lot and headed home. Halfway there, she pulled out her cell to check her calls. She'd felt it vibrating while she and Dex ate lunch but was having way too much fun to interrupt the flow of conversation.

I hope it wasn't about the girls, she thought guiltily.

She was relieved to see it was just a message from Bill letting her know what time to pick him up at the wharf.

I'll text him back when I get home.

Putting her cell back in her pocket, she continued on to the house on the hill, a smile on her face, thinking about her afternoon and how she hadn't wanted it to ever end.

FIRST DAY ON THE JOB

Bill's first day at work was spent in orientation, although, after meeting with Phil the week before, he felt he knew the lay of the land at Omicron as well as anyone. However, this day in the office would give him a chance to get to know who the players were within the company. His goal was to get into R&D as soon as he could and, to do that, he knew he might need some inside help.

As planned, he arrived in town early and stopped off at a deli for coffee and a snack. As he sat and sipped his drink, he tried to concentrate on Omicron's product line and all he had learned about their position in the software industry. Looking at his notes, his mind kept slipping back to that night at the dance and the sensation of Maggie's warm body pressed against his.

You gotta stop this, he told himself. *You love your wife. Remember Julie and all the trouble that caused you. You don't want to go there again.*

Standing up, he checked his watch - it was time to go to work.

At the office, Mr. LeFleur greeted him warmly and escorted him to a conference room where other new recruits, from various departments, were gathered. Thus began a morning filled with lectures regarding benefits, company policies, company history, goals, etc.

During the mid-morning break, a young man dressed in faded jeans, a Red Sox sweatshirt, and dirty Nikes approached Bill in the coffee room.

"Hi," he said. "You Andersen?"

Bill smiled and offered his hand. "Yes, I'm Bill Andersen. Who's asking?"

"Gerry Davis, R&D," the man answered. "I hear you're a hotshot developer from Silicon. That so?"

Bill laughed. "Well, I don't know about the 'hotshot' stuff, but, yeah, I used to work in the Valley. Victim of the recession. Times are tough out there."

"Well, their loss, our gain," Gerry replied. "Glad to have you on board. You're in Sales now, but we should be opening up a bit soon and we'll see what can be done. Shoot me off your CV and keep in touch. Hope you're a Sox fan, that always helps! My office is down the hall on the right. When you're inside on Friday, stop by and I'll show you what we're working on now. Can always use some fresh input. And I'll intro you to the rest of my team."

Bill thanked him warmly.

The morning break over, it was back to the conference room for more boring lectures. At lunchtime, he tried to reach Karen on her cell, but got no answer. This surprised him. She usually carried her cell everywhere and always picked up. He left a voicemail letting her know when he would be home and returned to the conference room.

In the afternoon session, the new recruits were divided up by department and spent the rest of the day reviewing the specifics of their positions. Bill and LeFleur went over his territory map and client list, and discussed prospective new accounts. They reviewed, in detail,

Omicron's product line and LeFleur was impressed with Bill's knowledge.

"You've really done your homework," he said, obviously pleased. "Phil told me you two had a sit down last week. I think you're going to do fine here, and I see that Gerry has already tracked you down. I'll probably be losing you soon, but I hope I'll get some gas out of you before then."

LeFleur looked at his watch. "It's almost four, I think we can knock off now for the day, think you've got everything down pat. Good luck tomorrow and I'll see you on Friday. If you need anything in between, don't hesitate to call."

LeFleur shook Bill's hand and escorted him to the lobby.

As he left the building, Bill felt totally jazzed, energized. Things had gone so much better than expected - the brief meeting with the head of R&D and the complimentary discussion with LeFleur.

Finally, things may be turning around for me.

The only thing nagging at him was Karen's absence when he'd called.

I wonder what she's up to. It's probably nothing - she was most likely out in the garden, vacuuming, or something and didn't hear the cell.

He was about to call her again, when his phone buzzed. He checked and there was a text from her acknowledging his call and confirming his pickup time. She made no mention of why she was so late getting back to him. Bill sighed and put it out of his mind. He thought again of the contacts he'd made at Omicron.

Yes, indeed, things are looking up for me and for my family.

Smiling to himself and feeling truly happy for the first time in a long time, he headed for the wharf and the ferry home.

Karen was waiting in the parking lot when Bill arrived home. As they drove, he told her enthusiastically about his day. Glad that things seemed to be going well for him at last, her mind kept straying to her adventure with Dex. *Should I tell him about it? I know I should, but it might upset him and I don't want to spoil his mood.*

"Karen, earth to Karen!" prodded Bill.

Startled out of her thoughts, she turned to him. "Sorry, just thinking about dinner. Did you say something?"

"Yes. I asked you where you were this afternoon when I called. I know you're anal about carrying your cell because of the girls. When I couldn't reach you, I got worried."

Karen's mind raced for a plausible answer. "Sorry, I didn't mean to upset you. I went to the store to pick up some laundry detergent and left my cell on my dresser. I thought it was in my jacket pocket and didn't discover it wasn't till much later. Guess I'm beginning to get a little dotty in my old age."

Bill laughed. "Maybe your mind's just going on 'island time' - you know, 'Don't worry, be happy' and all that!"

Karen laughed with him, glad the interrogation was over.

As she pulled into the drive, the girls ran out to greet their father and Bill enjoyed telling them about his day. He changed all his new co-workers into different animals and soon had them rolling on the floor in hysterics.

Karen only half listened to them as she prepared dinner, her mind still wandering back to her afternoon with Dex. *What will I do if he really meant it about the boat? No, he couldn't of, he was just teasing. But what if he really did mean it? I'd have to turn him down politely, of course.*

However, deep down, she knew turning him down was the last thing she wanted to do. She hoped he would come and take her out on that boat of his and the sooner the better. She had enjoyed his company so much.

How would he get in touch with me anyway? I didn't give him our number and I can't go looking for him. No, all those yahoos at the store would have a field day if I did. No, I can't go back there for anything, not even the detergent I forgot to get. Well, I'll probably never hear from him anyway. I'll probably just run into him at all the 'yahoo' functions. We'll say hello and that will be that.

She sighed regretfully and forced herself to concentrate on the meal she was preparing. Almost done, she called the girls to set the table and asked Bill to open a bottle of wine.

Walking past the washer in the mudroom, Bill noticed dirty laundry piled on top of it. He returned to the dining room and set the open bottle of wine on the table to breathe.

"Thought you said you were picking up detergent this morning at the store. Doesn't look like you got to the laundry, if that pile of clothes on the washer means anything."

Karen couldn't stop herself from blushing. "They didn't have the brand I use," she stammered. "I'll get some next time I go to town."

Bill made note of the blush. *Her explanation is surely plausible; the store's merchandise is limited. But why is she acting so funny about it, blushing like that?* He shook his head. *You're getting paranoid, Bill. Karen has no reason to lie.*

BACK TO NORMAL

The next couple of weeks went by swiftly for the Andersens. With Bill back at work, they settled into a comfortable, familiar routine. Karen drove him to the wharf each day to see him off, then went back home and got her girls ready for school.

Alone, the days were her own. Sometimes, she stayed home and worked in the gardens. There was no recurrence of anything like the incident on the trail and that "experience" began to fade from her mind like a bad dream. Other days, she took the ferry to town, where she shopped, visited museums, and explored the downtown area.

On one such trip, she met a couple that owned a summer home on the island. They were great tennis enthusiasts and had their own court. They were delighted when Karen told them how much she missed the game and invited her to play when they came to stay for the summer later in June.

However, most days she found herself sitting alone staring at the sea, her mind full of questions about her husband, her marriage, and sometimes Dex and how he fit in to that whole scenario.

I love Bill - at least I think I still do. It's better now that he's back to work. Almost like before, but not quite. No, something's not completely right - maybe it'll never be right again. Is it me? Have I changed that much? Or is it him? Or maybe him and that girl? Am I wrong to worry about that? Or is it Dex? What's going on there is a mystery to me but somehow I'm drawn to him. But I can't let that happen. My family comes first - always. Somehow I have to make things right again. But how?

On Saturday, as promised, Bill and Karen had their "date night" in town. They had a wonderful time and Karen remarked to him that it was "almost" like being back in California. However, deep inside, she knew that was a lie. It would never be California again - of that she was certain.

They made love that night and their coupling had that pleasant familiar quality of two people who have been together and loved each other for a long time. However, when it was over and they separated, Bill's thoughts turned to that night on the beach and the feel of a young woman's body pressed tightly against his. And Karen - she remembered how it felt to ride behind Dex on that bike - the wind in her hair, her hands resting lightly on his hips and a smile on her face.

HOOK, LINE, & SINKER

    Alone again, Karen stood staring out the bedroom window, trying to decide what to do to pass the time until her children came home from school. She'd spent the day before in town at a farmers' market so there was no shopping to do, the house was clean, and the laundry was done. It looked like a good day to go to the beach but the spirit didn't move her in that direction. Sighing to herself, she decided to stay home and work in the gardens. They needed weeding and fertilizing and she wanted to check the vegetables for pests.

    As she knelt in the perennial bed pulling out the grasses that had proliferated between the flowers, she heard the roar of a motorcycle coming up the drive. She looked up, startled to see Dex parking his bike behind her car.

Oh Christ, I must look like the wrath of God!

    She was dressed for the gardens. Her hair was pulled up, hidden by a floppy hat, and she had on Japanese gardening pants that were baggy and soiled. Her face was clean, but without makeup.

As he approached, she stood up, pulling off her gardening gloves.

"Hey, princess," he drawled, smiling. "Long time, no see. Where you been keeping yourself?"

She felt her cheeks begin to redden.

Why does he always seem to have that effect on me? She took a minute, trying to pull herself together before she replied.

"No place special, Dex. I've been right here. Sometimes I go to town, but mainly I'm here."

"Thought I might have seen you at the store or the yard. Was wondering if maybe you've been avoiding me?"

Karen's blush began to deepen. "No, I haven't been avoiding you. What would make you think that? I haven't had any need to go to the store. And why would I go to the boatyard? I don't have a boat."

Dex laughed. "Well, I've been hanging out those places most every day hoping to get a glimpse of those beautiful blue eyes of yours."

He looked straight at her, locking his eyes with hers, then slowly looked her up and down, enjoying her obvious embarrassment.

She glanced down at the ground, trying to get control of herself.

If I get any redder, he'll mistake me for a beet.

She pulled off her floppy hat, letting her sun-streaked hair tumble out.

"Well, to what do I owe the pleasure of this visit today?" she asked, trying to change the subject and lighten the atmosphere, which had grown heavy around them.

Dex laughed. "Well, princess, my boat's back in the water and I thought you might want to go for a ride, try your hand at fishing. See if you can land yourself a bluefin. They can make a mighty fine meal."

Karen glanced down at herself then looked up at Dex.

"Sweetheart," he commanded, "just go inside and throw on a pair of jeans, a sweatshirt, and your sneakers. No need for you to fuss with your hair or your makeup - you're beautiful enough just as you are. And don't worry, I'll get you home in time to greet those cute little girls of yours when they get off the bus."

Karen hesitated, knowing she should politely refuse, but she wanted to go - wanted to spend another day in the company of this man.

"Okay, just give me a minute."

She picked up her gardening gear, turned, and walked up the steps to the house. She was back in a few minutes wearing faded jeans, a T-shirt with a hoodie on over, and her Adidas. She had a scrunchie in her hand and pulled her hair back into a low ponytail as she walked over to the bike.

"I damn well better catch a fish," she laughed as she took his helmet and put it on her head.

When they arrived at the boatyard, Dex stopped in the store and picked up some sandwiches and beer. They boarded his punt and motored out to his mooring. His boat was an old 45' wooden converted lobster boat, everything on it meticulously maintained. The decks were teak and gleamed in the morning sunlight.

He helped Karen aboard, tied the punt to the mooring, and prepared to motor out to sea. Once they were clear of the boatyard, he motioned her to join him in the wheelhouse. He took a tube of zinc oxide out of one of the drawers and squeezed a dab onto his fingers.

"Now, princess, I know you already have a bit of a tan, but the sun reflecting off the water can be pretty fierce and I don't want to send you home with a bad burn." He reached for her face with his fingers. "Don't move. I don't want to get any of this goop into your eyes." Gently, he smeared her cheeks and nose with the sunscreen, taking his time, enjoying himself.

When she felt his touch, she couldn't help but shiver.

"You cold?" he asked, a wicked smile on his face. "If you need, there are sweaters down below. Just feel free. Also, some slickers should the sea kick up a bit."

Moving away from his touch, she shook her head. "No, I'm fine and thanks for the sunscreen."

She leaned on the rail, turning her back to him, and looked out to sea, trying to widen the distance between them. Dex smiled watching her, then turned his attention back to the boat and taking them away from Mateguas.

They motored silently for about a half hour. Dex finally slowed the boat down and went about getting the fishing gear ready. He explained to her he mainly went after tuna, in particular the lucrative bluefin. He took the poles and expertly baited the hooks then set them in the rod holders at the stern of the boat. He instructed Karen how to stand and what to expect, then he went back to the helm to move the boat around, looking for fish. After a while, he went below to get some cold drinks.

Waiting for her drink, Karen was beginning to wonder what all the hoopla was about when it came to fishing. So far, it had been a big nothing. Getting bored, she stood holding the rod, the line resting lightly between her thumb and forefinger the way Dex had shown her. Suddenly, she felt a series of small bumps on the line. She stood still as it began to play out. She tried to reel it back in, but her catch was too heavy.

"Dex," she cried. "I need help. I've got a bite!"

He quickly came up behind her, placed the drinks down on the deck, and put his arms around her, laying his hands on the pole over hers.

"You go, girl!" he said, laughing. "Let's tire him out a little bit before we try to reel him in."

They let the line play out and, as the fish struggled to get free, Karen began to feel a distinct sense of exhilaration.

"Now!" cried Dex. "We reel him in now!"

Karen pulled on the rod, leaning back into Dex. As she did, she became aware of his body behind hers and the physical reaction he was having to her touch. She could feel his arousal and, without thinking, leaned back harder into him.

Dex pulled on the line and, in an even motion, yanked the fish onto the deck. As it lay there flopping, Karen turned toward him.

Dropping the pole, he stared at her, his need etched across his face. He crossed the short distance between them and took her in his arms. She weakly protested but he ignored her and pressed his lips to hers in a passionate kiss. Halfheartedly, she tried to pull away, but he was too strong and she found herself being swept up by the emotion she was feeling. She put her arms around his neck and kissed him back, her passion matching his.

They stood locked together, desire growing as the kiss went on. Dex slid his lips down to nuzzle her neck, murmuring her name as his hands began to caress her body. The sound of her name brought Karen back to reality and she pulled away from him. Struggling to regain control of herself, she backed up until she was leaning on the rail of the boat. Breathing heavily, panic and desire in her eyes, she faced him.

"No, no, I can't, I can't," she cried as much to herself as to him. "I'm married, I have children. I can't. I just can't."

Dex saw tears threatening to spill over onto her cheeks and he struggled to get his emotions under control, angry with himself for breaking his vow to respect her marital status. But she had looked so beautiful standing there, hair all a mess with a smudge of zinc oxide still on her nose, smiling so brightly. He wanted her so badly it hurt.

"Karen, I'm so sorry. Please believe I would never do anything to cause you pain or distress. Can you find a way to forgive me? It won't happen again, I promise. Please. I don't want to lose...to lose our friendship."

She pulled herself together and looked up at him. One tear coursed down her cheek and she absentmindedly wiped it away. "It's okay, Dex," she said carefully. "It was as much my fault as yours. I wanted it, too. But, you understand, I can't. I just can't."

He nodded and spoke, his voice tinged with regret. "I understand. It won't happen again. You have my word."

She gave him a shy smile.

They stood for a moment staring at each other silently, each trying to figure out a way to keep their blossoming friendship from falling apart.

Karen broke the silence. "Well, what do we do now with this fish? What kind is it anyway? Is it a tuna?"

Breathing a sigh of relief, Dex turned his attention to the fish that was still flopping around on the deck. He unhooked it and put it into the cooler compartment on the boat.

"No, it's a bluefish. About ten pounds, I'd say and it's all yours. I'll fillet it after I get you home and bring it over tomorrow, if that's all right with you? I have some good recipes my mom left me. I'll photocopy them and bring them over with the fish."

"That'd be great," she said, feeling relief that they had somehow been able to put their desire behind them.

It was close to one o'clock so Dex put the fishing gear away then motioned Karen to follow him down into the cabin. Once below, he got out sandwiches and beer and set the table for lunch. As they ate, Karen told him of her upbringing in California, her parents' divorce, and the effect it had on her.

She didn't understand it, but for some reason, she felt she was able to tell him anything. She began talk about her marriage and the problems she and Bill were having and about the events that occurred just before they made the decision to move to Mateguas.

"It was hard, Dex. Everything was falling apart. We were going to lose our house, our cars, everything." She hesitated for a moment then went on. "The only job Bill could find was part time at an electronics store and that was just on commission. No salary, no benefits, and the checks were few and far between."

She paused again, clasping and unclasping her hands and staring down at the table. Dex sat silently watching her, knowing she was building to something.

"We were fighting all the time; we weren't communicating at all. We owed everyone so much money. I was going to have to apply for Medicaid for the kids, which upset me. I didn't know how we were going to survive and then..." Again, she stopped and took a breath to steady herself.

"I...I found out I was pregnant."

She sat quietly for a moment. Dex reached out and took her hands, holding them gently.

"I didn't know what to do. I couldn't bring a child into all that. We had no insurance and were about to lose our home."

She hesitated again, and then spoke, her voice barely audible. "So, I made a decision. I ended it."

The words now began to tumble out of her mouth, her body racked with silent sobs. "And when I got home; oh God, Dex, when I got home, Bill was there and he said we were saved - that his aunt had died - that we were moving here. Oh God, if he'd just told me sooner."

Her words hung in the air between them like a dark omen. She couldn't believe she'd just told this man, who she really hardly knew, the secret she'd kept bottled up for so long and could barely even admit to herself. She stared down at her hands, enfolded in his, waiting.

"Karen, look at me."

Slowly, trembling, she raised her head and looked into his eyes.

"If you'd known, you would have done things differently. But you didn't know. Hindsight's great, but you can't live your life wishing you could go back and change things. You did what you felt you had to do. That's all. End of story. You did nothing wrong."

He let go of her hands and gently reached out and brushed away a tear that was slowly sliding down her cheek.

She saw compassion in his eyes and heard the calm acceptance and understanding in his voice. "Thank you," she said softly. "Thank you."

Dex smiled at her, surprised at the depth of emotion he was beginning to feel for this woman. He had the overwhelming desire to protect her and keep her safe. What had started as a mere flirtation was beginning to become much more and he found himself starting to envision a life with her by his side.

"Now," he said, "how about some dessert to top off that lunch?"

Not waiting for an answer, he got up and walked into the galley. When he returned, he placed a tin box in front of her.

"Pete's wife, Louise, makes just about the best fudge in New England. She sells it at the Ladies' Aid and I always keep a supply on board. Help yourself."

Karen took a bite of the rich, chocolaty confection. "It's delicious. I'll have to ask her for the recipe."

Dex laughed. "I think it's a family secret, but you might be able to cajole her out of it." Reluctantly, he glanced at his watch. "I think we'd better head on home soon if I'm going to get you there to meet the school bus."

Karen nodded and stood up. As Dex turned to go topside, she laid her hand on his arm, stopping him. "Thank you again for listening and for being so kind."

Dex took her hand in his. "Princess, I have no right to judge you. As I said, you did what you had to do. And, it's over now. Don't keep beating yourself up about it. And, be assured that nothing you said will ever go any further. It stays right here - between you and me - on this boat."

She leaned forward and kissed him gently on the cheek then let him go topside to motor them back to Mateguas.

When they arrived at Karen's home, she handed him back his helmet and smiled. "Thanks for the day and for the fishing lesson."

"I'll be by in the morning with the fish YOU landed," he laughed. "And the recipes; I won't forget those."

Then, as he'd done at the end of their previous outing, he bowed low, took her hand, and gently kissed the back of it. "Princess, thank you for taking pity on this mere mortal by spending the day with him. It was one I will not soon forget."

His words were not lost on her and softening in her eyes, she smiled. "Nor will I, sir knight, nor will I."

SECRETS KEPT

The school bus arrived not long after Dex left. Karen spent some time talking to her daughters about their day over cookies and milk until it was time for her to pick up Bill.

"How was your day, hon?" he asked her on the way home.

"Oh, I just worked in the garden. Nothing really interesting."

Once home, Bill went upstairs to change while Karen started dinner.

Another little lie. I'm actually getting quite good at this. I don't know why I don't just tell Bill the truth about Dex. Nothing really happened between us, she thought, reliving the kiss in her mind. *I stopped it, didn't I? We're just friends, aren't we?*

But she didn't want to share his friendship with Bill. *No, I want him all to myself. This is something I can't share. And, I'll have to lie again tomorrow to explain the fish.* She shook her head. *Oh, what a tangled web we weave and all that.*

Dinner ready, Karen called the girls and Bill to the dining room. Bill talked animatedly about his day and the girls talked happily about their schoolwork.

"And, Mommy, tomorrow we get out of class at noon!" exclaimed Sophie. "They call it an early release day."

Relishing the chance to spend an afternoon alone with her children, Karen smiled. "Bill, why don't you take the car to the wharf tomorrow. That way you won't have to depend on me picking you up. The girls and I won't need it. We can go to the beach or work in the gardens here."

"Are you sure?"

"Yes, and you might get home early, too, and that will make it easier for you."

"Okay, great."

After dinner, the girls were hustled off to do their homework and Karen busied herself cleaning up the kitchen while Bill, as usual, worked on his laptop. After all was put in order, Karen, tired from her eventful day, excused herself and went up to bed.

When Bill came up, he kissed her goodnight and lay down beside her.

Karen's eyes were closed, but she wasn't sleeping. Her mind was on Dex and how it felt to have his strong arms around her, his lips on hers.

And Bill was also thinking of someone else and of a stolen kiss on the beach. His thoughts arousing him, he reached for his wife and though they made love, they were anything but together.

LITTLE GLOOSKAP

The next morning after breakfast, Bill kissed his wife goodbye and drove down to the wharf. When he arrived at Omicron, he quickly finished his sales paperwork and made his way down to Gerry's office.

He and Gerry had hit it off right away, the younger man recognizing Bill's potential value to him and the company. For the past couple of weeks, they'd gotten into the habit of hanging out Friday afternoons to brainstorm, tell stories, and dream up new ideas. Today, however, Bill was disappointed. Gerry was not in his office. Bill asked one of the members of the R&D team where he was and was informed Gerry had gotten a last-minute invite to speak at a conference in Boston and was there for the weekend. Bill, his sales work done, left the building and began to stroll down to the wharf to catch the next ferry home.

Arriving early, he found he had about a half an hour to kill until the next boat so he stood outside the terminal watching the activity down below on the docks. A small punt came in, expertly maneuvered by a young woman. She was wearing a thin cotton dress, her hair tucked into a baseball cap. As she steered the boat into the dock, the wind pressed the dress around her thighs and tight against her bosom. Bill noticed several of the men working on the wharf stop what they were doing to stare at her, the effect of the wind and the dress rendering her virtually naked before their eyes. As she leaned over to tie up the boat, her cap fell off and masses of red curls fell out. She shook out her hair, glanced up, and saw Bill watching her.

"Hey, California," she yelled at him. "Can ya give a girl a hand?"

Laughing, Bill ran down the stairs to help. Whether she really needed his assistance or not was a question he knew was up for grabs, but he came to her aid anyway.

Once the punt was secured, he offered his hand to help her up onto the dock. She was barefoot and, before she stepped from the boat, she slung a backpack on one shoulder. Once on solid ground, she pulled a pair of flip-flops from her bag and put them on. She gave him a gorgeous grin.

"So, what ya doing here, California? Waiting for the ferry?"

Bill nodded. "Shouldn't you be at home teaching my kids?"

"Teacher's afternoon off. I needed to pick up some supplies, so I sent the kids home early. Hope your wife's there to greet them and not gallivanting around again with Dex!"

Bill cocked his head and looked at her questioningly. "What do you mean? Dex and Karen?"

"Oh gosh, me and my big mouth," she said with a twinkle in her eye. "My bad! Thought she would have told you about it."

"Well?"

"Why don't you come with me while I pick up my stuff, then take me for a drink and maybe, just maybe, I'll tell you."

"You're on," he replied and they walked together away from the wharf.

They strolled, chatting, till they came to a store where Maggie purchased the supplies she needed. She tucked them away in her backpack and turned to Bill. "Okay, California," she said taking his hand in hers. "Let's go get us a drink and I'll fill you in on the gossip about your wife."

She led him up the cobblestone side streets until they came to a small tavern. The wooden sign hanging outside said "The Sternman."

"This is my favorite place in town," she said, leading him inside.

The interior was dark, with a long, polished mahogany bar and several tables and booths in the back. An old jukebox sat in the corner.

The bartender greeted her warmly and it was obvious to Bill she frequented this establishment regularly. There were just a few customers in the bar, all men, and they eyeballed Maggie appreciatively.

"George, give us a couple of tequila shooters with Coors back," she said, leading Bill to a booth in the back.

Sitting down across from her, Bill leaned forward. "Okay, what's the deal with my wife and Dex?"

"Shhhh," she said putting her finger to her lips. "Drinks first, revelations later."

They sat silently, watching each other until the bartender brought their drinks.

"Salut!" she said as she knocked back the shooter.

Not to be outdone by this girl, Bill picked up his drink and tossed it back. They sipped their beers as Maggie indicated to the bartender for another round.

"Okay," she finally said, "you've earned your gossip. Rumor has it that a couple of weeks ago, on a Monday I think, your wife met up with Dex at the general store. Whether it was planned or not, I don't know. Anyway, he proceeded to sweep her off her feet, making her forget all about her groceries, and took off with her on his motorcycle."

The bartender brought them another round of shooters. Digesting what she had said, Bill tossed his back. *Was that my first day at work? Was that why she didn't answer her cell?*

"Go on," he said to Maggie. "There must be more."

Maggie tossed her shooter back, smiled at him, and continued. "Well, the guys at the store who watched the whole thing were taking bets as to whether your wife would go with him or not. But she didn't hesitate. She just hopped on that bike, put her arms around his waist, and off they went!"

"So, big deal. She went for a bike ride. That's nothing to get upset about."

Maggie thought carefully before she spoke. "Bill, Dex has a rep with women. He doesn't have female 'friends,' except for me. He took your wife for a ride and it wasn't just a fifteen-minute 'once around the island' - no, it was all day. They were seen having lunch down at the boatyard, too, laughing and apparently having a good time. I'm sorry, but that's how it was."

Bill sat quietly, sipping his beer, thinking about Karen and wondering what she was up to.

After a minute or two, Maggie reached out and took his hand. "You okay, Bill? I didn't mean to bring you down. You're right - it was probably nothing. Just island gossip."

Feeling the warmth of her hand, he looked up and the memory of the kiss they'd shared the night of the dance washed over him. That memory alone was enough to arouse him and he gazed at her hungrily. She sensed the change in his demeanor and pressed his hand lightly.

"Have you had lunch?" she asked. "George, the bartender, makes some of the best burgers in town."

"No, but it sounds like a good idea," Bill agreed as he motioned to the bartender.

They placed their order for lunch and another beer each. As they waited for their food, Maggie entertained him with stories about growing up as an islander, carefully omitting the episode with the professor.

By the time their food arrived, they were both famished and they quickly polished off their meal. Sipping his beer, Bill glanced down at his watch. "I guess if I leave now, I can make the next ferry home."

"Oh, don't worry about that. I'll take you back in my punt."

"That'd be great," he said, glad of the chance to spend more time with her. He paid the check and they left the bar together and walked back to the wharf. He took her arm and helped her into the punt, relishing the opportunity to feel the warmth of her soft skin.

Once on the open sea, Maggie turned to him. "Do you need to get back right away? There's a place I'd like to show you."

Bill hesitated for a moment before replying, thinking about Karen going off for a motorcycle ride with Dex. *What's good for the goose and all that*, he told himself. *If she can go gallivanting about, then so can I.*

"I got time," he said to Maggie. "And you're the captain of this vessel. I'm just the lowly deckhand. You plot the course!"

"Okay," she laughed, steering the punt away from Mateguas. "Okay!"

Soon, they arrived at a small island. "You're going to be blown away by this," she said enthusiastically. "This has to be the most God-fucking beautiful place in the world."

She brought the boat to a halt a few yards from shore. "You'll have to take your shoes and socks off. There's no way to avoid wading to get ashore."

"What is this place?" he asked as he obediently removed his footwear and rolled his jeans up to his knees.

"It's called Little Glooskap Island," she replied as she anchored the punt. "It's really just a rock, not big enough to actually be called an island."

Barefoot, Bill got out of the punt and gave Maggie his hand as she joined him. The water reached mid-calf and was cold as they waded quickly to shore. Laughing, Maggie led him up a short sandy trail. At the top was a small meadow surrounded by jagged rocks that were the foundation of the island. The meadow was dotted with purple, blue, and yellow wildflowers interspersed haphazardly amongst tall grasses. As they walked, the sand felt warm and soft against the bottoms of their feet and the grasses brushed seductively against their calves.

Bill hopped up onto one of the rocks and gazed off into the distance. He reached down, taking her by the hand, and helped her up to stand beside him. From their vantage point, they could see Mateguas and several of the other islands glistening in the afternoon sun.

"This view is spectacular, Mags. Thank you for bringing me here."

Smiling, she turned to face him. A gentle breeze mussed her hair and several of the shiny red curls fell across her face. Bill reached up to brush them away from her eyes and found his hand on her cheek. He started to say something but she put a finger to his lips to quiet him. Aroused by her touch, he put his arm around her waist, leaned down, and kissed her softly. She opened her mouth slightly and, teasingly, licked his lips with the tip of her tongue. His passion intensifying, he kissed her deeply, pulling her close. Sinuously, she began to move her hips against him, enflaming his desire even further. Unable to stand it, he slid his palms down to her buttocks, cupping them, and lifted her in the air. Moaning, she wrapped her legs around his waist, and pressed her sex tightly against his.

Feeling the force of his arousal, she cried out. "Yes, Bill, oh yes!"

His hands found their way under her skirt as he laid her on the ground. Ripping away her panties, his fingers probed her wetness.

"Now, Bill, now!" she cried as she arched her back to meet him.

In an instant, he was inside her and could feel the pulsing of her orgasm. Astounded by the depth of his hunger and need for her, his arousal heightened and soon, unable to hold back any longer, he cried out her name as he spilled his seed into her. Spent, they both lay panting on the bed of grass.

Soon, Bill raised himself up on his elbows and looked at her. Her eyes were closed and there were small beads of sweat on her upper lip. He leaned down and licked them off.

God, he thought, *how I want to know and taste every part of her.*

Her eyes opened and she pulled his head down to her chest. "Make love to me, Bill," she moaned.

Unbuttoning the front of her dress and finding her braless, he laid his cheek against her bare breasts. Slowly, he began to suckle at her nipples, pulling on them gently as they hardened.

They made love again, but this time without the frantic hunger of their first encounter. Bill relaxed, relishing the experience of her, determined to bring her to new heights of passion. They moved slowly, teasing and tasting one another, until they both could stand it no longer. As they came together, Bill cried out her name and pulled her body tightly against his. Exhausted, they lay entwined in each other's arms, giving way to sleep.

Bill woke as the sun was creeping down toward the horizon. He stood up, the reality of his situation washing over him. He was alone on an abandoned island with a young girl he hardly knew and they had had sex, not once, but twice!

Maggie began to wake up and looked up at him, her eyes still soft and unfocused in the afterglow of lovemaking. He felt himself begin to stir again.

My God, he thought. *What is happening to me?*

Shaking his head, he looked down at her. "Mags, wake up. We have to get going. I'm late as it is and I haven't let Karen know I'm going to be late. I'd better call her now."

As he pulled out his cell and began to dial, Maggie reached out and stopped him with her hand. "No, don't call - text her. That way your voice won't give you away."

"You're right. Yes, you're right. I'll text her."

Quickly, he formulated a message for his wife.

*Karen, sorry I'm late. Went out for a drink with
Gerry and time got away. Should be home soon.
Love u, Bill.*

169

Maggie watched as he sent the text. She stood, buttoned her dress, and put her ruined panties in her pocket. "Tide's gone out a bit and the punt is probably grounded. We'll push it out and take off. We'll be home in no time, you'll see."

She walked over to him and tried to straighten out his shirt. He put his arms around her, relishing the feel of her body close to his. Then he pulled away, took her hand, and together they returned to her punt. They got the small boat into deeper water and Maggie quickly motored them back to Mateguas.

As she docked, she motioned to him to get out. "You go now, Bill. I know you need to get home. I'll take care of the boat."

He watched her as she tied up to the wharf, unable to move.

God, she's beautiful, he thought.

She looked up and their eyes met for an instant. He started to say something, but she silenced him with a gesture.

"Go, Bill. We'll talk later."

He nodded, turned, and jogged to the parking lot.

As he got in the car, he surveyed his appearance. He knew his hair was mussed, dampened by the sea spray, and his shirt was wrinkled and probably grass-stained.

What will Karen say when she sees me? I could explain the hair. But how will I explain grass stains?

As he started his car, he realized he didn't have his glasses. He checked his pockets but they were nowhere to be found.

Did I leave them on the island or in the boat?

Technically, he realized, it wasn't really a problem - it was just a short drive home and he knew he could make it all right without them. He had another pair at the house he could use until he found a way to contact Maggie. However, the frames on the old pair were different and Karen would notice.

I'll have to tell her I left them in the office on the mainland. That's plausible, but how will I explain the way I look?

He sat for a moment, thinking, but no solution presented itself. With no other option available, he drove home carefully and pulled up the drive. The house seemed quiet. When he entered, he was surprised to find it empty. On the refrigerator was a note from Karen:

> *Bill - The girls have a tide pool assignment and we've gone down to the beach so they can finish it. Love u, K*

He took a deep breath, feeling relieved. *Maybe, just maybe, I can pull this off.*

Rushing upstairs, he stripped off his clothes, and jumped into the shower. As he washed, he thought about his liaison with Maggie, wondering why it had happened.

I've never really stepped out on Karen before. At least, not totally. Yes, I've flirted with Julie and others, but it never got really outta hand like today. So, why? Why did I step over the line this time? Granted, Maggie is decidedly beautiful and sexy, but I've known beautiful, sexy women before and, while I may have been tempted, I never really strayed. I love my wife.

His thoughts turned to Karen and her coolness to him during the past two years.

She made me feel like I wasn't a man anymore. Only now that I'm working again is she starting to warm up to me and maybe that has nothing to do with me. Maybe it's all because of her new friend, Dex. Could she be having an affair, too?

He shook his head. *No, I don't believe that. She wouldn't. But Mags - she makes me feel like a man. She doesn't try to emasculate me like Karen does.*

He stepped out of the shower and took a good look at his clothing. His shirt was indeed grass-stained. *Those stains will never come out. I'll have to trash it.*

His jeans were also stained, but they were marked with bodily fluids, both his and Maggie's. He started to put them in the hamper, noting it was full. *I'll do the wash. Tell Karen I wanted to help; yes, that might work.*

Changing into his sweats, he took his old pair of glasses out of the dresser drawer. He gathered up the dirty laundry, including his jeans and underwear, and took it all down to the washer and started a load. The stained shirt he took out to the trash barrel and made sure it was fully hidden by other refuse. Pleased with his handiwork, he took another deep breath.

Next time, I'll have to be better prepared. Then his mind shuddered. *Next time? God, after this narrow escape, am I really thinking of seeing her again? God help me, I am.*

It was like she was a drug and after one hit, he just had to have more.

I have to see her again, at least one more time - to look into those eyes, so soft, so seductive - to feel her heat, just one more time.

With some effort, he shook the image of Maggie lying in the grass out of his mind and examined his reflection in the sliding glass door. *Normal. I look perfectly normal. I can pull this off. Karen's sharp, but will she suspect me of cheating? I don't think so. If I can keep my cool and I'll be all right.*

He left the house and walked down to the beach finding Karen and the twins out on the rocks examining the contents of one of the tide pools.

"Is this a private party, or can anyone join?" he asked as he approached, surprised at how normal he sounded.

Karen looked up and smiled.

Sophie and Terri yelled in unison, "Daddy, Daddy, come see what we found!"

Sophie ran toward her father and gave him a big hug and Terri was not far behind. Bill embraced his daughters, holding them tightly.

"Sorry I'm late, hon," he said as he extricated himself from the girls' embrace. "Did you get my text?"

Karen nodded. "Yes, I got it. I was beginning to get worried. Next time you take off with Gerry, let me know when you go, not when you're on your way back! I know you tech types can get wrapped up in your work and forget about time."

She stood up. "And speaking about time, I think our tide pool explorations have to come to an end for the day. We don't have much light left." She looked closely at him, a frown appearing on her face. "You've got your old glasses on. Where are the new ones?"

"I must have left them in the office. Gerry and I got so involved in shoptalk we lost track of time. We went out for a beer and when I realized how late it was, I decided just to come home and not go back to get them. And, oh, I have a surprise for you. After my shower, I took my clothes down to the laundry and started a load of wash!"

Karen's eyes widened. "YOU - you started a load of wash? You? Has my husband been replaced by some sort of alien pod person? I am completely at a loss for words!"

Bill managed a chuckle. "I'm trying, I'm trying. Give a guy a break, won't ya?"

Karen laughed and reached for his hand. Sophie took her other hand as Terri took her father's and, as a family, they headed up the beach to the road. As they walked, Bill glanced down at his wife.

I do love her, he thought. *But I've crossed a line now and I know I'll do it again - at least once more.*

When they got home, Karen sent the girls up to get washed while she started dinner. They were having hamburgers despite the fact that the freezer was full of freshly filleted fish. Dex had stopped by, as promised, but he didn't stay long, to Karen's keen disappointment. He had a full day's fishing ahead of him and he needed to get out to sea while the tide was right.

"Dinner's ready, everyone," she called.

As they sat down, she turned to Bill. "Is Gerry married, hon?"

"Yeah, and I think they have a son, about three years old," he replied.

"Why don't you invite them over here some weekend. They might enjoy a day on an island. We could barbecue early so they could make it home in time for the little one's bedtime."

"Good idea," Bill replied. "I'll feel him out on it next week. Oh, and about next week, I may have to stay over Thursday night. I'll know for sure on Monday."

Karen nodded. This was part of his job, she understood, but the faster they got him into R&D, the better. She knew the value of networking and the importance of social contacts to one's career and inviting the head of R&D and his family over was part of it.

After dinner, the girls in bed, Karen sat down in the overstuffed chair to read while Bill worked on his laptop. It wasn't long before Bill, claiming major fatigue, went up to bed. Karen, however, stayed up, listening to the melodic sound of the surf hitting the shoreline and thinking about the fresh fish in the freezer.

MAGGIE & DEX

Karen wasn't the only one listening to the sound of the surf. Maggie sat on the beach where she and Bill had enjoyed their first kiss, alone with her thoughts, playing the day over and over again in her mind. She knew she would see him again soon. She'd found his glasses in the boat and he would want those back.

But I wish he would just call me 'cause he wants to see me. Because he wants to talk to me - not just to get a pair of glasses back.

She sighed.

"Now that's a sad sound," came a voice from behind her, startling her out of her reverie. She turned. Dex was coming down the path toward her, a load of firewood in his arms. He dumped the wood on the beach and began to build a fire.

"Saw your car in the lot. Thought you could use some company and some warmth, kitten. There's a bit of a chill in the air tonight."

When the fire was going, he turned and sat down next to her. "Okay, girl. Spill. Have you taken a bite of that forbidden fruit yet?"

Feeling color seep into her face, Maggie bowed her head down, hoping Dex would not see. But she was too late. In the glow of the fire, he saw her cheeks turning red with embarrassment.

"Oh ho!" he laughed. "So you have! Was he as good as you thought he would be? Give me the particulars, where and when? Come on, girl, you know your secret's safe with me."

Maggie laughed. "You found me out. It was today, on Little Glooskap, and it was better, way better, than I imagined it would be. Way better!"

"Little Glooskap?" he chuckled. "Boy, you sure do know how to turn a man's head around. On Little Glooskap, how could he resist?"

"Oh, Dex," she protested. "You make it sound like I planned it. It just happened. I bumped into Bill in town, he took me to lunch, and I just wanted to show him how beautiful it was there. And, it just happened."

"Girl, you're talking to Dex now. You know you don't take a person of the opposite sex to Little Glooskap unless you got hanky-panky in mind. That grass there is so soft and I swear it's from all that fertilizer it gets, and I don't mean the kind that comes from the garden supply store!"

Maggie laughed. "Well, what about you and the wife? I heard the talk - you taking her for a ride on your bike, buying her lunch. What happened in between? You give her another sort of ride?"

Dex stiffened at the mention of Karen. That subject was out of bounds. He would not have her name sullied. "Now, Maggie," he said, choosing his words carefully. "I just gave her the nickel tour of the island. Nothing happened, nor will it. She's a lovely lady, but she is a lady, a very married lady, and I don't mess with that, unlike some other folks I know."

Maggie bristled at his words. "Are you going to go all judgmental on me, Dex?" she asked, anger seeping into her voice. "I bet you'd tap that blonde any day of the week if you got the chance. Don't go getting all holier than thou on me. With Bill and me, well, it's not just sex. It's more, I know it."

Dex shook his head. "He's married, Maggie, M-A-R-R-I-E-D. He has two little girls. You think he's going to leave all that for you? You've been down that road before and where did it get you? You got left holding your hat in your hand, alone and broken. Don't let that happen again. Just don't let it. Enjoy him a couple of times, get your itch scratched, then YOU leave him."

Now it was time for Maggie to shake her head. "No, Dex," she protested. "It's not like that. It's not. We're meant for each other, I know it. We fit, believe me, we fit."

Dex shook his head again as they sat quietly staring into the fire, each deep in thought. He knew nothing he could say would dissuade her from the path she had chosen. He put his arm around her and stayed silent, knowing he would be there to help her pick up the pieces when her world fell apart.

Maggie, equally as silent, thought about a future she was so sure was hers for the taking. She wanted the brass ring this time around and all she had to do was reach out and grab it.

DOWN THE RABBIT HOLE AGAIN

On Sunday morning, the Andersens all slept in. Since it looked like it was going to be a good day, warm and sunny, Bill suggested they go beach exploring. Karen begged off, stating she needed to work in the gardens.

"Well, munchkins," he said to his children. "Guess you're stuck with your old dad. What'd ya say we go down to the beach and look for sea glass for Mom?"

Terri and Sophie jumped up and down, happy to spend some time alone with their father. They ran upstairs to wash and dress as Karen cleaned up after their meal.

"Sure I can't interest you in the beach?" Bill asked her one more time.

"No, hon, you go ahead. I'm about beached out from yesterday. And it will do you and the girls good to have some quality time without me."

The girls came stampeding down the stairs, ready to go. Bill kissed his wife on the cheek then took his daughters' hands and headed out, down to the shore.

Finished in the kitchen, Karen donned her gardening gear and went down the back steps to the raised bed gardens. She knelt down, put on her gloves, and began weeding. She worked steadily for about a half hour when she was startled by a sharp squeal coming from behind her. She turned just in time to see a large owl swoop down from the branches above and pick up a small animal in its talons. She shivered as the owl passed over her and she was suddenly afraid. The bird had been so close, she could feel the air move as it flapped its wings. She remembered the owl in the woods that stole her hat and wondered if this were the same one.

Aren't owls supposed to be nocturnal? she asked herself and made a mental note to look it up on the Internet when she finished her weeding.

Suppressing the anxiety she was beginning to feel, she turned back to the garden and continued working. Suddenly, she had the distinct sensation that something or someone was watching her. Slowly, she turned around.

What the hell? Am I going nuts?

A large rabbit was sitting on the lawn in front of that horrible bush, staring at her. Unable to tear her eyes away from the creature's gaze, she sensed an intelligence in it that was somehow beyond comprehension.

For what seemed like an eternity, the rabbit remained motionless, its eyes locked with hers. Then, very slowly and deliberately, it stood up on its hind legs, opened its mouth, and smiled. Karen started in amazement - the sight was so bizarre - a rabbit smiling at her.

She rubbed her eyes, afraid she was hallucinating again. When she opened them, her body went rigid with shock. She was no longer in the garden. She was back on that damned trail. Somehow, inexplicably, she had been transported into the forest.

How did I get here? Why can't I turn around and leave? Why can't I stop myself? Oh God, won't you please help me!

Against her will, something or someone was compelling her to move ever deeper into the woods. Crows began their horrific shrieking above her and trees seemed to reach out, their branches like gnarly claws, scratching and grasping at her arms. And, despite her efforts, she kept moving forward knowing she was getting closer and closer to that malignant swamp and to the danger it held.

Her mind screamed for her feet to stop but they would not obey. A sense of dread washed over her. The trail was now full of shadows that seemed to move unnaturally and the forest seemed to be closing in on her, all light being extinguished. In the developing darkness, she struggled to keep her footing.

As she continued to be propelled forward, her nostrils were assailed by a vile and unnatural stench that was getting stronger and stronger. The odor was so rank she had to gird herself to keep from vomiting. She heard the savage hoot of an owl coming from the canopy above and her terror escalated. Finally, fearing for her life, she focused all her strength and threw off the panic that was threatening to devour her. Digging deep into her soul, she gathered her courage and shouted at the shadows ahead and at the owl above. "I WILL NOT. I WILL NOT GO ON. YOU CANNOT HAVE ME!"

Her voice drowned out the sound of the crows above her. Then, suddenly, it was silent. To her surprise, she stopped moving forward. Her body was hers again. Whatever had possessed her was now gone. She stood tall and turned to retrace her steps, to go home to the safety of her own backyard.

"I am not afraid," she said in a loud, strong voice. "And I will NOT run!"

Slowly and purposefully, she began walking back toward the strange bush that marked the beginning of the trail. As she approached, her eyes widened in surprise. The bush's thorny branches were opening up ahead of her, leaving a pathway so she could pass unharmed.

Bewildered, she stepped out of the woods into the yard. The rabbit was still there, nibbling on the grass, and looking completely normal. She stared at it, waiting. Nothing happened. It was just a rabbit.

"Well, I'm certainly not going to let the Easter bunny scare me!" she said loudly, trying to keep her voice from shaking.

The rabbit looked up, startled, then scampered off into the woods.

Suddenly overcome with fatigue, Karen slowly picked up her gardening basket and headed back toward the house. "I'm really losing it," she said to herself as she tried to wrap her mind around what had just happened.

Once inside, she walked to the living room and plopped down in the overstuffed chair. Her eyelids were heavy and her legs felt like lead.

Why am I so tired? she asked herself. No answer in sight, she tucked her weary legs under her body, leaned back, and closed her eyes.

While Karen was enduring another experience in the woods, Bill and the girls were building a sandcastle. On the pretext of looking for some shells for decoration, Bill wandered down the beach. When he was out of earshot, he pulled out his cell and quickly dialed Maggie's number. Expecting his call, she answered on the first ring.

"Mags, it's me. Did you by any chance find...."

"I got 'em," she replied. "They must have fallen out of your pocket in the boat. Where are you now?"

"I'm at the beach across from the house with the girls. Karen's at home."

"Mmmm," she said, thinking. "I think Freckles could use a run. We'll be there and gone before you know it."

"Thanks, Mags, thanks," he said with relief. "And, um, I have to go to Camden on Thursday to meet with a client and, um, I'll probably have to spend the night on the mainland and I was wondering if, I mean, if...."

"I know just the place," she quickly replied, realizing what he was struggling to ask. "It's about halfway between town and Camden, very private and not expensive. Islanders never go there. I could meet you around six? I'll make the reserves so your name is not involved. When I get to the beach, you give me your contact info and I'll text you the particulars. Okay?"

"Great!" he said, laughing. "See you soon."

About ten minutes later, Maggie's VW pulled up at the beach. She released her dog, who ran happily down to the water and over to the girls.

"Whoa, Freckles," she yelled chasing after her dog. "Sorry, girls, if he wrecked your castle, but he comes from a whole line of castle wreckers that go way back!"

The girls seemed delighted by the intrusion and began throwing sticks in the water for the dog to retrieve.

Seeing his daughters were well occupied, Bill walked over to Maggie and she carefully slipped a package in his jacket pocket. She handed him her cell and he quickly added his info to her address book.

When he handed it back, she gave him an alluring smile.

"Well, California, I'd better get Freckles to poop or it's a wasted walk for him." She mouthed the word "Thursday," turned, and trotted off after her dog. She collared him and proceeded to walk back to her car.

Bill shook his head, amazed by her beauty, and watched until she drove out of sight. Then, he turned his attention back to his daughters and to rebuilding the castle that Freckles had wrecked.

DREAMS

When Karen finally woke up, she could see the sky was beginning to darken.

Why, I've been asleep all day, she thought, amazed. Sitting up, she heard the muffled laughter of her husband and daughters coming from the kitchen. Carefully she got out of the chair, her legs cramped from being in one position for so long. As she rose, the memory of the incident in the woods came rushing back at her and she had to steady herself to keep from falling.

It must have been a dream. Yes, it was just a dream. It must have been. If not, I'm going to be spending a good bit of time on some shrink's couch.

She walked to the kitchen, where her husband and children were preparing dinner. Bill had taken out four of the fish fillets and was busy seasoning them for the grill while the girls put together a salad.

He turned when he heard her come in. "Finally wake up, sleepyhead?" he asked, leaving the fish and coming to her side. "You feeling okay, hon? You were so deeply asleep. And you were dreaming something. You kept moaning and saying 'no, no.'" He put his palm on her forehead, feeling for warmth.

"I'm okay, Bill. I did have some weird dreams. Maybe I got too much sun or something this afternoon. In any case, I'm up now but it looks like you've got everything under control."

"Yup," answered Bill, nodding. "The girls and I are rockin', aren't we?"

Sophie giggled. "Yes, Daddy. We're going to pretend Mommy's a princess and wait on her tonight!"

Karen started at being called 'princess,' Dex's pet name for her, but she quickly shook it off before Bill noticed.

"Where did this fish come from, hon? It looks so fresh and there's an awful lot of it. Did you buy a whole fish?"

Karen's mind raced for an answer. "I bought it at the farmers' market. They were having a tasting and I liked it. And, yes, I bought the whole fish. The price was just so reasonable. They filleted it free, too. Oh, and they gave me those recipe cards." She pointed to the index cards Dex brought with the fish. Bill apparently found them on the counter and was following one of them.

"Well, good for you," he said. "Now that we practically live on the water, we should partake of the bounty of the sea more often. Isn't that right, Terri? Tomorrow night we'll be having snails and jellyfish!"

Terri and Sophie broke into peals of laughter. "Oh, no, Daddy," said Terri. "Not me!"

Karen laughed with them and began to take a step toward her daughter when she was caught by a wave of dizziness. Bill quickly reached out to offer support and helped her to a chair.

"You sure you're not coming down with something?" he asked, feeling her forehead again. "I think it's up to bed with you right after supper. Ter, Soph, and I can clean up, can't we, girls?"

"I don't know what's wrong with me," Karen answered. "Maybe I am getting something. Thanks for taking over."

Bill smiled and kissed her on the cheek, "Anything for you, princess, anything."

The next morning, Karen had to drag herself out of bed, still unable to shake off the fatigue from the day before. She dressed in jeans and a sweatshirt and pinned her hair on top of her head. Looking at her reflection in the mirror, she noted the dark circles under her eyes. Her face looked thin and gaunt. She got on the scale and was surprised to find she'd lost three pounds.

How could I lose so much weight in one day? Maybe Bill's right. Maybe I have a bug. Yet, I don't feel sick, just tired - so very tired.

Sighing, she pinched her cheeks for color and went downstairs to make breakfast for her family.

At the table, Bill watched her closely. "Hon, you don't look so hot," he said, concerned. "Take it easy today. Don't press yourself, okay?"

Karen nodded as she picked at her food. Her appetite seemed to have vanished. She thought about the weight loss and forced herself to eat some eggs and toast.

Breakfast over, she made sure the kids were set for school before she drove Bill to the wharf.

"Remember what I said," he admonished her. "You take it easy today. Rest. Promise?"

"I promise," she said with a small, shaky smile.

He gave her a quick kiss and was off to the ferry.

After the girls got on the bus for school, Karen decided to soak in a hot bath. She filled the tub, stripped off her clothes, and stepped in, letting herself sink down into the hot water. Soon, she felt her body relax, as muscles she didn't realize were tight unwound. She leaned her head back and closed her eyes, letting the heat from the water soothe her. She saw the rabbit again, on its hind legs with that awful grin on its face, its eyes intense.

When she opened her eyes, she was shocked to find she had slipped under the water.

I'm drowning, she thought as she struggled to shake off the ennui that seemed to have taken over her body and mind. Finally, she jerked herself up, freeing her head from the water, coughing violently. She lurched out of the tub, leaned over the toilet, and retched.

I almost killed myself. What in God's name is the matter with me?

She retched again, bath water spewing from her lungs. Finally, she stood up, dried herself off, and threw her clothes back on, her mind focusing.

I need to see Dex. I don't know why, but I do. He'll be able to ground me somehow, help me make sense of what's happening.

She towel-dried her hair and pulled it back into a braid as she studied her reflection in the mirror. Surprisingly, she looked more alive now than she had earlier that morning. She added some blush to her cheeks, put on some lip gloss, and went downstairs and out to the car.

She drove by the store first but neither his bike nor his truck was outside.

He's probably out on his boat, she thought as she turned the car to go to the yard. Once there, she parked outside the small store where they'd eaten lunch. A group of men were standing and talking across the yard by a boat that was dry-docked. She couldn't tell if Dex was with them or not.

If he's over there, he'll see me. I'll wait.

She went into the store and was greeted warmly by the teenager who had waited on them the other day. Karen helped herself to coffee and, suddenly feeling famished, bought a big blueberry muffin to go with it. She paid, went outside, and sat down at one of the tables to wait for Dex.

As she sipped her coffee, she thought about the events of the past twenty-four hours - the extreme fatigue, lack of appetite, weight loss, and, finally, the near-drowning in the bathtub. Then she remembered the rabbit.

That damned rodent is responsible for everything. I know it. But how can that be? That's insane.

"Penny for your thoughts, princess?" asked Dex as he strolled over to the table. He'd seen her arrive, but not wanting to cause any more talk about them, had taken his time extricating himself from the men he was with.

She looked up at him surprised, confusion and fear evident in the expression on her face.

He saw the haunted look in her eyes and immediately frowned. "Something's wrong, Karen," he said flatly, his voice serious for once. "You finish that coffee, get in your car, and drive down to Eagle Point. You know where that is?"

She nodded.

"I'll hang around here for a bit," he continued, "so those yahoos over there don't start talking about us and ruin your reputation. Then, I'll meet you there. Can you do that, princess? Can you wait for me there?"

"Yes," she said faintly, as she put down her coffee, and got up to leave. Dex gave her a quick nod and ambled into the store.

Soon, she arrived at Eagle Point and parked her car. Not waiting for Dex, she got out and walked toward the rocks overlooking the sea. The braid in her hair was too tight and giving her a headache, so she undid it, untangling the coils with her fingers. She shook her head, hair finally free, and breathed deeply. The air was invigorating. Suddenly, she felt lighter, like a weight had been removed from her chest, and she marveled at how precious and fragile life really was. She reached down and ran her hand through a clump of seaweed that clung to the rocks and was amazed at its silky texture.

She walked along the rocks, relishing the fact that she was alive - thankful she had not succumbed to the water in the tub or to the forces swirling around her. She'd come close to death but she'd survived - survived by the strength of her own will. She had been alone and she had triumphed. She felt she was looking at this world through new eyes, seeing the beauty and magnificence of the rugged coastline for the first time.

As she walked along the shore, Dex's truck pulled into the parking lot. He saw her and rushed to join her. As he approached, he sensed a change in her. Unaware of his presence, she stood tall looking out over the sea, her hair a soft, curling mantle on her shoulders. She was so beautiful; it almost hurt to look at her. He stood silent, transfixed by the vision before him.

Finally, she turned, the sun behind her creating a halo around her head. A beatific smile broke out on her face when she saw him.

Dex was amazed. How could she have changed so much in the short time since he'd seen her at the boatyard? The haunted look was gone, replaced by a calm confidence.

Slowly, they made their way toward one another. Karen took his hands in hers then put her arms around him and held him tight. In a daze, he held her, not wanting this moment to ever end.

Finally, she pulled away, took his hand, and sat down on the rocks. Slowly, she told him about what had happened to her in the woods, about the rabbit and the owl, describing these events as dreams. Then she told him about almost drowning in the tub that morning. She did not look at him as she spoke, but rather, kept her attention focused on the sea and the waves pounding against the rocky shore. She spoke calmly, her voice steady with no hint of hysteria.

Dex was shocked by her revelations, but he tried to keep his face neutral and not show the fear he felt for her. As she talked, he wondered if, somewhere in her subconscious, she knew about her husband and Maggie and this knowledge was what had been plaguing her mind, causing what he believed was her attempt at suicide. It angered him to think that her husband's dalliance could cause her such harm. It was all he could do to keep from taking her in his arms. He'd wanted her from the first moment he'd laid eyes on her that day on the wharf. But now he wanted to protect her, keep her, and never let her go. He knew he loved her, loved her so much he felt he would burst. She was his end all, his be all; he would keep her safe at the cost of his life, if need be. However, he knew he had to keep all his feelings to himself, hidden from her. This moment was about her, not about him.

When she finished her recitation, she turned and looked at him. "Do you think I've lost my mind?"

He looked her steadily in the eyes. "No. I think you're just about the sanest person I've ever met. I just think you've been having a rough time at home since you got here. All that pressure and stress is making your mind play some tricks on you. But don't think you're ever alone. I'm here, princess. I'll always be here for you."

Karen smiled and squeezed his hand. "Okay, yes, okay. And, thanks - thanks for being there, for being you."

She squeezed his hand again, and then turned her attention seaward once more and Dex followed suit. They sat quietly, hand in hand, watching the waves till it was time for her to go home, each knowing and accepting that they were, somehow, bound to each other.

He walked her to her car, wishing there was some way he could tell her how he felt, but he knew that would be wrong. She had a life, a husband, children, and he would have to be satisfied with whatever crumbs she cared to throw his way. However, he knew it was worth it for moments like these. Yes, it was definitely worth it.

He opened the car door and helped her in, bending low over her hand and kissing it ever so gently. She laid her hand on his cheek. "M'lady," he said.

"My knight," she replied.

"You take care, now. If you need me, just holler. I'm never too far away."

She nodded as he closed the car door and gave him one last smile as she started the car and headed home to her family.

Worried about his wife, Bill hitched a ride home from the wharf so she wouldn't have to come pick him up. When he entered the house, he was surprised to hear music and laughter coming from the family room. He stood in the doorway astonished to see Karen and his daughters dancing to music from a video game. Karen looked radiant - her hair curly and carefree - smiling and laughing as she moved to the beat of the music.

"Hi," she said when she saw him. "Get out of those uptight old work clothes and join us."

"Boy, you sure made a rapid recovery. I expected to find you in bed or on the couch curled up under a blanket. Guess maybe it was just a twenty-four hour bug. Glad to see you're feeling better. I'll change and be right down."

He skipped up the stairs to the bedroom. Stripping off his work clothes, he thought about how beautiful Karen had looked and how glad he was that she was feeling her old self again. Then, he remembered his planned liaison with Maggie.

I should just call her and cancel - break this off before it really begins.

He pulled his cell from his pocket and opened up to Maggie's number. He was ready to dial when, in his mind's eye, came a picture of her lying in the grass, her face framed by red curls, small beads of sweat on her upper lip. He closed down the phone.

Just one more time. Just once more, then I will be rid of her.

His mind made up, he tossed on his sweats and went downstairs to join his wife and children.

Later that evening, he received a text from Gerry apologizing for being absent the previous Friday and asking Bill to join him for a beer the following week. Bill wrote back in the affirmative and, as Karen suggested, invited Gerry and his family over to the island for the day on Sunday. Gerry texted back enthusiastically saying his wife, Samantha, and son, Little Gerry, would be totally delighted to spend the day on the island but that Sunday wouldn't work for them and suggested Saturday instead. Remembering Karen's reaction when he'd changed their date night plans before, Bill broached the subject with her before replying.

"No problem, Bill," she answered with a smile. "Your career comes first, but I appreciate your asking."

"Thanks, hon. Oh, and Gerry mentioned that he and I will be watching the Sox game while you and his wife and the kids go to the beach! He also hinted that he had something important to talk to me about on Friday. Maybe it's the move to his division."

"Hope so, hon, you're wasted in Sales."

Bill nodded and laughed. "I'll text him back. And thanks again, Kar. You're the best."

CELLAR MYSTERIES

The next couple of days were dreary as rain and fog blanketed the island. At the Andersen home, the sound of the sump pump greeted them in the morning and said goodnight to them when they went to bed. Karen and the girls began complaining of the damp musty smell that crept up from the cellar between the floorboards into the main house. Bill did some searching online and found a modestly priced dehumidifier, purchased it, and arranged for it to be delivered on the ferry the next day.

When it arrived, he took it downstairs to install. The cellar was indeed damp and the smell was awful. He brought in a couple of cinder blocks to elevate the machine in case of flooding and set it up with the drainpipe going into the sump pump hole. Happy with his handiwork, he plugged it in and set it on high. As he turned to leave the cellar, he remembered the symbols etched on the foundation wall in the far corner that he had noticed when they first arrived.

He walked over to the stone and hunkered down to get a better look. On what appeared to be a piece of the original foundation were etched a crescent moon, a jagged line that looked like a lightning bolt, a tear- or raindrop, and three stick figures.

Looking at the symbols, Bill's curiosity was aroused. He wondered how old the etchings were and what they could possibly mean. Deciding to investigate further, he pulled out his cell and took several pictures of the carvings.

When he returned upstairs, he sat down at the computer and printed out the photos and took them to the living room where his wife was seated, reading. "Hey, hon, take a look at these."

She put down her book and studied the photos. "What are they? And where did you take them?"

"I took them a few minutes ago - down in the cellar. These symbols are etched into the foundation of our house. Pretty mysterious, isn't it? Maybe they have something to do with that swamp hag story Pete told us about."

"I don't know. Those carvings look awfully old. And that stone they're carved on, it's huge. Do you think it could have been here before the house was built?"

"What do you mean?"

"That it was part of the landscape and was incorporated into the foundation because it was too heavy to move. They didn't have equipment back then and who knows if they had oxen or horses here on this island."

"Mmmm, you might be right. Remember those Indians, the Aben-something, thought this land was sacred because it was closest to the Great Spirit. Maybe these are symbols of their god? Think I'll do a little research on the Web and see what I can come up with."

Karen handed the photos back to him as he sat down at his desk with his laptop. After a little while, he came over and sat next to her.

"Found something, hon. See here, the moon curved like this? That's called its 'waning crescent phase' and it's a universal symbol of fertility, related to life and death. It's also sometimes called 'the old moon.' And this other symbol - the lightning bolt - in Native American mythology, it's hurled by male gods to fertilize the earth. Haven't found anything specific about the rain- or teardrop yet, but, if it is a raindrop, then the earth needs rain for things to grow so it might also be related to fertility. And the stick figures look like a family - man, woman, and child. So they have been - what's that old biblical phrase? Oh, yeah, fruitful; they've been fruitful."

Karen looked at the pictures again. "Okay, if these symbols all have something to do with the ability of the earth to provide sustenance, how would they relate to Pete's swamp hag story?"

"Don't know," said Bill as he glanced at his watch. "It's something to think on."

He leaned down and kissed her on the cheek. "I feel beat. Think I'm going to turn in. And, hon, remember I have to stay over tomorrow. My meeting with the Camden customer won't be over till late and may involve drinks. I don't want to be making that drive in the dark with alcohol in my system. I'm going to go up, pack a bag now, and try to get a good night's sleep. This could be a pretty big sale and it could put some extra bucks in my paycheck."

Karen nodded. "Text me when you know when you'll be home on Friday. I know you're having drinks with Gerry and may be late."

"Got it," he said as he went upstairs to bed.

The next morning was an ordinary one in the Andersen household. Bill got ready for work and, after a quick bite, Karen drove him to the wharf. Overnight bag in hand, he kissed his wife goodbye, promising to call, and boarded the ferry for town. Once on the mainland, he drove up the coast to Camden for the meeting that was actually scheduled for lunchtime, not late afternoon as he had told Karen. Once the meeting was over, he planned to do a little sightseeing before meeting Maggie at the inn at six.

As he drove, his mind wandered. He thought about his parents, his upbringing. He had always taken a backseat to his older brothers. Sure, he was the one who was on the honor roll, who got straight A's, but that didn't cut the mustard with his dad. No, his sons weren't worth their salt unless they played, and excelled at, football, baseball, hockey, or any of the other big high school team sports. Track, in his father's eye, was a sport for pansies, guys who couldn't make it as "real" athletes. And girls, yeah, he'd had his share, but they were always the ones his brothers, or jocks like his brothers, didn't want or ones they had already had. At least that's the way it was until Karen. She was the ultimate cheerleader goddess and he had won her. And the frosting on the cake was that she was a virgin to boot. He got to go, for once, where no man had ever gone before. He smiled to himself as he remembered their wedding night - she was so shy, so innocent, and they were so much in love.

Yes, he'd had everything, for once, and then it had all gone to hell and he was back to being second-rate again. His oldest brother had offered to float him a loan when things were at their worst, though he could ill afford it himself. But Bill had turned him down, not because of his brother's fragile financial status, but because he didn't want to be beholden to him, to be riding on his coattails once again. And now, finally, things were beginning to come together. He knew he'd get the R&D job and, with a little bit more money coming in, Karen would come around and they'd be a golden couple again.

But what about Maggie? Maggie, that beautiful but slightly used and bruised type of girl who was the object of most male fantasies. Well, he had her, too, didn't he? Sure, he planned that tonight would be the end of it, but deep down, he knew better. Yes, he wanted it all, and for better or worse, that "all" included her.

MAGGIE

Maggie glanced at the clock on the wall of the classroom. It was time to go. She drove home to shower, change, and pack her overnight bag and headed for the wharf where her punt was tied up. She motored over to the mainland and started the hour-long drive to the Seaside Inn where she'd made reservations for the evening. This inn had been a favorite of hers when she was involved with the professor. It was cozy, private, and unassuming. The restaurant, as she'd told Bill, was quite good and the bar could have a lively crowd on any given night.

She felt nervous, wondering if the magic of Little Glooskap had worn off. Would he regret having made this date with her? Well, if he did, she would just have to change his mind.

She loved him. She didn't know why, she barely knew him, but she was sure. Would he ever love her in return? She had to acknowledge to herself that his wife, however much she disliked her, was stunning and he had those two adorable little girls. How could she compete with that? She was just an island girl. Yes, she was educated, maybe not as well as Karen, but she was smart. And she knew she had an intangible something that set her apart from other women, something men wanted. Yes, she had an aura about her that drew men to her, sometimes for the better, but usually for the worse. Dex was the only man who seemed immune and she was glad of that. She needed a male friend in this world.

Her thoughts whirled about her as she drove. Soon, she saw the inn's sign and she pulled into the drive, parked, and went inside. It was five-thirty. Bill was supposed to meet her at six. As she checked in, she told the clerk she was expecting a gentleman to join her and, if he asked, she would probably be waiting in the bar. Business taken care of, she went to their room, freshened her makeup and hair, put her things away, and headed to the lounge for a much-needed drink.

Bill arrived a little after six. He consciously got there late, not wanting to appear to be too eager. He stopped at the front desk and asked if she'd checked in. The clerk gave him her message. Bill thanked him and headed toward the bar.

Standing in the doorway, he scanned the interior of the crowded lounge for her. Finally, he caught a glimpse of red hair at the far end of the bar. As he approached, he noticed she was engaged in animated conversation with a good-looking young man about her own age. Bill stood still until he caught her eye. Immediately, she broke off the conversation, smiled, and headed over to him. Bill noted with some satisfaction that the young man she'd been talking to seemed surprised at her quick dismissal.

She was wearing a dark turtleneck that clung to her body and a short denim skirt. Her legs were bare and on her feet were the usual flip-flops. She had painted her toes and fingernails a bright pink and her hair, freshly washed, floated freely about her head. She wore a minimal amount of makeup, just lip gloss and a little blush. She looked ravishing and Bill was pleased she had taken such pains with her appearance for him.

When she joined him, he put his arm around her waist, leaned down, and kissed her.

"Let me grab your drink and let's sit down," he said as he

directed her to the back of the bar where a booth sat empty. He sat her down then strolled over to get her drink and order one for himself. As he approached, the young man she had been talking to finished his drink, got up, and left. Bill smiled to himself as he placed his order and went to join Maggie in the booth.

As they sat sipping their drinks, he told her about his meeting and the sale he'd made. He was in a jubilant mood, knowing that this day's work would bring his family something extra in his paycheck. They talked about his daughters, Maggie filling him in on their progress at school. His heart swelled with pride as she went on about their intellects and their social skills. He talked lovingly about them and his hopes for their futures.

Soon, the waitress brought menus and they ordered dinner and a bottle of wine. They ate quickly, each eager to be alone with the other. After the plates were cleared away, they sipped the remnants of their wine as they waited for the check.

"I can't wait to get you alone," he said softly, taking her hand.

The waitress came over and, the bill settled, they left the restaurant. Bill put his arm around her shoulder as she showed him the way to their room. He took the key from her and opened the door, propelling her inside and taking her in his arms. He kissed her passionately, using one free hand to shut the door. Responding to his ardor, she wrapped her arms around his neck.

"Oh, Bill, I, oh I..." she stammered as he kissed her, his hands roaming her body.

"Say it," he urged as he bit her neck, softly. "I want to hear it, to hear you say it."

She pulled her head back and looked at him, her eyes soft.

"Yes, I love you," she cried. "Oh, Bill, I do. I love you. I know we only just met, but I know. I love you."

He silenced her with a kiss, knowing he'd heard what he wanted, and led her to the bed. Much later, their lust well satisfied, they fell asleep entwined in each other's arms.

Bill woke just before dawn with a wicked hangover. He got out of bed as carefully as he could so as not to disturb her.

She lay on her stomach, her legs tangled in the sheets, a soft snore coming from her nose. She was beautiful. He dressed in his running gear and grabbed a piece of paper from the desk in the room and wrote her a note, the same note he had written to Karen hundreds of times in similar situations. He wrote without thinking and put the note on the pillow next to her head, pulled on his Nikes, and went out the patio door.

Half awake, Maggie heard the door close and reached out to the other side of the bed. When she realized it was empty, panic began to set in. She sat up, trying to shake off her sleepiness, and scanned the room. No Bill. She got up and checked the bathroom. No Bill. Feeling upset, she sat back down on the bed again, looking around the room. Relief washed over her when she noted that his overnighter was still there. Lying back down, she saw the hastily scribbled note left on the pillow beside her.

"M -
Gone for a quick jog, be back soon.
Luv u,
B

Her heart leapt. He'd written "love you" to her! She felt like dancing around the room. Smiling, she picked up his shirt from the floor where he'd left it and put it on. It came almost to her knees. She made a pot of coffee and went out on the patio to wait for him to return.

Feeling refreshed, Bill jogged back to the Inn. When he approached their room, he saw Maggie standing outside, wearing his shirt, a coffee cup in her hand. The oversized shirt made her look small - delicate - and he became immediately aroused. He slowed his pace and, when he reached her, put his arms around her, cupping her buttocks and lifting her tightly to him. She wrapped her legs around his waist as he carried her into the room.

When their passion was again sated, Maggie checked her watch. "I'm going to be late for school," she said, as she hurriedly got dressed.

When she was ready to go, he got up and gave her a quick kiss.

"I'll be in touch, Mags," he said as she grabbed her things and headed out the door.

Alone, Bill made himself some more coffee and turned on the TV. Sitting back down on the bed, he noticed a piece of paper and realized it was the note he'd left for Maggie. He picked it up and looked at it.

Oh Christ, he thought when he saw what he'd written. *Why did I put the 'luv u' there? Now she'll think I love her and that could lead to complications.*

He shook his head. *Maybe I should just break this thing off.*

But as that thought crossed his mind, he knew he intended to do no such thing. He crushed the note in his hand, disgusted with himself, and threw it in the wastebasket.

KAREN

While Bill was driving to his liaison with Maggie, Karen busied herself cleaning house and doing laundry. They were expecting the man she hoped would be Bill's new boss and his family on Saturday and she wanted everything to be perfect. She made a list of groceries she would need to pick up in town on Friday.

Bill called late in the day. He told her he was about to meet his client and wanted to talk to her first in case he forgot later. He told her he thought he would be back in the office Friday morning, early, and would leave the car keys with the lot attendant. He hoped to be home by six and would call her if he could not find a ride.

"Wish me luck," he said. "I love you."

Later, after she put the girls to bed, Karen poured herself a glass of wine and sat in the overstuffed chair listening to the waves pounding on the shore.

She thought about her husband and prayed everything would work out for him, that he would succeed. Then her thoughts turned to

Dex and their strange connection, wondering when she would see him again and hoping it would be soon.

He's always there to bail me out. When I'm falling apart, he shows up to save me. How does he know? It's like we're on the same wavelength or something. We're connected to each other - it's almost like we're part of the same person.

She shook her head and glanced down at the end table. Lying there were the pictures Bill took of the foundation rock. She picked them up and studied them again.

I hope we're not sitting on top of some damned Indian burial ground like in that old movie, she thought, chuckling to herself.

Tired, she tucked her legs underneath her and turned again to listen to the sea, her mind now filled with jumbled thoughts about her marriage and Dex and how she didn't want to let go of either.

BILL

On Friday, as promised, Bill parked their car in the lot by the wharf and left the keys with the attendant. Back at the office, he sat down to complete his paperwork for the week and, when it was done, walked down to R&D to see what was going on.

"My man!" exclaimed Gerry, hopping up and clapping Bill on the back. "Good to see you. I missed our confab last week, but duty called and, as they say, 'if you don't talk, you won't get heard!' Listen, I got some stuff to take care of right now. Let's get together in about thirty? I'll take you to lunch."

Bill smiled and nodded his agreement and returned to his desk. A half hour later, they went to a sports bar that was in close proximity to the office. They stopped on their way in and got drinks before taking a table in the back, away from the TV screens. The waitress came by and took their lunch order. As they waited for their food, they sipped their beers and talked.

"Okay, Bill," began Gerry, serious for once. "Before we start talking about R&D and your possible place in it, I have to tell you I spoke with Greg Sloane."

Bill's heart sank. It was all going to go south again. Another bad reference from Sloane and he'd be lucky if he kept his job in Sales.

"Ger, let me explain," Bill started but the younger man stopped him with a wave of his hand.

"Let me finish, bro. He regrets what he did to you. He was pissed - something to do with you and his ex."

"His ex?"

"Yeah, I guess shortly after you left he found her with the pool boy or something, in flagrante delicto! Booted her ass out. Told me he was wrong to let you go, that you were the real deal. So that's all water under the bridge, okay?"

Bill breathed a sigh of relief and nodded his head.

Gerry smiled. "Okay, now that that's out of the way, let's talk about Omicron. I had a sit down with the CFO last week. He's the man to see if you want to get anything done and he knows it's R&D that keeps the company afloat. I told him I wanted, no, needed, you on my team - that you were wasted in Sales. I told him about our Friday afternoon brainstorming sessions and how much you've helped me focus in on problems we've been having with the software. He said he's heard from LeFleur you were crackerjack at sales, too."

Gerry finished his beer and indicated to the waitress to bring them another. "Now about Sales, Bill. You gotta cool it there. You don't want to be more than a B+ there. No more of this A+ shit! You keep on excelling and that little prick, LeFleur, is going to fight to keep you. So, slow down, my man, slow it down."

The waitress brought their beers. Gerry took a sip before continuing. "Now the CFO, he agreed with me that I need more help, but he's a stickler for the rules and says you gotta finish your probationary period before he moves you. So, you're stuck with LeFleur until the end of October. Between now and then, I want you with me every Friday afternoon and I've convinced the CFO to put a little something extra in your paycheck to recognize your contribution to R&D. So, my man, the plan is to get you inside before the snow flies! What do you think?"

Bill was ecstatic. He would be in R&D before winter. Things were moving much faster than he'd thought they would. And the extra in the paycheck - they could really use it.

Their lunches came and, as they ate, Bill and Gerry talked shop. When the meal was over, Gerry glanced at his watch and called for the check.

"I've got a meeting at four," he said. "Got to tell you, Sam is really looking forward to tomorrow. I usually keep her home watching the Sox with me. She really wants to go to the beach. And it will be good for Little Gerry, too."

"We're looking forward to having you. I don't think Karen's made too many friends on the island yet so it's kinda lonely for her and she really enjoys entertaining. We'll pick you all up at the noon boat. Okay?"

Gerry nodded.

"And thanks for all the support, Gerry," Bill continued. "I really appreciate it and I look forward to working with you and your team. I promise I won't let you down."

The two men shook hands. Gerry paid the check and left to walk back to the office. Bill checked his watch. He could make the four o'clock boat, get home early and surprise Karen. He jogged to the wharf, full of confidence and enthusiasm, thinking to himself that this move to Maine had surely worked out well for him.

Yes, he admitted to himself, he wanted it to have it all and, finally, it looked like Mateguas was going to give it to him.

SATURDAY AFTERNOON & LITTLE GERRY

As promised, Bill met Gerry and his family at the noon boat. Gerry's wife, Samantha, was a pretty, petite brunette and Little Gerry, fondly known as L.G., was a chubby toddler with big brown eyes.

Karen greeted them warmly, introducing the girls and giving them all a brief tour of the house and property. The ballgame was starting soon, so the men sat down in the family room to watch the pre-game show while Karen, Sam, and the kids went to the beach.

As they watched the game, Bill got a sense of why Gerry wanted him so badly. Gerry was one of those brilliant guys whose mind was always operating full speed, but in all different directions at the same time. He was unable to keep his focus. Bill had seen guys like him before; they always kept a couple of steady, calm individuals on their team to ground them, to keep them on track. Bill was one of those types.

During one of the many commercial breaks, Gerry turned to Bill. "Hey, man, you play golf?"

Bill was surprised. He'd played often back in California, but that was before he'd lost his job. His set of clubs had to be sold with most of their other belongings to finance the move to Maine.

"Yeah, a little," he replied, "but I haven't played in a while. Don't have any clubs anymore."

Gerry nodded. He was sure Bill was a skilled golfer. He knew people and those Silicon types played as hard as they worked. In fact, most of the time, work and play were the same things to them. Gerry was an excellent golfer and looked forward to playing someone who could challenge him.

"Well, I've got a spare set. What do you say, if the weather holds, we play next Saturday? Afterward, we can pick up the little women and go out on the town, dinner and dancing."

"Sounds like a plan," agreed Bill. "Let me run it by Karen and I'll let you know on Monday."

"Great!" said Gerry, turning his attention back to the ballgame.

By late afternoon, the women and children returned from the beach. Outside, Little Gerry was keeping his mother busy and the girls were playing croquet on the lawn. Ballgame over, Bill brought out a chilled chardonnay and poured wine for the adults.

So far, he thought, *the day has gone extremely well. The weather's perfect and everyone's having a good time. Karen seems to like both Sam and Gerry and is delighted at having a toddler around again.*

"Gerry," said Sam, "you watch L.G. I'm going inside with Karen to help with dinner."

"Sure, babe," he replied taking his son and tossing him in the air.

He played with the little boy for a while then turned back to Bill and began talking shop again.

When Sam came back outside, Gerry and Bill were immersed in conversation by the grill and Little Gerry was nowhere in sight.

"Not again!" she cried, addressing her husband. "Where is he? Have you lost him again?"

Gerry looked up, surprised. "Babe, he was just here a second ago. He couldn't have gone far."

Karen, standing on the porch, heard the exchange and immediately took charge of the situation.

"Bill, you and Sam go down toward the beach. Gerry, you stay here in case he returns. I'll look around back."

They all began to search and call for the little boy as Karen ran around the house to the backyard. When she turned the corner, she glimpsed a rabbit hopping from the lawn onto the trail behind that strange bush.

Hearing a shout of glee, she turned her head and saw the toddler running as fast as his chubby legs could carry him toward the path, his finger pointed at the rabbit. Karen's mind reeled - he was heading for the trail! She watched, stunned, as the branches of the bush slowly moved until they were open just wide enough to admit the little boy. Crows began to shriek in the treetops.

For a split second, she stood frozen, watching as the scene unfolded before her. Then she acted.

She sprinted with all she had in an attempt to cut between Little Gerry and the trail - the trail that led to the swamp - that led to the owl. Just as the toddler was about to step behind the bush, Karen, with lungs bursting, swooped down and enfolded him in her arms. She lifted him in the air, running with him away from the woods, toward the house. When she felt they were safe, she stopped, holding the toddler tightly to her chest while she caught her breath. The little boy began to wail.

Hearing his son, Gerry ran to the backyard and Karen handed the toddler over to him.

"Where was he?" asked Gerry as he tried to comfort the boy.

Karen thought quickly. She couldn't tell him about the rabbit, the owl, and the path. He would think she was insane. Then, she noticed berry stains on the boy's shirt.

"He was eating berries," she said. "Guess I overreacted and scared him. I was afraid he'd go into the woods."

"No, you didn't overreact," Gerry replied gratefully. "Thanks for finding him. I'd better go get Sam and let her know he's all right and face the music, if you know what I mean."

Gerry ran down to the beach with his son in his arms as Karen began to slowly walk back to the house. Before she turned the corner, she glanced back - back at that strange bush.

Sitting in front of it now was the rabbit. She locked eyes with the little creature for a second, as time seemed to stand still. Finally, the rabbit nodded its head to her in some weird sort of acknowledgement and then turned and hopped back into the woods.

She shook her head, trying to understand the conflicting feelings of fear and wonder she was experiencing.

Sweet Jesus, what is happening to me? Am I losing my mind? I'll have to think about this later. Later, when I'm alone.

Trying to put it all out of her mind, she turned her back on the woods and walked to the front of the house. Bill and their guests were coming up the drive. Samantha was carrying the little boy and talking at her husband.

"You are toast, you know," she said meaningfully. "Absolute toast! I leave you with him for ten minutes and you lose him. And eating berries. If he has the trots all night, it's on you, mister, not me!"

Unsmiling, she stomped up the front stairs, taking her son inside the house. Karen followed behind, hoping to be able to calm her down and save the evening.

Gerry looked at Bill, shrugging his shoulders. "Guess Big Gerry's not getting any tonight. Or any other night soon, for that matter."

Bill clapped him on the back. "She'll get over it, my man, she will."

"How the hell did you do it with two of the little monsters at the same time?" asked Gerry. "I take my eye of him for a second and he's gone. Sam wants another, but, man, I tell her we got to wait till L.G.'s in school!"

Bill laughed. "I wouldn't want to do it again. Those girls were a handful, you know. But, now they're older, it's a lot easier. You'll see, it will come."

Bill poured him another glass of wine as Karen and Sam emerged with the steaks and hamburgers for the grill.

"Where's my heir?" Gerry asked his wife.

"He's taking a nap. I think he's pretty much had it for the day." She walked over to her husband and gave him a kiss on the cheek. "Sorry if I overreacted, but, if it happens again..."

Gerry nodded, smiling at her. "I know, I know."

The tension of the situation eased, the rest of the evening went extremely well. The meal was delicious and the conversation lively. When it was time to go, Bill and Karen drove the Davis family down to the wharf to catch the nine o'clock ferry.

As they watched the boat leave, Bill turned to Karen. They looked at each other for a moment and then they both burst into laughter. Laughing so hard tears were in her eyes, Karen got into the car.

"God, that Gerry - that guy can wear you out with his talk," she said, catching her breath. "Is he like that all the time?"

"Yeah," replied Bill. "It's like he's on speed and coke at the same time. Thought Sam was going to kill him over the boy. Glad she mellowed out."

"She was mad. Guess it happens all the time. She says he's a for-real genius and could have written his own ticket anywhere, the Valley included. They met in Boston, but she's from Maine and wanted to move back, so he picked Omicron. She says he has an agreement with them that lets him consult with other firms as long as there's no conflict of interest. Spends about a third of his time doing that for big bucks. That's why he needs you so badly. His plate is overflowing."

Bill smiled and told her of Gerry's suggestion for the next weekend - golf, dinner, and dancing.

Karen thought for a moment. "You know, when we get that first little something extra in your paycheck, we should use it to invest in a good set of clubs for you. You realize what he's doing, don't you?"

Bill nodded as he pulled in the driveway. "If I can cut the mustard as his golf partner, then he'll have me working at least six, if not seven, days a week, five in the office and one or two on the links. Been there, done that, got the T-shirt!"

Karen laughed. "Life back in the fast lane!"

Back at the house, Karen went directly to the kitchen to finish the cleaning up. As she reached for a dishtowel, Bill caught her hand, turning her around to face him.

"Seriously, Kar," he said, "thank you for tonight. It was all you. Everything. You were great."

She smiled at him, but he did not let go of her hand. "I love you. I don't think I say that often enough, but I do."

Her eyes softened, a slow smile coming to her face. "I love you too, superstar," she said, squeezing his hand.

She reached up and gave him a quick kiss, then turned her attention back to straightening up the kitchen. However, as she worked, she could not stop reliving in her mind the way that bush had opened up for Little Gerry and how the rabbit had somehow acknowledged her.

Am I losing my mind? Or is there really something inhuman out there testing me? And, if I am being tested, did I pass?

She had no answers, only questions, and, as she tried to put it all aside, she shuddered to think what would happen to her, and her family, if she was found wanting.

MAGGIE & DEX & KAREN

On Sunday, Maggie spent the morning working on her lesson plans for the upcoming week. School would be out soon for the summer break and she was looking forward to having more free time. In the afternoon, her work done, she drove over to Dex's house, but he was not at home. She finally caught up with him at the boatyard and asked him if he had time to talk. They walked over to the store, got coffee, and sat down.

"Well, sugar," he said looking at her carefully. "You look like the cat that caught the canary. Tell old Dex what's happening now."

"Oh, Dex," she whispered. "He loves me."

Dex raised his eyebrows. "Now what makes you think that, kitten? He hire a skywriter to plaster it all over the big blue? If he did, I sure missed it."

"Now, Dex, don't make fun," she admonished him. "He said it. Well, no, that's not exactly right. He wrote it."

She told him about the note, reciting it from memory.

Dex couldn't help but laugh. However, seeing the look on her face, he forced himself to get serious.

"Kitten," he said slowly. "That sounds an awful lot like a note he's written a thousand times, but not to you, to his WIFE! Only difference is he started it this time with an M, not a K. It means nothing, girl, nothing."

She looked at him, her eyes flashing with anger. "Why are you always trying to bring me down?"

"Sugar, you need to get outta this place," he said firmly. "You need to take that teaching degree of yours, go up coast or down to New Hampshire, Vermont, hell, even New York. Anywhere but here. Find yourself a nice, SINGLE, young man around your own age, settle down, have little red-haired babies. Have a life. Don't throw all you have away on some lousy married man who's just trying to get his rocks off, you hear?"

She shook her head. "It's not like that," she protested. "If you could see him with me, you'd know. If his wife found out and he had to choose, I think he'd choose me. I know it!"

"Maggie, you don't have it in your head to let his wife know about this thing you're having with him, do you?" he asked, suddenly afraid for Karen.

"What'd you care?" she demanded, raising her voice. "Although, it would give you free rein with that snooty blonde, wouldn't it? You would be able to put all your high morals, your principles, aside and go after her - the wronged wife! Bet you'd like that!"

His mind raced. She was right. Karen knowing about Bill's affair might clear the path for him to pursue her. But it was wrong, not the way it should be. Somewhere deep within him a voice told him it was his job to protect her, not to make love to her, at least not now. He was her knight, not her lover. Maybe, someday that would change, but for this moment in time he was her protector and that meant he had to keep Maggie from doing something foolish - something that would hurt both of them.

He chose his words carefully. "Listen, sugar, I have no inclinations toward that woman. None at all. I like her, but as a friend. I enjoy her conversation. And, as I have said before, she is a married lady and I respect that and I would hate to see her hurt. Just as I would hate to see you hurt. Don't do anything stupid, girl. You'll lose him and, possibly, everything you've worked for. You think she's going to let you go on teaching her daughters or anyone else's if she finds out what you've been doing with her man? Come on, sugar, you're smarter than that!"

Maggie sat still for a moment, weighing his words, a frown on her face.

"Okay," she sighed. "You're right. I won't do anything to upset the applecart. I'll be patient, wait for him to tell her. Will that satisfy you?"

"What would satisfy me most, kitten, would be for you to dump that philandering asshole, but somehow I don't think that's going to happen, so I guess I'll have to settle for what I can get."

He finished his coffee and stood up. "I've got to get back to work. You take care and think about what I said about getting outta here. That's the answer. Leave that asshole, leave this God-awful rock, and make yourself a good life. You can do it. You deserve it."

He leaned down and gave her a hug.

She hugged him back. "I will, Dex, I promise. I'll think on it. I will."

He heard her words but sensed there was no truth in them. She was not going to waver. She had chosen her course and would irrationally pursue it despite the rocks, shoals, and rough seas that blocked her way. No good would come of it, of that he was certain. However, of Karen he was sure. He would protect her. He had to.

The Andersen's Sunday was relaxed after the festivities of the day before. There was still cleaning to do and forgotten homework for Sophie and Terri to complete.

After dinner, the girls and their father retired to the family room to watch television. Karen was still straightening up the house when her eye caught the photos of the carvings that Bill had taken the other evening. She picked them up, examining them with renewed interest. As she studied them, her mind returned to the incident with Little Gerry the day before. If she had not been there, he would have run into the woods, onto the trail, and, maybe, never been seen again. She shuddered at the thought and made a decision. She would find out the truth about this house - this property. The safety of her family depended upon it.

Resolved, she folded the photos and put them in her pocket. *I'll start at the library in the morning.* Nodding to herself, she left the room and went to join her husband and children.

INTERRUPTED DREAMS

Much later, Sophie rolled over in bed, half awakened from a deep sleep. She'd been dreaming her daddy had gotten her a puppy and they were all playing at the shore. It was a happy dream and she closed her eyes tightly, hugging her pillow, trying to bring it back. But it was no use - the dream was gone. She opened her eyes and sat up, looking over toward her twin's bed. It was empty.

Scanning the room, she noticed there was a light coming from the inside of the closet. Curious, she got out of bed and tiptoed over to it. Terri was inside, sitting cross-legged on the floor, the wooden box in her lap. At her side was her flashlight, illuminating the wall in front of her.

"What're you doing, Ter?" Sophie whispered.

Her twin didn't respond. She was staring intently at the box and running her hand slowly back and forth across the carved symbols. Sophie could see her lips moving and she leaned closer to hear what Terri was saying. To her shock and surprise, she heard her twin, very softly, reciting the words to the prayer they'd found inside the box.

"Oh, Mateguas Grand Père de la Mort, entend ma prière.

Entendre la prière de cette mère pour sa famille.

Ce soir, la Mskagwdemos manèges la tempête.

Elle lance l'éclair, elle hurle el tonnerre, elle lave la terre de ses larmes, et elle a faim pour la famille de cette mère.

L'homme qu'elle appelle pour qu'elle puisse coucher avec lui et de lui voler sa semence."

Sophie's mouth opened in amazement as she listened. How did Terri remember it all? How could she know how to pronounce all those words? They weren't English.

Suddenly frightened, Sophie put her hand on her sister's shoulder. "Terri, I'm scared. What are you doing? Answer me."

At her sister's touch, Terri shuddered and shook her head slightly, as if awakening from a deep sleep.

"Soph," she said in a whisper. "How'd I get here?"

"Don't know. You were reciting that prayer - the one to the dad of the dead."

Terri looked down at the box, a wave of revulsion washing over her. She pushed it out of her lap onto the floor.

"Put it away," she pleaded. "I don't want to touch it again. Just put it away."

Sophie leaned in front of her sister, picked up the box, and put it under a pile of T-shirts in the back of the closet.

"You okay? You want me to get Mommy?"

Terri shook her head. Slowly, she got up and took her sister's hand. "Thanks, Soph. Let's go back to bed and pretend this was just a dream. Okay?"

Sophie nodded. She tucked her sister into bed and then got back in her own. "You sure you're okay?" she asked before lying down.

"Yeah, I'm okay," Terri responded in a soft voice. "Let's just go to sleep."

With one last look at her sister, Sophie lay down and pulled the covers up to her chin. However, sleep didn't come easily and it wasn't until she heard her sister softly snoring that she was able to let herself go and return to a happy dreamland.

HISTORICAL DISCOVERIES

The next morning, Karen put the photos and a notepad in a satchel and drove over to the library. She enlisted the help of the librarian, explaining she wanted to do some historical research into the property she and her husband inherited. The librarian thought a good place for her to start would be the property tax records and explained to her how to access the files on the town's website. She quickly found her property and made notations of the various owners' names and the dates when the property changed hands. It was a long list. On one of the documents, dated 1933, she found handwritten notes indicating that some surveying had been commissioned. She was surprised to find that the area to be surveyed was not the knoll on which the house stood, but, rather, the woods behind the house and beyond. This piqued her interest and she delved deeper into the records and found that not one, but three surveying firms had been engaged by the consortium that owned the house.

That doesn't make sense, she thought. *Why would anyone engage three different firms to do one job?*

She jotted down the names of the surveyors and then continued recording ownership until she got to Bill's aunt's name.

Finished with the town database, Karen again sought out the librarian.

"I noted that back in the nineteen thirties, the corporation that owned the house commissioned some surveying. What I don't understand is why they would have engaged three different companies to do the same job. Do you know anything about these three firms?"

The librarian looked at the names. "Well, that first one was a guy from Cumberland, I believe, and he is long gone. The second firm still exists and does work here occasionally, but the one from New York, well, I never heard of them."

She thought for a minute still looking at the names Karen had given her.

"You know I know just who you should talk to - Madge Parker. If anyone knows what went on with that surveying, she does. She's about ninety years old but still sharp as a tack. She's in a nursing home on the mainland. I'll get you the address and phone number and, if you want, I can give her a call and let her know you'll be contacting her. You'll enjoy her, too. She's a real hoot."

The librarian promised to get in touch with Madge later in the day and Karen hoped to be able to set up an appointment to talk with her on Friday. Content she'd done all she could for the time being, Karen returned home, for once full of optimism and hope.

BILL

While Karen was doing research, Bill was heading off for a planned liaison with Maggie. Heeding Gerry's warning about not being too good in Sales, he had slacked off some; not much, but just enough to give him some spare time in the afternoon. Once he knew he would be free, he sent a text to Maggie asking her to meet him at a motel close to town. She replied that she would work something out.

He ate a leisurely lunch then picked up a bottle of wine and headed to the motel. As he drove, he thought again about why he was doing this. He loved his wife and family and things with Karen were decidedly better than they'd been for the past two years. So, why? Why Maggie? Why now? He'd had chances to cheat before, but had never really been tempted, had he?

Okay, he told himself, *be honest - there was Julie. I might have crossed the line with her if I hadn't been laid off.*

He thought back again to that party two years ago. He remembered standing by the bar waiting for a refill when he felt a tap on his shoulder. He turned to find Sloan's wife, Julie, standing behind him, an empty wine glass in her hand.

"Get a girl a drink, Bill?" she asked with a soft smile on her face.

"Sure, Julie," he replied taking her glass from her hand, their fingertips brushing. He got her a drink and thought that was the end of it when she grabbed his hand.

"Come with me, Bill," she said with some urgency. "I want to show you something."

He'd known that to go with her was a colossal mistake, but he did it anyway and let her lead him out of the barroom by the hand. She took him quickly down a dark hallway, opened a door, and pulled him inside. He'd known at once where they were - the men's locker room, deserted now at this late hour. He leaned back against one of the lockers taking a sip of his drink.

"Now, what was so important, Julie?" he asked, taking her in with his eyes.

She was wearing a very short skirt and halter-top that left little to the imagination. Her breasts pushed deliciously against the thin fabric of the halter and the tight skirt showcased her firm round bottom. Her legs were long, shapely, and perfectly tanned.

She smiled and turned her back to him. With one hand, she reached up and deftly undid the halter-top. With the other, she held the flimsy fabric up against her breasts to keep it from falling off.

"My shoulder," she whispered. "Look at my shoulder. I just had it done."

In the dim light, Bill had had to lean down to look at her. On her shoulder he saw a small tattoo of a hummingbird. It was exquisitely drawn.

"Very nice, Julie," he said, leaning back again and taking another drink.

She looked over her shoulder at him, smiling seductively. "Isn't it beautiful? Don't you want to just touch it, Bill? You can, you know. Don't be afraid."

There was just a hint of a challenge in her tone and though he'd known he should just get the hell outta there, the combination of the booze and the heat emanating from her body were too much for him. So, he'd reached out tentatively and brushed her soft shoulder with his fingertips. When she felt his touch, she'd moaned and seemed to melt backward toward him, their bodies now just inches apart.

Unable to resist, he'd slid his hand from her shoulder, under her armpit until his palm was resting against the exposed side of her warm breast.

She began to turn toward him, the movement causing her plump breast to literally leap into his hand, when a sound shattered the moment.

A toilet flushing.

Julie, always quick on her feet, had recovered first, putting some distance between the two of them, struggling to retie her halter-top. But it was too late. Marty Grimgold emerged from the washroom and took in the scene before him, a sly smile blossoming on his face.

"Hey, Bill, Julie," he leered. "Hope I'm not interrupting anything important."

Bill remembered standing mute, his painful erection rapidly wilting away. And Julie, she had just blushed furiously and whispered a barely audible, "Hi, Marty."

Marty laughed then winked at Bill and left the locker room.

As the door closed, Julie turned to him, a hint of panic in her eyes. "What are we going to do, Bill?"

"You're going to leave and go back to the party," he said with a false calm. "Act as if nothing happened. After all, nothing did. Have a good time. I'll follow in five."

She nodded and swiftly left the locker room. Deflated, he'd sat down on the bench and took another sip of his drink, but now it just left a bad taste in his mouth. He knew he'd really screwed up this time.

If only it had been anyone other than Marty, I'd be okay.

Marty had seniority over him, having been with the company since its inception. But Sloane had passed him over to make Bill the lead developer on this project and Marty was not happy about it.

He'll use this against me for sure, Bill remembered telling himself as he'd finished his drink and stood up, ready to go back to the party.

But now, driving to meet Maggie, Bill knew that if it hadn't been for Marty, he probably wouldn't have stopped with Julie and that might have cost him his wife and his kids.

Yeah, he admitted, *that prick Marty probably saved my marriage.*

But what about his attraction to Maggie? How was it different? Julie's appeal was easy to explain. It was all about power, not sex. She was the boss's wife and the thought of having her was a definite turn-on. So, what was it about Maggie other than great sex? What was it that kept him coming back? Was his ego so fragile that he depended upon, and needed, the adoration of a young girl? He hoped not. One thing he was sure of was, it wasn't love. No, Karen was the only woman he had ever loved and he didn't think anything would ever change that. He shook his head, admitting to himself, that, at least for now, he was apparently committed to a course of action that could destroy everything he held dear.

Feeling depressed, he pulled into the motel parking lot, went in, and registered. The room was nothing special, just a cheap motel room. He opened the wine and poured himself a glass, then turned on the TV and waited for Maggie.

She arrived late, full of apologies and excuses. She was wearing a light cotton dress and sandals, her hair pulled back haphazardly in a scrunchie. Bill got up, took her in his arms, and loosened her hair. He kissed her and began unbuttoning her dress.

They made love passionately, each hungry for the other's touch. When their desire was satisfied, Bill poured her a glass of wine and checked his watch. "Gotta go, babe," he said. "Sorry this was so quick, but it's all I can manage."

Maggie looked at him as she lay naked on the bed. For the first time things seemed tawdry - a cheap motel and a two-hour liaison with a married man who couldn't wait to get back home to his wife. She felt used. She thought about Dex's warning.

No, it's not that way. He loves me. This is all he can do for now.

As Bill headed for the shower, she put out her hand to stop him. "You know, I heard some more gossip about your wife and you know who."

Bill turned around and sat down on the bed. He took a sip of her wine. "So, spill," he said. "What's Karen been up to now that I don't know about?"

Maggie sat up, took the wine glass from him, and sipped. She was going to make him suffer a bit. As she shook out her hair and stretched, she could tell he was getting impatient.

"Well," she drawled, "rumor has it your wife went for a little boat ride with Mr. Pierce. And it wasn't a short ride. No, they were gone for several hours and when they got back, he took off with her on his Harley."

She paused, taking a sip of the wine, to let the rumors sink in. "And, when he came back to the yard, without her, he retrieved a cooler from his boat. So, one would have to surmise they caught some fish, among other things."

Bill thought about those fresh fillets he'd found in the refrigerator and Karen's story that she'd gotten them on sale at the farmers' market. It didn't ring true to him at the time - that fish was much too fresh for a market sale.

So, she lied to me, again, he thought. Turning his attention back to Maggie, he smiled. "Is that it?"

"Yeah, that's all I know. Wasn't anyone else on that boat but her and him so I guess they're the only ones who know the whole story. But think - if it was all innocent, why didn't she tell you about it?"

Bill didn't answer, just stared off into space, thinking. He still didn't believe Karen would cheat. He was the only man she'd ever been with, of that he was sure. And, with the way she felt about marriage given her parents' divorce, well, he just didn't think she could live with herself if she went that route. No, she might be having a flirtation, but a full-blown affair, no way.

"Thanks," he said. "You let me know if you hear or see anything else. Now, I gotta get going!"

He leaned forward and gave her a quick kiss on her forehead and headed to the bathroom.

Maggie sipped her wine, in no hurry to leave. She hoped she'd driven, or begun to drive, a wedge between Bill and his wife. She was sure she had planted a seed of doubt, and she was hopeful it would grow. She wanted Bill to confront his wife and let her go back to California with those little girls. Then, she would have him and they would live together in that house on the hill. Yes, it was not just the man she coveted, but also the house. She had always loved it, wanted it, and now, yes, now it was within her grasp.

Bill came out of the bathroom, got dressed, and sat down beside her. "Stay as long as you like," he said, indicating the key on the nightstand. "It's paid for through the night."

He blew her a kiss then headed out the door.

She poured herself some more wine. *Yes, it's going to happen this time. I will have him and the house, too. Yes, I will.*

KAREN

Tuesday morning, Karen called Louise to ask if she knew anyone who could babysit the girls that weekend. Louise suggested her niece, Amy, who worked down at the boatyard. After she hung up, Karen decided to head down to the yard to talk to Amy in person about Saturday. She knew she could probably take care of things with a phone call, but there was always the chance she might bump into Dex and that she wouldn't mind at all.

When she got to the yard, it looked deserted. Disappointed, she went into the store where she found Amy behind the counter, making coffee. Karen bought a cup and engaged the girl in conversation about Saturday. Amy was happy to have the job. She told Karen she was saving for college and anything that could bring in extra cash was appreciated. That settled, Karen took her coffee and walked back out to her car and was surprised to find Dex leaning against the hood.

"Hey, princess, what are you doing down here this fine morning?"

Karen explained to him why she was there.

"You can't go wrong with her," he drawled. "Amy's a great little gal, very level-headed and responsible. She'll take good care of your little ones. Now, to change the subject, how about you, what have you got planned for the day?"

Karen shrugged. "Not much. Same old, same old - clean the house, work in the garden. Nothing exciting."

"Well, how about I change that? How would you like to go for a sightseeing ride, this time on the boat? No fishing today, just a tour of the island from the sea."

She thought for a minute. Getting back on that boat with him could be dangerous, but she wanted to, so she smiled and nodded. "That sounds like fun. Am I dressed okay?"

He looked her over. She could be wearing sackcloth and ashes and still look gorgeous. However, what she had on, jeans, sweatshirt, and topsiders, was fine for what he had in mind.

"You look great. If it gets chilly or wet, I have sweaters and slickers on board. Come on." He took her hand and led her to his punt and they motored out to his mooring. As she climbed aboard the boat, Karen felt a strong wave of emotion wash over her, remembering the passionate kiss they had shared. The emotion was so intense, she wavered and thought she might fall. Dex saw her movement and quickly reached out to steady her, practically lifting her into the boat.

"You okay, princess?" he asked, watching her closely.

"Yeah, I'm fine now. Just felt a little off-balance for a second. Thanks for keeping me from falling."

Dex laughed. "That's what I'm here for. I'm your knight, remember?"

Karen laughed and walked over to the rail to watch him get the boat ready to head out to sea.

They rode around the island, Dex pointing out different houses and beaches and other points of interest. Karen found it fascinating to see the same places she'd seen from the road from the opposite view. She was surprised to see how imposing her own house looked from the sea.

The morning rapidly disappeared and Dex suggested lunch at an inn on a neighboring island. His description of the place sounded wonderful and, having not eaten much for breakfast, Karen agreed. Dex got on the radio to the inn, made reservations for a table on the porch, and secured a mooring number. He told them the "Polly Ann" would be there in about twenty minutes and to have the launch ready to pick them up.

"Who was Polly Ann?" Karen asked, referring to the name of his boat.

"Polly Ann was my mother. This was my dad's boat. He lobstered with it. After they died, I fixed the boat up and converted it for fishing."

"Why didn't you follow in his footsteps and be a lobsterman?"

"Never could stand setting and pulling all those traps," he said, shaking his head. "I worked summers with my dad on the boat and I just didn't enjoy it. And you gotta enjoy what you do, you know, otherwise it's not worth it. Life's too short and all that stuff."

They were soon approaching another island. Dex pointed out an impressive building on a hill in front of them and indicated to her that was where they were going. He moored the boat and in a couple of minutes, a launch from the inn came by to pick them up.

Once inside the restaurant, they were seated at a table on a screened-in porch overlooking the bay. The view was wonderful. When the waitress brought menus, she called Dex by name, so Karen surmised he was a frequent guest here. Dex took Karen's menu from her hand.

"Will you trust me to do this?" he asked, indicating the ordering of lunch.

Karen nodded and when the waitress returned, Dex took over.

"Okay, we'll start with the steamed mussels, then the Caesar salad and the pan-seared Casco Bay scallops. And we'll have a bottle of the Pinot Gris to go with, well chilled. That work for you, princess?"

"Sounds wonderful," she said unfolding her napkin and putting it in her lap.

The waitress brought the wine in an ice bucket and left the bottle and two glasses on the table. Dex tasted the wine and then poured a glass for Karen. As they sipped their drinks, they talked, conversation coming easily, as if they had known each other for a lifetime. Their food came and they both dug in, Karen amazed at how good it all was. Their main course finished, the waitress approached them with dessert menus.

"This is my pick," said Karen, looking at the menu. "We'll split the crème brulee."

Dex nodded, "Just perfect. I would have picked the same."

When dessert was finished, Karen excused herself to go to the ladies' room. She had felt her cell vibrating halfway through the meal, and, assuming it was Bill, did not want to answer it in front of Dex.

It's like I want to keep them in separate compartments, she thought. She checked the phone and found she was right. It was a text from Bill.

> *Coming home early. Be on the 2:30 boat.*
> *Will catch a ride home.*
> *Luv u, B.*

Oh Christ, she thought as she checked her watch. *He'll be home by three and it's two-fifteen already. How will I explain this?*

She rushed back over to the table. "We have to go now, Dex, now," she said, urgency apparent in her voice. "Bill's coming home early; he'll be on the two-thirty boat."

Dex saw her distress and signaled to the waitress, who rushed over.

"Listen," he said, "we have an emergency and have to leave right away. Can you put this on my tab and signal the launch that we're coming?"

"No problem, Mr. Pierce," she replied and rushed off to do his bidding.

"And put twenty on that tab for you, sweetheart," Dex called after her.

She turned briefly, smiled, and nodded at him.

The launch was ready for them when they got to the wharf and took them out to the "Polly Ann." Once aboard, Dex untied the boat from the mooring and took them out to sea.

Karen stood next to him in the wheelhouse. "Seems you're a regular at that inn. You go there often?"

"Well, I can get pretty sick of my own cooking," he answered. "So, I like to go there for dinner at least once a week."

"I bet all the ladies you take out enjoy that."

As soon as those words tumbled out of her mouth, Karen felt a blush starting. *What the heck am I doing?* she thought. *Am I fishing to find out if he's dating someone? Oh, lord, what will he think of me?*

Dex stared straight ahead. "Well, princess, you're about the only member of the opposite sex I've been with lately. Shows you the sorry state of my love life, but I wouldn't change it, hell no, not for the world."

He glanced at her out of the corner of his eye. She was looking out to sea so he could not see her face, but he saw her shoulders relax ever so slightly as she leaned into the rail and he took that for a sign that his words pleased her. He smiled to himself.

"We're almost there. I'll bring the boat up to the wharf. You can jump off and head home."

Karen nodded and did as he instructed. She started to jog toward her car then hesitated and turned. Dex was standing in the boat watching her. She raised her arm, pointed at him, and mouthed one word: "You." Then she smiled her brightest smile, turned again, and ran toward her car.

BILL & KAREN

Karen arrived home about ten minutes before she expected Bill. She dashed upstairs and quickly assessed her appearance. Her hair was windblown and her cheeks and nose were sun burnt.

Easy enough to explain, she thought.

She brushed her teeth and used mouthwash to try to eliminate the smell of garlic and alcohol from the meal. She combed out her hair and rushed back down to the kitchen and started to clean up the breakfast dishes.

That was how Bill found her when he got home, at the kitchen sink washing dishes - completely ordinary. He walked in and came up behind her, giving her a quick kiss on the back of her neck.

"Hi, hon, it's nice to get home early for a change. How was your day?"

She turned and smiled at him. "It was good. I worked outside. Got a little sunburn."

Bill watched her, thinking about what Maggie'd said, and thought he'd try something to see how she would react.

"Hey, I had an idea on the way home. Maybe we could charter a boat and take Gerry and Sam out fishing someday. Maybe that Dex character from the dance could take us out. As I recall, he has a fishing boat."

At the mention of Dex's name, Karen's hand jerked, causing the glass she was washing to slide out of her grasp, smashing into the sink. She reached down to try to catch it and came up with a nasty slice across her thumb. Bill saw the blood dripping from her hand and rushed over to her. He wrapped her thumb in a towel, propelling her to the bathroom despite her protests. He checked her hand for any pieces of glass, then made her run it under cold water while he got out the first aid kit. He gently dried her thumb and applied a bandage.

"Gosh, I'm such a klutz," laughed Karen. "Thanks for taking care of me."

Bill studied her. *She certainly reacted to my suggestion, but cheat on me? No, I don't and won't believe that. She's having a flirtation, but she hasn't betrayed me - at least not yet.*

"Well, what do you think of my idea?" he asked, probing further.

"About what?" she replied, innocently.

"About Dex and chartering his boat?"

"I don't think Dex Pierce takes charters. He's a commercial fisherman and very successful from what I hear. But there are others that do. I've seen advertisements at the boatyard."

"At the boatyard? What have you been doing at the boatyard?'

Karen was ready for the question and told him about her conversation with Louise concerning babysitting help.

"I wanted to eyeball the girl myself before making any commitments," she explained. "At the store where she works, there's a bulletin board. That's where I saw the ads about chartering."

"Okay, but how do you know so much about this Dex?"

Karen's mind raced. *Has Bill heard gossip about us? Is that why he's questioning me so closely?*

She steadied herself. "I asked Louise about him. I wanted to know something about the guy who got my husband drunk at that yahoo benefit dinner."

Bill grinned. "So I'm still paying for that?"

"Yeah, you are!" she laughed. "Now let me get back to cleaning up the kitchen before the girls get home. They're due any minute."

"Oh no. You don't put your hand in that water again. I only bandage one thumb per day. You go meet the girls and I'll finish up the dishes."

She gave him a kiss, murmured her thanks, and, breathing a sigh of relief, went outside to meet her children's bus.

KAREN & MADGE

On Wednesday, Karen called the nursing home where Madge Parker was a resident. She spoke briefly with the old woman and made a date to come out and talk to her on Friday.

When Bill got home in the evening, she informed him she would need the car, telling him she was going to visit a nursery outside of town. This was not a total lie. There was a garden center near where Mrs. Parker lived and Karen did plan to stop there after her interview. Bill told her the car was hers for the day and not to worry about him.

On Friday, after seeing the girls off to school, Karen headed into town. The nursing home was about an hour's drive north and she'd told Mrs. Parker she would be there around eleven that morning. The drive was a pleasant one and Karen enjoyed the coastal scenery. She arrived at the home on time, went inside, and asked for Mrs. Parker.

She was led to a pleasant patio that overlooked the ocean. An old woman was sitting in a wheelchair staring out at the sea. She was bundled up in a wool sweater that looked handmade and had a lovely blue afghan across her lap. Her hair was sparse, but long and silver gray and it blew softly around her face in the sea breeze. As Karen approached, she could tell Mrs. Parker had once been a lovely woman and her blue eyes, now watered down with age, still revealed a lively intelligence.

"Mrs. Parker?" Karen asked softly as she came up beside the woman.

The old woman looked up. "Ayuh, that'd be me," she replied. "And the name's Madge, none of that Mrs. Parker shit. You must be Karen."

She extended her hand and indicated for Karen to sit down beside her. "I know it's a bit chilly out here, but I just love to watch the water," she said wistfully. "Brings back memories of home. Now what is it you want to pick this old brain about, young lady?"

Karen explained that she and her family had recently moved into Jane Morgan's old house and that she was interested in finding out more about the property's history. She told Madge she had heard talk about the alleged murder of an Indian woman and her child by the first owner, Fergus Maguire, and about subsequent disappearances in the swamp behind the house. She told her what she'd found in the library about the attempts at surveying the property in nineteen thirty-three.

"I wonder if you remember anything about that surveying?" Karen asked. "Hiring three companies to report on the same piece of property doesn't make sense; at least to me, it doesn't."

Mrs. Parker nodded, "I remember that. The company that owned the house, they got it into their heads that if they filled in that swamp and cleared the land, well, they thought they could build on it and make a bundle of money. Island land was booming back then. I was about thirteen and a very curious young lady," she laughed. "I overheard my folks talking about it. The company wanted to put in a row of cottages and rent them out during the summer. They were going to turn the main house into a restaurant. But before they built anything, they needed to know if it was possible to fill in that swamp. So, they hired surveyors.

"The first one who came out was local, from the mainland. He went into those woods one morning and wasn't seen again for two days. When he came running out, his hair that was black as pitch when he went in had turned solid white! He refused to talk about what had happened in those woods - just said there was something not right about the place. He returned the company's money, saying he wanted nothing to do with anything involving that property. He passed a few years later, a fairly young man. Can't remember from what.

"After the story about the first surveyor got around, there was no one in the county who would take the commission. So, the company hired some guys from Bangor. They came down, two of them. They went into them woods and came out about an hour later, one man supporting the other who was bleeding heavily from his head. Seems an owl, largest the man had ever seen, had swooped down outta the trees and landed on the guy's head, dug in its talons, and tried to take off with him! Guess the guy was a might too heavy, so the owl let go, taking with it most of his hair. You might say the owl scalped him!"

As Madge related this, Karen shuddered, thinking about the owl that had taken her hat.

"So those guys," Madge continued, "like the first one, refused to survey the woods. By now, there was no one in the great state of Maine that was willing to take on the job, and no one in New Hampshire either! One of the company's officers was from New York and he was tired of dealing with what he called the 'New England halfwits,' so he hired a surveying firm from his hometown to come up here. Well, they arrived and went into those blasted woods with their equipment. They came out later in the day and, very quietly, packed up their stuff and left without a word to anyone. I heard my daddy say the company finally got a report from them just saying that there was no way that swamp could be drained or filled and it would be a fool's errand to try. You might try contacting that firm if you want to know more. I think they're still in business and might have that report on file somewhere. And that's about all I know about that."

When the old woman ended her tale, she looked up at Karen. "Would you mind asking the nurse for some juice for me? I'm about parched to death with all this talk."

Karen hopped up and got the woman some juice and held the cup for her as she sipped through a straw.

"Now tell me - Karen, is it?" Madge asked as Karen nodded. "What have you heard about the Mskagwdemos?"

Karen looked at her, surprised by the question. "That's the swamp hag, right?"

The old woman nodded, indicating for her to continue.

"Well, we heard a story that claimed that after that Indian woman who owned our land was murdered by Maguire she asked the

God of the Dead to make her a Mskagwdemos so she could take her revenge. Then she killed Maguire and, after that, just kept on killing. At least that's the way we were told it."

The old woman chuckled. "Oh, that old story. Not true, no, not true. Let me tell you how it really was. And I got this from my daddy who got it from his daddy and so on. First, you have to understand about that Indian woman. She wasn't an ordinary woman - she was a bruja."

Karen looked at her puzzled. "A bruja?"

"Yes, a medicine woman, a witch. It was her mandate to tend to the sacred land, your property. She did not live there - no, she lived in the woods, next to the swamp. Karen, the land your house sets on, that Fergus Maguire built on, was, and is, steeped in the mysticism of the Abenaki. The place has powerful juju."

As she spoke, she looked directly at Karen and held her hand. She gestured for more juice and Karen again helped her take a sip or two.

Clearing her throat, the old woman continued. "It was told that she performed sacred rituals on the land that sits in front of your house, every month, at the time of the waning crescent moon. You know, the waning crescent is also known as the 'old moon' and is thought to symbolize the wise and all knowing."

Karen pulled out the pictures of the etchings and showed them to Madge. "My husband found these carvings on a stone that's part of the house's foundation. Is that a waning crescent moon?"

"Ayuh, it is. See how it's curved?" replied Madge, tracing the arc with her finger. "These symbols, they're the symbols of Mateguas, God of the Dead. He's the one she performed the rituals for, made sacrifice for. See that lightning bolt, well, that represents his manhood. And the single drop of water stands for the tears he sheds for his people. Now, you heard that the bruja had a son?"

"Yes, and he was murdered by Maguire, too. Right?" replied Karen.

"Yes, that's right. But you must understand, he was no ordinary boy. You see, the bruja was a virgin when she birthed him."

"A virgin birth?" questioned Karen. "Like Jesus?"

The old woman nodded. "Yes, just like Jesus. Virgin birth myths are fairly common in most cultures and predate Christianity. Odin impregnated the Scandinavian, Frigga, and the result was Balder, the healer and savior of mankind. Dionysus, Krishna, and Buddha were all purportedly the offspring of virgins. In Native American culture, there are legends of the Great Peacemaker who was also the product of a virgin birth. Hiawatha was an acolyte of his."

Karen, impressed with the breadth of this woman's knowledge, made a note to look all this up when she got home.

"So now where was I? Oh, yes. It was told that the Indian woman had been celibate, like most mystical beings throughout history, and had never known a man in the biblical way. One night when she was performing her ritual, Mateguas threw down a lightning bolt that struck her right between her legs, in her womanhood. And with that, the boy was conceived.

"After the lightning bolt, the woman lost all the hair on her body and was never seen again without a mantle over her head. The blessed boy was born nine months to the day after the lightning hit her and the child, as he grew, well, he was special.

"Physically, he was a beautiful child, perfectly proportioned, with no visible scars or blemishes. Even as an infant, it was said his touch was magical, that it could cure the body and heal the soul. And his eyes - they were a deep brown, but with flecks of gold in them that shimmered in the sunlight. It was said that he could see into a man's soul and find the good or evil therein. In addition, after he was born, the land was blessed with amazing fertility. There was a promise in that child and it is a shame that it was not allowed to come to fruition, because then along came that awful Maguire man and everything went to hell in a hand basket."

"But what does that have to do with the Mskagwdemos?" Karen asked.

"Patience, my dear, I'm getting to that. Okay, now where was I? Oh, yes, Fergus Maguire. Well, he bribed the local government officials so he could acquire the woman's land. She tried every way she could to keep the property, to keep it for The People, the Abenaki, but the white man's law prevailed and the sacred land was lost. The Abenaki were being forced off their land all over Maine at that time so what happened here was not an uncommon occurrence. Most of The People moved to Canada, to Quebec, and that's where their descendants live today. But that bruja, she and her son didn't leave. They stayed in the woods and tried to sabotage the building efforts by setting fires, stealing tools, and the like. Finally, Maguire just got sick and tired of that woman so he and his friends went into the woods, found her, raped her, tortured her, and then killed her.

"That sweet boy had to watch and, when his momma was dead, he went to her and kissed her on the lips. It is said that at that moment, she stirred, but Fergus' men saw the movement and they dragged her deep into the swamp and held her under till she died a second time. Then, they took that sweet boy and brutalized him, if you know what I mean, an obscenity. After, they tied rocks to his hands and feet and threw him in the swamp where he, too, died."

The old woman gestured for more juice so Karen got up and brought her some, helping her sip from the straw.

"Well, as you can imagine," Madge went on, "all this did not sit well with the great Mateguas. His bruja and his son murdered, his sacred land defiled. Yes, he was good and pissed. So, HE conjured up the Mskagwdemos to take his revenge. He cursed Fergus Maguire and his sons and his sons' sons for all eternity. The Mskagwdemos lured Maguire into the swamp and he was never seen again. His kin moved off the land or that hag would have got them, too. But, seein' she's an evil being by nature, she was not content with just Fergus, so over the years she took others, innocents, or tried to take them. Nowadays, that Mskagwdemos still abides in your swamp, waiting. For what, I don't know, but she's there all right."

"But nothing's happened there in years from what I hear," said Karen. "No disappearances, no deaths."

"Last disappearance I heard tell of was about fifteen years ago," Madge replied. "A young girl, out picking berries in Janie's backyard, went into those woods. She was missing about two hours or so, but, finally, just came waltzing out on her own accord. Funny thing, though, she didn't remember anything from the time she went in to the time she came out. And that's pretty much what I know about that. I haven't thought of this stuff in years."

She gazed off into the distance for a minute or two, then turned and looked directly at Karen. "Now you been asking all the questions, girl, so I figure it's my turn. Your husband's kin to Janie Morgan, right?"

Karen nodded. "Yes, she was his aunt."

"Now, did you know Lisbeth?"

"Lisbeth?" queried Karen. "Do you mean Jane's partner, the poet?"

"Yes, Lisbeth Boucher," the old woman said. "She was ma bonne amie, both of us being French Canadian and all."

Karen looked at the woman, thinking that the name Madge Parker surely didn't seem French.

"I know what you're thinking, dearie," the old woman chuckled. "But my maiden name was Morin and I was brought up as a Marguerite, not a Madge. My family moved to the island before I was born, but we spoke French all the time at home. When I got married, I had to give up my first language and it wasn't until Lisbeth and Jane moved here that I got a chance to speak it again. Jane, now she didn't like to speak French much, but Lisbeth enjoyed her native tongue so the two of us got together often to sit and talk in the language we were brought up with."

Karen nodded politely, wondering where all this was going and what it had to do with the legends surrounding her property.

"Well," the woman continued, "Lisbeth was extremely interested in the history of the property and the stories about it. This was probably because she was part Abenaki on her mother's side. She did a lot of digging into those old tales, I can tell you that. She and Jane got along extremely well on most things, but Lisbeth's interest in the property was a sore point for Jane. She just didn't understand it.

"When they were both getting on in years and Lisbeth's cancer returned, Jane started talking about leaving the property to your husband. I have to tell you, Lisbeth was adamantly against it and it was over this decision they had their most bitter argument. Lisbeth told me she was going to write down her thoughts on this and made Jane swear to give them to your husband should she be foolish enough to actually leave the property to him. Have you seen these papers?"

"No," Karen admitted. "If Bill's seen them, I don't know, but I know I haven't. But what does that have to do with anything?"

"Patience, dear, patience," she replied. "I need some time to think on all of this. There's more I need to tell you, but I have to try to get the pieces in place first and I'm feeling a bit too tired right now to do so. Can you help me get back to my room so I can lie down for a while? After I've had time to do some ruminating, I'll give you a call and we can go further, if that's okay with you?"

"Sure," said Karen, slightly disappointed. She helped the old woman to her room and got her settled in bed.

"I know you're confused, Karen," she said, "but I really need time to think. This is all like a jigsaw puzzle. Leave your number on that pad on the bedside table. I'll call you for sure when things are straight in my mind. And you look for those papers Lisbeth left. They're important, I know."

Karen wrote down her number then leaned forward and kissed the old woman on the cheek. "Thank you again for helping me. And I'll look for those papers."

The old woman smiled and squeezed Karen's hand. "I don't get much company. My kids are all out west. They only come by about once a year. This has been a real pleasure for me, Karen."

After leaving the nursing home, Karen drove to the garden center she wanted to visit, bought a couple of plants, then headed home. On the way, she thought about all the old woman had said. She wondered how much was based in truth and how much was outright urban legend. She also wondered about the girl Madge spoke about who got lost in the woods, whether she was still on the island, and if she ever remembered what happened to her. But most of all, she thought about that owl and it scalping the surveyor. That part of the woman's story, she believed 100%. But the Boucher papers, well, she'd have to ask Bill about them.

Back in town, she parked the car and caught the next boat home, trying to put thoughts of the house and the Mskagwdemos out of her mind. As she sat on the hard wooden bench, she tried to convince herself that it was all just crap - stories, like Pete said, to keep kids from going into the woods. But she knew she was just fooling herself. She thought about the trail, the swamp, the owl, and the rabbit. Dreams? Maybe, but all too real; yes, all too real for comfort.

A NIGHT ON THE TOWN

On Saturday, Bill left on an early boat to meet Gerry for their round of golf. Karen spent the day with her daughters, exploring different parts of the island. She took them to the boatyard for lunch and they sat and watched the boats come in and out. There was no sign of Dex and, for once, she was grateful.

A little before five, Amy arrived at the house to sit the girls. Karen dressed carefully for the evening, knowing it was important to Bill's career.

"There's a casserole in the fridge," she told Amy. "Just put it in the oven at three fifty for about a half an hour. Hope you like chicken. You're not a vegetarian, are you?"

Amy laughed and assured Karen that she was not. Karen advised Amy they expected to be home around ten. Then she kissed her daughters goodbye, grabbed her coat and purse, and headed down to the ferry. Sam picked her up in town and took her to the restaurant where they would be meeting the boys.

Bill and Gerry were already there, having a drink. They were full of stories about their day on the links so the evening got off to a jocular start. They all enjoyed a fine dinner then went to a little club nearby to listen to music and enjoy an after-dinner drink. All too soon, it was time for Karen and Bill to return to the wharf to catch the last boat home. With promises all around to do it again soon, they took their leave of Gerry and Sam. When they got home, they found Amy watching television, their daughters tucked away safely in their beds.

Bill peeked in on them on his way to bed. "They're sleeping like angels," he said as he entered the bedroom.

"Yes, and I think we've found a good sitter in Amy," said Karen as she took off her shoes. "Unzip me, please?" she asked, turning her back to him. As he unzipped her dress, he slid his arms around her waist. She shrugged off the dress and turned in his embrace.

"Think we had a successful evening, don't you? Wish they would let you move to Gerry's department sooner, hon."

"Yeah, so do I," he said, pulling her closer. They kissed and slipped into bed, following patterns that were old and familiar to them both. When their lovemaking was over, Karen turned on her side, away from him, and drifted off to a dreamless sleep.

Bill, however, lay awake, unable to keep himself from comparing the gentleness of Karen with the passionate response of Maggie. He told himself again that he would end the affair, all the while knowing that he was just kidding himself. He wasn't finished with Maggie yet, not by a long shot.

Finally, he drifted off to sleep, but his slumber was not dreamless. No, his dreams were troubling and tinged with a malignancy that, if allowed to grow, had the potency to devour and destroy him.

ICE CREAM SOCIAL

The next day, the girls were helping out with an ice cream social Maggie and the other teachers were staging to benefit the school. Sophie and Terri had volunteered to dish out ice cream and apply toppings. After breakfast, Karen dropped them off at the school to help set things up. On the lawn were two tent-like structures, erected side by side. Tables had been set up to serve as a counter at the front and the coolers containing the ice cream were to be set on benches behind them. Maggie would be bringing the ice cream and toppings later, just before the event started.

Bill slept in that morning, his sleep disturbed by dreams he could not remember. He woke up feeling lousy. He tried to go back to sleep, but was unable to rest. He finally got up and shuffled downstairs.

"Well, Rip Van Winkle rises at last!" exclaimed Karen as he entered the kitchen. "You look terrible. How much did you have to drink yesterday anyway? I know about the wine and pre- and post-dinner cocktails, but did you find some of that hooch, too?"

"Don't tease, Karen," he replied testily. "I slept terribly. Had dreams, bad ones I think, but I don't remember them. Don't think I got more than two hours' real sleep all night. Where are the girls?"

"It's Sunday. Remember the school ice cream thing? They're helping set up and are going to be serving. I took them over about fifteen minutes ago. Probably was the sound of the car that woke you up. We're going to the event around noon. Here, have a cup of coffee. Maybe that will get you going."

Bill nodded as he took the cup. "I'm probably going to need more than one. And how about something to go with it? Eggs? Toast?"

Karen laughed and started to make breakfast for her husband.

By the time Bill and Karen got to the school, the event was in full swing. Most of the townspeople were there, lining up for sundaes. Others were sitting at picnic tables talking and enjoying the companionship of their friends and family. Karen looked over to where the girls were scooping out ice cream and caught sight of Maggie.

"Good lord!" she exclaimed under her breath to Bill. "Look at what's teaching our children!"

Bill turned to see what Karen was talking about. Maggie was wearing short cut-off blue jeans and a pink tank top. It was obvious she was braless, her nipples showing through the thin material. On her feet, she wore flip-flops, with toenails painted a bright pink. Bill felt himself stir at the sight of her and he quickly looked back at his wife.

"Come on, Karen, lighten up. She's just a kid herself; they all dress like that now."

"Well," Karen responded, "I'm surprised she doesn't have a tattoo showing and I bet she's pierced you know where!"

Bill laughed and Maggie looked up. When she caught sight of him, she very lightly flicked out her tongue to lick her upper lip and then smiled knowingly. Bill frowned and shook his head slightly, indicating for her to cut it out before looking away, back at Karen.

"Look, hon," he said, trying to divert her attention from Maggie, "there's Pete and Louise. Let's go join them."

Bill guided Karen over to their friends. They chatted for a bit then Bill and Karen got in line for ice cream, promising to come back after they were served. When they reached the counter, Terri took over, trying to act professional.

"What can I get for you?" she asked her mother, trying hard not to laugh. Sophie was already breaking up, unable to contain herself.

"Mmmmmm, what do you recommend, young lady?" Karen responded.

"I think you should have chocolate and strawberry with sprinkles and whipped cream!" exclaimed Terri.

"Well, Terri-bug," said Karen, laughing, "then that's what I'll have, but don't make them big scoops!"

Terri scooped the ice cream while Sophie applied the toppings. Bill ordered the same, and, as the sundaes were being made, sauntered down to where Maggie sat at the cashbox.

"How much for two sundaes?"

Maggie smiled. "It's five dollars each. I know it's a bit steep, but it's for the school."

Bill pulled out a twenty and handed it to her. When she reached for it, she lightly brushed his fingertips with hers. He cocked his head, signaling her to look down. She glanced at the bill he had just given her and saw he had written one word on the end: "Tuesday?" Smiling, she gave him a brief nod as she placed the bill in the cashbox.

"Keep the change," he said.

As he spoke, Karen joined him, handing him his sundae. She exchanged brief pleasantries with Maggie, then walked with her husband back to where Pete and Louise were sitting. As they neared the table, a truck pulled into the parking lot catching Karen's eye. It was Dex's. She took a bite of her ice cream watching as he and a young man emerged from the vehicle. They had on work clothes and she guessed they were on a break.

Dex saw her, said something to his friend, and began to stroll toward the table where she sat.

Bill, noticing Karen's attention had been diverted over to the parking lot, glanced that way to see what had captured her interest. When he recognized Dex ambling in their direction, a pang of jealousy hit him in the gut. Trying to shake it off, he noted that Karen, while taking a bite of her sundae, had left a dab of whipped cream on her nose. Knowing Dex was watching, he leaned over and lightly licked it off.

243

"You got a little sweet on your nose, hon," he said by way of explanation when she pulled back, startled.

Blushing, she frowned at him. "Bill, please."

Another islander also noted with interest Dex's arrival at the social. Maggie smiled to herself as she watched him approach Karen and Bill.

This could be interesting, she thought. *Dex just better not do or say anything about me.*

Dex had a wicked grin on his face as he walked up to Bill and Karen.

"Hey, bro," he said, proffering his hand to Bill. "What's shaking? All this sweet stuff can cause a man to develop a mighty thirst! Can I interest you in...?"

Bill stood up and shook his hand, laughing. "Just enjoying some ice cream with my wife. Nothing stronger this afternoon, so don't you try to tempt me! She's still making me pay for the last time!"

Dex laughed at Bill's reference to the hooch. Then he turned to Karen. "Now, talking about sweet stuff, how are you this afternoon, princess?"

Karen felt a blush begin to spread on her cheeks. Trying to hide her embarrassment and anger, she took another spoonful of ice cream and looked up at him.

"I'm fine, thank you," she said stiffly. Then she turned to Bill. "I think I'll go over and see how the girls are doing."

As she walked away, she looked back over her shoulder. "Nice to see you again, Dex."

He smiled at her and turned his attention back to Bill. They engaged in small talk for a few minutes, then he excused himself to go get some ice cream.

At the counter, Dex chatted with Maggie and teased the girls, all the while keeping one eye on Karen, who was tossing the remains of her sundae in the trash barrel.

Back at the picnic table, Bill kept watch on both of them. He'd noticed Karen's blush when Dex called her "princess" and wondered if that was a pet name he had for her. Grudgingly, he admitted to himself that there might be more going on between the two of than a mere flirtation. Yet, he still couldn't make himself believe it. She wouldn't cheat on him. He watched Dex stop and chat with Maggie and wondered if they had some sort of romantic history, too.

Trying to keep from being consumed by suspicion and jealousy, he walked over to his wife, who was standing alone by the trash barrel. He put his arm around her and whispered in her ear. She nodded and walked over to Terri. Bill went in the opposite direction, toward the parking lot.

"Hey, Terri-bug," she said. "Dad and I are going home now. I'll be back to pick the two of you up at four. If you want to come home sooner, you call me on the cell. Okay?"

Terri nodded, gave her mom a quick kiss, and went back to scooping ice cream. When Karen turned around to go, she almost bumped into Dex, who was standing close behind her.

"Sorry about calling you 'princess,' Karen, but I just couldn't help myself," he said contritely, taking her hand in his. "Hope you won't hold that against old Dex."

He smiled down at her, clasping her hand tightly in his.

Karen laughed, her irritation dissolving at his touch, and gave his hand a slight squeeze. "I won't," she whispered. "I've got to go now. See you soon?"

"Anytime you want, princess. Your wish is my command," he replied with longing in his eyes.

She nodded, still smiling, and gave his hand one last squeeze before dropping it and moving away from him, toward the parking lot to wait for her husband.

Maggie watched the exchange and the handholding. *Something is definitely going on there,* she thought. *Whether or not they've done the 'deed' is irrelevant. There is for sure sexual tension between them. I'll have to probe Dex again, try to find out how far they've gone, and talk to Amy down at the boatyard. She might have seen something. Yes, Dex and that woman have something going on for sure. Wait'll I tell Bill about it!*

When Bill and Karen got home, he noted there was a message on their answering machine. He listened, jotting it down and then called to his wife.

"Hon, someone named Madge Parker called for you. Said she had remembered something and you were to come by anytime, not to worry about calling back, that she wasn't going anywhere. Just to come by when you can. What's that all about?"

Karen thought quickly. For reasons she couldn't fathom, she wasn't ready to share what she'd found out about the property with Bill.

"Oh, she's from that garden supply center I went to last week. She was getting some information for me. Think I'll run down there again on Friday, if the car's available."

"It's always yours on Friday, hon," he replied, coming up behind her and putting his arms around her and nuzzling her neck.

She pulled away. "Bill, not now. I just ate a huge ice cream sundae and I feel anything but sexy."

"Well, you look pretty damn hot to me and I think you looked hot to Dex, too. I don't know if I like the way he looks at you - sorta like he's ready to eat you up."

Karen forced a laugh. "Oh, he's probably just trying to make an old married lady feel good. More than likely he's got the hots for your braless girlfriend in the pink tank!"

Bill started at the word "girlfriend."

"Oh, come on now," he protested. "Why are you calling our daughters' teacher my girlfriend?"

"Well, she sure stares at you a lot. If she keeps it up, I just might have to call her out on it!"

They both laughed as if it was a joke, but in the back of Karen's mind, she knew it wasn't. Maggie did look at Bill hungrily, blatant desire and longing on her face. Maybe he didn't see it, but she did and she didn't like it. She knew, despite whatever it was that was going on between her and Dex, she was still committed to her marriage and family and wasn't about to let any sexy young girl break it up. No, she assured herself, she would keep her eye on Ms. Maguire and her husband - that was for sure.

RABBIT TIME AGAIN

On Monday morning, Bill laid out for Karen his work plans for the week. He told her he thought he would need to stay in town for a dinner meeting on Tuesday, but it wouldn't be overnight. As he left for the ferry, he told her he would firm up the meeting and let her know for sure that evening. He kissed her lightly and headed off for work.

After cleaning up the breakfast dishes and straightening the house, Karen decided it was time for her to venture into the gardens out back. She'd been avoiding them ever since her last experience there and the near-drowning episode that followed it. She told herself there was nothing to fear and that, if she was afraid, it would be healthier to face her fear than to cower away from it. Decision made, she changed into a pair of old shorts and a T-shirt, put on a gardening hat, and headed out to the garage to get her basket of tools.

When she reached the raised beds, she was amazed. Her tomatoes already had blossoms and some of them had the beginnings of fruit. Her peppers were the same and the squash was adorned with large yellow flowers. The lettuce was ready to pick and she saw cucumbers growing on the vines that wound around the periphery of the garden.

Everything's too early, she thought, puzzled. *The weather hasn't been that good.*

As she began weeding, she remembered Madge Parker's words about the son of the Indian woman, *"...after he was born, the land was blessed with amazing fertility,"* and about the property itself, *"The place has powerful juju."* She wondered about this as she worked, hoping Madge could shed some more light on things when she visited her on Friday.

The sun was hot and Karen soon wished she had brought a bottle of water with her to the yard. Her back was feeling cramped from bending over so she straightened up and stretched out her arms. When she did, she had the awful sensation she was not alone.

Her mind quavered. *Oh no, not again!*

Reluctantly, she turned around, a shockwave passing through her body. The lawn behind her was covered - literally covered - with rabbits chewing on the grass, apparently oblivious to her presence. She had a flash memory about an old horror movie in which hoards of giant rodents terrorized the earth. Beginning to feel afraid, she started to rise, hoping to make her way back to the safety of the house.

As if sensing her movement, all the rabbits suddenly turned, rose up on their hind legs, and stared at her. She froze in place as she watched the rabbits on the lawn before her. Then, to her amazement, they all smiled.

Transfixed by the scene unfolding in front of her, Karen stood rigid. Crows began their horrible screeching in the trees above and the sound caused her fear to intensify.

Seemingly out of nowhere, a large owl swooped down at her, its talons brushing the top of her head, knocking her hat off. Instinctively, she ducked down, covering her head with her arms. As she cowered, another owl swooped at her, and another, and another. She could feel the air move from the beating of their wings as they dove at her repeatedly, just missing her head with their vicious talons.

Seemingly unaware of the onslaught of the owls, the rabbits continued to stand upright, staring at her, their faces contorted in hideous grins. Karen tried to scream, to yell for help, but there was no one to hear. She pressed her body tightly to the ground in an attempt to get away from the owls, but they were coming closer and closer. The sheer horror she was experiencing paralyzed her as the attack continued.

Her mind began to scream silently as her body involuntarily curled tightly into fetal position. *Oh God, why is this happening to me? Won't someone help me?*

Another owl came at her head and, as it swooped down low, she could take it no longer and, feeling powerless, lost consciousness.

While Karen was being attacked in the yard, Dex was coming in from a morning's fishing. He'd had a good day and the cooler on his boat held not one, but two bluefins.

Smiling to himself, he hopped on his bike to go get some lunch. Motoring down the narrow road toward the island market, he decided to stop by Karen's and see what she was up to. As he approached the house, which seemed strangely quiet, he felt a strong sense of foreboding. Hopping off his bike, he ran up the steps. Alarmed to find the front door unlocked, he raced from room to room calling her name, but the house was empty.

Back outside, he thought about going down to the beach, but, somehow, knew she wasn't there. Then in a flash, it dawned on him.

The woods, those damned woods!

He ran around to the back of the house, praying he would find her perfectly okay, hoping he would have to swallow his pride and look foolish in front of her.

But his hopes were dashed when he saw her crumpled form by the raised bed. He sprinted over to her, taking her in his arms. She was unconscious, a thin line of spittle dripping from the corner of her mouth. He held her close, murmuring her name repeatedly, willing her to wake up. Finally, her eyes fluttered open and she looked at him, pupils dilated and unfocused.

A seizure, he thought. *She's been having seizures. That's what this has been all about.*

Gently, he lifted her, carried her to the house, and laid her down on the couch, cradling her in his lap. He felt relieved when she began to come around, her eyes beginning to focus. When she seemed to be able to comprehend that he was there, she threw her arms around him, burying her face in his chest. He held her close, trying to comfort her.

After a few minutes, she pulled back a little, coughing. Dex started to get up to get her some water, but she stopped him.

"Don't leave me," she cried. "Don't!"

"Never, princess," he said gently. "But I think you could use a glass of water. I'm not going far. I'll be right back."

She let him get up and he went into the kitchen and filled a glass with cold water from the tap. When he returned to her, she drank it down greedily.

"Go easy, girl," he said. "There's always more where that came from."

He took the glass from her, refilled it, and then sat down beside her.

After she drank, he took her hands in his and willed her to look at him. "Princess," he said slowly, "it looks to me like you might have had a seizure out there. When I was in med school, I did some reading in Neurology, and, well, that would explain all the things that have been happening to you."

Karen started to object, but he silenced her. "Now seizures are nothing to laugh about. They're serious stuff. I have a friend, a doctor, who I knew in school. He's a Fellow in Neurology here at the hospital in town. He's an excellent physician and a good guy. I want to call him and make an appointment for you, get you in there to have a CAT scan and all the other appropriate tests to rule out any kind of lesion, aneurysm, or tumor that might be causing this. You know I'm right, princess. You can't go on like this, not knowing. I know I can't. Do I have your permission to make the call?"

She knew he was right. If there was an organic cause to all this, she had an obligation to her children to find out what it was. In her heart, she didn't really believe there was anything physically wrong with her, but she knew she had to go through the motions anyway.

"Okay," she said, "on one condition. Bill doesn't know. I don't want him to know unless they find something. It will have to be our secret. Agreed?"

Dex nodded as he pulled out his cell and left the room to make the call. She could hear him talking to someone but couldn't make out the words. He was gone about fifteen minutes then returned to her, putting his cell away.

"You have an appointment tomorrow, at one," he said. "I'll take you over. They don't want you driving. Okay?"

"That was fast," she replied amazed. "Guess you really do have connections. And, yeah, it's okay."

She started to get up, but sat right back down, feeling a little dizzy.

"When did you last eat?" Dex asked, as he helped her back down on the couch.

"I had some toast for breakfast."

Dex checked his watch; it was going on two. "Let me get you something. You just rest and leave things to me."

He found some broth in the kitchen cabinet and put it on the stove to heat before adding some fresh herbs and a can of diced tomatoes. He pulled some scallions and a half of a zucchini from the fridge, chopped them up, and added them to the soup. When the concoction was heated through, he added the juice from a fresh lime and cilantro, and poured it into a bowl. On top, he crushed some tortilla chips and sprinkled some jack cheese. He brought the finished product to Karen, who was now sitting up and looking better, some color back in her face. He handed her the bowl, warning her to be careful. It was hot.

She took a sip. "My goodness," she laughed. "This is delicious. You never cease to amaze me, sir knight!"

Dex laughed, glad to see her feeling better. "No big deal. Just a quick, fresh soup I picked up on the Internet. Nothing magical."

When she finished, it was her turn to look at her watch. "The girls will be home soon. I think I need to freshen up before they get here. Take a shower."

Dex nodded. "You sure you're going to be okay if I leave you?"

"I'm okay now. I don't know what I would have done without you. How did you know I needed help?"

"I don't know," he said, his puzzlement showing. "But I just knew you were in trouble. Maybe we're like Lassie and Timmy - you're Timmy and I'm the old dog who's always rescuing you. But, of course, you're much better looking than Timmy ever was!"

Karen laughed as she stood up.

"I'll pick you up at noon tomorrow, okay?" he said, preparing to leave. "We'll go over in my punt and I'll drive you to the hospital."

An anxious look appeared on Karen's face. Dex smiled at her. "It's going to be okay, princess," he said, taking her hand in his. "You'll like Josh and he's the best there is, medically speaking. We'll get you straightened out. Don't worry, I'm not going to let anything bad happen to you, ever!"

She nodded as he leaned forward and kissed her on the cheek. Then he turned and left the house.

Karen picked up her soup bowl and put it in the sink. She went upstairs and turned on the shower and stripped off her clothing and stepped in. The hot water felt wonderful. As she washed, she thought about what had happened, about the rabbits and the owls. The owls threatened her, but somehow, they seemed unable to touch her, to cause her physical harm. And the rabbits, the smiling rabbits; what did they mean? Was she having seizures? She didn't think so. No, this was something else entirely.

She remembered Madge Parker's words again, *"The land your house is on, that Fergus Maguire built on, was, and is, steeped in the mysticism of the Abenaki."*

She nodded as she stepped out of the shower. *Yes, I'll go through the motions tomorrow, allow myself to be poked, prodded, and scanned. But they won't find anything. No, this is nothing physical - nothing you can fix with a pill or a good diet. This is something else and I have to find out what it is. My family, my life -yes, everything I care about depends upon it.*

HOSPITAL TIME

The next morning, after Karen cleared the kitchen table she turned to Bill. "Why don't you take the car today, hon. I have nothing planned and I'm not going to need it."

"You're sure? Remember I'm going to be home late. I don't want to inconvenience you."

Karen smiled. "It's okay. I'll be fine."

Bill examined her closely. She looked pale and tired. "Okay, Kar. You take it easy today. You're looking a little off. Stay out of the sun and get some rest."

She nodded. "You worry too much. I'm fine. Now you have a good day and drive carefully."

He gave her a lingering kiss, and left for the ferry. After he was gone, she walked her daughters to the bus.

"Girls, I might not be here when you get home this afternoon. I have an appointment in town. Terri, you have the cell and here's a key to the house. I'll call you when I know for sure when I'll be back. And, girls, this is a secret. I'm doing something special for Daddy and I want it to be a surprise. Okay?"

The girls nodded as Terri carefully pocketed the key and got on the bus.

Alone, Karen dressed carefully for town. Dex picked her up at noon and they headed to the boatyard where his punt was tied up at the wharf. He motored them over to the mainland and drove to the hospital. They arrived early, which was good since there were so many forms to fill out. Soon, a nurse came to get her.

"Dr. Rosen has ordered an EEG, some blood work, and a CT of your brain, Mrs. Andersen," the nurse informed her as she gave Karen a smock to put on. "The doctor will be with you in a minute."

Karen changed and read a magazine as she waited. In a few minutes, there was a soft rap on the door to the exam room. "Come in," she said.

A nice looking man of medium build entered the exam room. He was about thirty-five years old, clean-shaven, with sandy brown hair.

"Hi," he said. "I'm Josh Rosen, Mrs. Andersen. Or can I call you Karen?"

"Karen's fine," she replied, smiling, "as long as I can call you Josh."

The doctor laughed and nodded. "Okay, Karen. Now Dex has told me a bit about what's been going on with you. But, why don't you tell me in your own words?"

Karen took a deep breath and began to describe for him some of her "experiences" and their aftermath.

"Do you ever have any strange olfactory responses? I mean, do you ever smell something odd just before one of these experiences begins?"

Karen shook her head. "No, mainly it's just the visual, the rabbits and the owls. Sometimes there's an odor of rot and decay, but I smell it during the experience, not before."

"Well, it's unusual, but the brain is a complex organ," he said, putting her chart down. "Okay, let's see if we can find out what's happening to you. First, we're going to need a little blood to rule out any abnormalities in your glucose, sodium, calcium, or magnesium levels. We're also going to check out your thyroid for anything out of whack there. Then, we're going to perform an EEG - that's a brainwave study, and, finally the pièce de la résistance, a CT of your brain. The CT will show us if there are any brain lesions, tumors, or vascular abnormalities that might be causing you to seize. Hopefully, these studies will give us a good picture of what's going on and then we can fix it. You ready?"

Karen nodded and the doctor called the nurse back into the room to draw blood.

"I'll see you again when you get down to CT," said Dr. Rosen as he shook her hand and left the room.

Josh Rosen checked in with his office, then walked down the hall to the waiting room to find Dex.

"She's getting blood work, an EEG, and a CT," he told his friend. "Pretty weird stuff, rabbits and owls. Never heard anything like that before. What's your interest anyway? She's got a husband, right?"

Dex nodded. "She's a friend and I like her. You just see she gets the best."

"I will," the doctor responded. "You know this might not have an organic cause. It doesn't fit any of the usual scenarios. You might be looking at something psychogenic. Have you thought about that?"

Dex nodded again. "Her husband's having an affair. I don't think she knows it on a conscious level, but maybe, her subconscious knows and is playing tricks on her. I've thought about it."

"You seem awfully involved for just a friend," Josh replied, watching Dex closely, sensing that he held strong feelings for this woman. "Come on, I'll buy you a cup of coffee and we can catch up. Karen is going to be tied up for a while. They'll page me when she's in CT."

They went to the cafeteria and got coffee. Sitting at a corner table, Josh gently questioned his friend, trying to assess the depth of feeling he had for Karen. He was surprised at what he intuited. He'd known Dex for years and there had never really been what he would call a serious girlfriend, one that Dex wanted to spend his life with. Oh, there had been lots of girls, but none that really stuck. This woman, Josh could tell, had stuck. Yes, he could see that she had a hold on Dex's heart and was not going to let go. He worried for his friend.

"You know," he said, "affair or no affair, he's still her husband with whatever baggage comes with that. How do you know about it anyway?"

"It's with a friend of mine on the island," Dex replied.

Josh laughed. "That inbred little island of yours again! You know you're still young, my friend. Go back to med school. Leave that place. You know my sister still has the hots for you. I wouldn't be surprised if she'd support you if you moved to Boston. But then, where would I get my sashimi-grade tuna? No, on second thought, stay on that island!"

Dex laughed. "And you got some coming your way next week for helping me out here, bro. My way of saying thanks."

Josh clapped Dex on the back then leaned back in his chair, serious again. "You know, that husband of hers might not just want to slip quietly away into that good night if we find something organic wrong with her. He might just step up and take care of her."

"Yeah, I know," Dex said. "And if that's what she wants, then that's what I want, too. I just want the best for her. If that should include me, well, that'd be the frosting, you know."

"Well, bro," said Josh, "I'm hoping for a simple, small benign tumor that could be excised by an intern or a tiny aneurysm that can be lased. Anything else and you're talking trouble and that includes not finding anything. The psychogenic route is a tricky one and can be worse than a malignancy in my book."

As he spoke, his pager went off. He pulled it out and looked at it. "That's CT," he said. "Gotta go." Josh shook Dex's hand and walked swiftly away. Dex remained seated, his hands around his coffee cup, silently praying it was something benign, something fixable, and that he would not lose her.

BILL

At the same time Karen was being wheeled into the CT machine, Bill had his fingers in Maggie's panties on a secluded section of beach about an hour from town. Sensing he couldn't go the cheap motel route again so soon, he'd invited her out for an early dinner at a place by the shore. On the way to the restaurant, they stopped and walked along the beach until they came to an indentation in the rocks where they could satisfy their hunger for one another, unobserved. Later, when they arrived at the restaurant, they sat in a corner booth and ordered tequila shooters with beers back.

As they waited for their order, Bill talked about his job and his hopes to move into R&D before winter came. He was excited about his prospects and shared his enthusiasm with her. She gave him her undivided attention, happy that he was confiding in her. When the drinks arrived, they tossed the shooters back and then sipped their beers.

"Okay, enough about me," he said. "Any new gossip about my wife and that fisherman?"

Maggie, relishing the chance to tell him what she'd seen, smiled. "You asked me to keep my eyes open, you know, and I did. I saw something on Sunday at the ice cream social that I think you should know about."

Bill was puzzled. He'd been at the event and he'd seen nothing to be worried about. Dex was somewhat familiar with Karen, the way he talked and looked at her, but that was his modus operandi. He was known to be an outrageous flirt. There was the way he called her 'princess' and Karen's reaction to it, but Bill had convinced himself that this was just more flirting, nothing serious.

"Go on," he said curious as to what Maggie had seen.

"Well, it was right after you left to get the car. I saw them together, talking. They were standing real close to each other, closer than most people would. I couldn't make out what they were saying, but it looked intimate. Then, he took her hand in his and held it kinda tight. They talked a little more; she was smiling at him and I saw her squeeze his hand a couple of times and nod."

As she spoke, she leaned across the table and took Bill's hand in hers, trying to convey her sympathy and concern, but he seemed unaware of her touch.

Maybe it is true, he thought. *Maybe Karen is cheating on me.* He recalled how she reacted to his romantic overtures when they'd returned home after the social. *She pulled away, rejecting me.*

His mind flashed to a picture of Karen and Dex together, intimately, and the thought made him physically ill. He pulled his hand out of Maggie's grasp abruptly, excused himself, and went to the men's room. The shooter and beer were churning in his stomach and he leaned over the toilet, retching violently.

Pull yourself together, he told himself as he rinsed out his mouth and splashed water on his face. *There's probably nothing going on. You know Karen. She wouldn't. Maggie's probably embellishing.*

He checked his appearance in the bathroom mirror then went back to the restaurant.

"Are you okay?" Maggie asked when he sat down.

"Yeah, I'm fine and I'm hungry," he answered, looking at the menu. "Let's get this show on the road and order."

KAREN

Karen's head was in the CT machine when Dr. Rosen entered the room. He indicated for her to stay still and walked over to speak with the technician and watch the screen. When the exam was over and Karen had been wheeled out of the machine, he helped her up.

"I had the blood work done stat and it all looks fine. The EEG and CT will be read this afternoon. I should have the results by this evening. Do you want me to call you at home?"

Karen nodded and gave him her cell number.

"Well, that's about it then for today," he said. "Take it easy, and no driving or using any heavy machinery till the results are in, okay?"

Again, Karen nodded.

"It's been a pleasure meeting you," he said, shaking her hand. "Wish it could have been under more pleasant circumstances, but don't worry, we'll get you sorted out. And you take care of that buddy of mine and remind him about the sashimi he owes me!"

Karen looked at him quizzically, "Sashimi?"

Josh laughed. "He'll explain it to you. And if we find anything, don't worry; I'm good at what I do."

He turned her over to the nurse, who escorted her back to the exam room to change back into her street clothes.

When she was dressed, she joined Dex in the waiting room. It was three-thirty and she sent her daughters a text, telling them she'd be late, to start their homework, and, if she wasn't there by five, to help themselves to some milk and cookies. There were no messages from Bill, so she assumed he would still be home late.

Knowing she was anxious to get back to the island, Dex took her straight to the wharf, helped her onto the punt, and motored off. They arrived at the wharf a little before five.

At her request, Dex parked his truck at the end of her driveway. Before she got out, she turned to him. "Thanks for your help today. I don't know how I would have done it without you."

"Josh going to call you tonight?"

"Yes, when he gets the results."

"Will you call me? Let me know?" he asked, trying to keep the emotion and fear he was feeling out of his voice.

She handed him her cell. "Put your contact info in there and, yes, of course, I'll call you. After me, you'll be the first to know."

She leaned toward him and kissed him lightly on the cheek.

He took her hand and squeezed. "It's going to be all right," he said. "It has to be."

BILL & KAREN & DEX & MAGGIE

Bill and Maggie finished their dinner in silence. He had lost his appetite for her the moment she told him about Dex and Karen. He just wanted to get home. When dinner was over, he hurriedly paid the check and escorted her to the car. Once inside, he checked his watch - it was a long drive, but if he hurried, he could still make it home before his daughters were in bed.

They drove in silence, each lost in their own thoughts.

When they arrived at the pier, Bill helped her into her punt and she motored them back to Mateguas.

"I'm sorry about this evening," he said as he helped her tie up the boat at the wharf. "I know I wasn't the best company at dinner. I'll make it up to you."

"It's okay," she replied. "I guess I shouldn't have stuck my nose in where it didn't belong. If anyone should be sorry, it's me. You did nothing wrong."

Bill smiled and gave her a quick peck on the cheek then jogged to his car, anxious to get away from her and home to his family.

On the island, Karen was getting her children ready for bed when her cell rang. She checked the caller ID - it was Josh Rosen. She took a deep breath, hesitating slightly before answering.

"Karen?" he asked when she picked up. "It's Josh Rosen. All your results are in. I went over the CT personally with the radiologist. I'm pleased to tell you everything looks completely normal. No tumors, lesions, or vascular abnormalities and the EEG was completely normal as well. So, that leaves us with two other possibilities."

Karen held her breath as he continued. "Dex told me you live near a marsh or swamp. Is that right?"

"Yes, it's a swamp, I think, and it's behind the house, in the woods."

"And the incidents you told me of, they took place behind the house in close proximity to the swamp?"

"Yes," she replied.

He hesitated for a moment, thinking, and then continued. "Well, there's the possibility of an environmental factor triggering the seizures. I mean, say someone used that swamp to dump toxic waste of some kind and you are outside, near the waste, and you breathe in some toxic element that's in the air and then that element triggers a seizure. Does that make sense to you?"

"Yes, but how would I know? I mean, how can I find out if that's the cause?"

"Talk to Dex. He knows just about everything that goes on there. He'll know, or can find out if someone's been dumping. In addition, see if you can find out if anyone else who ever lived on or near that property suffered from seizures. Look for a cluster effect, that is, people getting sick for no apparent reason who live in close proximity to the swamp. If you find out anything in the affirmative, you get yourself and your family out of there pronto. Let the government take over and clean it up."

"Okay," she said. "But you said there were two possible causes. What is the other one?"

He hesitated before answering. "Okay, it's the dreaded psychogenic cause. Stress and emotional disturbance, well, they can trigger fugue-like states that can be similar to what you describe. Moreover, if the environmental route does not pan out, it's my opinion that you should see someone. Attempted suicide is nothing to fool around with. I know it may be hard to accept that your mind may be doing this to you, but these dreams, these experiences, could be your brain's way of letting you know you need help. I'll be dictating a letter to you tonight confirming all this. In it, I'll include the names and numbers of two people I would highly recommend should you feel the need to talk to someone. Will you promise me you'll at least consider this?"

Now it was Karen's turn to hesitate. "Yes, okay," she finally agreed. "I promise I'll consider it."

Sounding relieved, Josh added, "I'm always here for you, too. Let me give you my private line. That way you can contact me whenever you feel you need to."

He gave her his number then said goodbye, promising to get that letter out to her the next morning.

She poured herself a glass of wine, thinking about what the doctor had said. Environmental pollution was a long shot. The booby hatch was the more likely alternative. She sighed and picked up her phone to call Dex. He answered on the first ring.

"Karen?" he said, his voice full of emotion.

"Yes, it's me. I just got off the phone with Josh. All the tests were negative. My brain apparently is in good working order. He asked, however, about the swamp behind the house, about whether there might have been toxic waste dumped in it that could be triggering seizures. He said you might know if someone was dumping. Also, he asked me to check on prior residents - look for seizure activity, or malignancies, that could have an environmental cause. The only incident I know of was Jane's partner, Lisbeth. She got breast cancer while living here."

"That's it?"

She hesitated before answering, taking a deep breath. "No, if the toxic waste angle turns up nothing, he wants me to see a shrink. The men in white coats will come and it will be off to the loony bin with me. Maybe, they'll have me bite on a rubber plug while they shoot waves of electricity through my brain, turn me into a veggie.

Alternatively, maybe, I'll just take up residence in a padded room wearing a fashionable straightjacket. More likely, I'll end up zonked out on downers, my hair a greasy mat, and drool dripping off my chin. A pretty picture, it isn't."

Dex had to laugh. "I don't think you're anywhere near that, princess, but if it happens, I'll be there to wipe that drool off your face. But, seriously, talking to someone might not be a bad idea. You've been under a lot of stress what with a life-changing move and everything."

She sighed, "Yes, I know you're right. I promised Josh I'd think about it and I will."

As she spoke, she heard the sound of a car in the driveway. "Just a minute, Dex."

She put the phone down and listened. She heard a car door slam. Bill was home. She looked at her watch - he was early.

"Dex, I have to go - Bill's home. Can I meet you tomorrow and talk about this toxic waste angle?"

"Sure. I'm fishing early. How about you meet me at the yard at one o'clock? We can grab a bite to eat and talk. And I'll think about the dumping while I'm out on the water."

"Great. Gotta go. See you tomorrow." She hurriedly hung up, took her glass of wine, and sat down in the living room to wait for her husband.

Bill ran from the car to the house, feeling a sense of urgency. He wanted to see his wife, to see his children. He found Karen in the overstuffed chair looking out at the sea. She looked tired, but still beautiful. He kissed her softly.

"Are the kids asleep yet? I don't want to wake them, but I do want to see them."

"I just put them to bed. You go on up. They'll be happy you're home."

He smiled, kissed her again, and ran up the stairs to say goodnight to his girls. He came back down about fifteen minutes later.

Feeling exhausted, he walked back to the living room where his wife sat. As he gazed at her, in his mind's eye, all he could see was Dex holding her hand. The image sickened him.

Could she betray me? And how can I even think to question her when I've betrayed her so many times? And why am I doing that anyway? I meant to break it off, but each time I try, something inside me seems to want that girl more. Am I that lost?

It seemed so. He desperately wanted to confess to Karen, to take his knocks, to try to make things right, but then that image reappeared, Karen and Dex laughing, holding hands, and shutting him out of the world that had once been his. Depressed, he said nothing, kissed her again, and told her he was tired and went up to bed.

Karen stayed downstairs for a while, thinking about the events of the day. She thought about her husband, who looked so worn out and distressed, and about her marriage, which seemed to be falling apart around her. And what about Dex? What did he mean to her? Then she thought about her sanity, or lack thereof, and what would happen to her daughters if she lost her mind.

But, most of all, she thought about the rabbit and the owl and what they meant and how she might have to protect herself and her family from them.

BILL & KAREN

Bill got up quietly before sunrise. Karen was still asleep, curled up in a fetal position, hugging a pillow. He watched her for a minute then walked over to the window and stared out at the sea. The questions of the night before were still plaguing him and had robbed him of a good night's sleep. He pulled on his sweats, went downstairs and made himself a cup of coffee, then walked outside in the dark, across the street to the beach. Once there, he sat on a rock waiting for the sunrise, sipping his coffee and listening to the waves hit the shore.

He did not want his marriage to fail, but he seemed to be helpless to steer it away from the course it was headed on. And Maggie? He knew he didn't love her, but he did need her. She fulfilled something in him, something that had been missing in his life for the past two years. And Karen? He had always loved her and still did. But could he forgive an infidelity? He didn't know. And, his daughters? God, how he loved them. He would never let them go, never.

He finished his coffee as the sun peeked over the horizon, promising another beautiful day. He got up slowly and turned to head back to the house, no decisions made, just questions - questions of love and loyalty and how it had all gone so wrong.

Karen woke up and found Bill was not in bed. *When did he get up? Where did he go?*

She stood up and walked over to the window, thinking about him. His sleep had been restless, as if plagued by demons he could not control.

She looked out at the sea, then over toward the road. The sun was just beginning to rise. As she watched, she saw a lone figure come up the drive. It was Bill. He held a coffee mug in his hand, his shoulders hunched and his head bowed. To Karen, he looked as if he carried the weight of the world on his back and she felt a wave of pity for him. He had had so much promise. How battered and beaten his self-esteem must have been and how hard it must be for him to regain the confidence that had once been so natural to him.

And what was my role in all this? she asked. *Did I help him? Did I support his fragile ego, make him feel like a man? No, I only eroded his confidence further with my anger, my bitterness, and my resentment.*

Whatever nadir they had come to, she acknowledged, he would not have to shoulder that blame alone. No, she shared equally in the unraveling of their marriage and, if it were to be saved, she would have to try to repair the damage she had done.

Resolved, she threw on her robe and went downstairs to greet him, to put on a pleasant, loving face for him, to be his wife once more.

As Bill walked in the door, she smiled at him, handing him a fresh cup of coffee. He thanked her and sat down.

Is she meeting her lover today? Maybe I should just pretend to go to work and follow her to see what she does. No, I can't do that. I can't stoop to that level.

As he watched her, he remembered how they used to steal days for themselves. He would call his office and say he was working from home. She would drop the kids at school and then come home to him. They would loll around in bed, making love all morning. After, they would, like children, run out somewhere to explore something new - a restaurant, a beach, a museum, a movie. Then they would come home and make love again. How long had it been since they did that? What would she do if he suggested it?

He sipped his coffee. "Hey, hon, how's about we play hooky today? Like we used to?"

He waited for her reply. Her back was to him but he could almost see the wheels turning in her mind, trying to find a polite way to refuse. It broke his heart.

She turned around, about to speak, but he beat her to it. "Ah, I really can't today anyway. I have a client at noon. Think I'll make a sale. That'll put a little extra in the paycheck."

He got up from the table, noting the confused look on her face that was mixed with relief.

"We'll do it another time," he said. "Well, I'm going to shower."

"Don't you want something to eat?"

"Naw, I'll get something in town," he answered as he left the room.

Karen watched him go, puzzled by his behavior but glad he'd changed his mind. She needed to talk to Dex about the toxic waste angle.

If only Bill had suggested it another day - I would have leapt at it. Lately, we always seem to be at cross-purposes. How can I change that?

Reluctantly, she shook her head, knowing the answer to her question was right there in front of her. *Yes, I should come clean with him. Tell him about the seizures or whatever they are, about the tests, and about Dex. But I'm not ready yet. I need more information, need to understand myself what is happening before I discuss it with him.*

She sat silently thinking, trying to decide what to do.

I'll talk to him after I speak with Madge on Friday. I'm going to stop holding back with that old woman - I'll tell her everything - the rabbits, the owl, everything. And if she thinks I'm crazy, then so be it; it'll be off to the shrink with me. But if she doesn't - if she believes what has been happening to me is real - oh, gosh, I don't know what I'll do then. But I have to tell Bill. If I don't, there won't be any future for us. I can't live with all these lies any longer. And I'll have to tell him about Dex, too, and let the chips fall. Maybe he'll forgive me.

Her decision made, she checked her watch and went upstairs to get her daughters ready for school.

Later, she drove down to the boatyard to meet with Dex. They bought sodas and sandwiches from the store and sat at the picnic table out front.

"So, were you able to come up with anything?" she asked. "About the toxic waste angle, I mean."

Dex took her hand. "No, princess, I haven't. This is a small island and if someone was using it as a dump, it'd get around. I've asked some of my buddies about it and no one knows anything. There are trails back in those woods, but they're all footpaths, not wide enough to take a truck or even a small car. It would be almost impossible for someone to transport a bunch of toxic waste to that swamp. Sorry, princess, but I just don't see it."

She sighed. That left the psychogenic cause - straightjacket time. "Thanks for trying. I guess it doesn't make much sense hoping for toxic waste, but I was. I just don't want to go the psych route, if you know what I mean. Antidepressants and all that jazz. I don't think there's anything wrong with my mind."

"I don't either," he replied. "But stress shouldn't be underestimated and this might be a temporary thing and talking to someone could help."

She nodded. "I am going to talk to someone - Madge Parker. I'm seeing her on Friday."

"Madge Parker? What does that old lady have to do with anything? Isn't she senile or something?"

"She's not senile. She's sharp as a tack," she answered a bit indignantly. "I've spoken with her before and she's a bright old lady who knows an awful lot about the history of my property. I'm going to tell her about the things I've been seeing. If she tells me I'm loco, then I'll see a shrink, but I want to hear what she says first."

Dex shook his head. "Are you buying into all that old Indian legend crap? Karen, use your head! That's just a bunch of bunk, stories to frighten children."

"Dex," she said evenly, "I've told you what I'm going to do. If you think I'm off on a wild goose chase or just trying to avoid the inevitable, then so be it! But I'm going to do what I'm going to do!"

"Okay, okay," he replied, trying to calm her down. "You do what you need to. Just know I'm here for you, okay?"

Karen nodded briefly and began to concentrate on her sandwich. They ate silently and when she was finished, she stood up. "I've got to be getting back," she said, obviously still angry. "Thanks for meeting me."

As she turned to go, he reached out and grabbed her hand. "Now, princess, are you going to stay mad at me? I don't think I could stand that."

He looked so contrite, she had to laugh, her anger dissipating. "No, I guess I'm not. How could I stay angry with my knight in shining armor? He just might decide not to rescue me next time!"

The tension between them eased, he walked her to her car. As he closed her door, he leaned in the window. "Let me know what old lady Parker says, okay?"

Karen nodded, patted his hand, and backed out of the parking space and headed for home.

Dex watched as she left, wondering what she was getting into, delving into all the old legends. He hoped she would soon give it up and come to the realization she might need professional help.

Troubled, he walked over to his truck thinking about Maggie and Bill. That knowledge was a potential bombshell that could destroy her and he was determined to stay close so he could be there for her should that happen.

MADGE PARKER & BETRAYAL

On Friday, Karen headed to town, driving to the nursing home. When she arrived, she found Mrs. Parker in the same place, sitting on the patio, watching the sea. Karen pulled up a chair beside her.

"Hi, Madge," she said softly, trying not to startle the old woman. "Remember me, Karen Andersen from Mateguas?"

Madge turned her head to Karen. "Honey, I'm not senile. Of course I remember you." She patted Karen's hand.

Karen smiled at her. "You said you remembered something."

The old woman nodded. She was about to speak, but Karen silenced her with a gesture. "Before we go there, Madge, I have to tell you I haven't been completely honest with you about why I'm interested in all this."

Madge turned and looked at her, puzzled. "Go on."

Karen took a deep breath then began relating the details of her experiences in the woods, about the rabbit and the owl, the near-drowning, and saving Little Gerry. The old woman watched her intently as she spoke. When Karen finished, Madge took her hand and held it tightly.

"Oh, my poor child, my dear child. It all fits, you know. Yes, it all fits."

She continued to hold Karen's hand as she sighed, struggling to find the right words. "What I wanted to tell you, what I remembered, it fits. Remember what I told you about the blessed boy?"

Karen nodded.

"Well, he had other abilities, other attributes that defied logic. He could, now what do you call it? Shift, yes, he could shift."

"Shift?" asked Karen. "I don't understand."

"No, shift isn't right. Shape-shift! That's the term. Yes, it was told that he could shape-shift, or turn himself into almost any animal form. It was amazing. He could fly over the island as an eagle or run through the woods as a fox. But the animal he shifted into most frequently was the rabbit, his father's totem. I'm afraid, my child, that he has chosen you. He has been appearing before you. Smiling upon you. And he has been testing you, testing your courage, your resolve. And he is pleased. Yes, he is pleased with you."

"But chosen for what?" asked Karen. "For what?"

Madge smiled and patted her hand. "Why, to do battle with the Mskagwdemos, what else? To be the protector of your family. To send that hag back to the swamp where she belongs.

"Now, the owl, it could never hurt you?"

Karen nodded, "No. It came close. I could feel the beating of its wings, but it didn't hurt me. It scared me, yes, but not hurt."

"The owl in folklore has many meanings," the old woman went on. "I'm not sure what it means in your tale, but it seems it is a creature of the Mskagwdemos, trying to cause you harm so you cannot protect your family. It is trying to frighten you so you will not be able to find the courage to save your children, your husband. But it has not succeeded because your will is strong.

"You ARE strong, Karen Andersen, and you will prevail. You must believe in yourself, that these things you have been seeing, have been experiencing, are real. Trust your intuition. Find those papers, the ones left by Lisbeth Boucher. Believe me, they are the key."

Karen stared at the old woman, trying to comprehend. This woman accepted her tale as true, not a figment of her imagination, not seizures or hallucinations, but as real happenings. She *had* really seen the trail, the rabbits, and the owls. It was real. She knew now. But *chosen*, why? Why her? And doing battle with the swamp hag - how was she to know what to do? The questions swirled in her mind.

Madge watched her, knowing this young woman was struggling to absorb all this, to make sense of it, and to *believe*, yes, to believe.

"Find those papers, child," the old woman repeated. "It will make sense and you will know what to do."

Karen nodded and stood up. "Thank you for your time and, most of all, for believing me."

She bent down and kissed the old woman on the cheek.

"When you have defeated the Mskagwdemos, come back and see me," the old woman said softly. "I will want to hear the tale."

Karen nodded then took her leave of Mrs. Parker. Worried and confused, she returned to her car for the drive back to town, knowing, if she hurried, she could catch the afternoon ferry.

Arriving early, Karen parked her car and walked to the ferry terminal. She still had a few minutes before the boat was to leave, so she walked outside and stood by the rail, looking down on the busy waterfront. Her mind was in turmoil, trying to digest all that Madge had told her.

As she watched the activity below, a familiar figure appeared, walking down the wharf. Recognizing it was Bill, she was about to call out to him when she saw him stop to help a woman tie up her punt. The woman was laughing as he helped her out of the small boat and, once ashore, she put her arms around his waist and leaned her body into his. Karen's mouth fell open in shock as she watched her husband lean down and softly kiss the woman on the lips. Accepting his kiss, she tilted her head back and, as her hat fell off, a mass of red curls cascaded around her face. It was Maggie!

Karen jumped back away from the railing, not wanting them to see her. Gasping for breath, her mind struggled to accept what she had just seen. Her husband and that schoolteacher. Maggie. Together. Kissing.

That bastard! That lousy cheating bastard! With that girl, that tramp! How can he do this to me!

She leaned against the wall, trying to calm down. *Why am I hiding?* she asked herself.

Angrily, she moved again to the rail, wanting to scream accusations at them, but they were nowhere in sight.

She stood silent, her shock and anger giving way to grief. Suddenly, she heard the sound of the ferry's horn.

"Oh crap!" she moaned. "Now I've missed the damned boat."

Quickly, she pulled out her cell and, hesitating only for a second, called her daughter. Before she spoke, she took a deep breath trying to remain calm.

"Honey, it's Mom. Sorry to interrupt your school, but I missed the ferry so I won't be home when you get there. You and Sophie just let yourselves in. There's a key under the mat. You can have two cookies each with a glass of milk while you wait for me. The cookies are in the jar on the counter. I'll be home on the next boat. Okay? Can you do that for Mommy?"

Her daughter replied she could and after hanging up, Karen tried to comprehend what had just happened - Bill, her husband of ten years, was obviously having an affair with that girl.

I need a drink, she thought, checking her ferry schedule. She had two hours to kill.

She left the ferry building looking for the first bar she could find and she did not have to go far. The sign said "The Sternman" and it promised to be an establishment where a strong drink could be had, no questions asked.

The interior of the tavern was dark. The place was about half full and all of the customers appeared to be workingmen. Several of them turned to stare at her as she walked in. Ignoring their looks, Karen sat on an empty stool at the end of the bar. When the bartender came over, she ordered two fingers of Jack Daniels, neat. She stared at her drink for a couple of seconds, then picked it up and tossed it back. Trying to choke back the tears that were beginning to well up in her eyes, she relaxed as the warmth of the alcohol slid down her throat. She indicated to the bartender for another, this time on the rocks.

How could he do that to me? How?

Deep in thought, she was startled when she felt a tug on her ponytail. She turned around, surprised to find Dex standing behind her, smiling.

"Hey, princess, better go easy on that stuff," he said, jokingly.

As she looked up at him, he could see the tears in her eyes and the look of devastation that was etched upon her face. He picked up her drink, took her hand, and led her to a small table for two in the back of the bar. He sat down across from her, keeping her hand securely in his.

"Now what's up, princess? I can see you're upset. What's happened to ruin this fine day for you?"

Karen took a gulp of her drink and looked up at Dex, words tumbling out of her mouth as tears streamed down her face.

"That...that creep, that bastard I'm married to and that schoolteacher, that slut. I saw them...right out in the open. I saw him kiss her! They're not even trying to hide it...I had to stand there and watch, watch him kiss that slut. I, I...."

Dex squeezed her hand. What he had feared had finally happened. The shit had hit the fan.

Karen took another drink, anger again overtaking her despair. "I'll kill him, I will. If he thinks he can get away with this, well, he's got another thing coming. I can't believe it. He's with that whore right now. Then he's going to come home to me, to me and MY children; that lousy lying creep."

"Easy now, no talk of killing anyone, you hear. There are other worse ways to deal with him. You just calm down. Don't rush into anything."

Karen looked at him, nodded, and took another drink.

"All this time, I've been trying, trying to love him, trying to stand this place, trying, Dex, trying. And he - he's been with that whore, the two of them laughing at me," her voice broke. She took another gulp of her drink and sat silently for a couple of minutes, staring at the table.

Then she looked up into Dex's eyes, recognizing the longing and love in them. He was such a kind, gentle man, and he cared for her so much. And, she admitted to herself, she had feelings for him, too. They had not acted on them out of respect for her marriage, a marriage that now appeared to be nothing but a sham.

Slowly, she leaned forward across the small table and kissed him softly on the lips. He pulled back, startled by her action.

"Take me somewhere, Dex. To your boat, to a motel, I don't care where. I know you want me. I want you, too. Just take me away and make love to me. Help me to forget."

Dex's eyes opened wide in surprise. He stared at her for a second and then took both of her hands in his. He leaned across the table, his face close to hers, never breaking eye contact with her.

"Now, Karen, that's the best offer I've had all day and there's nothing I'd like better, but, no, not this way.

"If you want me to come home with you while you pack your bags, I'll do it. I'll take you away, anywhere you want to go. But, somehow, I don't think you're ready for that. I want you, yes, you know that, but not for one night. I want you for always. And when and if you're ready to come to me, fully and completely, then, and only then, will it be right, will it be good. If we did something now, out of anger and revenge or because you're hurt, you would only regret it later and so would I. No, princess, this is not the time."

Karen stared at him, listening to his words, and nodded. "You're right," she said, reaching for her drink.

Dex deftly moved the drink out of her reach and turned and asked the bartender to bring a pot of coffee and a cup for Karen.

"Now, we need to sober you up so you can go home to those little girls of yours," he said as he poured her a steaming cup of coffee.

Karen looked at her watch. "Oh, my God, I'm going to miss the next boat!" she exclaimed, frustration overwhelming her.

Dex patted her hand. "Hush now, don't you worry. You get a couple cups of java in you and then I'll get you home in my boat. We'll make it there before that old ferry docks, don't worry. I will take care of you, Karen. I will."

She sighed with relief and dutifully drank the hot coffee while Dex sat quietly, watching her. When she was feeling a bit more sober, he signaled the bartender for the check, paid, and escorted her from the bar.

As they walked back to the wharf, he kept his arm around her, keeping her close. When they reached his boat, he helped her on board. She was only wearing a lightweight jacket, so he draped his coat across her shoulders and helped her to a seat. He untied the punt and maneuvered it out to sea. Once clear of the wharf, he went full throttle back to Mateguas.

As they motored home, Dex watched her out of the corner of his eye. *My God, what is wrong with that man? How can he hurt her so? If she were mine, God, I would cherish her, protect her, and never, never stop loving her.*

As promised, they beat the ferry back. Once tied up and on the wharf, Dex led Karen to his truck. "I don't want you driving," he said. "Not in the state you're in."

Just before they got to her house, Karen asked him to pull over.

"I don't know what I would've done if you hadn't been there," she said, turning to him. "Thank you for your kindness, for taking pity on me."

"Pity had nothing to do with it, Karen," he said, taking her hand in his. "I meant what I said back in the bar. You come to me fully, wanting ME, not revenge on that asshole husband of yours, and I'll move heaven and earth for you. I'll love you and protect you and keep you and your children safe and warm from any storms that may try to batter you."

She looked at him, trying to comprehend what he was saying, what he was offering her. She reached up and laid her palm on his cheek. Her eyes softening, she leaned forward and kissed him gently.

Dex returned her kiss, restraining himself from taking her in his arms and never letting go. She was fragile now and he would not take advantage of that fragility.

Slowly, she moved away from him, the kiss ended. He stared at her, again surprised by the depth of emotion he was feeling. Yes, he wanted her, that he had known from the first moment he laid eyes on her, but now, every time he saw her, he loved her more. No, he didn't want her just for a few nights' pleasure - he wanted her for always, wanted to wake up each morning with her beside him, wanted to make a life with her. He had never felt this way before about anyone and he let the emotion sweep over him while he stared into her confused and swollen eyes.

"Let's get you home," he said hoarsely as he pulled back onto the road.

Once at her driveway, Karen turned to him. "What about my car? We forgot about the car. It's still at the wharf."

"Don't worry about that," he said, laughing. "Just let that no-good husband of yours bring it on home and when he asks you how you got home, well, you just tell him that Dex gave you a ride, but don't you tell him what kind of a ride! You let him think on that for a while, princess!"

Karen laughed genuinely for the first time since seeing Maggie and Bill together.

"Sure," she said. "And thanks again for being there for me, sir knight."

She left the truck and as she turned to walk up the drive, he yelled at her, "If you need me, call me, anytime. I'm there for you, Karen, and I always will be."

She smiled at him and nodded and, with one last lingering look at her, he reluctantly drove off.

Karen walked into the house not knowing what she was going to do next. She saw her daughters sitting at the table, dutifully enjoying their cookies and milk.

I have to think of them, she told herself. *They come first.*

She greeted her girls warmly then checked her cell. There was a text from Bill. He would be on the five o'clock boat. She told the girls to go upstairs and work on their homework, to stay in their room until she came to get them and, if they were good, she would take them to the Island Burger Shack for dinner. She watched as they obediently went upstairs, then poured a glass of wine and waited for her husband. Assuming he'd found the car, she expected him any minute.

She did not have to wait long. Soon, she heard him come up the drive and the car door slam.

Bill walked into the kitchen, a confused look on his face. Karen was seated at the table staring at him, her cell phone in front of her. He started to speak, to ask about the car, but she silenced him with a look and a gesture.

"Sit down," she said. "We have something to discuss."

Bill started to speak as he sat down opposite her, but, again, she silenced him.

"You don't get to talk," she said in a soft, but firm voice. "You just get to listen and then act."

He looked at her, puzzled. "Okay, go on."

"I saw you today, you and that whore, kissing right out in public view. You just couldn't keep your hands off her, could you? Okay, so you've had your fun, but now it's over. You hear me? It's over. If not, I'll take the girls, go back to California, and my father's lawyers will make certain you never see them again. Do you hear me?"

Bill sat at the table, shocked, speechless. All he could do was nod his head.

Karen continued. "So, now you are going to call that slut and tell her it's over, that you are never going to see her again. And after school's out next week, our daughters will NOT be back. I will not let her get her hands on them! Do you get it?"

She slid her cell across the table to him.

He hesitated then picked it up and dialed. Maggie answered on the first ring.

"Mags, it's Bill," he said haltingly. "Karen knows about us. She saw us. It's over, Mags. I love my wife. I've never stopped loving her."

As he said this, he glanced up at Karen to see her reaction, but her face was a frozen mask.

"I know it all meant more to you," he continued. "But, for me, it was, well, just an attraction. Made my ego feel good - male menopause or something. But it's over now. All over. I love Karen. I'm staying with her, if she'll have me. And we'll be taking the girls out of school. Karen doesn't want you teaching them. We'll be home schooling or finding a school on the mainland. I'm sorry. I screwed up and hurt everyone. It's on me. I'm sorry. Goodbye."

He hung up and stared at his wife, his shock at her discovery of his affair slowly being replaced by anger and jealousy.

"Now," he said to her, "I've done what you wanted, it's over for me and her. I meant what I said - I love you. I won't see Maggie again, but Karen, what about you? Don't you think I've heard the rumors? You and Dex, going for motorcycle and boat rides. Where did that fish really come from, Karen? Where? And holding hands with him in public while my back was turned. What was that about, Karen? What about you?"

Surprise showed on her face. She hadn't expected this. "Dex is just a friend, Bill, we never...," she stammered.

"If he's just a friend, then why lie?" Bill asked, raising his voice. "Why not invite him over for dinner? We could all go out on his boat with him. Why lie to me, Karen, if he's just a friend? You know how I felt when Maggie told me you were holding hands with him at that ice cream thing? When I went to get the car. Do you know? I was sick, physically ill. I had been telling myself that it was all just gossip - that you would never cheat on me, that it was just a flirtation.

"And do you know how it felt for me for the past two years, you being so cold? I lost my job due to the economy. The economy,

Karen! It wasn't my fault. I tried to get a new one. God, I would have flipped burgers, if anyone would hire me. But they wouldn't. I was overqualified. But did you support me or help me get through it? No, you treated me like dirt, like it was my fault somehow. Then, I got us here for a new start, but you hated it. I know you hated it. I tried, Karen, I tried, but you wore me down, you broke me. So, when this young girl came along thinking I was just about the greatest thing since sliced bread, well, Karen, I jumped at it. Yes, I admit it, I did.

"I'm sorry. God, you don't know how sorry I am. But it didn't happen in a vacuum. I didn't just get up one morning and say to myself, 'mmmmm, today I think I'll cheat.' No, it was the culmination of two years of crap. I wish it hadn't happened, but it did. But what about you, Karen, what about you and Dex?"

Karen listened as all the bitterness, all the rancor, he had been bottling up spewed forth and she knew he was right. She had treated him like dirt, like the termination was his fault. But did that justify his affair? No, it didn't - but he was right about one thing, she had been having her own little something with Dex and even though they had not made love, there still had been plenty that passed between them. Yes, he was right. He had good reason to be angry and hurt, too. They had wounded each other so deeply, she wondered if there was any hope left for them.

Bill finally stopped, exhausted. He put his head in his hands, on the verge of tears. "You're right about how unfairly I've treated you," she said softly. "I was wrong to take it out on you, about the job and everything, but that does not excuse what you did with Maggie. No, there is no excuse for betraying me, betraying our marriage, in that way. I have not betrayed you with Dex or any other man. You are the only man I've ever known. Now, I don't know if we can repair the damage we've done to one another, but, for the sake of our daughters, we have to try. I have to try to forgive you, but it's going to take time. I can't trust you now. Can't you see that? How long it will take me to trust you again, well, I don't know."

Bill looked up at her and nodded.

"Thank you," she said. "Now go upstairs and see our daughters. I don't want them hurt any more than they already have been. And you are on your own for supper tonight. I don't think I can sit across the table from you and carry on a regular conversation right now. The girls and I are going to the Island Burger Shack. You can make up some excuse for why you're not going with us."

She got up and left the room.

Bill sat quietly at the table. His life had just gone down the toilet and he had no one to blame but himself. Slowly, he stood up, and, as Karen told him to, went to see his children.

Upstairs, the girls did not do as their mother had instructed. Frightened, they huddled on the landing, trying to hear what was going on between their parents in the kitchen. At first, the voices were muffled. Then, they heard their father's voice raised in anger.

"Oh, Terri," Sophie whispered, shakily. "They're fighting again!"

Terri put her arm around her sister and held her close as they listened, unable to make out the words, but sure something was very, very wrong.

When Bill got to the stairs, he saw his children on the landing, sitting close together in the corner and he knew they had overheard some of the fight he had just had with their mother. He saw the fear on their faces and it broke his heart.

This is what I've done, he thought as tears welled up in his eyes.

He put his head down and quickly wiped the tears away and forced himself to smile as he bounded up the stairs to his girls.

Terri and Sophie seemed to shrink back when he reached the landing, so he sat down across from them and held out his arms.

"What's up, munchkins?" he asked. "Why don't you slide over here and give Daddy a hug?"

Sophie and Terri leapt into his arms and he held them tight. Sophie turned her face to look at him.

"Are you going to leave us, Daddy?" she asked in a small, frightened voice.

Bill looked directly into her soft blue eyes.

"No, honey," he said firmly. "Daddy would never leave you. What made you think that? I'll always be here for you two. Mommy and I just had a little fight. But everything's okay. No one's going anywhere."

He hugged them again then sat back, watching for their reaction to his words.

When he saw them relax, he continued, "Except for the Island Burger Shack, that is! Daddy had a big lunch in town and isn't hungry so it'll just be you girls and Mom going out tonight. Also, I need to get some work done and, if I can get it finished while you're gone, maybe we can play one of those old board games or something when you get back. Would you like that?"

Both girls nodded their heads vigorously. Bill laughed, hugged them again, and told them to get washed and ready to go out to dinner with their mother. As he watched them go to their room, he felt a profound sadness. He and Karen had messed up so badly.

Feeling exhausted and depressed, he went to the bedroom and lay down, taking some small solace in the fact that she hadn't booted him out.

Maybe, just maybe, we can find a way to repair the damage we've done to one another and to our children. I know I really crossed the line this time, but she crossed a line, too, however much she denies it.

Sighing to himself, he closed his eyes acknowledging it was going to take a hell of a lot of work for them to put this Humpty Dumpty back together again.

MAGGIE

She sat on the floor, phone still in hand, her house of cards collapsing all around her. There were no tears. She was in shock. There would be plenty of time for tears, later. She could not believe it. She had spent the whole afternoon in his arms. And now he was saying he did not love her, that it was only sex?

How could he lie like that? We talked about a sort of future together, or at least, I thought we did. He wrote "Luv u" on that note. How can he deny me now, deny our love?

She got up slowly and walked to the liquor cabinet and poured herself a scotch.

How did that bitch find out anyway? He said she saw us. Where? It must have been today, on the wharf. Yeah, she was probably waiting for the ferry and saw him kiss me. That was stupid of him. Kissing me right out in public. But why hasn't she kicked him out? Does she still want him now that he's cheated on her? If it were me, I wouldn't let him stay.

Shit, I counted on her giving him the heave-ho. Figured she'd ask for a divorce, take the girls, and go back to California. Leave him and that house on the hill for me. Given all that's gone on between her and Dex, you think she would be glad to have an excuse to get rid of her husband.

Maggie couldn't sit still. She paced the room trying to straighten out in her mind what had happened.

The girls! That's it, the girls! Karen must have threatened to take his children away from him. It has to be that. Otherwise, he would never have made that call. He's a good father and loves his kids. Yes, he would do anything for them.

She poured herself another drink, knowing she had to see him, to talk to him. She couldn't let him drop her over the phone. That was just too cold - too disrespectful.

If I can just get him alone again, I can make things right. Maybe, even take him back to Little Glooskap where our love began. Yes, that's the ticket. I'll take him back there, back to the meadow where we first made love so passionately. I'll text him. Tell him it was not right for him to disrespect me that way. Tell him if he's going to dump me, he should be man enough to do it to my face. I'll make him feel guilty, maybe, even hint at suicide. Ask him to meet me at the boatyard and I'll make him go with me back to Little Glooskap. Yes, that's what I'll do.

She checked the tides then pulled out her cell. She stared at it for a minute, composing the text in her mind.

She smiled, confident she could get him back and that she would, once again, be in control.

Yes, it's still all there and it will be mine. All I have to do is reach out and take it.

KAREN

As she drove with her girls to the Island Burger Shack, Karen thought about what had transpired that afternoon.

Bill cheated on me; yes, he went where no man should ever go, but am I blameless in this? As he pointed out, I neglected and emasculated him ever since he lost his job. So, why am I so surprised he succumbed to the charms of that girl? And what was I doing while he diddled her? I was engaged in my own game of tickle with Dex.

Yes, I share in the guilt. But would I change things if I could? Go back in time and refuse to get on Dex's bike? No, I don't think I would. He and I are bonded to each other in some sort of strange mystical way and there's no way I can deny that connection. And what would I have done without him when all those weird things were happening to me? But, why did I turn to him and not my husband of ten years?

The answers eluded her.

Well, if Dex and I are bonded, then Bill and I are also bonded, by our years together and by the love of our daughters. Yes, for our twins' sake, I have to put my own longings aside. I will accept Bill back and, as hard as that might be, work to find with him the life we once had or, maybe, some new kind of life we can live together.

Resolved, she pulled into the fast food restaurant and, taking her daughters by the hand, walked up to place her order.

BILL

Exhausted and alone with his thoughts, Bill felt his cell vibrate. He pulled it out of his pocket and saw the text from Maggie.

> *You owe me. You can't dis me over the phone like that. Tell me in person, you owe me that much. Or I don't know what I'll do. Meet me at the boatyard Sunday at 7am. You know you owe me that much. M.*

Oh God, he thought. *What will I do?*

She was right, he owed her an explanation face to face. She had done nothing wrong. It was on him; he was the bad guy. She had just opened herself to him, loved him - and what had he done in return? He'd dropped her flat with no compassion, no feeling at all. It was wrong, but it was what Karen had compelled him to do to save his marriage.

He sighed. He didn't know how he could swing it, meeting her, but he would try - try to be the kind of honorable man he'd always believed he was.

He texted her back,

I'll try.

LITTLE GOOSKLAP REDUX

Somehow, Karen and Bill made it through Saturday. Bill tried his best to not upset or annoy her and Karen was polite, but cool to him. He'd slept on the couch Friday night and gone for a run early in the morning. He came home to find her cleaning up the breakfast dishes and the girls playing outside. She didn't speak to him or offer to make him breakfast, just finished what she was doing and left the room.

Guess I'm going to get some practice in the cooking department, he thought to himself as he reached for the frying pan.

The rest of the day followed the same pattern, Karen avoiding him when she could, only feigning warmth when the girls were present. Bill continued to give her space and spent most of the day out of her sight in the garage, tinkering with the old motor scooter he had found there. Dinner was the first meal that included him. The conversation was awkward at times, but somehow they all got through it.

On Sunday morning, he got up early, threw on his sweats, left Karen a note, and began his run down to the boatyard to meet Maggie.

The yard was only about three-quarters of a mile away and he kept a good pace. When he arrived, it looked almost deserted except for a lone figure standing on the wharf waiting for him. She was wearing running shorts and a sweatshirt, her red hair mussed by the sea breeze. When he approached her, she gestured to the punt that was tied up at the wharf.

"Get in," she commanded.

"Mags, I don't have much time," he replied. "Can't we talk here?"

Ignoring his question, she stepped into the small boat. "Get in now!"

Bill stared at her, suddenly trapped by eyes that seemed to flash with a strange combination of anger, lust, and something else that he was unable to put his finger on. He felt a warning light go off in the back of his head and he knew he should just turn around and jog home, but somehow he was unable to move. As if in a daze, his eyes still locked with hers, he stepped into the punt and sat down.

Maggie, a small self-satisfied smile playing at the corners of her mouth, untied the boat and motored, full throttle, to Little Glooskap.

When they arrived at the small island, she anchored the punt, took off her sneakers, and jumped out. Bill hesitated, wondering how in the world he had gotten himself into this situation, then, not knowing what else to do, took off his shoes and waded ashore behind her. Hoping to get this over with as quickly as possible, he followed her up the trail. When they reached the meadow, she turned to him.

"How could you do that to me," she cried, "hurt me like that?"

Now the tears came and she pivoted away from him, trying to hide them. He walked over to her and put his hand on her shoulder.

"Mags," he began to say, "I...."

She spun around quickly, catching him off-guard. The slap came out of nowhere. Her hand came up and, with the flat of her palm, she hit him as hard as she could. The sound of her hand making contact with his face echoed across the meadow. She glared at him.

"You can't disrespect me like that," she yelled. "You can't!"

She pulled back her arm to hit him again but was not fast enough. He stepped in and grabbed her by her wrists. As soon as he touched her, she tried to press her body against his, trying to arouse him with her near nakedness. He felt himself responding and he pushed her down, forcing her to her knees. Holding her in place, he moved closer to her. She saw the anger in his eyes and she was suddenly afraid.

"Is this what you want?" he demanded, releasing himself from his pants. All his pent-up anger burst forth as he pushed her head down and forced her to take him in her mouth. As she ministered to him, he kept one hand firmly on the back of her head, guiding her. When he felt he was about to explode, he pulled out and pushed her to the ground. He yanked off her running shorts, noting with satisfaction she was naked underneath, and entered her roughly. She cried out in pain and then fiercely wrapped her legs around him, her hips rising to meet his thrust.

It was over almost as quickly as it began, their passion spent. Bill pulled away from her and stood up, rearranging his clothing. Maggie still lay in the grass, spread-eagled, her shorts dangling from one ankle.

"Get dressed," he said to her, flatly.

Responding to the anger in his tone of voice, she pulled up her shorts and sat up.

"Now I'm going to tell you what's going to happen from now on," he said to her. "You do NOT call me, text me, or email me. I am trying to put my marriage back together - to keep my girls! Do you understand?"

Maggie nodded, meekly.

"And, if and when, I think it's okay," he continued, "then, and only then, will I contact you! Do you get it? I will not lose my children over you!"

Again, Maggie nodded as she stood up.

Bill nodded back then turned and started down the trail to the punt. Maggie stood frozen, stunned and seemingly shocked by his anger.

"You better get your ass in gear," he yelled without looking back at her, "or I'll motor back to Mateguas by myself and leave you here."

Sensing he meant it, Maggie pulled herself together and ran to catch up. They got into the punt wordlessly, and she took it full throttle back to the island.

When they got to the wharf, Bill hopped out, not taking time to help her tie up. He started to walk away but then turned and looked back over his shoulder.

"Remember what I said. No texts, no emails, no calls. And if, and I mean if, I can get things back to normal, then maybe, I'll contact you. You got it?"

He didn't wait for a reply. He glanced at his watch and began to jog home.

Maggie watched him leave, a smug smile growing on her face. Her plan had worked. She had him just where she wanted him. Now, all she had to do was wait. When he was out of sight, she stepped from the boat and walked confidently to her car.

Bill ran at full sprint until he was close to home, his anger dissipating rapidly as he thought about Maggie and what had just happened.

Good God, I practically raped her. That's not me. But she goaded me into it - she planned to seduce me today, that's for sure. But why did I let her?

His questions unanswered, he slowed down as he approached the driveway, getting his breathing under control. He was sure he would be okay. He hadn't been gone that long. As he gazed at the house, he thought about Karen and the family inside that he loved more than anything. He shook his head, feeling confused and knowing that for reasons he could not fathom, he'd put it all at risk again. He stood still for a minute, deep in thought, trying to understand his own behavior, then he walked up the drive and went into the house.

Karen was in the kitchen, on the phone, and the girls were sitting at the table having breakfast. Karen hung up and looked at him.

"Good run?" she asked. "Want me to make you something to eat?"

Bill shook his head. "Thanks, hon, but I probably stink. Think I'll take a shower and then take care of myself. No reason to trouble you. But I appreciate the offer. I really do."

"Okay," she replied. "And, that was Alyce Macintyre on the phone. You remember I told you about them. They own that big house on the north side. Well, they're here for the summer and she's invited me over this afternoon to play tennis. I told her I'd come. So, I'll need the car and you will have to watch the girls while I'm gone. Okay?"

"Sure, hon, anything you want," he replied, knowing he'd walk over hot coals barefoot right now if she asked him to. Taking care of his girls was a no-brainer.

"Good," she said as she sat down with Terri and Sophie to finish her breakfast.

Bill nodded and went upstairs.

Stepping into the hot shower, his mind again replayed the scene on Little Glooskap with Maggie.

Why? he asked himself. *Why do I keep reacting to her? I don't love her - hell, I don't even think I like her very much. But no matter what I do, she seems to be able to wield some sort of sexual power over me. I didn't want to get in that boat - I knew it was a mistake, but I did it anyway. What's the matter with me? I've always been able to control myself before. And, why did I let her think I'd contact her again? I'm not going to do that, am I?*

He stepped from the shower and gazed at himself in the mirror.

Maybe Karen's right - maybe there is something wrong with this place - something just a little off. Some kind of force or influence that pushes you in the wrong direction; making it so you can't resist.

As he thought about this idea, he couldn't help but laugh.

"You're starting to lose it, Bill," he said to his reflection. "Blaming your own lack of control on some kind of voodoo or supernatural mumbo jumbo. That's the coward's way. It's all on you and you know it. You have to just buckle down and remember what's important - your family."

KAREN & DEX

Karen did go to play tennis with her new friend, but she had other plans for the afternoon after the match ended.

Thanking Alyce, she made her excuses and left early. Following her island map, she pulled up the driveway of a modern-looking house built on a ridge overlooking the sea. It did not appear to be anything special from the road, but she knew that, seaward, it was a wall of glass, giving its occupant a spectacular view.

Dex's truck was in the driveway. She parked and sat in the car for a minute, gathering her courage. She hoped he was home. Girding herself, she walked to the door, knocked and waited. There was no answer. She paused for a moment, taking a deep breath, and knocked again. There was still no answer.

Feeling disappointed, she was about to turn away when the door opened. Dex had apparently just gotten out of the shower. His hair was wet and he had hastily thrown a towel around his waist. She felt her face redden as she stared at his well-muscled torso. The words "washboard abs" resounded in her mind and her knees felt weak. She had the overwhelming urge to reach out and run her hand over his chest, to caress him, to know every part of him. The struggle she was having with her emotions was plain on her face as they stood staring at each other.

Dex finally broke the silence. "Princess! What a surprise! Come on in. Make yourself comfortable. I'll be down in a second."

He led her into a spacious room and, as she suspected, the view from it was unparalleled. By the windows were two comfortable leather swivel chairs, each with a telescope mounted nearby.

Dex went upstairs to a loft that apparently served as his bedroom. Alone, Karen looked around, noting that it was a house reminiscent of those in Northern California at places like Sea Ranch or Bodega Bay. It was a warm and welcoming place and she loved it immediately.

Dex same down shortly dressed in jeans and a T-shirt, still drying his hair with a towel. He noted the tennis dress she had on, appreciating how the stretchy material clung to her willowy form. "Looks like you've just come in from the courts. Have a good game?"

Karen nodded and told him about meeting Alyce, her new tennis connection.

He laughed. "Well, welcome to my humble abode. Can I get you something? A drink?"

"Um, a glass of wine would be nice."

"Red or white?"

She asked for red and was surprised to see him open a door and go down a narrow stairway. He came back up in a couple of minutes and presented her with a bottle of Pinot Noir from an obscure boutique winery in the Willamette Valley. Her surprise showed on her face.

"Now, princess, you didn't take me for some backwoods yokel who does know a cab from a pinot, did you?"

She laughed. "Well, I must admit, I wasn't expecting a wine cellar!"

Smiling, he poured the wine and gestured for her to sit in one of the swivel chairs while he sat in the other. Karen sipped her drink silently, staring at the sea in front of her.

Dex watched her. He was afraid he knew why she had come to see him and he prayed he was wrong.

After a time, she put her wine glass down, stood up, and walked over to where he was seated. He stared at his glass, waiting, unable to look at her. She knelt on the floor in front of him and put her hands on his knees.

"Look at me," she said softly. "You know what has to happen."

He nodded as he gazed down at her.

"But not just yet," she said, standing up in front of him and taking his hands in hers. "Just once. Just this once, Dex. And, not out of revenge. No, oh no. Out of love, Dex, out of love."

Barely comprehending what she was saying, he stood and took her in his arms, pulling her tightly to him. He leaned down and kissed her.

"Oh, Dex," she cried returning his kiss, her senses overwhelmed by all the pent-up emotion she'd been denying for so long.

Tenderly, he lifted and carried her up the stairs and gently placed her on his bed. He lay down beside her and kissed her again as he ran his fingers reverently over her body, tracing every line, every curve, as if trying to memorize everything that was her.

She shivered at his gentle touch, waiting as he continued his exploration, her passion mounting. He rolled down her tennis dress, exposing her bare flesh, then leaned over and kissed her softly in the hollow of her throat.

Unable to stand it any longer, she took his face in her hands and looked into his eyes. "I won't break, Dex," she whispered as she pulled him to her.

As they kissed, she moved her hands under his shirt, luxuriating in the warmth of his bare skin. At her touch, he pulled away and hastily tore off his T-shirt then crushed her half-naked body to his.

She arched to meet him as they reached hungrily for each other.

Much later, when they were both spent, he held her gently, cradling her, not wanting to ever let her go but knowing he would have to.

It was dark when Karen got up and got dressed to leave. Dex did not stir. She knew he was not asleep and that he didn't want to face what was to happen next. She was going home - home to Bill and to her children and she wouldn't be back. There would be no more lunches at the yard, no bike rides, nothing. He was losing her before he ever really had her and it was something he could not face.

When she was ready to leave, she sat on the bed and put her hand on his shoulder.

"Thank you," she said, "for everything, for loving me. If things were different, well, I...I would never let you go."

He sat up and held her with his eyes. "I love you, Karen, and I'll go on loving you. Nothing can ever change that. You complete me. I know you have to go and I respect that. I hope things work out for you, for your family, because I know that's what you want and, what you want, I want. But, if they don't, you come on back to me. Come back to me and let me love you."

He got up and walked her to the door. With tears in both their eyes, they embraced and then she left. As she ran down the drive to her car, he stood in the doorway watching her and feeling more lost and alone than he'd ever felt in his whole life.

At home, Bill sat in the family room playing video games with his daughters. He was worried about Karen. When she hadn't come back from tennis, he'd called her new friend, Alyce. She told him Karen had left around four o'clock and that was three hours ago.

He checked his watch and thought about trying her cell again. He'd tried earlier, but apparently, she'd turned it off. Worried she'd been in an accident, he was thinking about calling the police when he heard a car in the driveway. He went to the door and saw her emerge and slowly come up the walk to the house. When she got to the door, he opened it and started to ask her where she'd been. She silenced him with a look.

"I was ending something," she said. "That's all you need to know."

He closed the door and watched her as she left the room.

She broke it off with that guy, he thought, feeling a sense of relief. *Now it's just her and me.*

IT'S RAINING RABBITS

On Monday, Bill went off to work at his usual time. He and Karen were still careful around each other, knowing that one wrong move could cause irreparable damage. Bill planned on a full day on the road, visiting clients, but he also planned to check in with her at regular intervals to let her know where he was and what he was doing. He knew he needed to regain her trust.

At lunchtime, he received a text from Gerry inviting the whole family to his club on Sunday. There would be golf for the adults and swimming for the kids. Bill forwarded the message on to Karen for her approval before accepting. It sounded good to Bill, a step toward normalcy, but he would not do it if Karen weren't on board.

At home, the girls, now out of school for the summer, were playing outside in the yard. Karen was in the house reviewing brochures for summer camps when she heard Sophie yelling.

"Mommmmmmy, Mommy come, come quick!"

Karen dropped the brochures on the floor and ran out the door. She scanned the front yard but they weren't there. Then she heard Sophie calling again. The girls were in the backyard! Frightened, she rounded the corner of the house and saw Terri running toward her, her face spattered with blood.

"Terri, what happened?" Karen asked when she reached her daughter. "Are you hurt?"

Terri's T-shirt was covered with bloodstains and the little girl was crying and incoherent. Karen quickly looked her over and could find no wounds to explain the blood. She grabbed her daughter's hand and ran over to where Sophie was kneeling in front of that strange-looking bush. On the ground before her was the limp body of a rabbit, its back bleeding from multiple wounds.

Karen knelt down by her daughter. "Sophie, what happened here? How did this animal get hurt?"

Sophie looked up at her mother, tears in her eyes. "We were just playing and then this big old owl came swooping out of those trees over our heads," she said, pointing above her. "It had ahold of the bunny and it dropped him almost on Terri! Is it going to live, Mommy? Please make the bunny live!"

Karen looked at the rabbit. She didn't think it could survive such wounds, but for her daughters, she would do what she could. "Sophie, Terri, you go into the house and get me some towels and a basin of water. Now, go now, and hurry!"

The girls ran to do their mother's bidding. Hesitating only for a second, Karen gently put her hand on the rabbit's head. When she touched it, the creature stirred and turned to look at her. Her mouth fell open in amazement. Its eyes were brown with flecks of gold that shimmered in the sunlight. Such intelligence and compassion she saw in them. The rabbit held her gaze for a minute and then slowly smiled.

The blessed boy! she thought, stunned.

As if it could read her mind, the animal nodded slightly, then closed its eyes and was gone.

The girls returned with towels and water, but their mother looked at them and shook her head. "I'm sorry, sweeties, but the bunny was too hurt. He didn't make it. Terri, you give me that towel to wrap him in. Sophie, you run to the garage and get me my gardening trowel. Let's give this poor creature a proper burial."

Karen gently wrapped the rabbit in the towel, and, with her daughters' help, dug a small grave at the edge of the woods. They placed the body of the rabbit in the grave and covered it over with dirt, gathering stones to put on top to ensure that it would not be dug up in the night by some other predator. Sophie picked some flowers and they placed them on top of the grave. Finally, they said a prayer, wishing the rabbit's spirit Godspeed on its way to heaven.

"Okay, girls," Karen said. "Let's go in the house and wash up. It's almost time for lunch. And, Terri, let's get you out of those bloody clothes and put them to soak so they won't stain."

She took her daughters by the hand and they all went back into the house. When the girls were cleaned up and sitting down to lunch, Karen checked her cell and opened the message from Bill about the weekend. She texted him back to go ahead and tell Gerry "yes" for Sunday as long as the weather held. She added the latter because she'd heard something on the news about a bad storm heading up the coast that might make landfall in New England on the weekend.

After lunch, Karen settled the girls down in front of the TV watching Animal Planet. She sat down in the living room to mull over what had happened that morning.

The owl and the blessed boy.

Yes, it was the boy inside the rabbit, of that she was sure. She remembered Madge's urging, *"...find those papers, the ones left by Lisbeth Boucher, they are the key."*

She tried to recall where Bill had put the correspondence about the inheritance, but was unable to remember. *I'll have to ask him tonight when he gets home. Yes, after the girls have gone to bed, maybe we can talk.*

She leaned back in the overstuffed chair and closed her eyes. Something was going to happen, and soon. She could somehow feel it building. Her thoughts strayed to Dex. How she wished she could talk to him and feel his calm presence. But that was impossible now.

She sighed and tried to let her mind grow blank, to let sleep come to take her worries and cares away. But it would not. So, she just tried to rest, gazing out at the sea, hoping she would be prepared when whatever was going to happen, happened.

THE BOUCHER PAPERS

Bill got home at five-thirty. He hitched a ride from the wharf with Pete and surprised Karen and the girls with a large bouquet of flowers.

"Thought we could use some color in here," he said, handing the flowers to his wife. He leaned forward to give her a kiss, not knowing if she would accept it or not. She allowed him to kiss her on the cheek then turned to put the flowers in water. He poured himself a drink and sat down with his daughters, eager to learn about their day.

As Karen began preparing dinner, Bill walked into the kitchen.

"Heard you had quite a bit of excitement here today. And a funeral! What was that all about?"

Karen told him the facts about the owl and the rabbit.

"The girls were upset," she said. "That owl dropped the rabbit right on top of Terri. She was covered in its blood. I tried, but I couldn't save it. Its wounds were just too great. We buried it, laid flowers on the grave, and said a prayer. That's it. If it could have lived, it would have been great, but it didn't and I couldn't see just throwing the poor creature in the trash. And the girls need to know all life is valuable and has meaning."

Bill nodded. "You did the right thing," he said, taking her hand and squeezing it. "You always do, for the girls."

After dinner, when Sophie and Terri were safely tucked away in their beds, Karen broached the subject of the inheritance papers.

"Bill, I was wondering. What did you do with all the documents on the house and land?"

"Huh?" he replied, puzzled. "They're in a box in the hall closet. What do you want with them?"

"Oh, I was just wondering where they went to."

Bill put down his laptop and left the room. He came back a few minutes later with an accordion file in his hands.

"Here they are. Actually, I'm glad you brought them up. There's some correspondence in here from Aunt Janie I should have read a long time ago. I've been putting it off. Guess I'm afraid she will reprimand me from beyond the grave for not keeping in touch."

Karen's heart leapt - correspondence! Maybe, just maybe, there was something from Lisbeth, too.

Bill began rifling through the papers until he came to a large Manila envelope. He opened it and pulled out two smaller envelopes that were both addressed to him.

"This is from Janie," he said, holding up one of them for Karen to see. "I recognize her handwriting. The other one, I don't know."

Sighing, he opened the envelope and began to read aloud.

My Dearest Bill,

If you are reading this, then I must be dead. I have instructed my attorneys to be sure you receive this first, before you make any decisions about the property I am leaving to you. Whether or not they do this, well, attorneys are attorneys after all. I am, I suppose, now on my journey to the great beyond or whatever is the heaven du jour of the moment. I am sure, however, that Lisbeth and I will be reunited, maybe not in body or soul, but I believe that the energy of such love as we had will not, cannot, die and so I go happily on.

But, to the matter at hand. I know of your troubles, the loss of your job, your house. Yes, your father has kept me informed. Your parents wish they were in a position to help, but, alas, they are not. There is barely enough for them in their retirement. In any case, I plan to name you my heir. There is the property, a couple of autos (one, however, is probably not worth a red cent), and a small bank account. But it is because of the property that I write to you now, and because of my Lisbeth and the promise I made to her.

Before she passed, Lisbeth was most emphatic that I not leave you the house. "Sell the house," she said. "Give him the money, but non, ma chère, do not give him and his lovely family this place. It will be no good, I tell you, no good."

I did intend to respect her wishes, sell the property and leave you the cash. But, as I am sure you know, the bottom fell out of the housing market and I knew there was no way in hell I could sell this place before I died. So, I have decided to leave the property to you - lock, stock and barrel. I love this island and I hope you and yours will learn to love it, too.

However, before she died, Lisbeth put down in writing her fears for you and your family should you move here and I promised her I would pass them on to you. So, I ask - please read what she has written before you make any decisions. Her thoughts are written in French, and I hope your wife, who I know is fluent in languages, will be able to translate.

Bill, I love you with all my heart. I always thought that if I'd had a son I would have wanted him to be exactly like you.

Guard and protect your family always, for that is your job.

With Love from the Great Beyond,
Aunt Janie

Karen leaned forward in her chair, listening intently to the words of Bill's aunt. There were papers from Lisbeth! This was what she needed. Why, she wasn't sure, but she believed Madge and the things she had told her.

Bill sat silently, holding the letter in his hands. Then he put it down and picked up the other envelope. He tore it open and several sheets of paper fell out. He leaned down and picked them up, handing them to Karen.

"Like she said, they're in French. Honey, can you translate?"

"I can try," she answered taking the papers from him, her hand trembling slightly. "I may be a bit rusty and there are differences between French Canadian and the European variety, but I'll give it a try."

She looked the papers over for a few minutes, translating in her mind. Then she began to read aloud.

Dear Bill,

You may not remember me, but I remember you. You and I met a long time ago when you were just a young man, but you impressed me then as a sensible man with excellent character. Jane says you have grown up to be a good husband and loving father. She says when she dies, if I am no longer alive (which because of the cancer I don't expect to be), she will leave our home on Mateguas to you. It is because of this I write. It is because of my fears for you and your family that I write. Jane does not share these fears, for she is a great lover of this island, of this home. I love this place, too, and it has been good for us, but that is because of who and what we are. For you and your family it will be different. You will be easy prey for the Mskagwdemos and it is this I fear.

I write this to you as a descendant of the great Abenaki tribe who first settled in what is now called the State of Maine. My great grandmother was full-blood Abenaki and her blood, though thinned, still flows in my veins. So, you see, ma chère, I understand the legends that have been passed down for decades. The Abenaki have many tales of spirits, most of them benign, but some of them are pure evil. The most vicious of the latter is the Mskagwdemos and it is of her I write.

The Mskagwdemos is known in the vernacular as "swamp woman" or "swamp hag" because it is in the swamps that she makes her home. She is a malevolent being who is sustained by the blood and flesh of her victims. To entice poor souls to her, she makes mournful cries for help and these cries are manifested deep in her victim's subconscious. Thus, her prey is lured to her out of a sense of pity and, once he enters the swamp, may be lost forever.

And what does this swamp hag look like, you ask? No one knows for sure, but it is claimed she appears as a wild woman, wearing only bark. Her hair is moss and her naked breasts are pendulous. She is tall, an imposing figure, and in her mouth are rows of sharp pointed teeth with which she tears her victims to pieces. This does not paint a pretty picture, non? However, in paradox, she possesses a strange, almost supernatural beauty and is irresistible to men.

And, it is because of her ability to bewitch mortal men, that they become her most common victims. She uses this psychic-sexual allure to seduce them and lure them to their deaths within the swamp. A man under the spell of the Mskagwdemos will never be satisfied with a human woman again. And once she has a man in her clutches, the hag seeks to steal from him his male essence, his seed, always in the hope of begetting a child from her own loins.

It is also believed she can kill children with just one touch. It is told she intentionally lures children to their deaths out of spite or so that she can eat them. However, some legends paint her more sympathetically as a woman whose calls to children come from her terrible loneliness and bereavement for her own lost child. In any case, once she has lured a child to her, the child will fall victim to her deadly touch, leaving the Mskagwdemos all the more lonely and lost.

Women, however, especially those who have borne children, are strangely immune to her. They do not hear her calls and they are not lured into the swamp. This is why your aunt and I have led an uneventful life here for so many years and it is also why the Mskagwdemos is now ever so much more dangerous, as her loneliness and hunger have been exacerbated by the lack of a victim for so long. She will hunger to touch your sweet little girls and devour them and she will use all her wiles to lure you to her, to take your essence so she may bear your child. And, once she has sucked you dry, she will discard the husk that remains into the swamp for snakes and other vile creatures to dispose of.

You will think me mad when you read this, think the cancer had eaten my brain, non?

But, what I tell you is true and, if you come here, you will have to face the Mskagwdemos and defeat her. But how do you defeat her, you ask? How, when I tell you that you will surely fall victim to her spell? The answer is simple: you don't. It is only the woman who can defeat the hag - the woman who loves the child, who loves the man. Is it not so throughout the world? Is it not the mother who suckles the children and protects the family? Is it not the mother who is revered in myth and fables in every language, in religion? Oh, yes, ma chère, it is your wife who will have to do battle with the hag, who will have to take up the mantle to protect her family. Is it not the way of life - the mother always protecting her little ones, her home?

But how, you ask? How can my wife do what I cannot? Again, you will laugh at this old French Canadian woman, saying the cancer has eaten her brain, that she grows paranoid in her old age. But, I say to you that I am as sane as you, more likely saner. Why saner you ask? Saner, because I can see all the possibilities in life. Yes, I, who am on the verge of death, can see beyond the rational into the irrational. Oh, yes, ma chère, the irrational, the insane, it does exist.

But, you ask again how does my wife defeat the hag and save my family? The answer is simple. I have prepared for her all that she will need. In the closet in the back bedroom there is a loose board at the base of the far wall. Behind this board is hidden a box. The box is very old and full of powerful magic. On the top are carved three symbols: the lightning bolt, the teardrop, and the waning crescent moon. These symbols represent the Great Mateguas, overlord of the underworld, and he will aid your wife, if she follows my instructions.

But when you find the box, it will be locked! Yes, I have locked the box so no one but the woman who will battle the hag can open it. I do this because only that woman will have the strength to harness its magic - magic that could bring harm to anyone else. And, there are two keys needed to open the box. One, you will find on the key ring with the island car key. The other is secreted under a floorboard in the bedroom, beneath the bureau. Again, all your wife will need is in that box.

So, if you do not heed my warning and sell this house and live your life safely in California or anywhere but here, then I leave you what you need to keep your family from the clutches of the Mskagwdemos.

Oh, and, ma chère, one more thing. In the back of the house, there is a bush that appears to be out of place. It is an odd-looking bush with very long, sharp thorns. But, it is really not a plant at all. Non, it is not a natural thing. It is a creature of the Mskagwdemos. It either hides or reveals a trail into the woods. Do not go down that trail! It leads to the Mskagwdemos. The trail may look very inviting, but do not succumb to its beauty, for it is false!

Ah, Bill, please believe this old woman who is soon to die. Stay away from Mateguas. Keep your family safe. For what is there other than the family?

So, bon soir, my chère. May you, your wife and your children live to be as old as this one.

Your friend always,
Lisbeth Boucher

Bill listened quietly while Karen translated. When she finished the letter, he let out a long sigh.

"Whoa! What a hoot!" he exclaimed. "I think the cancer just might have eaten her brain. Can you believe all that? Are you ready to do battle with an irresistible hag, hon?"

Karen forced herself to laugh, but merriment was the last thing she was feeling. The words scared her, scared her to her core. How could she do this? She was just Karen Andersen from California, not some Abenaki sorceress. She put the letter down on the table, noticing her hand was shaking. Not wanting Bill to see her fear, she quickly tucked it under her thighs.

He looked at his watch. It was going on midnight.

"Gosh, it's late, hon. All this supernatural mumbo jumbo can make you lose track of time. I'd better hit the hay if I'm going to be any good at all at work tomorrow."

He got up and started for the couch in the family room. Karen put a hand on his arm to stop him.

"Bill, I think you'll get a better night's sleep upstairs. But don't expect anything more than sleep. I'm not ready for that yet."

Bill looked at her gratefully, leaned forward, and kissed her cheek lightly. "That's more than I deserve. Thank you."

She nodded, her mind a million miles away, lost in the storm that was yet to come. She looked back down at the papers written by Lisbeth, as if by doing so she could make them disappear and erase from her consciousness the words written within them.

Looking up and gazing out the window, she sighed. There was nothing she could do now.

I'll have to be Scarlett again and think about it tomorrow and, maybe, in the light of day, I can make some real sense of it all.

She stood, turned out the light, and began to ascend the stairs - to lie down beside her husband and try to get some sleep. But her mind was full of questions and she knew sleep was unlikely and that this night, real rest was but a dream.

BUT WHERE'S THE BOX

The next morning, after Bill left for work, Karen sent the girls outside to play. Once sure they were occupied, she took the Boucher papers and her car keys and went upstairs. The letter said the box was hidden in the back of the girls' closet behind a loose board and she would need two keys to open it. She had one, on the island car key ring; the other was hidden under a floorboard. Reaching down under the dresser, she ran her hand along the wooden planks until she came to the knothole. She pulled on it revealing Lisbeth's hiding place, but the recess was empty.

She sat on the floor shaking her head. *Oh, crap! Well, if I have to, I can always pry the box open.*

Getting up, she walked over to the closet to look for the hidey-hole. Removing the girls' shoes, she quickly found the loose board and opened it. She reached in and felt around inside but found only dust and mouse droppings. Disgusted, she replaced her girls' shoes and stood up.

Maybe there is no box. Maybe it's just all a bunch of hooey. An old woman on the verge of death, hallucinating.

But, deep down, she knew she really didn't believe that. Too much had happened to her that defied explanation. She sat down heavily on Terri's bed feeling depressed.

If everything Lisbeth and Madge said is true, how am I going to protect my family now? The tools I need are missing. I can't conjure up Lisbeth for a sit down but I can go see Madge again on Friday. Maybe, she can help me figure it all out.

By Wednesday, the newspapers and local TV news were full of warnings about the storm that was forming in the Caribbean that was expected to move up the coast. Most projections had it making landfall in Maine late night Saturday or early Sunday morning. High winds and subsequent power outages were expected along with a strong storm surge along the coast. Mainers were warned to make ready for possible extended power loss. Gerry called Bill to cancel their Sunday outing plans because of the storm.

"Hey, bro," he said to Bill. "We'll have to do it another time. This going be your first real nor'easter, isn't it? Well, get ready; it looks like it's going to be a whopper. You have a generator out there?"

"Yeah, we do. It's a portable, but it's hardwired into the house. I'll have to check it out tonight and see if it's in working condition."

"And get gas," advised Gerry. "Get plenty of gas. And water. I assume you're on a well out there in the boons?"

Bill replied affirmatively.

"Once the electric juice goes off, your well pump stops, and ergo - no 'wa, wa'. In case the generator fails, make sure you fill up the bathtub and sinks. You can use that water to flush toilets. Also, you're right on the ocean so you're going to get very strong winds. Pick up around the yard so you don't have debris flying all over the place. Just batten down those hatches, bro!"

They talked a while longer, Bill jotting down all that Gerry advised him to do. They made plans to reschedule the golf outing in a couple of weeks when things were back to normal. Gerry told him he would be out of the office on Friday, staying home with Sam and his son to make sure everything at their house was secure before the storm.

"You take off early and do the same. I'll try to check in with you on Sunday afternoon if there's any cell service - make sure this storm doesn't make you pack your bags and hightail it back to all those safe earthquakes in California!"

They shared a laugh and promised to try to connect the day after the storm.

At home, Karen made a list of items to pick up in town on Friday - batteries, candles, and bottled water. After she finished, she thought again about the missing box and key.

Why would Lisbeth go to all the trouble to write that damned epistle and then not hide the box? Maybe sickness took her before she had a chance? If so, then why wasn't it right out in the open somewhere? It's not like we wouldn't notice a box with strange carvings on it. And one that was double locked to boot!

She sat down and read the papers over again until she was sure of her translation.

How am I even going to know when the battle is supposed to be joined? Is the Mskagwdemos going to knock on my door and call me out? Even if that was the case, how can I do battle without some help?

Again, she longed for Dex's presence. She yearned to be able to talk with him, to feel secure in his deep abiding love for her. She tried not to think about their last time together, but was unable to help herself. She'd never felt anything like that before. It had been as if they were part of the same being, joined for eternity in some strange, incomprehensible way. There had been such joy - it was almost magical. But she had to accept that it was over. She had obligations and she would fulfill them no matter how much it hurt. She shook her head, trying to erase the memories from her mind.

Feeling depressed, she went outside to check on Sophie and Terri. They were sitting on the porch looking sad and bored.

"What say we go to the beach, kids?" she asked. "And then, maybe, if you're good, to the Island Burger Shack for ice cream?"

Her girls leapt to their feet and hugged her.

"Yes, Mommy, yes," exclaimed Terri as she jumped up and down.

"Okay, okay," Karen said, laughing, "let's get into our bathing suits and get whatever toys or things you want to bring with you."

The girls ran into the house. Karen stayed on the porch for a minute, thinking that all the other stuff that had been going on had made her lose sight of what was really important - her children. She made a vow to herself she would not let that happen again.

Sighing, she went inside and changed, then took her daughters' hands and walked down to the shore to play.

STORM PREPARATIONS

After returning home and greeting Karen and the girls, Bill changed and went outside to check the generator. He read the manual that came with it and his aunt's handwritten instructions on how to get it started. He checked the gas cans, finding one empty and the other half full. He filled the generator with what he had to get it going and went into the house.

"Hey, hon," he said to Karen. "Be prepared for the power to crash. I'm testing the generator."

He went downstairs to the cellar, tripped the main, and crossed his fingers. Everything stayed on. He skipped up the stairs and walked into the kitchen.

"Looks like the generator's working okay," he said to Karen, who was busy at the sink. "I'm going to install a new sump pump now. And, oh, can you get the gas cans filled tomorrow?"

Without waiting for an answer, he returned to the cellar to install the new sump.

A few minutes later, he came back up the stairs. "Well, hopefully that will keep us from floating away. Hon, did you hear me about the gas cans?"

Karen, lost in her own thoughts - thoughts about the blessed boy and the missing box - was startled back to reality.

"Huh?" she asked. "I'm sorry, Bill, what did you ask me?"

"Gas cans, hon," he said, a little irritably. "Can you get them filled tomorrow? We'll need extra gas for the generator if the power goes out."

"Sure, no problem. Sorry, but my mind was somewhere else."

Bill looked at her closely. Was she thinking about that Dex character? Wishing she was with him? He felt a stab of jealousy, but tried to shake the feeling off. She'd told him she had ended it. He had to believe her.

He put down the old sump and walked over to her. "It's going to be okay," he said putting his arm around her. "It's just a storm. We've been through worse in California."

Karen stiffened instinctively when she felt his touch. Consciously, she forced herself to relax, to try to accept his affection. Then, she pulled away.

"I've made a list of stuff to pick up on Friday," she said, handing it to him. "Here, add anything you think I've forgotten."

"Sure, hon."

Later, after dinner, the Andersens spent the night talking and laughing about storms and earthquakes they had experienced in Los Gatos. What could really happen here that would be so bad? There would just be lightning, thunder, wind, and rain. Loss of power - well, they were prepared for that. So what else could happen?

The next day, Karen dutifully filled all the gas cans and secured an extra tank of propane for the grill. She brought down all the dirty laundry and got it done, including the bed sheets.

Telling herself she was prepared, at least, for a normal storm, she sat down and read through the Boucher papers again, hoping she would catch something she had mistranslated. Not finding anything, she rechecked the hiding places in the girls' room, just in case she had overlooked something. Nothing had changed. All she could count on now was Madge's memory.

Maybe I'm making a mountain out of a molehill. It will just be a storm. Probably a bad one, but just a storm.

FRIDAY

On Friday, after she dropped Bill at the wharf, Karen came home and prepared her children for a full day at the library. They were enrolled in a summer class that dealt with the ecosystem on the island. She packed them lunches and gave them money for juices and ice cream. She made sure Terri had her cell and, when they were ready, left them in the care of the librarian. She then drove to the wharf to wait for the next boat. While she waited, she decided to give Madge a call to let her know she was coming. The nursing home answered promptly.

"Hi," said Karen. "Madge Parker's room, please."

There was a pause on the line. "Who's calling? Are you family?"

"No, my name is Karen Andersen. I'm a friend. I've been visiting her recently." Karen waited, puzzled by the inquisition and the operator's tone of voice.

"Can you hold for a minute?" the operator asked.

Karen agreed, beginning to become concerned. Why didn't they put her through?

The operator came back on the line. "I'm sorry. I had to check before I told you. Mrs. Parker had a cardiac incident last night. She's been transferred to the hospital. She was in the ICU, but I think she's been moved to intermediate care now, but she cannot speak. She's in a coma."

Karen's heart sank. Her last hope was gone. Feeling helpless, she decided to go see the old lady anyway. It was the least she could do. She thanked the operator and asked for the hospital's address.

When she arrived, she was directed to the intermediate care unit on the second floor. A nurse escorted her to Madge's room. Looking down at the old woman, Karen was shocked to see how frail she looked. Her eyes were closed, but her breathing seemed steady and even. Karen sat down next to the bed and took her withered hand in hers. She squeezed, tentatively, hoping that, somehow, she would get a response, but there was none. Madge's hand lay limply in hers.

She sat by the bedside quietly for some time and then, in a soft voice, began speaking to the old woman, telling her of Lisbeth Boucher's papers, of the missing box, and of her fears. Throughout her recitation, she held the old woman's hand, willing it to show her some sign of comprehension. But still, there was none. Finally, Karen let go, rose, and leaned down and kissed Madge gently on the cheek.

"I hope you come back to us, Marguerite Parker," she said softly. "The world is a better place with you in it."

She gave the old woman one last look before leaving. Once in the parking lot, she sat in her car just staring at nothing for a while, then, with a sigh, drove to complete her errands. She finished quickly and decided to head on home. At the ferry terminal, she was surprised to find Bill in the waiting room.

"Hi. You got out early."

"Yeah, I hoped to surprise you - me picking you up for a change," he answered. "Get everything?"

She lifted her canvas bags in response. "Everything on the list. Don't worry. When this storm arrives, we'll be ready."

SATURDAY

Saturday morning, Dex was busy preparing for the storm that was now projected to hit late that night. He moved his fishing boat to the leeward side of the island for safety, as had most of the other commercial fishermen. That done, he pulled his punt out of the water to ensure it was not damaged by the wind and high seas.

All day, as he worked, he couldn't get Karen off his mind. He kept taking out his cell and staring at her number then putting the phone back in his pocket again. He was sure old lady Morgan had had a generator, but whether or not it worked properly, he didn't know. He wished he could go up there and see if she needed any help - if that husband of hers was taking care to make sure she was safe. He didn't like Bill, but he didn't sell him short. He knew he was an intelligent and savvy guy, except maybe where women were concerned. Still, Dex felt uneasy. Something was going to happen to Karen - something bad. He was sure of it.

He noticed Pete pulling his punt out of the water and went over to help. After they got the older man's boat securely on the trailer, Pete turned to him.

"Thanks, Dex, for giving an old guy a hand. Each year this stuff gets tougher. Let me buy you a beer, little buddy."

Dex laughed. "You'll be doing this when you're ninety! And, I'll accept your kind offer."

They strolled over to the yard store, chatting amiably. Pete bought two Coors and handed one to Dex.

"Everything the newsboys say seems to indicate that this weather is going to be a humdinger," said Pete.

"Yeah," replied Dex. "Hey, you're tight with the new folks, the Andersens? Do you know if they got themselves prepared? Got the generator up and running and all?"

Pete hesitated for a moment. He'd heard the rumors about Dex and Karen. He'd also heard gossip about Maggie and Bill. Up to this minute, he hadn't thought any of it was worth a grain of salt, but now, what with Dex asking about Karen and Bill, trying to sound casual, well, that just didn't sit right with him.

He looked Dex squarely in the eye. "I believe they are just fine, Dex. Bill's got the generator up and running, they have all their gas cans full, they got batteries and candles, a spare tank of propane, and Bill even bought them a new sump. Yup, they are just fine. Don't you worry your head over them. Bill has got everything under control."

Dex nodded, noting his interest was not appreciated. *Oh, well, I don't care. Pete might take offense, but at least I know now that all the physical safety steps have been taken. But why do I still feel so uneasy? It's kind of like how I felt before I found her passed out in the backyard. But it's more. Yes, there's something darker, something more intense about the way I feel now.*

He quickly finished his drink, thanked Pete again, and headed home to make sure his own property was secure. But his mind remained troubled - the thought of Karen being in danger ever present.

Pete watched Dex as he left the yard. *That boy is going to get himself in a whole lot of trouble over that woman,* he thought, shaking his head.

Then he, too, finished his beer and hurried on home to help Louise.

On the other side of the island, Maggie was with her mother

helping to clean up the backyard and move into the barn anything that might go flying off in the high winds that were predicted for late evening. As she folded up some lawn chairs, she thought about Bill. There had been no word from him since Sunday. She wasn't surprised. It would take more than a few days for Karen to have some confidence in him again.

I know it's too early. That woman is probably checking up on him all the time now. But still, I miss him.

She had almost called him on Friday when she was in town. She had her cell ready to dial when his words rang back at her, *"You do NOT call me, text me, or email me."* Remembering his anger, she quickly put the cell away. Calling him would be a mistake and could result in the end of their relationship. And now, more than ever, she could not let that happen. She had to keep the door open for him. And he would come back, of that she was sure. She had the upper hand now and he was hooked whether he knew it or not.

Unaware they were the focus of so many people's thoughts, Bill and Karen spent a normal Saturday. With the girls' help, they, like all their fellow islanders, cleaned up their yard, folding up lawn chairs, putting barbecues away, and securing any other items the wind might get a hold of. Karen made sure all the windows were securely locked and that there were fresh batteries in their flashlights, lanterns, and portable radio. They charged their cells and the backup battery for Bill's laptop. When their preparations were done, they ate lunch and headed to the beach.

The day seemed perfect with no indication of the storm to come. Karen watched as Bill and their daughters played in the water.

He takes such joy in them and they in him. How could I leave and deprive them of that? Her thoughts again turned to Dex. *Is he worth hurting my children for? No, nothing's worth that. But how can I stay here in this small, close-knit community where I'll bump into him at any time? And that Maggie creature - that slut - we'll see her all the time, too. At all the island social occasions, there she'll be, tossing her curls and laughing. How can I ever trust Bill again with that girl ever present, always available? And how can I trust myself with Dex living right around the corner? And Bill, how will he be able to trust me?*

She shook her head. *We sure made a mess of things. And what about the box and the swamp hag? Do they really exist? And if they do, how will I know what to do or when to do it?*

She gazed out at the sea, her mind swirling with questions that had no answers. *I guess I just gotta keep on keeping on,* she told herself. *The answers will come; they have to.*

She sighed and, with another shake of her head, got up and ran down to the surf to join her husband and children at play.

THE EVENING OF THE STORM

The wind picked up around four o'clock and the Andersens watched as the sea began to get rougher. Dismal gray cloud cover that foretold of the weather to come had replaced the bright sunshine of earlier in the afternoon. Karen, Bill, and the girls gathered up their belongings and headed across the street to their home. Once inside, Karen sent the girls upstairs to shower while she and Bill checked out the latest weather forecast. The storm was in the Boston area now and was still expected to hit around midnight.

"Maybe we'll sleep through the whole thing," said Bill, "and wake up to bright sunshine like nothing ever happened."

"I've got my fingers, eyes, and toes crossed for that," replied Karen. "Roast chicken for dinner work for you?"

Bill indicated it would be more than okay and sat down with his laptop while Karen started their meal. After dinner was over, they sat down as a family to play some old-fashioned board games. As they played, they could hear the wind outside and the ever-increasing sound of the waves hitting the shore.

At around nine o'clock, Karen sent the girls upstairs to get ready for bed. Once they were in their PJs, Bill went up to read them a story, complete with sound effects that had them giggling and laughing. When the story was over, he tucked them into bed and kissed them goodnight. Karen stood in the doorway watching.

"Now if you all get scared in the night," she said, "you come in and wake Mommy and Daddy, okay?"

"We will, Mommy," said Terri.

Karen kissed them both, then turned out the lights and went back downstairs where Bill stood looking out the window.

"It's picking up, hon," he said, gesturing her to his side. "See the whitecaps?"

Karen stood next to him and nodded. Tentatively, he put his arm around her waist. It felt comfortable and she leaned into him.

He turned to look at her. "I've made such a mess of everything, Kar. You, well, you and the children are my world. I don't know if you can ever forgive me, but I'll try to make it up to you. I'm going to talk to Gerry next week to see if there's any way I can move inside earlier. And once I'm bringing in a bigger paycheck, well, we'll move off this island over to the mainland where the kids can go to a regular school. And, where you won't be reminded every day of what an ass I've been."

She was about to tell him she didn't want to hear about it when she saw the tears rolling down his cheeks. Wiping them away with her fingertips, she smiled.

"That would be good. I don't think we can ever get back to where we once were but maybe, just maybe, we can build something different, something stronger, out of all of this. If we both try, in time, we might be able to put things back together."

He nodded and then leaned down and kissed her chastely, barely touching her lips. She reached up and pulled him to her, returning his kiss with passion. His arms encircled her and he held her close. The rain began to beat against the windows and the sound of the wind became louder. She wrapped her arms around his neck.

"Make love to me, Bill," she whispered.

He picked her up and carried her to the couch. They made love, each being exceedingly careful with the other, wanting this to work so they could go on together. When it was over, they lay in each other's arms, exhausted and half asleep. The sound of thunder jarred them awake.

Bill looked at his watch. "It's eleven o'clock. The storm's going to be intensifying over the next few hours. We'd better get upstairs in case the girls need us."

Karen nodded as he helped her up. She took his hand and together they mounted the stairs to their bedroom. They checked on the girls, who were sleeping peacefully, and then went to bed.

THE GIRLS

A flash of lightning lit up the sky illuminating the L-shaped room where Sophie and Terri slept. The light was so bright, it startled Sophie awake and she sat up rubbing her eyes. When she could finally focus, she was surprised to see their room was suffused by a golden glow that lingered long after the lightning faded. As she gazed about the room in wonder, she saw her twin standing by the window that looked out to the backyard.

"Ter, what ya doin'?" she asked.

Terri turned her head, a bright smile on her face. "Soph, come see. It's beautiful. It's like a fairy world."

Sophie got out of bed and joined her sister at the window. Her eyes widened in amazement when she saw what was happening outside. Scores of fireflies were dancing around one of the bushes in the yard, their light sparkling and shimmering in the wind and rain.

"It looks like Christmas," said Sophie, her voice filled with awe.

"Yeah, Soph. See how they dance. And listen - I think they're singing."

Sophie pressed her face to the glass, straining to hear. "I don't hear anything."

"Close your eyes and really listen."

Sophie did as her sister instructed. In a moment, she nodded her head eagerly. "I hear it. I hear it. It's like magic. It's so pretty."

The girls grinned in delight as they listened to the sweet melodic song of the fireflies.

"What language is it?" Sophie whispered. "I don't understand it but I love it."

"I don't know. I've never heard anything like it before."

They stood quietly listening and watching the spectacle taking place before them oblivious to the storm that was raging. But in an instant, their joy was cut short by a loud crack of thunder that shook the house. The room plunged into darkness as the golden glow was extinguished and the fireflies disappeared.

"Look," whispered Sophie pointing her finger to the yard.

Terri gripped her sister's hand tightly as she watched a shadowy figure streak across the lawn toward the woods. A flash of lightning lit up the sky, temporarily blinding the girls and when their sight returned, the figure was gone.

They stood transfixed, waiting to see what would happen next. Then a soft mournful sob, barely audible at first, pierced the silence. Stunned, Terri and Sophie hugged each other in fear as the sobs became more desperate. The wind began to howl and mournful cries echoed in the night. Tears streamed down Sophie's cheeks as she recognized the voice that was now calling out her name.

"It sounds like Mommy, Ter! Is it Mommy? Please, is it Mommy?"

Terri leaned forward, her body rigid as she strained to recognize the voice calling to them. The sound was so familiar but not real, not like her mother. Yet, it was her.

"It is Mommy. She sounds in so much pain. I think she's hurt. We have to help her."

Sophie gripped her sister's hand tightly. The cries were becoming more plaintive now as if the caller was losing hope.

"We have to wake Daddy. He'll know what to do."

Terri shook her head. "We can't get Daddy. What if it's his fault? What if he hurt her again? You heard them fighting. No, it's up to us, Soph. We have to help her."

The girls stood staring at each other for what seemed a lifetime, then Sophie nodded. "You're right. Let's go. We have to find Mommy. We have to save her."

Terri took her sister's hand and squeezed it. Together they tiptoed out of their room and down the stairs. They stopped briefly at the hall closet, put their slickers on over their nightclothes to try to stay dry and grabbed a flashlight. Then, hand in hand, they opened the door and, without hesitation, went silently out into the storm.

THE STORM

Karen was startled awake as the room shook with the crash of thunder. She looked over at the clock. It was two a.m. Bill turned to her; the thunder had awakened him, too.

"I'd better check on the girls," she said. "And make room. We might have company."

As Karen walked down the hall to the girls' room, Bill got up and went to the window to watch the storm. It was wild out there.

"Bill!" Karen yelled as she came running back in the room. "They're gone! The girls aren't in their room. They're gone!"

"Did you check the bathroom?" asked Bill, walking toward his wife.

"Yes, they aren't there either. They're gone!" she cried, close to panic.

"Calm down, hon. They've got to be here somewhere. Let's look downstairs."

They split up and searched the house, but their daughters were nowhere to be found.

"Could they have gone outside?" asked Karen as she looked in the hall closet. "Oh, my God! Bill, their slickers are gone! Why would they go out into the storm! Why would they do that? Oh, Bill, why?"

Bill pulled on his sweats, grabbed his slicker and a lantern that was sitting on the side table, ready in case the power went out.

"I don't know. All those old stories about people going into the woods during storms, maybe they thought they had to see...oh, I don't know, honey."

He put his arms around his distraught wife. "I'll find them, Karen. I'll bring them home to you. I promise. You stay here in case they return. I have my cell. I don't know if it will work, but try to call me if they come home."

Thunder crashed as he kissed his wife then opened the door and went out into the storm.

Karen watched him through the window as he struggled with the wind. It looked like he was going to head down to the beach, but, unexpectedly, he turned and jogged toward the rear of the house. When he rounded the corner, she could no longer see him. Had he heard something? She prayed he had seen or heard the girls and they would soon be safe inside. She went back upstairs to her daughters' room and looked out the rear window.

Bill was in the middle of the yard, fighting the wind, the lantern swinging precariously in his hand. Karen watched, her anxiety increasing as the minutes went slowly by.

I should be out there with him. We could cover more territory. What if they went to the beach? I can't stay here and just wait.

She swiftly turned from the window to go downstairs. However, as she moved, her hip caught the corner of Sophie's nightstand, knocking over a pencil box and sketchpad. Despite her rush to join in the search, habit took over and she knelt down to pick up the scattered pencils. Returning them to the box, she reached for the sketchbook. Her mouth fell open in alarm when she saw the drawing on the top. It was a sketch of a box with symbols on the lid - a crescent moon, a lightning bolt, and a teardrop. Next to the box were drawn three sticklike figures, a jar holding something red, and a knife with a carved handle. Beneath the drawing, Sophie had written: *"Oh Mateguas, great dad of the dead, hear my prayer."*

Karen stood up, her full attention on the drawing as she remembered the words of Lisbeth Boucher, *"...everything your wife needs is in the box..."* and *"It is only the woman who can defeat the hag...."*

The girls found the box! she exclaimed to herself. *That's why it wasn't where Lisbeth put it. And the keys, they found the keys, too! And that hag wants them, has called to them. That's why they went outside and she can kill them with a touch. And Bill, oh God, Bill, he's gone out after them. He will be helpless before her. He cannot aid them and she will consume them all. Oh God, my family!*

Knowing she was acting irrationally but unable to stop herself, Karen began tearing the room apart looking for the box and the magic it contained. She looked under the beds and mattresses. She searched through the drawers in the dresser. She found nothing.

Finally, she turned her attention back to the closet and began to frantically go through it. About to give up, she found the box on the bottom shelf way in the back, hidden under a bunch of T-shirts.

She pulled it out and examined it. It was unlocked. She sat on the floor and with some trepidation opened it. On top were several sheets of notebook paper covered with translations from French to English written in her daughters' handwriting. She tossed these aside. She could translate. She looked at the rolled up parchment briefly, then focused on the papers that were in the envelope. The first sheet, written in Lisbeth Boucher's fine hand, was entitled, *"Mateguas Prière"* or, in English, *"Mateguas Prayer."* As she read, she translated,

> *"Oh, Mateguas, Great Father of the Dead, hear my prayer.*
>
> *Hear the prayer of this mother for her family.*
> *Tonight the Mskagwdemos rides the storm.*
> *She throws the lightning bolt,*
> *She screams the thunder,*
> *She washes the land with her tears,*
> *And she hungers for this mother's family.*
>
> *The man, she calls so she can lie with him and steal his seed.*

The child she calls to suckle at her breast.

This mother would keep her family safe.
This mother would protect the man and the child, as they are helpless to protect themselves from the fury of the Mskagwdemos.

This mother begs the Great Mateguas for mercy.

With this knife made from the bones of the sacred moose, this mother will make sacrifice to the Great Father of the Dead that he may take pity on her and restore her family to her.

Her blood shall make fertile the earth so that The People, who are so loved by the Great Mateguas, will prosper.

Oh, Great Father of the Dead, hear my prayer."

Karen folded the prayer and put it in her pocket. Then she looked at what appeared to be a list of instructions, again written in Lisbeth's hand, and the diagram that went with them.

She studied the sketch carefully. It contained a crudely drawn circle in which were placed the symbols that were carved on the box along with the cornhusk dolls. The four compass directions were noted along with the admonition to always face east. When she concluded her examination of the drawing, she turned her attention to the list. As she translated, her fear escalated.

Mateguas Prayer

1) *Draw a circle around you on the front lawn using the blood powder.*
2) *Inside the circle, draw the crescent moon, lightning bolt, and teardrop symbols.*
3) *Place the family (dolls) inside the circle, facing east.*
4) *Recite the "Mateguas Prayer," always facing east.*
5) *When you come to the sacrifice, take the bone knife*

and slice open your palm - do it good and deep because you must bleed into the earth. Press your palm to the earth while continuing to recite the prayer.

6) The earth must take your blood and be nourished by it.

7) Continue reciting the prayer and repeating the sacrifice until the sun appears over the horizon.

8) If you do all these things correctly, your family will be returned, unharmed to you.

But *ALWAYS* face east, no matter what happens, do not turn around!

Am I really supposed to do this? she asked herself, as she held the knife in her hand. *They'll put me in the booby hatch for sure.*

Resigned, she folded the instructions and diagram and put them in her pocket along with the prayer. The knife, jar of blood powder, and cornhusk dolls she quickly put in one of the girls' tote bags.

She stood up and took a deep breath. Lisbeth's words echoed in her mind, *"Is it not the mother who suckles and protects the family? Is it not the mother who is revered in myth and fables in every language, in religion? Oh, yes, ma chère, it is your wife who will have to do battle with the hag, who will have to take up the mantle to protect her family."*

Yes, she could do this, as insane as it seemed. She would go out into the storm, draw the circle, say the words, slice open her palm, and give blood to the earth. She would do this for her family, the family that was probably safe somewhere riding out the storm. But she knew she couldn't take the chance that they weren't. Too much had happened that defied explanation. If this Mskagwdemos really existed and she sat on her thumbs waiting for Bill and the girls to return, she would lose them forever and she was not going to let that happen.

And, as she made her decision, she accepted it all. She *knew* why she, and only she, had experienced those bizarre events. The blessed boy had been preparing her - preparing her for this moment - so she would not falter, would not waver. He had been testing her strength, her resolve. And, with each test, she had grown stronger. She only hoped he had made her strong enough - strong enough to save her family through the force of her own will.

Oh, yes, I will save them or die trying.

BILL

Bill fought the wind and rain as he looked and called for Terri and Sophie. His first instinct was to go to the beach and was about to head down the driveway when he felt an overwhelming urge to turn in the opposite direction.

When he reached the backyard, he was immediately struck by the vividness of one of the berry bushes. Its colors sparkled in the rain and the branches seemed to beckon to him. As he neared it, he saw there was a well-kept trail directly behind it.

Why haven't I noticed this before? he asked himself as the wind and rain battered him.

Staring at the bush and the path beyond, he remembered the words of Lisbeth Boucher, *"Do not go down that trail. It leads to the Mskagwdemos."*

He stood at the head of the trail, frozen in indecision, when he noticed in the mud in front of him a piece of fabric with the face of a teddy bear on it. Unable to stop himself, he stepped onto the trail and reached down, illuminating the scrap with his lantern. It was flannel - a piece of one of the twins' pajamas.

They came down here. Why?

He began jogging down the trail, calling for his children. At one point, he looked back and was surprised to see the path seemed to be closing up behind him. But still he went on. He had to find his children and take them home to Karen. He'd promised her and this was one promise he would keep.

Deeper and deeper into the woods he ran as the sky darkened and thunder crashed. He rounded a bend and a large owl swooped down at him and threatened to maim him, but he ducked, not breaking his stride. He ran on - for his children, for his wife, for his family.

Soon, the trail began to narrow precipitously and he was afraid that it would end. If it did, how would he find his children? He turned a corner and, suddenly, in front of him, he saw his daughters. They were standing at the edge of a malignant-looking swamp, black flies and mosquitoes swarming above their heads. Their posture was rigid, as if in a trance. They seemed unable to move or to acknowledge his presence.

"Terri, Sophie, it's Daddy," he called. "Come to me!"

At the sound of her father's voice, Sophie's eyes seemed to clear as if awakened from a deep sleep. She tried to run to him, but her feet would not move.

"Daddy, we can't," she answered tearfully. "That thing won't let us."

As she spoke, her eyes widened with fear and she pointed to something behind him. "Oh, Daddy, behind you. She's here!"

Bill turned to see what had frightened his daughter so. His mouth widened in amazement as the apparition stepped onto the trail behind him. He gasped, unable to believe what he was seeing and, paradoxically, while it horrified him, it also took his breath away.

KAREN

Karen gathered up her courage, put on her slicker, and ran downstairs to go out into the wind and rain. The storm was reaching its height when she opened the front door. A sudden gust tore the door from her hand and she screamed as it slammed against the side of the house. The wind was howling and she had to fight to get to the front yard, rain pelting her as she ran.

Finally reaching the middle of the lawn, she stared out at the ocean to the east of her. Whitecaps crashed against the shoreline and the sky was an angry grayish black color that was darkening with every minute. A lightning bolt suddenly lit up the sky and was followed immediately by a deafening crack of thunder.

Better get started before I'm blown away, she thought as she reached in the tote for the bottle of blood powder.

The wind screamed at her as she carefully broke the seal and untied the wire that held the little silver spoon in place. She took a deep breath, trying to calm herself. Her hands were shaking so much from the cold and fear that she was afraid she might drop the bottle at any minute. She kneeled on the ground as the wind whipped her wet hair around her head, making it difficult for her to see what she was doing.

Slowly and carefully, she dipped the spoon into the powder and, as she withdrew it, the wind caught hold of the talc and blew it straight into her face. Coughing, she swore, then took another deep breath and hunkered down closer to the ground. Again, she dipped the spoon into the powder, but this time, as she pulled it from the bottle, she shielded it from the wind with her other hand. With infinite patience, she drew the circle around herself. Lightning flashed and on its tail came a mind-bending roar of thunder.

That was close, she thought her fear escalating.

Lightning streaked between the clouds again and the wind screamed louder than before as she closed the circle around herself. As the last of the powder sunk into the earth, all around her suddenly became quiet. She looked up in amazement. The storm still raged, but somehow, in her little circle of blood powder, she was safe.

It's like being in the eye of a hurricane.

She shook off her sense of wonder and laid the cornhusk dolls on the ground beside her so they were also facing east. She picked up the bottle again and, with the spoon, continued drawing: the lightning bolt, the teardrop, and the crescent moon.

As the powder hit the earth, it began to glow an eerie reddish color and she seemed to be enveloped by that glow. It made her mind reel. Forcing herself to concentrate, she carefully finished the drawings and stood up as doubts again assailed her mind.

This is insane. I've gone insane. They will lock me away for sure. I'll spend the rest of my life weaving baskets and drooling because of all the medications I'm on.

With an effort, she pushed these doubts from her mind as her fear for her family overcame the fear for her sanity. To steady her resolve, she pulled from memory pictures of her girls who she loved so much. And ones of Bill, too - ones from the good times she had almost forgotten. Tears streamed down her cheeks as she accepted that she loved him, too, despite everything.

She pulled the prayer from her pocket. As she did, she remembered the rabbit - the blessed boy - standing on his hind legs, grinning at her, confident in her courage. Comforted by this thought, she reached down deep within herself for strength and, taking a deep breath, in a soft voice began to speak:

"Oh, Mateguas, Great Father of the Dead, hear my prayer."

As she spoke the words, her voice grew louder and more confident. Although she could not hear it, she was aware the storm around her was intensifying.

A lawn chair that was folded up on the patio suddenly was launched at her by the wind. The chair was coming directly at her head and it took all her strength and courage to stand her ground and trust in the invisible barrier that apparently protected her. The chair's velocity increased as it neared her, but when it crashed into the barrier, it fell harmlessly to the ground.

Karen didn't move. She continued reciting the words, words that would bring her family back to her. Lightning shattered across the sky and she could feel the earth tremble beneath her feet as thunder crashed. But still she went on.

"With this knife made from the bones of the sacred moose, this mother will make sacrifice to the Great Father of the Dead that he may take pity on her and restore her family to her.

"Her blood shall make fertile the earth so that The People, who are so loved by the Great Mateguas, will prosper."

After she recited these lines, she knelt on the ground, the bone knife in her hand. She took a deep breath and, without hesitation, drew the knife across her palm, cutting deeply. She cried out in pain as blood oozed from the vicious wound she had inflicted upon herself. Trying to ignore the pain, she pressed her injured hand into the grass. She felt frozen as the earth sucked at her wounded hand, greedily taking her blood as nourishment. She remained kneeling, feeling dizzy and weak, her palm pressed to the ground for several minutes.

Suddenly, the earth gave back and her weakness vanished. She felt an almost superhuman strength begin to course through her body. Feeling calm and powerful, she stood up and in a firm and steady voice, finished the prayer,

"Oh Great Father of the Dead, hear my prayer."

BILL

Bill stared at the apparition that had stepped out onto the trail behind him, his mouth agape. It appeared to be a woman, tall, naked - her body covered with decaying green moss-like hair. Her breasts sagged and hung down almost to her knees. The mossy patch between her legs seemed to teem with worms that undulated in and out of the cleft between her thighs. When she opened her mouth, he could see the razor-sharp teeth that lay within. The word *hideous* did not do her justice, yet, despite this, Bill found her wildly arousing and was shocked by his instantaneous erection.

The creature looked between his legs and began to laugh a wild, maniacal laugh that caused Bill's erection to deflate as fast as it had come and struck fear in his heart. He remembered Lisbeth's warning, *"...she will use all her wiles to lure you to her, to take your essence so that she may bear your child and, once she has sucked you dry, she will discard the husk that remains into the swamp for snakes and other vile creatures to dispose of"*.

This is real! he thought, amazed and terrified. *This is really happening!*

His aunt's words echoed in his mind, *"Guard and protect your family always, for that is your job."*

Standing as if frozen, he admitted to himself that he was frightened, more frightened than he had ever been in his life, but he had to save his children - save them for Karen. Pushing his fear aside, he lifted his head, faced the Mskagwdemos, and spread his arms wide in an attempt to shield his daughters.

"You will not have them!" he cried. "Over my dead body...."

As he spoke, there was suddenly a change in the atmosphere around them. The air seemed lighter, cleaner. Terri realized she was able to move and she grabbed Sophie's hand. Together, they ran to their father, somehow freed from the spell the Mskagwdemos had put on them.

The hag, whose eyes were locked with Bill's, suddenly turned and roared in the direction of the house, her attention diverted by something that had happened there.

"Run, girls, run!" yelled Bill as he pushed his daughters ahead of him and began running back down the trail toward home.

KAREN

Karen started the prayer again, her strength growing as she recited the words.

I think it's working. I can feel it.

Lightning lit up the sky as it struck the maple tree that grew at the end of the driveway, breaking off a large branch that fell to the ground. The earth trembled as it hit, but Karen was not deterred from her task. Then, out of nowhere, a sound from behind her pierced the barrier - a sound that struck fear in her heart.

"Mommmeeeeeeeeeeeee!!!!!!!!!!"

It sounded so like Terri's voice and Karen, unable to stop herself, turned her head ever so slightly in the direction of that voice. As soon as she moved, hideous laughter echoed across the sky, and Karen knew she had made a mistake - the instructions were very clear: always face east, do not waver! Quickly she turned back and with tears coursing down her cheeks continued the prayer. As she spoke the words, her mind raced.

Did I destroy my family by one lousy turn of my head? Or will the Great Mateguas take pity on me and forgive my error?

She did not know the answers but knew no matter what the consequences of that head turn, she had to go on, and continue on until sunrise. And so, she began again...

BILL

Bill held his daughters' hands as they ran blindly through the woods. The atmosphere around them had grown heavy again and their fear escalated. Sensing that something had gone terribly wrong, Bill slowed his pace and pushed his daughters behind him, shielding them with his arms. He stood still and watched as, up ahead of them, the Mskagwdemos stepped onto the trail, a horrible gloating smile on her face.

Again, as he stared at the hideous apparition, he could not help but feel a strong sexual attraction to it, but he fought his irrational desire with every ounce of his strength. The creature opened her mouth and they could see her tongues writhing within like a nest of angry snakes. The girls cowered, clinging to their father.

Suddenly, inside his head, a furious roar blotted out Bill's thoughts and he fought to keep from giving in to his fear. Then his mind cleared and he heard the creature's voice echoing throughout his consciousness.

"Your wife has failed, Bill Andersen. She is not strong enough. Her sacrifice will not appease the earth. The land cries out for more blood and must be fed. Now, it is up to you to choose. Give me the little ones and you can go free."

Bill shook his head vehemently. "No, never - you will NOT have them!"

Again, he heard the roaring in his head and it took all his courage to stand his ground. Without warning, an image of Karen flashed in his mind - Karen, as she was when he first met her, so young, so beautiful. Then, the Mskagwdemos' voice again resounded inside of him.

"If I cannot have the children, then give me your woman and you and the little ones can go free."

Bill stood silent as more images of Karen and their life together passed through his consciousness. Both the good and the bad times played repeatedly in his mind. Could he turn her over to this monster? And if he did, could he live with himself after? Finally, he knew - knew everything that had happened since he'd set foot on this island had been leading him to this - to this one moment - to this choice. He knew now it was his turn to sacrifice - for his daughters and for the woman he loved more than life.

"No," he said firmly and finally. "You cannot have her. My children and my wife will not be yours."

He turned to his girls, knelt down, and hugged them tightly. "Run home, my darlings. Run home to your mother. Know that I love you with all my heart. Remember that. And tell your mother that I love her - that I never stopped loving her and that I will love her always."

"Daddy, no," wailed Sophie.

Bill kissed his children, stood up tall, and stared at the Mskagwdemos. The hag nodded and stepped off the path, making room for the little girls to pass by.

"Go now," he said to his daughters. "Quickly, go! Do not be afraid. And do not turn around. Do not watch!"

He hugged them one last time and pushed them down the trail ahead of him. Reluctantly, they did as he asked.

Bill took one last look at his daughters, then, slowly turned to face the Mskagwdemos. He stood his ground, even though every fiber of his being told him to run - to run to safety. He held his head up high and stared at the apparition before him and nodded. And, as he accepted his fate, improbably he felt a lightness begin to surround his heart.

The Mskagwdemos stepped back onto the path. With a victorious smile on her face, she moved to stand before Bill. Then, she opened her mouth...

KAREN

Karen repeated the prayer over and over again, each time slicing open her hand and giving blood to the earth. Finally, she saw the sun begin to creep over the horizon. The wind calmed and the rain stopped. The clouds that had blackened the sky were dissipating rapidly. She finished her last recitation of the prayer and sank to her knees.

What now? Will my family be returned to me? Bill? My girls? Or will they come and take me away and lock me up in an asylum?

Exhausted, she lay crumpled on the ground, not moving, when out of nowhere she heard a faint voice calling her.

"Mommy!!"

This was not the terror-filled voice she had heard earlier. No, that had been an illusion designed to make her fail. This voice was the true voice of her daughter and she got up and ran to it, around the house to the backyard. She scanned the yard. There was no one there. She stopped, confused.

I know I heard it. I know I did! she cried to herself. Then, she heard it again - this time two voices, calling in unison.

"Mommy, mommy!"

The calls came from the woods beyond that strange-looking bush, from the path behind it. She ran to the bush and got there just as her daughters emerged from the forest. They were muddy from head to toe, but otherwise, seemed unharmed. She fell to her knees, arms outstretched, and surrounded them in an embrace. They hugged for several minutes, clinging wildly to each other, then Karen pulled back and looked into her children's eyes.

"Your father; what happened to Daddy? Where is he? Did he find you?"

Tears sprang into Sophie's eyes. "Oh, Mommy, she ate him! She killed our daddy!"

Karen's heart sank but she held her head high as she looked at her children. "Tell me what happened," she said. "Tell it to me this one time and I'll never make you tell it again. After this one time, it will just be a bad dream."

Terri straightened up and stared at her mother. Her eyes seemed old, no longer those of an eight-year-old child. No, now they looked ancient, burdened by visions no child should ever have to see.

"She had us, Mommy. We couldn't move. She had Daddy, too. He came to try to save us but he got caught, too. Then, all of a sudden, we were free. We could all move and we ran. Daddy held our hands; he protected us. Then she was there again, right in front of us. Daddy pushed us behind him, trying to keep us safe from her. Then, that thing stepped onto the path and he told us to run. We tried to get him to run with us, but he wouldn't. He told us he loved us and said to tell you he loved you, too, always. That thing, she stepped back in front of Daddy after we went by. Oh, Mommy, Daddy told us not to turn back, not to look. But we did. He was so brave, Mommy; he walked right up to her. But, when he got near her, she opened her mouth...."

At this point, Terri's voice trailed off. She closed her eyes to blot out the horror of what she had seen. After a minute, she took a deep breath, opened her eyes again and looked at her mother.

"She swallowed him, Mommy, sucked him into her somehow and, Mommy, he screamed. Oh, Mommy, how he screamed!"

Karen pulled her daughters to her again.

345

"Hush, hush, now," she soothed. "Never again, never think of it again. Your daddy drowned in the swamp. Tell yourselves that over and over again until it becomes real. Hush, loves, Mommy's here. Mommy will never leave you."

Slowly Karen got to her feet. She was so exhausted, but rest had to wait. She had to take care of the girls, to clean up the ritual area in the front yard, and to call the authorities about Bill. She would have to go through the motions, pretend to be the distraught wife of a missing husband. She knew he was gone - when she'd turned her head, she had sealed his fate. But he had been brave. He sacrificed himself for his children and she would always remember that. And she would always remember he had been a good man. It was this place, this island that had somehow perverted him, twisted him. Yes, he was a good man and she would remember him that way and she would be sure her children remembered it, too.

She took the girls upstairs and drew them a hot bath. Once she got them in the tub, she quickly bandaged her bloody hand and walked to the front yard. She gathered up the powder, dolls, and the knife and put them back in the tote. With her foot, she destroyed the circle and the symbols she had drawn. She returned to her children and wrapped their dripping bodies in large, clean, white terrycloth towels.

"Go get dressed, sweeties," she said. "I need to make a phone call."

She watched as Terri and Sophie walked slowly to their room, then she pulled out her cell and dialed 911.

KEEPING IT ALL TOGETHER

Karen made sure her children were okay, then waited for the police. Before they arrived, she re-bandaged her ravaged hand.

This will be badly scarred, she thought, *so I can never forget.*

When she heard the sirens approaching, she went upstairs to her daughters. "I want you to stay up here, girls. Don't come downstairs. If you get frightened or anything, call for me and I'll come up. Under no circumstances, tell anyone what you told me. Daddy drowned in the swamp - drowned trying to save you. That's all you need to know. Just stay here. I'll take care of everything."

Karen went downstairs to greet the police. She told them the story she had concocted, that Bill had gone for a walk in the woods before the storm struck and had apparently gotten lost in the confusion of wind and rain. She begged the police to search the wood. She knew their efforts would be fruitless, that they would never find her husband, but she had to play the game for her daughters' sakes.

Soon, her yard was full of islanders' trucks and cars. Pete and Louise were among the first to arrive and Pete, along with the police officer, began organizing the search. Louise walked over to Karen, who was watching from the porch.

"Oh, honey, I'm so sorry," she said giving Karen a hug. "How are the girls? What this must be like for your poor children. If there's anything I can do...."

Her voice trailed off when she noticed that Karen was not listening. She had turned her attention away from Louise and was staring intently at the driveway. Louise looked over her shoulder to see what it was that had caught Karen's attention. Immediately, she recognized Rusty and Emma's truck. She could see Rusty walking over to where Pete was organizing the rescue. Emma was standing by the truck door talking to someone inside. Then, a mass of red curls emerged from the vehicle.

Karen stiffened. "Louise," she said evenly, not taking her eyes off Maggie, "would you please do something for me?"

"Anything," replied Louise.

"Would you please go over there and tell that filthy slut to get off my property! And tell her if I catch her anywhere near my land again, I will get my husband's gun and I will shoot her. And, Louise, that is not a threat; that is a promise! Tell her that."

Louise's eyes widened in alarm hearing the fierceness in Karen's voice and she nodded and hurried over to Emma and Maggie. Karen watched as Louise conveyed her message and warning. The girl shook her head, laughing, and started toward the house. Emma, alarmed, grabbed her daughter by the arm and bodily threw her back into the truck. Emma then spoke briefly with Louise and quickly backed down the driveway.

As they left, Dex roared up on his Harley. He hopped off and sprinted to the front porch where Karen still stood. As he neared her, he saw the devastation on her face, but could find no words to console her. Then his eyes caught sight of her roughly bandaged hand.

"Girl, what have you done to yourself now?" he asked, taking her ruined hand gently in his.

She looked up at him with tear-filled eyes, all of the anger at Maggie's appearance drained out of her.

"I fell," she said.

He put his arm around her and led her into the house. He took her to the bathroom, where he sat her down and carefully undid the bandage. What he saw shocked him. Her palm was covered with knife wounds, one crisscrossing the other.

"Jesus, Karen, why did you do this to yourself?" he asked, looking deeply into her eyes.

She straightened up, wiping away the tears. "I fell," she said again, her voice firm. "Yes, I fell and that's all there is to it. Don't ask me again. That's it."

He looked at her long and hard and then nodded. "You fell. Well, let's get these wounds cleaned up properly so you don't get an infection."

As he spoke, he began to gently wash her damaged hand. He stayed with her a while and, when he was sure she was okay, went to join the other men who were searching the woods.

The search went on all day. Men and dogs combed the woods and the swamp, but there was no sign of Bill. At dusk, they called it off for the day, informing Karen they would be back in the morning with some equipment to try to dredge the swamp. Karen thanked everyone as they left. Dex came back to the house and sat quietly with her for a while, not talking, just holding her hand, trying to provide whatever comfort he could.

"I have to go to the girls," she finally said. "Make sure they're all right."

Dex nodded and put his arms around her and held her tight. "I'll be back tomorrow," he said softly. "But, if you need anything in the night, anything, just call me and I'll come back. Okay?"

She nodded as she slipped out of his embrace and gave him a small smile.

"Anything, Karen, anything," he said, reluctantly dropping her hand. He gave her one last look then turned and left the house.

Glad to finally be alone, Karen slowly mounted the stairs to check on her daughters. She had made sure the girls stayed in their room while the search was going on and brought them sandwiches and milk at lunchtime. Now, as she entered their room, she saw the sandwiches remained uneaten and Terri lay with her face turned toward the wall, her eyes blank and devoid of emotion. Sophie sat on her bed holding a sketchpad. Drawings depicting her horrific memories of the night before littered the floor.

Karen quietly sat down beside her, gently taking the sketchpad from her and enfolding her in her arms. The little girl's body became racked with silent sobs as she tried to find comfort in her mother's embrace. When she seemed calm, Karen laid her down on the bed, covered her with a blanket, and went to her other daughter, who appeared to be unaware of her presence. Leaning down, she kissed Terri softly on the forehead and covered her too. Then she slowly closed the door and went back downstairs.

She walked to the living room and sat down in the overstuffed chair, deep in thought. As she listened to the sound of the sea outside, she finally knew what she had to do.

THE BLESSED BOY

Just before dawn, Karen walked outside to the same spot she'd stood the night before. She remained motionless for a moment, her mind reliving the storm and its aftermath. Resolved, she turned, facing east, and opened her arms to the sky. In a firm, steady voice, she began to say the words - not the words given her by Lisbeth - not the *Mateguas Prayer*. These were her own words - her own prayer.

> "Oh Mateguas, Great Father of the Dead, hear my prayer.
> "This mother thanks you most humbly for the return of her children, but this mother grieves for them, for the memories they must now carry. It is a burden they should not have to bear. They are too young, too innocent.
> "This mother asks the Great Father of the Dead to let her carry the memories alone, that her children be freed from this burden, that they might keep their innocence.

351

> *"And this mother begs the Great Mateguas to provide sanctuary for the innocent children so they might mourn the loss of their father in peace."*

At this point, Karen ripped the bandage from her ruined hand and, scraping off a newly formed scab, forced it to bleed again. When her blood was flowing freely, she knelt down and pressed her hand to the earth.

> *"In return, this mother vows to make blood sacrifice to the Great Father of the Dead with every waning crescent moon for the rest of her days."*

She remained kneeling, allowing her blood to seep into the earth. Then she stood up and again stretched her arms to the sky.

"Oh Great Mateguas, hear my prayer!"

The sun was just peeking over the horizon as she finished. She watched as it rose up, a vibrant red orb, the sky around it bursting open in an aurora borealis of color. Red and pink ribbons of light streaked across the firmament intertwining with each other creating a magnificent display of color and light. Then, as quickly as it had begun, it was over. The sun cleared the horizon and the colors faded.

Karen stood tall with her arms outstretched, mesmerized by the spectacle that was unfolding around her. Then she heard a sound from behind her and turned in the direction of that sound.

A naked toddler, aged three or four, was crouched beside a mound of daisies that had been beaten to the ground by the wind and rain. He picked one of the flowers and stood up, the blossom lying limply in his hand. He turned around, looked at her, and smiled.

She sat on the ground, amazed, as the boy came to her and gently placed the flower on her bloody palm. When it touched her skin, inexplicably it began to come to life and seemed to regenerate. As drops of dew from its petals touched her wound, she was amazed to see the skin begin to come together and start to scab over. She watched in wonder as the flower changed and grew, taking on vibrant colors that seemed to pulse with light.

She looked from the flower to the child standing before her. He was perfect in every way. He said nothing, just stared at her with big brown eyes that sparkled with flecks of gold in the morning sun.

He nodded to her once and smiled, his eyes full of compassion. Then, as he turned to go, he laughed. To Karen, his laughter sounded like a thousand silver bells, immeasurably sweet and achingly melodic. She reached out to him, but he scampered off behind the house and was gone.

She stood up, astounded, as she stared at the wounds on her hand and saw them healing at an uncommon rate. In minutes, the crisscross of knife slashes faded, leaving only one scar in the center of her palm - a small waning crescent moon. She smiled, her mind clearer than it had ever been and, in that clarity, she knew what she had to do next.

She walked purposefully to the house, sat down at the computer, and scrolled through all their photo files. When she found the one she wanted, she printed it out and, photo in hand, walked into the girls' room and shook them awake.

"Sophie, Terri, come sit with me," she said as she gestured to Terri's bed. The girls sat on the edge of the bed looking at her with haunted eyes as she knelt before them. Smiling at them, she took their hands in hers.

"Look at me and listen to what I say. What I say will be the truth and you will believe it. Your father, who loved you more than life, went for a walk in the woods. He thought he would get home before the storm hit, but it caught him and he got lost and wandered off the path. He is missing now, but it is likely he fell into the swamp and drowned.

"You were NEVER in the woods. NEVER! You were here with me in the house waiting for your father to return. We played board games to pass the time. You never went out into the storm. And you never found that box - the one with the carvings on the lid. NEVER!

"Now, see this picture," she said showing them the print she had made. It was a photo of Bill and his girls, taken at the beach when they were about five years old. Bill had Terri on his shoulders and Sophie stood in front of him, wrapped in his arms. All three were beaming.

"Remember this day, this day at the beach, when your thoughts turn to your father. Remember how he loved you and the joy you brought to him. Remember him always as a good man, a good father, and a good husband to me. You will feel grief when you find he is not coming home, but it will be the normal and natural grief of one who has lost someone so beloved. Terri, Sophie, do you understand what I am saying?"

The girls, who sat as if in a trance, nodded in unison. Karen smiled at her daughters and nodded back. "Terri, tell me what happened last night."

The little girl seemed to wake up, blinking her eyes several times before she spoke.

"Mommy, you know what happened. You, Soph, and me sat in the living room listening to the storm and waiting for Daddy. Oh, Mommy, will they find him?"

She put her arm around Terri and turned to her other daughter. "Sophie, is that right? Is that what we did?"

"Yes, Mommy. We played a board game while we waited for Daddy. Will he be home soon?"

Pleased, Karen gathered her children into her arms and held them close. *Merci, Grande Pere de la Morte,* she thought. *Merci.*

THE NEXT DAY

The searchers returned early the next morning and Karen greeted them warmly. She noted, not without some satisfaction, that Maggie did not appear. The police officer in charge asked if he might speak with her for a moment.

"Mrs. Andersen," he said, "I know this is difficult but it will be necessary for me to speak with your daughters about the night Mr. Andersen went missing. I need to do this in order to collaborate your story."

Karen gave him a hard look. "My daughters are extremely upset right now. They miss their father and are worried for his safety. Does this have to be done?"

"I'm afraid so," the officer replied. "I can't close this case until I've interviewed them."

Karen shook her head slightly. "Okay, but you be gentle with them and I insist on being present. My girls are very fragile right now and I don't want them any more upset than they have to be."

The officer agreed. He'd heard the rumors about the Maguire girl and Bill Andersen and wondered about the possibility of foul play. For the record, he needed to hear the little girls confirm their mother's story. Not that he believed Karen Andersen could have murdered her husband and carried his corpse out to the swamp during one of the worst storms he could remember. No, he didn't believe that. But he had to have her story collaborated and her daughters were the only ones who could do that.

Karen brought the girls down to the living room to be questioned by the officer. In a soft voice, he asked them simply to tell him what happened the night their father went missing. They were very candid with him and completely believable when they told him the story Karen had planted in their minds.

Karen smiled to herself as she listened and again said a silent prayer.

After the officer had gone, Karen sat the girls down at the computer and got them started playing some games. When she saw they were well occupied, she left the room and stood alone by the phone. She stared at it for a minute, then picked it up and dialed a familiar number.

"Mom, it's me, Karen," she said. "I'm afraid I've got some bad news."

Calling her mom was difficult for Karen. They had been somewhat estranged since Bill lost his job. She and her mother had had words about her decision to stay in the home and not seek the employment that might have saved the struggling young family. They had not spoken since the move to Maine.

Karen told her mother about Bill's disappearance and probable drowning.

"I was wondering," she asked, "if the worst happens, would it be possible for the girls and me to come stay with you for a while after everything's settled out here? I won't want to stay here without Bill and the house will be a constant reminder of his death for us. Once we're settled, I'll take some refresher courses so I can get back to work. I know it might be an imposition, but we really have no other place to go. We can't stay here after all that's happened."

"You and my granddaughters are always welcome here," her mother replied. "But I just might have a better idea. Let me check it out and get back to you later. Now, let me talk to the girls."

Karen agreed and called her daughters to come speak with their grandmother.

A couple of hours later, her mother called back.

"Honey," she said, "when you and the children are ready to come home, there will be three first class tickets waiting for you at the United counter in Portland. And while I hope you choose to stay with me for a while, your father is offering you and the children his house in Monterey, the beach house. You remember the place? It's not large but it's warm and cozy and your dad wants you to have it. He and Christine have no use for it and were thinking of selling it anyway. And none of the 'evil spawn' is interested in it either. So, if you want it, it's yours and the children's. It might be the best place for you and the kids to recover and heal if it ends up that Bill is dead."

Karen was astounded. She had asked for sanctuary for her children and here it was. "Mom, that would be...that would be wonderful! I can't thank you enough."

"Your dad wants to be a part of your life, honey, yours and his grandchildren's. But this offer has no strings attached. You can let him in or ignore him. In either case, he still wants to help. I've gotten to know Nurse Christine pretty well over the years and, actually, she's not that bad. And, their children, the 'evil spawn,' are pretty much okay, too. It might do you good to get to know them all."

They talked some more and promised to stay in touch.

At about six o'clock, the police officer, accompanied by Pete, came to the door. Pete was carrying Bill's slicker and the lantern he had taken with him into the woods.

"We found these," said Pete, handing her the slicker. "This coat was caught on a tree branch deep in the swamp. Can you tell if it's Bill's?"

Karen looked at the jacket, tears springing into her eyes. "Yes, it's Bill's. Mine's the same brand. They come from a store in the Monterey Bay area. We bought them when we were on our honeymoon."

Pete and the officer both looked down at the ground, not knowing how to comfort this woman whom they had come to admire for her strength in the face of adversity.

The officer looked up first. "The lantern we found a little ways off the path, before you get to the swamp. The casing on it is cracked and it doesn't work. Mayhap he tripped and fell, breaking the lamp, and then abandoned it when he found it wasn't working. That's all we've found, the jacket and the lamp. I'm sorry to have to tell you this, but it seems apparent he drowned in the swamp. That bog is so deep in places and there are all sorts of vines and debris on the bottom that can tangle a man up.

"I'm sorry, but I can't see any reason to go on searching. We've gone over every inch of that wood. If he were there, we would have found him. Again, I'm sorry, Mrs. Anderson, for your loss."

"If there's anything we can do, Karen," said Pete, putting his arm around her and giving her a hug, "just call us and we'll come running."

Karen nodded and brushed the tears from her eyes. She took the slicker and the lantern and put them aside. She shook hands with the police officer, thanking him for all he and his men had done. Then she turned to Pete.

"Thank you and Louise for everything. I think the girls and I will be leaving the island once all the legal things are taken care of. We'll be going home to California. The memories, well, they aren't all that good here. My father has offered us a place to stay and I think a change of scenery might help the girls and me recover from this loss."

Pete nodded, not surprised, and gave her another hug. "We'll miss you," he said as he turned and walked to his truck.

Later that evening, after her children were in bed, Karen sat in the overstuffed chair listening to the sea. In her hands she held a picture taken at her wedding - one of her and Bill just after the ceremony. Tears slipped down her cheeks as she stared at it.

We had so much promise, she thought, *and I ruined it all.*

Absently, she wiped away the tears and placed the photo on the end table beside her.

I killed him. Not by turning my head - no, that was just a mistake. I killed him with my resentment, my anger, and my bitterness. I destroyed him slowly over the past two years, acting so selfishly, concerned only with myself and my own feelings. If I'd just swallowed my pride and gone to my father or stepped up and gotten a job - he would still be alive. We never would have come to this place and he never would have met that girl.

A soft sob escaped her lips.

Now I have to live with this guilt. It will never leave me. It's a part of me now. It's my penitence.

Nodding to herself, she slowly stood up. She glanced down at the picture one last time then turned and mounted the stairs to go to bed - alone.

AFTERMATH

Over the next few weeks, Karen kept busy making preparations to move. Dex was a frequent visitor, often dropping by in the evening after she'd put the girls to bed. They sipped wine and talked late into the night. They were together and yet, apart, Karen trying to come to grips with her guilt over the loss of her husband. Often, they just sat quietly, his hand in hers, watching the sea, each alone with their thoughts.

One evening, close to the day when Karen and her daughters were to leave Mateguas forever, they sat outside watching the evening sky. Karen turned to him and took his hand.

"You know," she said softly, "you can fish the Pacific just as well as you can fish the Atlantic."

He looked up at her, surprised. "What are you saying, princess? Are you inviting me to go with you?"

She nodded. "I know you love me. Why, I'm not sure. I'm no prize. I'm selfish and petty and, now, I have demons. There are things I have to keep bottled up inside, things I can never share with you. But, yes, come with me. You know I can't stay here. The girls don't need constant reminders of what happened to their father. But I don't want to lose you. Come with us and start a new life. We're leaving next Tuesday. Come with us."

Dex looked deeply into her eyes. "It's a big decision, Karen. I have the boat, the house - my life is here. But I don't want to lose you either. I have to think on it. Can you give me that?"

She nodded then turned her head again to watch the sky. "Our plane leaves from Portland at ten a.m. on Tuesday morning. I hope you'll join us."

The next few days were filled with packing and getting the house ready to go on the market. Dex was strangely absent. He did not stop by or call. Karen was deeply disappointed for she felt they were connected, bound to each other. She didn't call it love; the loss of her husband was a wound that still was too fresh for that. But she found it hard to think of a life without his strong presence. She thought about looking for him or calling him, but it was his decision and, maybe, it was time for her to close that chapter of her life, too. She could not stay and he could not leave. That was that.

Karen contacted a local real estate agent and put the house up for sale. She instructed the agent to sell the "monstrosity" for whatever the market would bear.

On the morning they were to leave, with the car full of their belongings, Karen made one last trip into the house. From her bedroom closet, she retrieved the carved box. She removed one item from it, put it in her pocket, and then took the box to the girls' room. She locked it with key and padlock and returned it to the hidey-hole where the girls had first found it. One key ring she put back under the floorboard. The other would stay in the car after they left.

As she exited the house for the last time, she walked out to the front lawn, facing east. She stood there for a few minutes remembering, then nodded, turned, and went to join her girls in the car.

At the airport, she stood at the window, watching as their plane pulled in. The girls were seated behind her, busy playing games on her cell. As she watched the plane dock, her thoughts were far away, remembering what her life had been and wondering what the future held for her and for her children.

Suddenly her reverie was broken by a tug on her ponytail. Startled, she turned to find Dex standing behind her, leather satchel in hand, a mischievous grin on his face and a sparkle in his eyes.

"I sold the boat to one of the summer people who's always wanted it," he said, taking her hands in his. "I'll get a 'west coast' boat when we get there. The house is on the market and the hog is being shipped to a dealership in San Mateo. I can pick it up there next week. So, that's it. Right now, money-wise, I'm a pretty poor prospect, princess, but where you go, I follow."

She smiled and squeezed his hands. "My mom's going to fall in love with you! We'll stay with her a few days. She's in Palo Alto, not far from San Mateo. After you get the bike, we'll head down the coast to Monterey. I know I didn't tell you, but my dad's given me his beach house there. It's free and clear and I have the check from Bill's life insurance. So, I think we'll be okay till you can get something going."

"Monterey? Why, that's a fishing town! How'd you swing that, princess?" he asked, astonished.

Karen just smiled. "Let me introduce you properly to my girls."

The girls said hello to Dex and he sat down between them. In no time, he had them laughing and giggling.

Karen watched, a smile on her face.

It's all coming together, she thought as her lips formed a silent prayer.

MONTEREY BAY, CALIFORNIA

SIX MONTHS LATER

Dex woke up and rolled over, discovering Karen was not in the bed beside him. He checked the clock - it was happening again. It had happened every month since they'd moved here, when the moon was in what was called its "waning crescent phase." Just before dawn, she would disappear outside to perform what he thought of as "her ritual." What the ritual was for, he did not know. All he knew was that, somehow, it was connected to Mateguas and the death of her husband.

The first time it happened, he'd questioned her about it. She'd sat him down and told him he could ask her anything except for two things. He couldn't ask about the night Bill died and about what she had done outside the night before. Those subjects were closed. She'd asked him to promise her he would not question her again and said if he refused or if he broke his promise, she would be done with him. He could tell by the tone of her voice and the look in her eyes that she meant it. So he had promised.

He sighed and rolled back over. There was nothing he could do. She would be in soon and he would hold her in his arms until her shaking stopped.

As he tried to return to sleep, Karen stood on the beach facing east. She stared at the horizon, watching for the sunrise while the crescent moon peeked out between the clouds. As the sun began its ascent, she stretched her arms out to the sky, the small bone knife in one hand. And, in a strong, steady voice, she began....

"Oh Mateguas, Great Father of the Dead, hear my prayer...."

EPILOGUE

DECEMBER, MATEGUAS ISLAND

The woman sat in the old rocker looking out at the sea. She had replaced the overstuffed chair with the rocker because she liked the movement, the gentle back and forth. There was a fire going in the woodstove, giving the room a cozy, warm feeling.

There will be snow tonight, she thought as she watched the waves relentlessly hit the shoreline. She thought about the house and how much she loved it. When it went on the market, the asking price a steal, she'd snatched it up, making sure, however, Karen didn't know who was buying it. That had been difficult, but she'd done it.

So, now she had the house and more - she had Bill; he was inside her. She put her hands on her huge belly, the life within beginning to stir. It was a boy, she was sure. Yes, it would be a boy, like Bill and like the other.

As she rocked, she thought about Bill and Karen. As much as she disliked Karen, she had to admit the woman had turned out to be a worthy adversary, strong and brave.

I would have had them all but for her strength, she thought.

But, she had what mattered most - the child that was growing within her, and this house, this land, returned to her at last. All was as it should be. She closed her eyes.

Maggie woke up, startled, and looked around her. *Jesus H. Christ! How'd I get here?*

She looked out the window - it was getting dark outside and just beginning to snow. She glanced at her watch - it was six o'clock.

Last thing I remember is closing up the schoolhouse and getting in my car to come home and that was around four-thirty! An hour and a half gone - just gone! How'd I drive home?

She glanced down at her belly as she felt the baby move. *Thank God, he's all right.*

As she absently caressed her bulging stomach, she remembered how it was right after Bill died. Word of her involvement with him spread rapidly through the island's close-knit community and, at first, she was outcast - shunned for her indiscretion. Then, as her pregnancy became apparent, the tide turned and the community embraced her. After all, she was one of theirs and Bill was from away and, as such, suspect - not to be trusted.

She got up to make herself a cup of tea, her thoughts turning again to the lost time. She had been losing time ever since she'd found out she was with child. At first, it was just five minutes here, ten minutes there. She'd attributed it to the change in hormones because of her pregnancy. But, one-and-a-half hours - that was getting serious.

Time loss was nothing new to her. It had happened before when she was a young girl. It all started after she'd wandered into the woods - the same woods Bill got lost in - the woods behind what was now her house.

As she poured her tea, she thought about those woods. She'd been picking berries when she'd seen a path behind one of the bushes. It had seemed to beckon to her, so she'd put down her basket and stepped right onto it. That was the last thing she remembered before coming to in her father's arms. After that, snatches of time just seemed to get away from her.

Yeah, I lost time back then, too, but all that stopped when I got my first period. Hormones - it's gotta be the hormones.

But, thinking back, she remembered how it had frightened her then, just like it was frightening her now.

She took her teacup and sat back down in the rocker. *It'll all go away once the baby's born.*

At least that was what she kept telling herself. But, now she wasn't so sure anymore. Lately, when she came back from wherever her mind went when she lost time, she could remember thoughts that were not hers and she had visions of things she'd done that she knew she couldn't and wouldn't do. And, those images - they weren't very pleasant, either.

Yes, she had to admit, she was getting scared. The lapses were getting longer and coming more frequently.

It's like someone or something is taking me over. Like, soon Maggie won't exist anymore. I'll just be a shell with someone else living my life.

She shivered.

And sometimes, deep in the back of her mind, she could hear laughter - wild maniacal laughter - and when that happened, she was afraid. Oh, so very afraid...

THE END

ABOUT THE AUTHOR

Born in Norwich, Connecticut, author Linda Watkins moved to Michigan when she was four years old. After graduation from college (Carnegie-Mellon University '70), Ms. Watkins relocated to the San Francisco Bay Area where she lived most of her adult life. A Senior Clinical Financial Analyst at Stanford University School of Medicine, Linda was always writing. At work, she created 'long forms' and business plans; at home, she wrote whimsical stories, poems and songs for the delight of her friends and family. In 2006, retired, she moved to Chebeague Island, Maine where she wrote her first novel, *Mateguas Island*.

Today, she resides in Muskegon, Michigan with her three rescue dogs (Splatter, Spudley and Jasper) and is actively working on the sequel to *Mateguas* as well as two other novels.

For more information or to view some of her other works,
please stop by her personal website

www.LindaWatkins.biz

Or her novel website

www.MateguasIsland.com

You can also follow her on Facebook:

www.facebook.com/pages/Linda-Watkins-Author/412758982152044

If you enjoyed reading *Mateguas Island*, please take a few minutes to post your review on Amazon.com, Goodreads, iBooks, or wherever is most convenient for you.

Other books by Linda Watkins

Secrets, A Story of Love and Betrayal
Secrets, a novelette, serves as a prequel to *Mateguas* and is available at Amazon.com, iBooks, and as a NOOK Book.

BUT WAIT - THERE'S MORE......

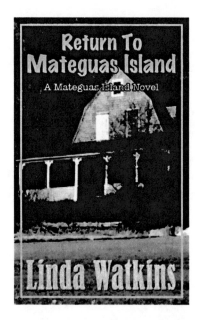

COMING FALL/WINTER 2014:

To read an excerpt from *Return to Mateguas*, visit

www.MateguasIsland.com

CPSIA information can be obtained at www.ICGtesting.com
Printed in the USA
LVOW10s1511091015

457650LV00001B/177/P